THE RELIC RUNNER ORIGIN STORY

A DAK HARPER THRILLER ANTHOLOGY: BOOKS 1-6

ERNEST DEMPSEY

138 PUBLISHING

OUT OF THE FIRE

A DAK HARPER THRILLER

ERNEST DEMPSEY

GET A FREE STORY

Visit ernestdempsey.net to get a free copy of the not-sold-in-stores short story, RED GOLD, featuring former government agent Sean Wyatt.

You'll also get access to exclusive content not available anywhere else.

ONE

HAMRIN MOUNTAINS, IRAQ, 2015

Dak stared through the night vision goggles at the terrorist camp on the opposite ridge. He and his team had been sitting there for over an hour, waiting until it was dark enough to move without being easily detected. Their window was short due to the cycle of the moon. In thirty minutes, the earth's satellite would start climbing into the sky and cast its eerie glow onto the desert mountains. It would still be dark enough to carry out the operation, but the light of the moon would make Dak and his team much easier to spot as they navigated up the slope toward the terrorist's camp.

"How many you count, Haus?" a man named Bo Taylor asked crouching next to Dak. He was about the same height as Dak, around two inches past six feet, but his hair was blond, cut short in the military fashion, but his tanned face was wrapped by a thick beard. Four of the six men on their team had grown beards during their time in the northeastern mountains of Iraq. The only two that didn't sport beards were Carson and Luis. Carson, a black man from the Bronx, had worn a beard for years before joining the military and eventually Delta Force. But he cut it off when he signed up and never grew it back. No one was sure if Luis could even grow a beard or not.

"Hard to tell which ones are going in and out, or if it's others who were already inside," Dak answered after several seconds of watching the entrance into the cave. "Details like that aren't as easy to make out from this range."

"I'm having the same issue," Bo confessed. "But if you had to guess?"

"Fourteen. Not counting any that might be inside we haven't seen yet. I'd go ahead and plan on double."

"Twenty-eight targets?"

"Better to plan on too many than not enough."

Bo snorted. "I guess. Sounds pessimistic to me."

Dak didn't reply, instead tightening his focus on the camp.

Several canvas tents dotted the top of the hill around the cave's entrance. Fires burned outside of some, where men tended them while doing their best to keep warm. Taking watch at night in the Hamrin Mountains was a cold, thankless task, and one that the men in Dak's sights didn't seem to be diligent in performing.

"I like those odds," Carson quipped from Dak's left.

Carson Williams, a tall, muscular black man, was about one inch taller than Dak. His head was shaved clean, same as his face, and he spoke with a deep baritone.

"I bet you do, weirdo," Luis said. His voice contrasted the big man's with a tinny, higher pitch. He was the shortest of the group, around five feet and nine inches. His thick, black hair fluttered in the chilly mountain breeze. Luis Martinez may have been lacking in the physical size department, but the man was resourceful, cunning, and a bulldog in a fight.

Billy Trask and Nathan Collier rounded out the remaining members of the six-man team. They were in a back position, about fifteen yards up the hill from the other four. Billy, a gangly sniper from Western Kentucky, was in a ditch with his MK 21 ASR rifle propped up on a tripod. Nathan squatted next to him, an M249 aimed into the darkness toward the terrorist camp. The light machine gun was better suited for covering fire in this situation, where the sniper rifle would provide accurate elimination of enemies.

Billy had used this very model of the weapon to take down targets from twice as far away, so to say he was comfortable shooting from this distance was an understatement.

"Always better to be safe than sorry," Billy said into the radio upon hearing Dak's comment.

Dak Harper had a reputation for doing things by the book, but he also wasn't afraid to go with his gut when the instance called for it.

He knew that, based on their surveillance of the enemy camp, things would settle down about this time, which made their entire operation a waiting game until the word go.

Nathan said nothing. He was always the quiet one, sometimes in a disturbing way. There had been more than a few occasions where Dak found the bulky man sharpening the twin knives he always kept on his belt. The way he went about honing the blades was disconcerting. Dak witnessed him sliding the weapons back and forth, watching them like he might a dancer with ribbons floating and twirling around her body. Dak never mentioned it, though he'd considered many times asking about the fascination with knives. Husky and built like a tank, Nathan was the heaviest of the group. He could carry more than anyone else, which was why he was assigned to the light machine gun, though the term "light" didn't accurately describe it in terms of weight.

"Looks like all the hens are home to roost," Dak said as he watched two guards disappear into the cave entrance two-thirds of the way up the other hillside.

"I still see four guards stationed outside of the tents above the cave," Bo said.

"We eliminate them first," Dak answered. "Then we go in. Everyone ready?"

"Yes, sir," the group answered as one.

"Okay, then. Let's do it."

TWO

HAMRIN MOUNTAINS

The group maneuvered silently up the hillside, split into two groups to flank the encampment at the top of the hill. Billy remained in his sniper nest, while Nathan pushed up the center, heading down into the ravine and then making the exhausting trek upward toward the shrouded entrance of the cave, covered by desert camouflage nets to keep it out of view of the spy drones that constantly scoured the mountain range for extremist camps and training facilities.

Dak and Bo took the right flank and reached the top of the ridge first, nearly a minute before the left flanking pair of Carson and Luis reached their spot.

"We're in position," Carson breathed into the radio.

"I have one target acquired at the front of the cave," Billy said.

"Keep him in your sights," Dak ordered. "Take him out on my command."

"Ten-four, driver."

"Team two, you ready?" Dak asked.

"Ready when you are," Carson said.

"Take out the guards. Use your knives and keep it quiet. We don't want all Hades breaking loose before we get a chance to look around the cave."

"Roger that," Luis said.

The four men moved as a single, precise instrument of death. Dak maneuvered to his right toward a guard standing by a fire pit outside of two tents. The other three moved similarly to him, each taking the enemy nearest them.

The unit moved with deadly precision and the guards never stood a chance. Dak reached his target without so much as a twig snapping. The terrorist guard stood by the fire, staring into the bright orange flames. The mans hands were out in front of him, fingers covered in tattered gloves. His AK-47 hung around one shoulder from a strap, dangling low by his hip.

He never had a chance.

Dak stepped out of the shadows and inserted the sharp tip of the knife into the base of the man's neck and drove it up into his brain, severing the spinal cord in the process before scrambling vital organ with a quick twist. Death came instantly for the guard. The most the man felt was a sharp sting on the back of his neck before succumbing to the sudden darkness.

Dak felt the guard grow instantly heavy as his legs gave out, forcing Dak to hold him tight with one arm around the dead man's chest as he dragged him back into folds of the rocks and scraggly bushes just behind the tent.

"Target down," Dak said into his radio.

"What took you so long?" Bo asked with chagrin. "Mine's down."

"Target three down," Carson's voice entered the conversation.

No one said anything for a long moment, and for several seconds, Dak wondered what was taking Luis so long. He maintained silence until the radio crackled and Luis spoke.

"My guy is down, though I'm not sure why I got the biggest one."

"Enough chatter," Dak said, a hint of chastisement in his voice. "Eagle one, what do you see at the entrance?"

"Same two targets as before, sir. Ready to eliminate them on your order."

"Into breach position," Dak ordered the others.

The men moved silently through the dark and met at the top of the ledge that hung over the cave's entrance. The camouflage netting hung with stakes hammered into the hard ground. The fabric stretched out over the landing below and dropped over the next ledge, held in place on the lower side by large rocks.

From the air, the covering probably looked like nothing more than a dusty slope on the edge of the hillside.

It was nearly the perfect cover, but not so perfect that Dak and his team couldn't find it. These terrorists were the ones responsible for an attack on a village about twenty clicks away. They'd murdered innocent people for the meager resources the villagers possessed. The only survivors were those who'd escaped or been out in the hills with their flocks of goats and witnessed the attack go down from a distance.

Their village wasn't the only one hit.

This band of brigands was responsible for at least six such attacks on small, outlying, defenseless villages over the last month. And it was time to shut them down for good.

Dak knew that it was an endless battle. Even when everyone inside the cave was dead, another terrorist cell would pop up some-where else in the next few weeks and the deadly game would start all over again.

There was no time to think about such matters. Dak and his team had a job to do. He inched his way forward, crouching low. He stopped when he reached the edge of the cave entrance roof. The camo fabric at his feet would do nothing to stop the high-velocity rounds from Billy's weapon.

"Nathan?" Dak spoke just above a whisper into the radio.

"In position and ready to lay them out if anyone comes out of the cave."

"Light 'em up, Billy."

Billy stared through his thermal scope at the two figures standing on either side of the cave door. He selected the man on the right first. Billy always waited for a target to turn their head when there was a choice of two. The one who moved and took their attention away from the field of vision with the other in it would be the one who lived longer, albeit only a few seconds.

The guard on the left had taken a step away from the opening into the mountain and was looking off into the ravine. Billy lined up the target, having already compensated for wind, distance, and drop.

He squeezed the trigger as he exhaled and the colorful figure in his scope dropped as a red splatter escaped through the back of the man's skull.

Predictably, the other guard spun around quickly at the sound. He'd no sooner laid eyes on his dead compatriot when a bullet cracked through the back quarter of his head and ejected out of the front left corner.

The man dropped instantly in a heap.

"Clear," Billy said. "Targets down."

Dak motioned to the other three, and the four men descended onto the cave entrance.

THREE

HAMRIN MOUNTAINS

Bo took the point, leading the other three into the cave. Nathan remained outside, a safe distance from the entrance, but with his machine gun ready to take out any reinforcements if the terrorists were clever enough to have people in reserve.

The four Delta Force men opted for their pistols in the tight quarters of the cave corridor. While the M1s offered more firepower, they were bigger and less maneuverable in the confines of cave passages. All of their weapons were equipped with suppressors to give them every edge they could muster on the mission.

Bo's muzzle popped from up ahead. A thump followed the sound as the body of another guard hit the floor.

A moment later, Dak stepped over the dead man as he followed Bo into the dim passage.

The cave was lit with ancient lightbulbs dangling from the walls, held up by old concrete screws with the wires wrapped around once before continuing down the wall to the next bulb. The terrorists usually got their electricity from generators, which was inefficient, but necessary so far from civilization.

Carson and Luis brought up the rear, checking behind often to make sure no one slipped past Nathan's guard at the entrance.

The cave corridor narrowed before it reached the first switchback where it curved to the right and then back to the left again, going deeper into the mountain. At the second bend, the path gradually angled down and Dak could see a brighter light shining off of the wall below. He heard voices too, men barking in gruff tones—either in Arabic or a close relative to it.

Dak understood some of it, though the individual words were difficult to hear from where he stood. He and the others in his group spoke the language fluently. One of his early assignments had been flying around in a helicopter on night missions over the city of Baghdad, listening for potential insurgents' conversations.

He and Bo crept down the passage until they could see where it opened up to the left, expanding into a huge underground chamber.

The voices echoed through the tunnels now and it was easy to hear what the men were saying. Several of them were joking about having their way with some of the women in the village before killing them in front of their husbands.

Dak glanced at Bo and saw the man's reaction. Fury burned in Bo's eyes. Dak had seen the look before and knew the man's temper was getting the best of him. No amount of elite training could burn that out. They had constructed it long ago, and nothing would tear it down now. The only way it was altered was by fueling it, and these extremists had just done that.

Dak shook his head silently at his partner, but he already knew it was too late. Fortunately for Dak, Bo's directed his anger at the bad guys.

"Go," Dak said, unleashing the reins.

The two men holstered their pistols and raised the M1s. They stepped around the corner with the weapons raised, and took aim at the first targets they spotted, lining up the terrorists with the holosights fixed to the guns' rails.

Their weapons popped with every squeeze of the trigger as Dak and Bo stepped into the room, one going left and the other two the right.

Luis and Carson moved in next, taking the center of the room and eliminating panicked extremists as their comrades fell to the barrage of hot metal the soldiers unleashed.

Four, six, ten men died within the first five seconds. The ones in the back of the cave heard the commotion, the gunfire, and tried to rally to their arms that were carelessly lying around on top of crates or leaning against the wall.

The room filled with a fog of gun smoke and the bitter scent that came with it. Some terrorists screamed in anger as they desperately tried to defend themselves. Others begged for mercy, putting up their hands as they yelled in broken English at the Americans descending upon them.

They would have no mercy this night.

Bo took out at least seven of the terrorists while the rest of the team mopped up the others.

The gunfight took less than a minute. When it was all over, two dozen bodies lay strewn around the room. Some of the dead were heaped on top of one another, the men dying in piles as they fell under the hail of bullets.

Bo looked around through the smoke and gave a satisfied grin. He nodded over at Dak who was also sweeping the area to make sure they had missed no one.

Dak returned the look and then spoke into the radio. "All clear. Tangos down."

He moved deeper into the cave's room, spotting something in the back corner in a wooden crate. Five crates sat there, all sealed except for the one on the floor with the lid propped up against it. Something glimmered from within the box. Dak drew to it like a moth to the flame and he cocked his head curiously when he reached the crate and saw what was inside.

He lowered his weapon and stared blankly at the contents. There, packed inside loose bits of straw and paper, was a two-foot-long, golden statue.

"What in the world?" Dak said out loud.

FOUR

HAMRIN MOUNTAINS

He turned in time to see Bo sidle up next to him, his eyes also fixed on the crate. "Looks like we hit the jackpot this time," Bo huffed. Pride beamed from his eyes.

"What?" Dak asked.

The other two joined them by the pile of wooden boxes and gazed into the open one.

"Wonder what's in the other four," Luis said.

"More loot," Bo answered confidently.

"You guys know we can't keep any of this, right?" Dak informed. "This stuff is probably stolen from a museum or a dig site. These artifacts are probably pretty valuable."

"No kidding," Bo said. "And now it's time for us to get a nice little bonus to our measly paychecks."

Dak chuckled. "Yeah, sure."

"Why not?" Bo asked. He met Dak's eyes with sincerity. "No one knows this stuff is here. There was nothing about it in the reports, the mission briefing, the objectives. We completed the mission, Dak. And it looks like we just got lucky."

Dak didn't like where this was going. "You know that's against the rules. Our job was to eliminate the cell and call in the cavalry to assess the situation. That's it."

"I know the rules," Bo said. "But we're the good guys. And I say it's time for the good guys to get a little pay day."

Luis and Carson agreed.

"What's going on?" Nathan asked into the radio. "You guys find something?"

"Yeah," Bo said. "Something that could send us to an early retirement."

"Really?"

"No," Dak interrupted. "We aren't stealing this stuff. Right now it's evidence and after the area is cleaned up, it'll probably be taken to the antiquities authorities in Baghdad."

Bo leveled his gaze at Dak, clearly unhappy with his team leader's plans.

He changed his methods in hopes of converting him. "Dak, come on man. Think about it. If the other crates have similar stuff to this, we could be talking about millions. Maybe more. All of us are nearly done with our time in the military. What were you going to do? Start working for private security firms? Go out and get a real job?"

None of that sounded like what Dak wanted. If he was honest, he really just wanted to find a nice place in the mountains to settle down, somewhere quiet. With the money he could scoop from these stolen artifacts, he'd have a nice little nest egg to get him all of that, and still have plenty left over.

He eyed the statue with a measure of curiosity. He'd studied ancient history in his spare time and found it fascinating while he was in school, earning a minor in history and a major in political science before shipping off to training, then Officer Candidate School.

Dak had served with these men. He'd developed trust with all of them. Things were never perfect, but they rarely clashed, and when they did it had more to do with strategies or planning than anything else. Those disagreements typically ended amicably and with everyone on the same page.

This, however, was a different situation.

Dak knew that everything Bo was saying made sense, but these artifacts didn't belong to them. And after a quick look at the statue, Dak immediately recognized the design as deity from the ancient Sumerian culture. He felt his stomach turn at the realization that these relics were easily more than five thousand years old, probably closer to six. Still, that fact wouldn't change the minds of his men. They were thirsty for something better, an easier life after the military. One that didn't involve 9:00 to 5:00 jobs or protecting wealthy elites on their exploitative missions to dangerous areas of the world. He could sympathize with that, but he knew his men couldn't sympathize with his argument. Still, he had to try.

"Guys, I don't even know where we could move artifacts like this. You'd have to have a connection in the antiquities black market to fence things like this, and I'm not sure any of you have those contacts."

"I'd be willing to work at it," Bo countered. He stepped closer, a look in his eyes unlike any Dak had seen before. He and Bo had been on more missions together than he could count. Actually, that wasn't true. He knew exactly how many. Twenty-six. They'd performed twenty-six dangerous, covert operations together. And not one time had Dak ever seen this look in Bo's eyes.

"I'm sure you would," Dak said with a snort. "Seriously, though, guys. We need to get out of here, report back to base, and get this place cleaned up."

"No," Bo said. "We're taking those crates."

"Guys?" Billy said into the radio. "What's going on in there?"

"Shut up, Billy," Bo said, using his sniper's real name through the radio. It was a no-no in their line of work, but Bo was done playing by the rules. Dak could see it.

"Bo," Dak interrupted, "we're not stealing these artifacts. Okay? They belong in a museum or in a lab for research. And like I said, even if we could take them, there's no way we can move them. Who's going to buy them?"

"Leave that to me."

Dak's eyelids narrowed to slits. "Stand down, Bo. That's an order."

Bo turned away for a moment, frustrated. "Fine," he said. "Have it you way. Mr. Always Play By the Rules. You go on home to the states and get your college tuition paid off. Maybe they'll have you stand up at one of the football games this fall so everyone in the stadium can clap for you and thank you for your service."

"Bo, stop it."

"No, I'm done playing by the rules, Dak. We deserve a score like this. We've given everything, sacrificed everything. And what do we get? A standing ovation when we board a commercial airline? A gas station attendant thanking us for our service?"

"We didn't sign up for this job for the money. Or the glory. We do it because we can, and because no one else is capable."

"Maybe," Bo said. "But I think it's time we take a little something for ourselves."

He spun around and drew his pistol, aiming it straight at Dak's head.

Luis and Carson flinched and took a step back, uncertain what they should do.

FIVE

HAMRIN MOUNTAINS

"Bo?" Luis said. "What are you doing?"

"Taking what's owed to us," Bo answered. "You going to stand in my way, Luis? Or are you going to get what's coming to you?"

The long silence told Dak that Luis was mulling it over.

"Dak is our friend," Luis countered. "He's been with us through everything. We can't do this."

"I offered Dak the chance. He said no thanks. That means we're splitting the loot five ways instead of six."

"Bo? What's going on in there? What loot?" Billy asked through the radio.

"Shut. Up. Billy." Dak's voice rumbled as he issued the order.

"I say we take it," Carson chirped. "Like Bo said, we've been on the front lines, doing stuff no one even knows about back home. And he makes a good point." He swore. "Most of what we do doesn't even get back to the president, much less the people. We work in the shadows, risking our lives every single day. And for what? They say thanks for your service. Those civilians don't even know what service we've done." He raised his weapon and pointed it at Dak. "I'm in."

Luis's eyes darted from the two men to his leader and back again. "Seriously? Can we just talk about this?"

"No time," Bo said. "You're either with us or you aren't, Luis. One way or the other, these crates are coming with us."

"How are you going to transport them?" Dak asked. "These things have got to be a few hundred pounds each."

"We take one of the terrorist trucks up at the camp," a new voice said from the edge of the corridor. Nathan stepped into view, lugging his machine gun over his bulky shoulder.

Luis' head spun again, this time to account for the man at the door. "You're supposed to be outside."

"Yeah, I know," Nathan said without caring. "But I heard the commotion and had to see it for myself. Don't worry, I swept the perimeter again. There's no one else coming. Besides, Billy's got an eye on things. Right, Billy?"

"Roger that. Although, I'm still trying to understand."

"So, that's three of us. Luis? You want to make some money or not?"

Dak looked over at Luis, pleading with the man's dark brown eyes.

"You always said you wanted to help your family back in Mexico, right?" Bo prodded. "You could do a whole lotta helping with the money from artifacts like these."

Dak could see the conflict in Luis' eyes, and the side of good was losing the fight.

Luis took a deep breath and nodded. "You're right. Besides, who will know about it? We get this stuff out of here, hide it somewhere until we can sell it, and then go on with our lives. It's a victimless crime, Dak," he reasoned. Then he looked around at all the dead bodies on the floor. "Well, relatively victimless."

"They killed innocent people, Dak," Bo pressed. "What do you think our government will do with these relics? You think they'll donate them to some museum or historical preservation society? No way." He let out an expletive. "You know all too well what they will do with this stuff. The higher-ups will commandeer it, claim it was being used for terrorist funding, and then be lost to the evidence locker. Meanwhile, the top brass will do the same thing with it I'm suggesting. They'll sell it on the black market to the highest bidder and every single one of them will laugh about it the entire time. They'll make jokes about us, the grunts who found it—all while they're sipping on glasses of $500 bourbon while we're trying to figure out how to pay our medical bills. Does that sound fair to you, Dak?"

The cave flooded with silence. Dak pondered the question, Bo's points, and the scenario. He was trapped. No two ways about it.

"It does," Dak said finally. He noticed the men holding the guns visibly relax. Instinctively, he shifted to the side, doing his best to look nonchalant. "And I don't think anyone could blame you for taking that path."

Bo nodded and his weapon started to fall to his hip. That was Dak's only chance. He made a move for his pistol, but something struck him in the back of the head. The force of the blow snapped his head forward. As Dak felt his knees give way, he could see Carson's face blur by before the spinning world vanished.

SIX

HAMRIN MOUNTAINS

The first thing Dak noticed before his eyes peeled open was the terrible throbbing radiating from the back of his skull. When his eyelids cracked it took a moment for him to adjust to the overwhelming, utter darkness surrounding him. He'd been in dark places before, but nothing like this. He felt as though it squeezed him like an anaconda.

Dak's eyes blinked in slow motion. He was alive. That much he knew. Or everything he thought he knew about purgatory was wrong.

The pounding in his head continued at the same steady rhythm. The agonizing pain caused him to wince, squeezing his eyelids together for several seconds. While his eyes were closed, he focused on what happened prior to waking up in this hellish limbo.

The terrorist cave. He and his team had infiltrated the cave. They'd taken out the targets. Then what? He recalled the next series of events; the memories getting clearer with every passing second.

There was a treasure horde—crates with artifacts in them. It was an assumption that all the crates carried ancient relics. Having seen the golden statue in one, however, made it easy to believe the rest contained similar valuables.

Dak and the others got into an argument. Guns were pointed. Then Dak had made a play for his own weapon. That's when he realized what happened. Carson was the nearest face he'd seen as he collapsed, mere moments before passing out. Carson must have knocked him out. He was the only one in a position to make that move.

Dak grunted and felt around on the ground near him. His fingers hit something small, cylindrical, and metal. The object clinked when he flicked it away. Spent shell casing from the firefight.

The rough-hewn, uneven floor offered no comfort, though something had smoothed the surface over the years—water perhaps, or maybe foot traffic from those seeking shelter.

How had he let himself get into this situation? One moment, he and the team he'd served with for 26 missions were taking down a bunch of terrorists. The next moment, they were turning on him. A familiar lump rose in his gut and he swallowed hard to fight the urge to vomit. A million questions ran through his mind. He propped himself up and felt around for a wall. When his fingers brushed against a hard, vertical surface, he twisted around and leaned his shoulder blades against it. The wall wasn't the most comfortable surface, but it allowed him to rest for a moment while he fought the swirling dizziness that only worsened in the suffocating darkness.

He needed to get out of here. The crates were long gone, as were the men from his team. That much was a simple certainty.

Dak told himself to focus. Not on getting out, but on the more immediate need. Light. He needed to find light.

His rifle had a light attached to it, but it was long gone. He felt for the cell phone in his pocket, but it was gone. Dak sighed in frustration. With his weapons and phone gone, that left few options for finding anything that could light up this tomb.

Tomb. That's it.

The realization hit him. He'd considered the cavern a metaphorical tomb, not thinking about the fact that—at the moment—it was literally a place of death. The bodies of the terrorists they'd taken out during the mission would still be all over the floor, exactly where the men had fallen during the attack. There was zero chance the team took the time to remove all the bodies.

Dak fought against the aches and pains surging from his left shoulder and his head, and pushed himself forward onto his hands and knees. He recalled the layout of the cave room, mapping it in his head. He remembered being in the back where the crates were stacked before he blacked out. Odds were, his men didn't move him. They would have been in a hurry to get out of there with their loot. On top of that, they'd have to find a place to stash it—which wasn't a problem out here in the middle of nowhere Iraq, but it would take time. The team would be expected to report in at some point. He wondered how they planned on handling his mysterious disappearance.

Distractions. He had to stay focused.

Dak crawled forward on his hands and knees, inching his way along the hard floor. He hadn't gone more than five or six feet before his fingers nudged something soft. It was cloth.

The bitter, iron smell of congealed blood mingled with the limestone all around them, along with the musty scent of the mountain underground, and a still lingering hint of gunpowder.

He realized crawling around could have planted his hands directly into a pool of blood and immediately decided to conduct the rest of his search on his feet—if this guy didn't have what he needed.

Dak squatted like a baseball catcher as he felt his way through the folds of the man's garments, searching for a light or a phone, anything with some kind of artificial illumination.

He'd searched through the man's entire outfit and discovered nothing, so he shifted slightly to the right and shuffled forward until he felt his feet hit another solid object.

Dak kept hoping that his eyes would eventually adjust, as they did when he turned off the lights of his bedroom at night. That usually only took a minute or two, but five minutes into waking in the cave, he started to realize that luxury wasn't coming.

He was bathed in total pitch darkness and the only thing that would change that was a light.

He bent down and began searching the next body. The first guy smelled bad, but this guy reeked of weeks without a bath and it was all Dak could do to not throw up at the scent. That, combined with the looming aroma of death was nearly all he could take, but he forced himself to choke back the bile rising in his gut. He was about to give up and move on to the next body when he felt something solid in a pocket of the man's robes. He dug deeper and his fingers grazed against a smooth, hard surface.

A flip phone.

SEVEN

HAMRIN MOUNTAINS

Dak's heart skipped a beat. He pulled the device out of the dead man's clothing and flipped it open. The pale glow from the little screen and the numbered keypad may as well have been the brightest beacon, a lighthouse guiding him to safety.

The weak light cast an eerie glow on the macabre scene at his feet. Now he could see the bodies strewn around on the floor. The deathly silence hung over him like a thick fog, seeping into his lungs and coating his skin.

He scanned the room and noticed that most of the terrorists' guns, if not all, were still here.

"I guess Bo didn't think disarming them was necessary." The thought struck him as funny and even with the dire circumstances enveloping him, Dak chuckled for a second until the action caused the pain in his head to worsen.

Bo and the others had gone to the trouble of disarming him but left all these other weapons. Maybe his former partner simply wanted his guns and not the inaccurate Kalashnikovs the extremists preferred.

Dak bent down and picked up one of the rifles that didn't appear to have any blood on it and slung the weapon over his shoulder. He rummaged through three more dead men's clothes until he found a phone with a brighter light on it. Then he pocketed the first light as a backup, then switched on the new one.

The device flashed a bright, white glow into the room. Dak shone the beam in every direction until he was certain he'd searched the entire area, then made for the passage. When he reached the corner, he glanced back one last time. He looked down at the watch on his wrist and noted the time. They'd entered the cave more than eight hours ago. By now it would be morning.

It was then Dak realized he could have used the glow from his watch to search for a better light.

He sighed, irritated with himself, and then proceeded up the corridor toward the cave's entrance.

Dak knew the rest of his team was long gone, but he hurried anyway, trotting up the path at a pace that caused his head to pound even harder than before. He pulled off the speed a little hoping to ease the throbbing, wondering if ibuprofen would be strong enough to take care of the pain. Not that there was any of that around here.

He weaved his way through the bends in the passage and then around the last curve, but what he discovered was even more troubling than the grisly scene of death down below.

Rubble smothered the cave entrance.

Huge rocks occupied much of the where the opening was before. Loose dirt and smaller rocks filled in the rest of the space, along with additional debris from what must have been a controlled explosion. Dak knew that the members of his team carried a small amount of ordnance capable of such a tactical demolition job.

A sickening feeling washed over him as he stared blankly at the blockade. Part of his anxiety came from the fact that he was trapped in a cave and no one was coming to help. There was another huge part of his mind, though, that focused on what happened. The men he trusted most in the world had betrayed him.

His mind wandered, as it tended to do at times, pushing his

thoughts to a faraway fantasy world where he tracked down the men who betrayed him. In that daydream, he exacts revenge on each one of them for what they've done.

Spending time and energy on such things was hardly productive. It didn't get him out of here and now that he was stuck, the clock was running. He'd have two or three days to survive without water. After that, he'd be dead.

He stepped to the sloped barrier of rock and debris and pulled at some of the smaller stones. They gave way easily enough, but the second he jerked them free, more dust and rock collapsed into the passage, making things worse than they were just seconds before. He looked up to the cave ceiling and realized that part of the roof was being held up by the boulders blocking the way out. Even if he could get them to move, the rock and earth overhead might crush him.

Dak put his hands on his hips and thought for a moment. He analyzed the walls and ceiling. They were hand-cut, not naturally formed by time and pressure. Someone had spent a great amount of time carving out these passages in limestone.

If they built one way in, perhaps there was another.

Dak hurried back down the corridor, making his way to the big room in half the time it took to get to the top.

The dozens of bodies lying on the floor greeted him again, but he ignored the sight and focused on his search, the only thing that might save his life.

The light on the phone panned across the room as he turned one way and then the other, scanning the walls for any sign of a door. Unfortunately, he found nothing.

He stepped over two dead men and stopped at the wall, then slowly made his way around the perimeter of the room, tapping on the rock with the butt of the Kalashnikov on his shoulder. Every time, the same sound resonated from the dense stone.

Dak was about to give up the search and return to the original cave entrance when he noticed something unusual. His skin tickled at the sensation and he spun around to find the source. A thin stream of air washed over his arms, causing the hairs on his forearms to raise.

"A draft," he said.

He froze again and waited until he could detect the faint sliver of air seeping into the room. Then he realized where it was coming from. He spied a huge metal supply box sitting against the wall, propped flush against it.

Cocking his head to the side, Dak tiptoed over to it, narrowly avoiding patches of drying blood.

He stopped and craned his neck, bending over at the hips until he could see behind the huge metal crate.

There, behind the backside of the box, was an opening in the wall large enough for him to crawl through. It only reached about three feet high and was probably that wide, but it was more than enough for Dak to fit.

He looked back over his shoulder. The darkroom seemed a fitting end to the terrorists, men who'd taken the lives of so many innocent.

It wouldn't be his end.

Dak wedged one leg between the wall and the metal crate and used his weight to push the heavy container away from the cavity until he had enough room to use both legs and his rear end. Once the box was far enough away from the wall, Dak got down on his hands and knees, pointed the light into the black opening, and started crawling.

EIGHT

HAMRIN MOUNTAINS

To Dak, it seemed like he was crawling for hours. His knees rubbed raw on the hard stone surface of the little tunnel. His hands and fingers, too, were worn to the point he could almost sense the skin peeling away layer after layer as he pressed forward into the mountain passage.

He noted that the walls in the confined corridor appeared to be similar to the ones in the paths he walked through before, cut in a seemingly hurried fashion. The sides and roof were jagged, undulating.

He found himself wondering why someone would cut through hard rock such as this, and not bother to continue carving through it in a way that would allow people to stand on their feet instead of crawling on their bellies.

Dak checked his watch as he reached a bend in the tunnel and noted he'd only been crawling for fifteen minutes. He sighed, frustrated, but didn't let those emotions deter him. He had to keep going.

His tongue felt parched. Every time he swallowed gave the sensation of sandpaper grating against the back of his throat. He knew he needed something to drink, but he was far from dehydration. Dak and the others had been deliberate about taking in plenty of fluids, both before the mission and during. Out in the desert dry air, moisture got sucked out of people faster than they realized, which meant diligence was a necessary component of staying on top of personal hydration needs.

He was thirsty, but he'd be okay. For now.

Dak pressed on, reaching another switchback in the tunnel that cut to the left. He contorted his body at a sharp angle to make his way around the corner and that's when he felt the cool breeze for the first time in earnest.

It wafted over him like a curtain, brushing against his face, hair, and arms. He pointed his light directly ahead, but all he could see was a deeper black beyond the frame of the corridor walls. Frowning, Dak pushed onward until he reached a lip at the end of the tunnel where the ceiling and walls abruptly ended. Something straight ahead of him glinted a shiny yellow color.

The frown on his face deepened, pinching his eyebrows together tightly as he tried to make sense of what he was seeing.

Dak emerged from the crawlspace and dusted off his pants and shirt before raising the light again and sweeping it over the new area.

He stood in a chamber, cut out of the mountain in a perfect square. The walls were smooth, unlike those of the corridors he'd seen thus far. The room was far more refined, and whoever constructed it had specifically reserved their best work for this space.

He turned around 180 degrees and held the light up so he could see what was written over the doorway.

Hieroglyphics unlike any he'd ever seen adorned the stone surface over the doorway. He recognized some of the cultural references in the drawings as coming from the Sumerian civilization. Amid the images of animals, people, deities, and shapes, Cuneiform script filled in some of the gaps between, giving the viewer not only a picture story of the past, but the words to go with them.

Dak couldn't help feeling a tingle of excitement as he stood there in the chamber, staring up at images and words that were carved and painted thousands of years go. This room was easily one of the oldest known archaeological sites in the world, at least based on the scant information he gleaned so far.

He spun around, shining the light on the rest of the interior, and found what looked to be a sarcophagus in the center, resting atop a solid limestone table. Vast treasures surrounded the burial table and sarcophagus. Golden statues resembling animals from all over the world lined the walls, along with gilded boxes, bowls, plates, and jewelry. One treasure chest to the right overflowed with riches, including diamonds and other precious jewels. Gold coins were scattered around on the floor at the base of the chest.

On the far end of the burial chamber, Dak noticed the two imposing, golden guards standing on either side of a darkened doorway. Each of the figures possessed the bodies of men, their heads covered by crowns with horns protruding out in two directions. The detail that went into creating the golden statues was astonishing, right down to the veins and muscles in their arms and necks. Dak thought for a fleeting second that the creatures might actually come to life if he disturbed the sacred room. But he wasn't superstitious, and the terrorists had already begun pilfering the chamber of its precious items.

Dak looked to the right and found two more figures just like them. To the left were two more. A seventh one stood at the head of the sarcophagus, as if hovering over the interred in permanent judgment of their earthly deeds.

"What is this?" Dak said out loud.

His feet moved involuntarily, carrying him deeper into the burial chamber. He paused when he reached the foot of the sarcophagus and gazed down onto its form.

The massive container stretched nearly eight feet long. It was at least three feet wide. The expertly carved lid displayed every possible detail of the dead man inside. The shirtless body exhibited huge pectoral muscles, biceps, and abs. A skirt draped over the dead man's private area, giving way to impressive legs sticking out of the bottom.

The figure's head wore a crown of golden leaves and a necklace that hung low around the neck with toothlike barbs clinging to it.

Dak reached out his right hand and ran his fingers along the smooth metallic surface. He crouched down low and pointed his light so that the beam illuminated the sides of the limestone burial table. He hadn't seen the designs carved into the stone before, but now he could see them clearly, and Dak couldn't believe it.

He stood and slowly ambled around the sarcophagus, inspecting every inch of the limestone table before coming to a stop where he began.

The images depicted a man, one of great physical prowess, standing on the bow of a boat, holding a staff to the heavens as a storm raged around him. Several people stood behind the man atop the boat's deck. The picture also displayed more animals, some of the varieties that could be seen on the walls of the chamber, but also with species that Dak had never heard of, save for in myths or legends.

"This isn't possible," he whispered, his voice suddenly taking on an air of reverence. "That was far too long ago."

He lifted the light and shone it on the walls, higher now than he'd looked before. Giant waves revealed themselves along every wall. Mountain peaks poked out from beneath the watery scene. Dak leaned close to the wall nearest him and narrowed his eyes. There were people in the water, some sinking beneath the surface, others still swimming for dear life.

Dak had studied this event many times in his life. The first time he saw it was as a child on his mother's knee as she read stories to him from the Bible. Later, he revisited the tale in high school, church, and then in college.

The story bore striking similarities in a vast number of other cultures and it seemed as though every nation in the world had one of their own—with varying degrees of differences here and there in the details.

No doubt flickered in Dak's mind. He'd let go of that long ago. He believed in the story, in one form or another. It didn't really matter to him if he was right or wrong about the details he'd been taught growing up. His beliefs belonged to him. Not someone else. They could do what they wanted.

It wasn't Dak's theological beliefs or his historical assumptions, that took a beating as he peered through the darkness at the golden burial plinth. What he had trouble believing, was who the man was buried just a few feet away from him.

Based on the writing on the wall, the hieroglyphs, and the location of the tomb, there was only one logical conclusion, and it shook him to the bone.

Dak had just accidentally stumbled into the tomb of Gilgamesh the Sumerian.

NINE

HAMRIN MOUNTAINS

Impossible? Evidently not.

Crazy? Absolutely.

Dak's breath came in huge, even gulps as he continued to stare in wonder at the sarcophagus.

"I discovered the tomb of Gilgamesh," he said, mesmerized by the weight of his realization. "Well, I didn't discover it. The... terrorists did. Still. Who am I talking to?"

He stopped and pressed his lips together.

How had this tomb, the burial chamber of one of the most legendary characters in history, go undiscovered for so long?

To be fair, they were out in the middle of nowhere, on top of a mountain in a backwater part of the world. He wasn't the best about keeping up with history and archaeology anymore. Life's tendency of making people busy went double for Dak. Still, he hadn't heard about anything going on in this part of the world. Most historians, archaeologists, and anthropologists would probably balk at the notion of coming to this place in the Hamrin Mountains, especially with so many extremist groups lurking around.

Still, some of those folks threw caution to the wind in plenty of dangerous locations. Typically, nothing happened, but now and then there was an attack or a heist.

Governments tried to keep incidents like that to a minimum. They needed the revenue from the tourist industry to keep things afloat, and if a bunch of archaeologists were killed or abducted and held for ransom, fewer and fewer would come. That would mean fewer artifacts, not as many headlines in the media. Tourism would suffer, at least that's what the governments believed.

The archaeological community didn't mind them taking that stance. That meant things would be safer during digs. Usually.

He wondered how the terrorists discovered the burial chamber. As far as his team knew, the extremist group had been in this spot for more than a month. His intel didn't go back farther than that, but they might have had been here longer.

"What were they doing here?" he wondered out loud. Since when did terrorists become grave robbers?

The first question would have to wait. It's possible the terrorists found the cave by accident while looking for a place to hide between operations, eventually turning it into their headquarters. Surely discovering the burial chamber was an accident. He doubted any of the extremist groups were students of ancient history or had unraveled some mysterious puzzle to lead them here.

The second question was much easier to figure out.

Terrorist organizations depended on money to fund their operations. There were travel costs to gather recruits, food to feed them, weapons, munitions, and technology that could be altered and used for nefarious purposes.

Dak had heard of terror cells abducting young girls and selling them to the sex slave trade. Human trafficking was a lucrative business in the tar pits of the underworld. Drugs were another revenue stream that filled extremist coffers. In this part of the world, heroin was one of the big earners, along with a few other opium-based substances.

Considering those sources of income, this group might have been planning on selling these priceless treasures to fund future terrorist attacks. Dak was no expert in pricing ancient artifacts, but his best estimate for this room was in the tens of millions, maybe more. That could buy a lot of bullets and ordnance for a group like this. They'd be able to recruit heavily in the region, and beyond.

Dak chewed on his lower lip for a moment. He looked down at the cell phone in his hand to check the battery life. It still had over 50 percent, which was plenty—if he could find a way out of here soon. Then another thought poked his brain. If the terrorists were going to sell these relics on the antiquities black market, he might find a contact on one of the dead men back in the other room. He loathed the idea of going through the crawl space again, but if he could do it once he could do it again.

First things first, he had to find the exit.

Dak drew a deep breath and marched over to the doorway between the two guards. He recognized them as two of the Anunnaki judges from Sumerian mythology—sons of the great sky god Anu or An, as he was often called. Funny, Dak thought, how certain elements from his education dipped in and out of his memory. It was most often the odd ones for him, the things that other people didn't care about or skimmed over in their studies. For Dak, those were the nuggets that made history so fun, so inviting. He'd once wowed a professor by including a tidbit about President William Henry Harrison on an essay, mentioning the detail that he was the president who gave the longest inaugural address and served the shortest term.

No one else even bothered to consider that fact, instead focusing on the president's few high points while in office.

Dak stepped between the Anunnaki guards and into the darkened corridor. He held the light out in front of him, figuring it was unlikely he'd need to shoot anything in an ancient—and until recently, undiscovered—tomb.

The passage angled up and then leveled out after about thirty steps. At the top of the rise, it cut sharply to the right, then back to the left. At the second turn, Dak started to see the residual glow of sunlight on the walls and floor of the corridor. The air, too, felt different—warmer. It brushed against his skin with a welcoming radiance even before the light touched him.

He felt his pace quicken as he neared the corner. He peeked around it, wary that it could be a trap. All he could see was blinding sunlight pouring into the corridor. As his eyes adjusted, he stepped toward the light. Emotions fought to take hold of his mind. Relief filled his senses, along with feelings of regret, anger, and the shock of being left to die, buried alive in an ancient cave.

Dak stopped at the exit to the cave and all of those emotions crashed down around him. He braced himself with his right hand, holding onto the edge of the cave's wall as he poked his head out. Just as quickly, he pulled back into the corridor, his heart full of devastating disappointment.

The passage exit perched dangerously on a cliff, sixty feet up from the desert floor.

TEN

HAMRIN MOUNTAINS

Dak stared down the side of the cliff for a moment. He briefly considered climbing down, but that would be foolhardy. Most of the cliff's face was smooth without many narrow ledges or hand holds to make the journey down even remotely possible. He'd done some rock climbing in his life. A few of the climbs were difficult, bordering on the expert level. This, however, was a death sentence. He wouldn't make it halfway before he slipped and fell, or got stuck on the face of the rock.

"So close," Dak groused.

He thought hard for a minute, weighing his limited options. Since climbing down the cliff didn't appear to be a good idea, he needed a safer way to descend the mountain. Rope would be good, but there was none to be found.

Then an scheme bubbled to life.

It wasn't a pleasant idea, and the execution of it would be even less so. Still, it was his only chance. When faced with survival or death, he would always choose survival.

Dak spun around and hurried back down the corridor. He passed through the burial chamber and returned to the crawlspace, got down on his hands and knees, and began squirming through the tunnel again.

He emerged back on the other side and raised the phone to shine the light around the room. The bodies still lay there where he'd left them, and Dak wondered how long it would be before the room began to stink of rotting death.

He swallowed hard and pulled his shemagh up over his nose and went to work.

First, he set about scouring the room for more lights. He searched every one of the dead men and found twelve more phones. Most of them were flip phones, but every little bit helped and he would save those in his cargo pants to use once he was out of here, but that plan would have to wait.

Next, he took two of the smartphones and turned on the lights, placing the devices face down on the floor. He also found several flashlights that he also placed around the room in the darkest areas. Within twenty minutes, the entire chamber was bathed in a dim—albeit inconsistent—light.

He grunted in satisfaction upon seeing the entirety of the room.

"Now comes the gross part."

He started with the body nearest him and began the unpleasant process of undressing the dead man. This one had taken a bullet to the head, so most of his blood loss stayed off of the clothes. Dak knew that specimens like this were few, and he didn't look forward to dealing with some of the messier corpses.

He removed the man's outer garments, leaving his underwear and shirt, choosing to only take the clothes that hadn't been tainted when the victim's bodily functions relaxed upon termination.

Dak piled up the clothing next to the entrance to the crawlspace and then went to the next body.

He repeated the process, removing the garments from nearly all of the dead men in the room. Satisfied he had enough to use, he removed a knife from one of the bodies and started cutting the robes and tunics in wide strips. This step took nearly an hour to complete after the forty minutes of stripping the corpses.

Once all of the clothes were cut to his specifications, he tied one end to the other, then repeated the knots with all the strips. By the time he was done—almost two hours later— he'd produced more than one hundred feet of "rope."

After grabbing the rest of the phones and lights, he stuffed them into every available cargo pocket, then tied one end of his makeshift rope securely to his ankle. Looking back one last time into the room, he sighed and then began the long crawl back through the tunnel toward the burial chamber.

His stomach grumbled. His fingers ached from pulling and rubbing on the stone. His knees were scraped. Despite all of this, along with an overwhelming thirst, Dak felt a renewed sense of energy pulsing through his body.

He reached the burial chamber in record time and clamored to his feet. Then he trotted up the corridor to the opening in the cliff and looked down.

Dak bent down and untied the rope from his ankle, then retreated back through the passage until he reached the burial chamber. Most of the rope still protruded from the crawlspace. That was a relief. He'd initially thought he would need to bring one of the heavy chests or perhaps a statue closer to the tomb's exit, but having created more than enough rope, that wouldn't be necessary.

He pulled on his creation until the last of the rope appeared through the crawlspace. Ignoring the blood stains on his hand from the dead men's clothes, Dak tied off the rope's end to the leg of the Anunnaki statue on the right. He pulled hard on the fabric, leaning into it from several feet away to make sure the statue didn't topple over and also insuring the cloth wouldn't rip.

Pleased with his handiwork, Dak grabbed the rest of the rope and returned down the passage toward the exit.

When he reached the lip of the cliff, he sat down and tied the other end of the rope around his waist, then dropped the bulk of the fabric over the precipice. He looked over the edge as the loop in the rope dropped almost to the bottom of the ravine, leaving less than twenty feet to the bottom. With that, combined with the rope around his waist, Dak figured he'd have to drop no more than six or seven feet to the bottom.

He secured the knife in his belt and then leaned out over the drop-off, tightening the slack in his rope until it went taut. Then, Dak took a breath, said a silent prayer, and took a step down the rocky face.

ELEVEN

HAMRIN MOUNTAINS

One foot after another, Dak lowered himself toward the bottom. His fingers weakened with every passing minute. The muscles in his forearms burned from the effort, but he didn't let go. With every step, he drew closer to safety.

The sun beat down on him from a cloudless sky. Sweat rolled down his face and jaw, forming little balls of perspiration before letting go and dropping into the abyss below.

He didn't dare look down now.

Heights weren't one of his phobias. In fact, few things in life caused Dak to be irrationally afraid. Such fears would prohibit him from doing his job. His mind drifted again, begging him to think about the five men who betrayed him and left him for dead.

Distracted, his fingers slipped on the rope and he dropped six feet before he was able to catch himself, clamping down on the rope with a strong grip. The act burned the skin on his fingers from the friction, but the injuries were negligible and he kept going, hand over hand, one foot at a time until he reached the end of the rope, about seven feet off the ground.

When the rope was taut, he let go of his tight grip on it and retrieved the knife from his belt, and started sawing. It didn't take much for the sharp blade to sever the fabric. When the last strands gave way, Dak dropped to the sand below with a thud. He landed on his feet and rolled to the side to cushion the fall, even though it was less than ten feet. He'd seen people get hurt with shorter drops than that and breaking an ankle out in the middle of the desert mountains wasn't his idea of a good plan.

Dak let out a sigh and looked back up the wall he'd just descended. The rope he'd created dangled loose in the breeze, swaying back and forth gently over the rocky surface.

His head still hurt, but the throbbing wasn't as bad as before. His vision had cleared, though now he wished for a pair of sunglasses to shield his eyes from the bright sunshine.

He stood and dusted himself off, then looked around. Hills and mountains surrounded him on all sides. The only sound came from the wind whispering through the canyon. The place where he and his team setup prior to the mission was only a few clicks away, but he knew there would be no mode of transportation there.

Dak recalled his men's plan regarding transporting the treasure crates. They'd mentioned using one of the terrorist trucks to move the chests, though there was no way to know where. Still, if memory served correct, he'd seen more than one pickup on the top of the mountain.

He looked up with disdain to the top of the mountain, then to the right where the ravine looped around in front of it and into the valley where he and his team had descended the night before to attack the camp. It would take another hour for him to get back to the top, to the scene of the crime, and he didn't like the idea of returning. Especially now that he was finally free.

It was either go back to the camp or risk dehydration and death in the desert. The base was too far from here and while he was in terrific physical condition, even Dak had his limits.

With no other options in play, he started toward the valley.

TWELVE

HAMRIN

Bo stepped out of his commanding officer's quarters and back into the hall. He never bothered to look back as he turned and stalked down the corridor toward the barracks.

He'd informed the colonel of what happened—how Harper had gone crazy, started talking weird, and eventually sided with the terrorists. The colonel had a difficult time believing the story, but Bo hadn't lied to him before—as far as he knew.

Bo explained how he and his men took out the terrorists and the traitor sympathizer. He even mustered a few tears that mirrored his disbelief at Dak Harper's actions.

"I... I just don't understand how this could happen, sir?" he'd said, doing the best acting job of his life. "I trusted Dak. We all did. I... I'm sorry, sir. We had to collapse the cave. Dak and all the terrorists died inside. It was the only way, sir. We had to get out of there. The place was booby-trapped."

The colonel eventually accepted the story and praised Bo for his leadership, his bravery, and quick thinking in a difficult situation. With Dak Harper gone, the man had to be dead, awol or had joined the dark side with the terrorists—as Bo had suggested.

Bo and his team would be given a short leave before they shipped back to the states, this being their last mission during their tour. Once he and the crew were back home, they would come up with a plan to retrieve the stolen artifacts and move them through the black market.

That was going to be difficult.

Bo had his fair share of shady connections, but the antiquities black market was a place he'd forged no kind of network. He honestly didn't know where to start, though he figured some of his acquaintances in the cybercrime community could help. Those guys were always dipping their toes into a wide assortment of shadowy pools, very often on the dark web. Bo would make a few calls and see where it led.

He veered right once he was outside the metal building the soldiers referred to as the "tin palace" and marched toward the rows of barracks across the courtyard. The immense, beige building was nothing spectacular in the way of aesthetics, but Bo had never seen a garrison that accomplished that feat.

He strode with purpose through the corridors until he found his men sitting in a little room in a more remote wing of the facility. Bo stepped inside and shut the door so no curious ears could hear their conversation.

The four men looked up at him, curiosity burning in their eyes.

"Well?" Carson asked.

Bo nodded. "He bought it."

A collective sigh filled the room, though Luis still didn't look relieved. He'd been acting worried ever since they left the cave. It was easy to see that what they'd done to Dak didn't sit well with him, but there was nothing he could do. If he'd gone against the rest of the team, he might well be stuck in the cave with Dak too.

Nathan nodded. "Good. What else did he say?"

Bo sauntered over to an empty chair around the table where the men sat and plopped into it. "Well, as you know that was our last mission. Nothing has changed in that regard. We're going home, boys."

"What about the—" Billy looked around and then lowered his voice before continuing. "What about the treasure? If we go back to the states, someone else could find it."

"I don't think so," Bo disagreed. "We took precautions. It's well-hidden, and only the five of us know where it is."

"So, what?" Carson asked. "We fly home, hang out for a bit, then fly back here and recover the stuff?"

"Exactly. And we do it together." Bo leveled his gaze, meeting the stares of each man so they understood there would be no backstabbing, no sneaking around and stealing the bulk of the treasure for themselves.

"That's probably best," Luis said. Regret and doubt filled his voice as he stared blankly at the table's surface.

"After that, we go our separate ways." Bo leaned back in his chair and draped an arm over the back of it. "I've reached out to a few of my morally loose friends. They have some connections in the arms black market, done quite a few deals in West Africa and Central America. I believe they'll be able to get us connected with someone who can move those artifacts."

"Perfect," Carson said, throwing up his hands. "When do we head back stateside?"

"Tomorrow morning." Bo looked around at the men once more, making sure he engaged each one. "It's been an honor serving with you, gentlemen. Here, in a few weeks, maybe a month, I suspect we are all going to be very rich."

The group joined in with a reserved but rousing collection of agreements and laughs.

"No day job for me when I get back," Billy said.

"What are you going to do with your cut?" Carson asked.

Billy thought for a moment. He rubbed his narrow jaw and shrugged. "I guess I'll buy the farm I always wanted. Been eyeing some land in Tellico Plains, an hour from Knoxville. It's at the base of the mountains. Ten acres. Not a ton of property, but it's more than enough for me and with the money we get from those sculptures, I bet I'll have plenty left for another life-time or two."

Carson nodded his approval.

"What about you?" Billy asked.

"Me?" Carson guffawed. "I'm gonna park my tail on a beach somewhere. Maybe Hawaii. Maybe South Florida. I'll figure that out when the time comes. I want to be somewhere warm and sunny with sand between my toes."

Billy chuckled. "You don't need to sell artifacts to get that. You got that all around you right here."

Carson laughed at the comment. The others did too. "Funny man." He turned to Luis. "What about you?"

Luis rolled his shoulders. "I don't know. I haven't thought about it, honestly. Not much, anyway."

"Come on. You never daydreamed about what you would do if you ever came into a bunch of money?"

Luis bobbed his head in semi-agreement. "Yeah, I mean, sure. I always said I would help my family back in Mexico, my distant rela-tives. But for me, I'll probably just get a nice house somewhere in the suburbs. Something quiet. Maybe on a cul-de-sac."

Carson rolled his eyes and looked to Nathan. "What about you, Mr. Quiet?"

Nathan's focus remained on the knife in his hand as he ran it back and forth across the belt. The thing couldn't possibly get any sharper. He perpetually worked on his blades, keeping them razor sharp at all times, but the way he went about it unnerved others.

Nathan never looked up as he answered. "I don't know."

Carson snorted. "What do you mean, you don't know?"

Nathan's eyelids lifted slightly. He peered threateningly at Carson from just underneath them. "It means I don't sit around thinking of stupid ways to blow my money. It's unproductive. I'll figure it out when the checks clear." The menace in his tone was enough to send chills through every man in the room. It especially unnerved Luis, who blew it off by focusing on Bo.

"What about you, boss? Any grand plans?" He offered an uncomfortable laugh with the question.

Bo's face remained cold, emotionless. "I'm going to disappear. Probably in a foreign country."

"Sounds like a good idea," Luis said. "We should probably all lie low for a while."

"Yes," Bo agreed. "lying low is exactly what I intend to do. I may get into a few business ventures here or there, but I plan to keep a low profile and enjoy my life. No more missions. No more taking orders from someone else. I'll get my life back. After that, I can do whatever I want."

THIRTEEN

HAMRIN MOUNTAINS

Dak wiped sweat from his brow with the sleeve on his forearm. He breathed heavily and accidentally kicked a rock as he trudged the last dozen feet to the crest of the mountain.

He hadn't seen the terrorist camp in the day, other than from pictures in the mission briefing. To his surprise, it looked remarkably well-organized. The tents were arranged in neat rows with a central fire pit for the men to gather around in the chilly desert evenings. At the end of the path between camouflaged tents, Dak spotted three Toyota pickup trucks parked in the dirt behind a cluster of boulders.

He shook off the fatigue from the ascent and trotted across the camp to the three trucks.

The vehicles sat under another desert camouflage tarp that made spotting the trucks much more difficult from the air since common practice for finding such training centers often utilized drones, spy planes, or satellites.

Dak slowed to a walk and chose the first truck to the left. He hadn't even considered the possibility that he might have to Hotwire the thing if he couldn't locate the keys. It was unlikely the extremists were kind enough to leave them in the ignition and there was no way

Dak would go back down the cave. Even if he wanted to, the only way back in was to descend the cliff face and hop in through the hole.

No. If he had to hotwire the truck he would.

He pulled on the latch and the door didn't budge. He sighed a disappointed breath and walked around to the passenger side. That door was locked too. Dak spun around on his heels and tugged on the driver's side door. It also didn't move. He'd exhausted half of his options already with no luck

He repeated the process with the two remaining trucks and found all the doors locked. He bit his lower lip and let out a frustrated grunt. He needed water. Distracted, he glanced over at the nearest tent. There was a small chimney sticking out of the back part of the roof signaling it was the camp's kitchen.

If this place had any water, it was probably there.

Dak gave up on the trucks, for the time being, knowing that he'd probably have to break one of the windows and strip some wires under the steering column to get the thing started. For now, he needed to treat his parched tongue.

He stepped into the tent, pulling back the flap as he passed through and found himself in a vast room held up by poles at both ends and in the center. Two tables formed an L shape on the right side of the tent's interior and several wooden folding chairs occupied the left side, along with a couple of plastic card tables for eating.

A fireplace made of stone and mud in the back connected to the chimney he'd seen from outside. Pots, pans, and utensils filled one end of the table that ran parallel to the back wall.

He surveyed the room and found what he was looking for. In the back left corner, a stack of bottled water cases bloomed like an oasis in the searing desert.

Dak rushed over to the water and ripped open the top case. He yanked a bottle out and twisted the cap off, discarding it carelessly on the dirt floor. The water dribbled down the sides of his mouth, rolling off his chin as he chugged the quenching liquid.

He polished off the entire contents of the bottle in less than ten seconds. He tossed the empty container aside and grabbed a second. Dak downed half of the second bottle more slowly and stopped when he was halfway done. Then he set the bottle down, picked up four more from the case, and stuffed them in his cargo pockets.

Satisfied he'd collected enough to keep him hydrated in case something went wrong on the way back to base, he whirled around and noticed something at the door to the tent. He hadn't seen the wooden pole on the way in, but it stared him in the face now.

He sauntered over to the pole and cocked his head as he gazed upon it. Four nails jutted out of the wood, each holding a set of truck keys. He nodded at the stroke of luck and took the set from the top rung on his way out the door.

A funny thought occurred to him as he walked back toward the row of trucks and he couldn't help but smile. Four keys had been hanging on the pole. That meant his team hadn't bothered to look and probably had to rig the wires to get the thing to start.

Good.

He had a few other savory words he wanted to express, but he pushed them aside. Back at the last truck in the line, he noticed that there were shards of glass scattered in a specific area on the sand. He figured it was where his team had broken the window to gain access to the pickup.

"Suckers," Dak said, though he realized that he too was a sucker for having let trust and friendship get in the way of seeing people for what they were.

Over the course of his life, Dak developed a general mistrust of most people. A large part of that stemmed from his youth. His father vanished when Dak was just a boy which placed the burden of raising him squarely on his mother's shoulders.

She was a drunk and often came home with a different man every weekend. Sometimes she'd hire a babysitter to watch him. Other times, she would just turn on the television, put a plate of macaroni and cheese out, and tell the boy to keep the doors locked until she came home.

Dak had only been five years old at the time, which made her actions highly dangerous and illegal.

Fortunately, Dak met some friends along the way and their families helped make sure he had a future when his mother continually dropped the ball on all fronts.

Dak shook off the thoughts of the past and inserted the key into the truck's door. He turned it and felt relief shower over him as the door pulled free.

He took a deep breath and exhaled, then climbed into the truck, set his waters in the four cup holders around the cab, and turned the ignition.

The engine rumbled to life, and he set his sights on the winding dirt road leading down the mountain. His mind raced with plans, things he would say and do when he got back to base.

He hoped Bo was there. He wanted to see the disbelief on the man's face when he saw the ghost of Dak walk into the garrison and inform the commanding officer that he'd been stabbed in the back by his own team.

Soon, Dak would set things right.

FOURTEEN

HAMRIN

The Toyota Tacoma slowed to a stop. The tires crunched on the loose rocks on the dirt road. Clouds of dust rolled out from behind the back tires. The wind grabbed the dust and swirled it around carrying it upward toward the mountains before it vanished in the air as each particle separated from the others.

Dak stared through the dingy windshield. He'd been forced to use the windshield wipers to clear away the layers of dust that built up on the glass. That act had spent what little wiper fluid remained in the reservoir, leaving him to dry wipe the windshield most of the trip back from the mountain.

He stared at the base in the distance and realized the danger of approaching a military installation in an unknown vehicle, a vehicle that was the transportation of choice by many terrorist groups worldwide.

No, driving up to the gate would be a bad idea. Even if he tied a white flag to the end of his gun barrel and held it out the window, he'd probably be shot dead by the time he was fifty yards from the gate—maybe a hundred if one of the snipers was on the job.

He'd have to approach on foot and leave the weapon in the truck.

Dak was approximately three hundred yards from the eastern gate of the base. Hardly a hike through the Appalachian Trail. He could do it without breaking a sweat.

He took one of the two remaining bottles of water out of a cupholder and stepped out of the truck. His boots hit the ground with a thud and sent small clouds of dust out behind the heels.

A gust of wind hit him and he pulled his scarf up over his mouth and nose to keep the flying debris from getting in.

Dak saw a glint of sunlight off of something glass on one of the watchtowers and knew that someone was looking his way. He didn't care that they spotted him. He was on their side.

He started toward the garrison on foot, trudging through the dirt and sand, shoulders stiff and head held high. He didn't expect a hero's welcome. There wouldn't be hundreds of his fellow soldiers gathered around outside the barracks, slow clapping as he entered through the eastern gate.

Dak didn't care. He wanted a shower, a soft bed and pillow, and a good meal. The water he discovered in the camp had taken care of his thirst and put his hydration levels back to optimal, but his stomach grumbled from hunger. Looking at his watch, he realized it had nearly been eighteen hours since his last meal before the assault on the terrorist camp.

Halfway to the gate, he saw movement.

The gates swung open and two Humvees rumbled out, speeding his way. The tires kicked up huge swells of dust that rolled chaotically into the sky.

Dak frowned. "Why are they driving so fast?"

He figured it was because they realized it was him, one of the missing men from the mission. But why were there gunners manning the .50-cals on top of the trucks?

The answer came to him in a way he never expected. The huge barrel ignited with flames. In an instant, the surrounding desert floor exploded in rapid bursts as it consumed the massive rounds being fired from the weapon.

Dak flinched, then covered his ears and head as hot metal rained down all around him. He dropped to his knees and curled into a ball. That didn't stop shards of exploding rock from splashing against his skin and cutting his neck and hands in several places.

Then, as quickly as the onslaught began, it ended. Silence poured over him once more. Dak winced against the dust flying all around him until it blew away in the breeze. When it did, he found himself staring into the barrel of the .50-cal; the gunner glaring back at him through wrap-around Oakleys.

The trucks sat motionless for a long moment. Dak dared to try standing, but the gunner shouted an order at him to stay on the ground. "Don't move until we tell you to."

"What are you guys doing?" Dak shouted back over the rumble of the Humvees' engines. "I'm on your side. I'm an American. You guys know me." He recognized the gunner as Private First Class Jonathan Haskins. "Johnny. You know who I am. What is this all about?"

One of the doors in the second Humvee slammed shut and a gray-haired man with a desert camouflage cap and matching fatigues stepped around the lead truck. Two armed soldiers escorted him, one on either side.

"Sir?" Dak said, still tempted to rise, but not stupid enough to do so. "What is going on?"

He looked into the colonel's gray eyes, pleading for answers.

"First Seargent Dak Harper, I am placing you under arrest."

"What?" The world spun around Dak in an instant. The mountains in the distance dipped at an angle and the earth at his feet followed. He felt bile rising in his gut. What was going on? Under arrest? Why?

"Sir, I don't understand. What are you talking about?"

"Oh, I think you understand plenty. We were told what happened during the operation, how you sided with the terrorists, turned your back on your team, and nearly got them all killed. To be honest, when I heard the story, I was glad you'd perished in the cave collapse, but now that I see you're alive, real justice can be given."

"Justice? Sir, I didn't betray anyone."

"That's enough, First Seargent. We'll be taking you into custody. You'll remain here until we find transport to the nearest military installation with proper holding facilities where you'll await your trial."

Trial? Holding facilities? Dak knew he wouldn't see such a place. Soldiers didn't take kindly to those who turned their back on their own.

"Sir, what are you talking about?" Dak ventured. He had nothing to lose. "Why are you doing this? We went to the camp as ordered. We took out the cell. But Bo and the others left me there. They wanted something out of the cave." He kept the secret of the treasure horde from the colonel, figuring that information was on a need-to-know basis.

"Don't lie to me, soldier. Five men have corroborated what happened. Their stories match up perfectly. You will go to trial. That is if you make it that long."

Dak knew what the man was talking about. From time to time, accidents happened. Soldiers who stepped out of line—went against the grain—ended up severely injured and sometimes worse. Such methods weren't mainstream. But out here in a backwater outpost, no one would know the difference if a traitor happened to trip in front of a Humvee.

He'd never seen it himself, but Dak had heard the stories and it sickened him that his commanding officer insinuated such. Not only that, these were his brothers and sisters soldiers he'd served with, sacrificed with, protected. Now they were treating him like a common street thug. Worse, actually.

Two more soldiers stepped around the colonel, moved behind Dak, and shoved him to the ground.

Dak didn't panic. That instinct had been bred out of him a long time ago. Now, though, he found himself fighting a wave of anxiety, confusion, and shock. How was he being arrested?

One resounding truth pounded at his brain as the soldiers behind him twisted his arms and prepared to zip tie his wrists.

Dak couldn't let them arrest him.

FIFTEEN

HAMRIN

The soldiers pressed Dak's head painfully into the dusty earth. The hard surface grated against his skin and a rock stabbed at his cheek, narrowly missing his eye. He struggled for a moment, but one of the soldiers pinning him down pushed harder and issued a warning, telling him it would be better for him if he didn't put up a fight.

Dak knew that wasn't true. If he let them arrest him, his life was over. He'd spend the rest of his good days in a maximum security prison with all the lowlifes of the military world.

That was something he couldn't abide. There was no chance he'd let them put him away for life.

The arresting soldiers had made a mistake when shoving him to the ground. They hadn't bothered to check him for weapons. It was standard procedure, yet they'd mistakenly forgotten.

He felt the knife against his skin, tucked under his belt and hidden from view by his shirt.

The soldier straddling him grabbed his left wrist and tried to bring it back to the other where he could bind the two together. He drove his knee into the small of Dak's back, using his weight to keep the prisoner down.

If he didn't make his move now, he'd never get another chance.

He subtly twisted his body to position the soldier's knee off center to the right. Knowing the grips, the pressure point moves, and the protocols the soldier would use came in handy as the guy tried to tweak Dak's wrist to a compromising angle. In a flash, Dak twisted his body one way, then the other, forcing the man's balance off kilter. The knee that was so solidly planted a second ago, slipped to the right, shifting the soldier's weight.

The abrupt move caused the men with guns to raise their weapons, but they couldn't fire for risk of hitting their own men.

As the arresting soldier slid to the right, Dak whipped both legs up, driving the heels of his boots into the man's middle back. He grunted in pain and his grip on Dak's wrists loosened.

Dak rolled hard, jerking his hands away and shoving one into his shirt where the belt lay in wait. In the blink of an eye, he unsheathed the weapon, while using the dazed soldier's torso for leverage to vault over and behind the man. Within two seconds, Dak went from nearly being arrested to holding the soldier hostage with a forearm gripped tightly around the man's neck.

Dak's feet shuffled backward as he held the soldier tight against his body as a human shield.

The other soldiers trained their weapons on the target, but he gave barely an inch of space as he poked his head around the hostage's right ear.

"Weapons down!" Dak shouted.

The men didn't move. Neither didn't the colonel, who simply stood there with his hands folded behind his back, watching the event play out.

"Did you not hear me? I said put your weapons down."

"You know what to do, men," the colonel said with a grim expression on his face.

The soldier in Dak's grasp now displayed sheer terror in his eyes, like a child jumping into a pool for the first time. He said nothing, though part of that was due to his windpipe being crushed under Dak's sinewy forearm.

"He won't kill anyone," the colonel continued. "Isn't that right, Dak? I mean, if you truly are innocent, you won't hurt one of your own. Right?"

The words seeped into Dak's soul, and deep down he knew them to be true. He wasn't going to hurt another American soldier, not these anyway. Bo and the others, that was a different story.

He pushed the sharp blade's edge into the man's neck and a trickle of blood dribbled onto the metal. The hostage swallowed and the blade sunk a little deeper.

"I wouldn't do that," Dak whispered into the man's ear. "Swallowing like that? You might cut yourself."

The man hissed an expletive through his teeth, directed at Dak.

"That's not very nice." Then Dak spoke to the gunmen. "I know you can live with killing me. Apparently, you've heard some bad information, so I'm going to tell you right now I did not betray anyone. If I turned my back on my team and joined with the terrorists, why would I come here?"

The men with the weapons aimed at Dak didn't answer, but the colonel did.

"Obviously, you were sent here to infiltrate the base or perhaps initiate an attack."

Dak snorted. "With a knife? Come on, colonel. Don't be stupid." He would have never spoken to a commanding officer that way, but at this point Dak figured he was no longer a member of the United States military. So, what difference did it make? "You men with the guns. If you kill me, you'll probably sleep fine thinking you killed a traitor. I'm no traitor. But can you sleep with the fact that you also killed one of you own?" He didn't know the soldier's name in his grasp, but he shook the man so they'd understand.

If the gunmen didn't put down their weapons, the hostage was going to die.

"Put your guns down or he dies. It's that simple. Then you'll kill me. Fine. Based on what the colonel said, I may as well be dead already. But this guy," he shook the hostage again, "he's one of your own. You know he didn't do anything wrong other than being here, today. So, what's it gonna be, boys? A lifetime of sleepless nights because you let one of your own die? Or are you going to do the right thing and put those guns down?"

The colonel didn't say anything this time. He had no answer for Dak's clever positioning.

Dak could see one of the gunmen was pondering the dilemma. The other still kept probing for a clean shot, but the risk was simply too great.

"I can stand here all day, Colonel," Dak chirped. "What about you?"

The truth was, Dak's legs felt like jello. He needed food and cursed himself for not grabbing something from the kitchen at the terrorist camp, though he wasn't sure he trusted any of their food. He was weak and needed to eat, but his will kept him on his feet and focused on the problem.

"Lower your weapons," the colonel ordered. The command came smothered in derision, but there was nothing he could do. He wished he'd ordered snipers to take out the traitor from the towers, but he'd mistakenly assumed the group he'd brought out onto the desert plains would be enough.

The men let the guns fall to their hips.

"On the ground," Dak said.

The men hesitated.

The colonel made no effort to hide his irritation. "Do as he says," the colonel sneered.

Each of the armed men put their weapons on the ground and stepped back, waiting to hear the next order.

"All of them," Dak said. "Sidearms too. And Johnny, you and the other gunner get out of the truck. Take more than five seconds to get out here with the rest of us, I kill this guy."

Johnny and the gunner from the other truck did as they were told and climbed down out of the Humvees. They placed their weapons with the others and joined their unarmed comrades in a group.

"Good man, Johnny. Thank you. Now, all of you step back."

The men did as told, except the colonel, who stood defiantly where he'd been since arriving.

He also still had a gun on his hip.

Dak inched his captive forward toward the gun cache. "Colonel, your sidearm, sir."

The commanding officer's eyes burned with fury. "You're going to die for this," he seethed. "I'll make sure of it, Harper. There isn't anywhere you can go I won't find you. You'll have nowhere to hide, no one to trust. You understand me?"

Dak caught a glimpse of Johnny's eyes dart toward the colonel, questioning his comment with an unspoken stare.

The colonel unholstered his weapon and set it with the others.

"That's my problem, sir. Now, if you don't mind, join the others over there." Once the man was with the others, Dak inched his way closer to the pile of guns. When he was standing next to them, he shoved the hostage toward the group and in one fluid motion, bent down and picked up two of the pistols. He aimed one at the colonel and the other toward the first man in line. Now, do me a favor." The colonel arched one eyebrow. "Grab as many of those zip ties as you can."

SIXTEEN

TATVAN, TURKEY

Dak stared quietly at Lake Van from his table in the back corner of the cafe. He sipped his second cup of Turkish coffee, chasing the last crumbs of baklava. A gentle breeze rolled across the lake's crystal surface. Mount Nemrut loomed in the distance, a few strands of snow trickling down the slopes of the massive, dormant volcano.

He chose a spot in the back of the cafe where he could see every exit and entrance—a habit he figured he would never break, especially now.

He wondered what the colonel was doing at that moment, other than rubbing aloe on his sunburned face and neck. Although that was an assumption, it was one that made Dak smile, at least for a couple of seconds.

He positioned the soldiers in a circle, handcuffed to each other with the zip ties that were meant for him—along with several more sets. He kept the two Humvees between the cluster of men and the line of sight to the base in case someone was watching. Someone was always watching. It was best to operate with that mindset. To do otherwise would be sloppy, careless.

At best, Dak figured he had maybe a thirty-minute head start on any pursuers, though he doubted it took that long for anyone at the base to think something was up when there'd been a lack of movement for over ten minutes during the ambush.

He'd probably only had fifteen to twenty minutes to get out of the area before the cavalry showed up to rescue the colonel and his men.

Twenty minutes for Dak Harper, though, was an eternity.

He knew how to disappear, to blend in, to vanish like an apparition. He also knew all the tricks the military would employ to hunt him down. The colonel's vast net could stretch across the globe. Still, Dak remained a step ahead, making his way farther north until he reached the Turkish border. He crossed under the cover of darkness, though the night provided little in the way of camouflage with a nearly full moon hanging in the sky above.

Once Dak was across the border into Turkey, he continued northeast until he reached the small town of Tatvan on Lake Van.

Tatvan was the town time forgot, which was easy to see due to its remote location. A valley stretched between mountains and hills, running until it stopped at the lake's lip.

The enormous body of water encompasses over 1400 square miles and is one of the world's largest endorheic lakes, meaning it has no natural outlet. Fish are rare in the lake, though one species—the Pearl Mullet—visits during the spring to spawn in the brackish waters.

Dak liked the location, but he knew he couldn't stay. Even though Tatvan was as good a place as any for him to disappear, that wasn't his primary objective. Not yet. Keeping invisible was paramount, to be sure, but he had another pressing item on his agenda: Bo Taylor and his crew.

It wasn't just about revenge, though Dak knew a measure of it was exactly that. But he also needed to clear his name. The colonel would—no doubt—go to the ends of the earth to make sure Dak was found, and that he paid for his crimes, crimes he didn't commit.

The colonel didn't know that, and Dak had to remind himself of that fact. In his mind, the colonel was merely doing his job, taking care of his fellow Americans in the face of a perceived threat. Dak didn't blame the colonel. The man needed proof, evidence that Bo and the others were the real villains in this scenario. That would come, though Dak knew he had to be patient.

He wondered if Bo and the others knew of his escape yet. Dak assumed that was the case, but they would pull their own disappearing act soon if they hadn't already.

It had been three days since his near arrest at the base. Bo and the others were slated to fly back to the states yesterday. They were long gone and finding them now would prove difficult. Dak didn't mind a challenge. In this case, he relished it. He was the hunter. Could he be more than that? Perhaps he wasn't just a hunter of people? Dak needed time to think about it. Since a network in the antiquities black market would be a necessity to track down Bo and the others, perhaps he needed to start there and become what he'd heard of only once before.

Relic runners were thieves who had a penchant for acquiring rare artifacts. Sometimes they sold the goods, other times they kept them for themselves until the value went up. Some relic runners worked for wealthy benefactors while others worked for no one else, choosing to go it alone.

Dak could see the benefits of either, but if this was going to be his new life, his new identity, he'd need to learn more about this unusual group of people.

He switched on the laptop he'd purchased earlier that morning from an electronics shop in the center of town. The laptop didn't have the latest or fastest components, but it would get the job done.

Dak had already moved his money, withdrawing a significant portion of his savings account at the local bank. He'd open shadow accounts with the cash as soon as he could procure a false identity, but that would take time. The only contact he knew of with those kinds of connections was his old friend Theo. Last Dak heard Theo was in Bangkok. That meant Dak would need to make a trip to Thailand soon.

He noted several tourists walking by with cameras and wondered where they'd been. The remote town didn't strike him as much of a tourist destination. The vistas overlooking the lake, the mountains, the valley, were spectacular to be sure, but he couldn't imagine coming all the way out here on a vacation. Not only was the town of Tatvan in the middle of nowhere, but it also played host to harsh winters, in part because of its elevation over 5000 feet above sea level.

The waiter returned—a young man with swept brown hair and a thin mustache. He was skinny and medium height, wearing a white button-up shirt and a black tie with matching black pants.

"Can I get you anything else?" the waiter asked with a pleasant smile.

"Actually," Dak said, "I was wondering about those tourists," he pointed at the group as they disappeared around the corner, pointing at buildings, taking pictures with their cameras and phones, and chattering in French.

The waiter followed his finger to the group as they meandered out of sight.

"Is there some famous spot around here they were visiting?"

The young man looked at him quizzically, then shrugged. "Nemrut Dag." Upon seeing the confusion in his patron's eyes, he explained further. "There are ancient ruins on top of the mountain. It is the place where King Antiochus I built his tomb and a temple, both to honor himself and the gods."

Dak's interest piqued at the information, but he wasn't here on a sightseeing trip. As much as he'd love to climb the mountain and examine this ancient site, he didn't have that kind of time. He had to get a new identity before the colonel's net closed in around him. Once he was a new man, he could re-establish his life for a while, drop off the radar. All of his assets would be tied up, locked down by the government. Fortunately, he'd been able to access most of his funds to give him a head start with his new—and hopefully temporary—life.

"This is your first time in Tatvan?" the waiter asked.

Dak nodded. "Yes."

"Well, the trip up to the top of the mountain is worth it if you have time, and if you're into ancient history. Most of the local towns-people think little of that stuff, probably because they've been around it their whole lives."

"I can imagine."

Dak paid his bill, and the man disappeared, grateful for the generous gratuity his patron added.

Maybe Dak would pay a visit to the mountain temple while he was here. The next train out of town wasn't coming for several hours and he doubted he'd ever visit this place again.

He glanced back at the laptop screen and then closed it. Dak was about to begin a dangerous game, but as the guy with nothing to lose, he liked his odds of winning. Bo and the others would slip up at some point. When they did, he'd be ready.

That reminded him. He had a phone call he needed to make.

He pulled up another tab and entered the words "International Archaeological Agency" in the search bar.

The IAA website popped up and Dak scrolled down to the "contact us" tab, clicked it, and then picked up the phone he'd purchased earlier. He'd bought two, one as a burner and the other for persistent use if needed, though at the time he didn't have anyone to call, save for this one to the IAA.

Dak met Sean Wyatt years ago on a mission in Pakistan. He knew that Wyatt worked for a clandestine agency, but he wasn't clear on who, only that the man had clearance well above Dak's pay grade.

Wyatt told Dak it would be one of his last missions and that he was transitioning to his friend's archaeological organization. Dak had heard of the work the IAA did to help secure some of the world's most valuable cultural artifacts. He respected Tommy Schultz, the IAA founder, and knew him to be an ethical man, though Dak had never met him before.

Dak saw what the IAA did to preserve important pieces of history, and all as a non-profit entity.

He entered the phone number for the IAA headquarters in Atlanta and pressed the phone to his ear. The receptionist answered with a pleasant hello and asked how she could direct his call.

The treasure in the Hamrin mountains was still there. He doubted Bo and the team would return to that exact spot. They had no reason to do so since they hadn't seen the tomb with its horde of riches. That didn't mean someone else couldn't find it eventually, and Dak wanted to make sure it was kept in the right hands.

"I'd like to speak with Tommy Schultz, please. I have some information about a potentially huge find in Iraq."

THANK YOU

Thank you for taking the time to read this story. We can always make more money, but time is a finite resource for all of us, so the fact you took the time to read my work means the world to me and I truly appreciate it. I hope you enjoyed it as much as I enjoyed sharing it, and I look forward to bringing you more fun adventures in the future.

Ernest

OTHER BOOKS BY ERNEST DEMPSEY

For Alexandre

YOU ONLY DIE ONCE

A DAK HARPER THRILLER

ERNEST DEMPSEY

ONE

ISTANBUL

Dak waited in the cool shade of the café's umbrella, sipping on his third coffee of the afternoon. Typically, such an indulgence didn't make it onto the menu so late in the day, but fatigue tugged on seemingly every fiber of his body. He needed the caffeine like a smackhead needs a spoon and a belt.

The table, adorned with two empty plates, a half empty glass of water, and the silverware he'd used to devour the baklava and Doner kebab, remained cluttered at his request, mainly to keep other patrons from occupying the empty chair opposite him. He couldn't afford distractions; except for getting more coffee.

The Turks took pride in their brew, and they made it strong—the way they had since its creation. A pinch of sugar was all they permitted, at least at the few establishments Dak had visited. He didn't mind; he liked his coffee strong—it sharpened his senses like a wet stone to steel.

Dak kept his eyes on the building across the street, particularly the door where he knew his quarry would enter.

He knew she had been at work all day, but quitting time had come and gone an hour ago, which told Dak she was working late, or was dilly dallying at one of the local hotspots for a few drinks. If he was a gambling man, he'd have bet on the latter.

Dak drained the rest of his coffee and set the cup on the table next to the empty plates. Although he craved a beer, especially in the warm afternoon heat, alcohol was the last thing he needed right now. But it was certainly tempting after the week he'd just endured.

Being left for dead by his comrades topped the list of bad breaks in the last seven days, but the betrayal by the army itself caught him completely off guard. Since his narrow escape from Iraq into Turkey, he tried not to focus on why this had happened to him and come up with a plan. A pity party wouldn't help anything. He was glad he didn't have a family back home that would have to endure all the rumors, the smearing. Dak lived a fairly solitary life, with only his sister and parents in the Florida Panhandle to consider. He loathed the lies they were being shoveled now, but he couldn't risk contacting them to tell them the truth, to fill them in on how the military they'd all sacrificed to serve was now tarnishing his name and trying to hunt him down like an animal.

No, he couldn't contact his parents, or his sister. Someone would expect that. Did they think he would be that stupid? Probably not. Whatever they thought, he was on his own.

That was why he came to Istanbul.

After he crossed the border, Dak stopped in Tatvan to lie low, get some new clothes, and figure out a plan. His assumptions proved correct when the colonel and his search parties went farther east on their hunt. Dak knew eventually they would recall those troops and resources, and then things would get dicey.

Dodging a bunch of newbies straight out of basic was one thing, but when the colonel had no choice but to call off the search, he would use more covert means to locate the AWOL Harper.

The colonel had a reputation for bending the rules and didn't try too hard to conceal it. He knew enough people to pull some of the best talent in the military for dark ops, missions that no one else could do. It just so happened that it was five of those guys who threw him into this boiling cesspool of a mess.

It could be worse, he thought. At least the coffee is good.

Maybe too good. He felt his bladder expanding and knew he'd soon have to vacate his table and head to the restroom.

"Come on," he breathed. "Where are you?" The need for a caffeinated buzz had turned on him.

The seconds ticked by as if pounded out by some brawny, muscle-bound blacksmith on an anvil. After another four minutes, he was about to surrender to the breaking dam when he noticed a young woman walking purposefully down the opposite sidewalk.

Her gait betrayed a sense of confidence and professional hustle, as is so often the case with people working in the tech industry. The brown satchel hanging from her shoulder dangled wildly as she strode, bobbing up and down with every step. Her carob-colored hair jiggled slightly with the same cadence.

"There you are," Dak said, rising slowly from his seat. He flipped two bills onto the table and set the empty mug on top so they wouldn't fly away in the breeze.

His eyes never left the young woman in the black, loose-fitting blouse and sandy-brown linen pants.

He moved like a panther, stalking its prey through an urban jungle. His shoulders tilted and twisted as he dodged pedestrians walking in both directions. Nearing the crosswalk, the light fortuitously turned red, and he darted across the street amid the flood of people.

The young woman neared the door to her apartment. As far as he could tell, she hadn't detected his presence.

She ascended the steps to the building and stopped at the brightly painted red door. Dak slithered through the oncoming foot traffic, covering ground faster now. The target slid her key into the door and he let go of caution, bumping and nudging past people, leaving angry scowls and profanity he didn't understand in his wake.

The woman entered the building and the door slowly swung

behind her, catching on the pneumatic cylinder overhead to slow its speed and prevent it from slamming shut.

Dak flew up the short staircase and caught the edge of the door before it closed.

He breathed heavily for two seconds before shoving the heavy door open. When he did, a surprise awaited him.

The woman stood steadfast with one hand on her hip and the other holding a Glock with a brushed metal slide atop the grip.

Dak sighed and shook his head.

"How did you know I was here?" he asked, unmoving.

"Normally, when someone has a gun pointed at them, they raise their hands."

"Well, this isn't normal. Or maybe it is for you. It's been a while."

She inclined her head. "Yes, it has, Dak. What, two years now?"

Dak stared at the woman he'd loved; it was the best four years of his life. Even with a gun in her hand, and definitely chambered, her stunning beauty shook him, just as it always had.

"That wasn't my call, Nicky," he said.

"You think it was mine?"

"You know I don't."

"Actually, I don't know that, Dak. I don't know why you left. I don't know why you're here now, but what I do know, is that wherever you go, trouble follows. And trouble isn't something I need right now." Her voice quivered in the way only a conflicted heart could.

When Dak left to join the military, she begged him not to, told him she could support them both. He wasn't okay with that. Not that he was opposed to her shouldering the financial burden, but he felt he should pull his weight, do his part—Dak was taught to take care of himself and those he loved. Only later did he come to regret that stubbornness, a relic of decades past. Many were the nights he'd wished he could unhinge his arrogance, his pride—go back in time and make it right. Those feelings led him to join the military anyway, the ultimate sacrifice to take care of those he loved. His sense of duty didn't help. Now, though, those beacons that guided him through the darkest nights of the soul stood cold and black, leaving him in a confusing fog like a ship charging toward a rocky shore.

"I know it was my fault," he admitted, his words full of gravel.

"So, that's what this is? You flew all the way from wherever you were to tell me it was your fault? Maybe apologize; hoping to get back together? You broke me, Dak. I spent two years of my life wondering if that morning would be your last while you were on the other side of the world fighting someone else's war."

"That's fair."

"I broke things off with you so I could start a new life and move on. I have a good thing going here. The last thing I need is you begging me to take you back. Because I have to tell you, it's not going to happen."

"I know."

Her brow furrowed, and the gun visibly sagged in her hand. "What do you mean? Why are you being so agreeable? No witty comeback? No snappy defense? And why do you smell like you haven't had a shower in three days?"

He raised his arm and took a whiff. It was appalling, though he'd become nose deaf to it.

"I haven't. So, if I could, I'd appreciate it. And second. No," he said, lowering his head for a long breath. "You're right about all of it. And it was unfair of me to do what I did. I know that now. While I don't regret serving my country—not much, anyway—I regret leaving you. If I could do it again, I might choose differently. I might not. But I'm not here to apologize, even though I am sorry for everything."

She hesitated. Her voice softened ever so slightly. "Then... why are you here?"

"I need your help," he said. Then added, "And I really need to use your bathroom."

TWO

RAMSTEIN AIR BASE

Bo Taylor stalked into the mess hall like a lion that just killed a gazelle for the pride. Most of the tables were empty, the base's occupants busy with their routine duties. Just days after Dak narrowly escaped the colonel's clutches, Bo and his team were sent to Germany to prepare for their return to the United States.

He sat down at a table in the corner where his team sat in tenuous silence. They all wore their standard issue fatigues, as always, though they seemed to fit some of the men better than others, specifically Billy. The camouflaged clothing draped over his skinny frame like a muumuu on a coat hanger.

"You look happy," Carson said in his usual deep, throaty tone. The huge man looked like a warrior, his taut muscles nearly bursting through the fatigues at every seam.

"Why wouldn't I be?" Bo said.

"So, we're going home?" Luis asked. The shortest of the bunch sat in the corner, hunched over steepled fingers. The words came out amid a nervous apprehension.

"We're going wherever we want, boys," Bo said with a rap on the table. "You can go home, to a beach, whatever psycho farmhouse Nate wants to go to."

Billy snorted a laugh, but the accompanying smile vanished with a predatory glare from Nathan.

Something about Nathan Collier unnerved all the men in their team, even Bo from time to time. Their leader blew it off with a casual "at least he's on our side" attitude, but he didn't trust Collier. The man's quiet demeanor as he went about killing would have caused a serial killer's stomach to turn. There was a grimness to it, something both spiritual and terrifying all at once. It didn't help that he had a tattoo of the fabled reaper on his shoulder, complete with black robes flowing beyond bony, skeletal feet, a scythe whipping around for the harvest, and hollow eyes peering out above a toothy grin.

"So, they didn't find out about—" Luis Martinez stopped himself and looked around. Even though he was in the corner and could see the entire mess hall from his vantage point, paranoia gripped him tight.

Bo shook his head, both at the question and at Luis' naïvety, to even think about saying it out loud, and at the volume he'd been using.

Leaning in close, Bo lowered his own voice. "We're even getting medals," he said with a measure of humor. "We're heroes. And we're rich. We can go wherever we want, boys."

"Assuming we can move the goods," Nathan groused in his usual monotone.

Bo sighed in irritation, but he didn't push the man's buttons. "I have a guy who can move them. You don't have to worry about that. What you four do need to consider is being careful with how you spend your share. Don't be stupid and go blowing it all at a club," he cast a warning glance at Billy.

"Hey," Billy protested and threw up his hands.

Carson chuckled. "He has you pegged, kid."

"Like you're one to talk."

"Shut it," Bo snapped. "Once the deal is done with my guy, I'll contact you."

Nathan snorted derisively. "I don't think so."

"What's that supposed to mean?" Bo stiffened his spine and did his best to look insulted.

"We're just supposed to let you walk off with all our shares of the treasure and assume you'll bring us our cut?" Nathan held a razor-sharp knife in his hand and cut through a ripe Fuji apple with expert and insidious precision. He popped the sliver into his mouth and chewed, keeping his eyes on the fruit as he sliced another piece.

"I'm disappointed in your lack of trust, Nate, but if that's how you feel, you can come with me. All of you can." Bo did his best to play the role of the peacemaker. "I was just trying to make it easy for you."

"Thanks so much." Nathan's gravelly response sent a chill through Bo.

Truth was, Bo couldn't wait to get away from the creep. Just being in the same room with him, at this close proximity, made him uneasy.

"When is this deal going down, Bo?" Luis asked.

"Tonight?" Billy asked. "How is he getting here so fast?"

Bo smirked, as if Billy should have known the answer. "He's local," Bo said. "Based out of Frankfurt."

"That's convenient," Luis said.

"A lot of the best businessmen in the world are in Frankfurt. Some of them have connections—connections we can use. My contact will be here tonight at twenty-two hundred hours. We'll make the exchange then."

All except Nathan exchanged excited, greedy looks.

"Wait," Carson rumbled. "How much are we getting?"

Bo rolled his shoulders. "He will make us an offer when he sees the goods. Don't worry," Bo reassured. "I'm sure we'll make out."

"And if we don't?" Nathan questioned.

"Then we find another buyer," Bo said. "If I can find one, I can find another. He's not the only fish out there, boys. So, relax. Have some of that good German beer nearby, and we'll leave here at twenty-one hundred hours, get to the rendezvous a little early to scope the place out, and then we do the deal."

"Sounds good, boss," Luis said, nodding.

"I have a few things to take care of before we fly out tomorrow. I'll see you guys tonight. We can leave from here."

"What about Harper?" Nathan asked. He made the query as if asking about the price of a pack of gum.

Bo inclined his head, the look on his face turning stern. "You may want me to tell you not to worry about him, but that's the opposite of what you should do. You need to keep him in the back of your mind. He's out there somewhere. Maybe he's dead in the desert. I doubt it. My guess is he went north across the border into Turkey."

"The colonel sent search teams through there," Billy offered.

Bo responded with a sincere huff. "You think those guys are going to find Dak Harper? He's a ghost, Billy. Just like us. No one is going to find him."

"You don't think—"

"Yes, I do think he will try to hunt us down. It's what I'd do. It's what you would probably do, Carson. I know it's what Nate would do," he gave a nod toward Collier, who was still meticulously slicing the apple. "Which is all the more reason you guys need to lie low. With the money we make from this deal, we're going to be able to disappear. I'm talking new identities, the works. Not even Dak Harper will be able to track us down once we go dark. You understand?"

The men nodded. He stood up and left the other four staring after him for a long moment until he rounded the corner into the hallway. Bo's anger flushed through him with every step. His plan hadn't been to rip off the members of his team, though the thought crossed his mind.

It would be easy to sell off the treasure and leave them all in

Germany wondering where in the world he went. With the kind of money he figured they'd receive for the lode, he could disappear—erase himself. For a soldier whose job was to blend in much of the time, doing so with a ton of cash would be even easier.

Still, he didn't underestimate his team. Bo knew all too well that they wouldn't sleep until they had tracked him down. Even as good as he could be at disappearing, it wasn't worth the risk—always having to check over his shoulder to make sure he wasn't in someone's sights. And with Harper still on the loose, that could be a perennial issue.

No, he would do the deal with the German. They would split the money and go their separate ways. Bo didn't tell them about the second part of his plan. He'd been wondering if they'd left the treasure site too quickly, and if there might be more. He told himself not to be greedy, but the thought had stuck with him since the night they'd left Harper to die.

Dak had escaped and tried to return to base. Fortunately, Bo's contingency plan worked. The colonel believed his story about how Dak went nuts and attempted to kill Bo and his men. How Dak had managed to escape the clutches of the men sent to arrest him, Bo still didn't know, but that wouldn't matter as long as he was careful.

Still, if Dak found a way out of that cave, that meant there might be other treasure chambers in there somewhere.

Bo would give it a few weeks, maybe longer, before he ventured back there. Things needed to die down. He would set up his new life first. When his compadres were spread out around the world and couldn't keep tabs on him, he would go back to where they found the horde and see what else was there. Dak's body would there. That was something Bo knew he'd have to deal with, but it was a small detail.

He turned down an adjacent hall and stepped through a door into a recreation area. A pair of basketball hoops hung from backboards on either end, surrounded by a high fence.

Bo continued walking, his pulse calming to its normal rhythm as he reveled in the joy of his victory. He drank in the warm afternoon air as the rays of bright sunlight radiated against his skin.

He would be a very rich man. And if his guess was right, he'd be even richer upon returning to the mountains of Iraq.

THREE

ISTANBUL

Dak opened the door and stepped out of Nicole Carter's bathroom, straight into a fiery glare. The arms crossed tight across her chest didn't make him feel any better.

"Thank you," Dak said, ignoring the barbs flying at him from her eyes. "I had, like, three cups of coffee at that café across the street. Really good stuff, by the way. Strong. Just like I like it."

"I hope you're ready to leave," Nicole spat.

His head drooped so his chin nearly touched his upper chest. His thick beard brushed against the black T-shirt he'd purchased in Tatvan, the name of the town prominently displayed across his pecs in white letters.

"I deserve that."

"Yep. So, thanks for stopping by to resurrect the pain I was beginning to forget about. I appreciate it." Nicole spun on her heels and marched into the narrow kitchen.

Stopping in front of a cupboard, she tugged on the handle. The door opened easily and she removed a bottle of Jack Daniel's.

Dak smiled in approval. "That was one of the things I always loved about you. You're a whiskey girl."

"Please go," she ordered. This time, however, her voice cracked.

That hurt more than the acrid attitude he'd received so far.

"Look," Dak said, his head hanging again, eyes locked on the bamboo floorboards.

She held the bottle in her right hand while she fished a tumbler out of the same cabinet. "Go on, Dak. Spit it out." She splashed three fingers of whiskey into the glass and set the bottle down, leaving the cap off. Dak knew what that meant. He'd hurt her with the simple act of coming here, and she was going to deal with it the way she used to.

"I need your help," he said, deciding to go with blunt honesty. The words came out of his mouth like hot ash atop of a swollen tongue.

She was in the midst of raising the glass to her lips when he said it. The words disarmed her, causing her to freeze. Nicole turned her head to face him, still holding the drink near her neckline. "What? Did I hear you correctly?"

"I don't deserve it. Okay? I know I screwed up. Big time."

She nodded and tossed the whiskey into her mouth with the expertise and showmanship of a career bartender. Her head snapped back, and she swallowed the warm liquid without wincing at the tingling burn as it crawled down her throat.

"Got that right," she said and tilted the bottle over the glass again. This time, she went for just two fingers and a slightly more careful pour. "So, I was right. You're in some kind of trouble."

"Not some kind," he said, risking a step toward her. He stopped by the kitchen counter, began. "The worst kind. The army is saying I went AWOL, turned my back on my team, and now they're looking for me."

She'd raised the glass to her lips and taken a sip when he said it. The whiskey spewed out in a fine, amber mist. Nicole managed to catch only a fraction of it in her palm.

"What did you say? The army? The United. States. Army. They're looking for *you*? And you thought it was a good idea to come here?"

"They don't know I'm here, Nicky."

"How did you know I was here?" Her voice raged in the confined space.

He blushed. "I... I never stopped loving you. I wanted to make sure you were okay, so... I kept tabs on you."

Her chin drew back against her throat, eyebrows reaching skyward. "You stalked me?"

"Okay, now that you put it that way. I guess I never really thought of it like that, but no, not exactly. I just—"

"You just stalked me." Her hands dug into her hips and her head tilted at an angle; an angle he'd only seen when she was beyond angry.

"No," he insisted. "I... I just asked Keri now and then how you were doing. That's all."

"Oh." It was Nicole's turn to feel ashamed.

"She said you moved here, to Istanbul. That was... that was a while back." His head hung; he couldn't hold eye contact for fear the dams in his eyes would burst. "She told me you were doing okay, that you'd taken a job for some big company." He picked up his head again and did his best to make eye contact without losing it. "I just had to make sure you were good. That's all. I wasn't going to bother you. Then this happened."

"What happened?" she asked, her tone softening. She didn't take a step toward him, even though her instincts told her to.

He took a deep breath and sighed. "I guess there's no harm in telling you since I'm a wanted man now, anyway." The words stung him right in the chest. He still didn't understand what happened, other than the lone theory rattling around in his brain. Bo must have convinced the colonel that Dak had turned on them. It was the only explanation.

"We had an operation in the mountains of Northern Iraq," Dak said. "The job wasn't an easy one, but we didn't anticipate running into much trouble. There was a terrorist camp, most of them holed up in a cave. They'd been hitting small villages and outpost towns for a while. Everything went according to plan until we got into the cave."

He paused, tempted to let her ask what they had found underground, but kept going. "We took out the targets. Then we found something, a treasure of some kind. Looks ancient, but I'm a little rusty on some of my history stuff."

One of her eyebrows arched slightly.

"Anyway, the guys thought it would be a good idea to loot the place, sell the artifacts, gold, jewels, all of it, on the black market. I argued with the guys, told them we needed to report it, but they were set on taking everything and making some quick cash. Because I didn't go along with their plan, they tried to kill me. I barely got out alive. And that was after they left me for dead in the cave."

"How... did you get out?"

"I found a place to hide where they couldn't get to me. With everything in a stalemate, they knew they couldn't stay there indefinitely, so they blew the entrance to the cave, effectively locking me in. Except I found another way out."

"And you came here?" She looked confused and apologetic at the same time.

"Not at first," Dak admitted. "I returned to base. I thought I could go back, tell the colonel what happened, and they would arrest the rest of my team. Instead, they tried to take me."

"But they didn't." She almost sounded proud of the fact.

"It was a close call, but I know Bo Taylor had to be behind it. He probably gave the colonel some story about how I tried to kill them, or that I went AWOL. I don't know all the details, obviously. What I do know is that the colonel will do everything he can to bring me in if he thinks I'm guilty."

"Do you think they know you'll come here?" she asked the question as if the possibility didn't concern her, even though it should have.

"No," he said. "They won't connect those dots. Besides, I'll be out of here soon."

"Yes, you will. Though I'm still not sure why you came here. You said you needed my help?"

He nodded and bit his lower lip. "I'm off the grid right now. Nobody is more on the grid than you. I have a pre-paid phone I picked up in Tatvan, but it has limitations."

"Would you just spit it out, Dak? You never used to beat around the bush before."

"Sorry. You're right. I need you to find someone for me." The glare in her eyes pushed him to elaborate. "His name is Will Collins. Last I saw him, he was in South Carolina, based out of Greenville."

"And what's so special about this friend of yours?"

Dak considered telling her the truth, that Will was a former military guy who made a living selling guns. Most of the time his business was legal, by the book, but Dak knew Will understood how to circumvent certain channels. Word on the street was that Will made a bunch of money in a short amount of time and dropped off the map, sold his company, and moved abroad. There was a chance he wouldn't be able to help Dak with his current predicament, but something told him Will would still have at least one hand in a shady cookie jar. Dak hoped it was the one he needed.

"Will knows how to get things and how to make things. One of those things is a new passport. He can get me the paperwork I need to start over." Dak blunted the truth. He needed new ID, papers, passport, all of that, but not to start over as a bartender somewhere in Europe. He had one goal in mind—to find his old team and eliminate them, one by one.

Nicole crossed her arms and tapped the right bicep with her index finger, as if trying to determine if he was telling the truth. That was one thing she'd always appreciated about Dak; he never lied to her. Not once. Right now, that honesty was probably the only reason she would consider helping him.

"Okay," she relented with a passing hand. "I'll help you locate your friend."

"Thank you," he gasped. "The minute you do, I'll be out of your hair."

Her body slumped slightly, almost as if disappointment and gravity shared a common bond. She quickly realized what she'd done and stiffened. "Do you need money?"

"I have a little."

She rolled her eyes and strolled over to the kitchen counter where a cedar cigar box sat in the corner. She flipped open the lid and took out a wad of euros, counted several bills on out onto the counter, then stuffed the rest back in the box.

Nicole picked up the money, padded back over to him, and held it out.

"I'm not taking your money, Nicky," he said. "I appreciate it, though. I'll be fine."

"If you didn't need it, you would have stopped me from counting it out. Take it. That should get you anywhere you need to go in Europe. Buy a train ticket. That's the best way to travel here."

He knew that, but didn't say so. "Thank you. I'll pay you back."

"Please," she said. "That's spare change I keep lying around the house. I almost never use cash, but it doesn't hurt to have it."

"I guess not." He lowered his head again, feeling ashamed for taking anything from her.

"As to your friend, I may be able to help you, but not until you get a shower." She looked at him like he had toxic waste dripping off his shoulders. "Leave your clothes in a bag and I'll wash them."

"You don't have to—"

"No, I really think I do, Dak."

The disgusted scowl on her face said it all. He chuckled. "Okay. I'll take a shower while you look for Will."

FOUR

RAMSTEIN-MIESENBACH, GERMANY

Yellow lights illuminated the dark green umbrellas hanging over the tables of the Forsthaus Beckenhof biergarten. The place would normally be packed with locals drinking tankards of beer and reveling in laughter, or philosophical conversations that would undoubtedly save the world.

This night, however, the giant patio was as a graveyard, silent and secretive.

Bo looked over the area for the twentieth time. They arrived early to scout the rendezvous point and choose positions for the rest of his team. Billy watched over his shoulder from a bell tower at the end of the street. Carson took his watch from a window above a bakery across the street. Nathan held a position in a thicket of shrubs near the back end of the biergarten. He was the closest if things took a dicey turn, and he could also cut off an escape down that end of the street. Luis was opposite him, directly behind Bo in the car they'd rented. His job was to be ready to cut off an enemy retreat if they took off that way.

Bo didn't think that was going to happen. His contact was a good businessman and he wouldn't risk a short-term gain for a long-term loss, although people's ability to do stupid or erratic things never ceased to surprise Bo. It was the one consistent element of humanity; they were full of surprises. Knowing that, Bo took precautions.

He stepped under the white, ivy-covered archway, topped with a sign that read "biergarten", and continued into the sitting area. Bo had seen many similar establishments in this country, and he often wondered why there weren't more like it back in the States. He briefly considered opening one, then remembered he probably wasn't going to end up in the US.

Carson was planning ongoing to Miami. The man loved white sand and azure water, and the endless warmth. Bo had joked with him about the sand; after all, they'd spent a sizable chunk of their tour in deserts.

Nathan hadn't been as forthright about where he was going. Bo was actually good with not knowing. Luis claimed he had friends in Mexico and he might go there. Billy had his sights set on a farm in Montana.

Bo surveyed the street to his right through the white fence that surrounded the biergarten. It too was wrapped in dark green ivy. No cars drove by, and he'd only seen three since arriving half an hour before. There would be fewer as the night wore on. Somewhere in the village, from around the corner opposite the drinking hall, a young woman's voice cackled in the night. A friend or lover must have said something funny. Or maybe she was just drunk and every-thing was funny.

An owl hooted from one of the trees behind the Forsthaus Beck-enhof building.

The breeze still and cool, tickled Bo's ears.

His senses were always high for something like this. It wasn't a mission, but he treated it as such. That kept him sharp, made certain he didn't get sloppy and make mistakes.

Bo strolled through the main aisle to the back of the patio and found a table in the corner where the only thing to his back was the fence, the corner of the building, and Nathan Collier with a Sig Saur

9mm XM17. Just because he didn't fully trust the psychotic Collier, didn't mean the maniac didn't have his uses.

"In position," Bo said into his radio.

No one responded per his orders. They were only to report on their positions and any suspicious activity they might witness. So far, nothing had been said.

Within forty seconds of finding his seat, Bo noticed headlights coming down the avenue next to the biergarten. The sound of tires on asphalt and moaning engines signaled the arrival of the German's entourage.

Bo noted the three BMW 8 Series Gran Coupes as they passed by. The three black sedans ground to a quick halt and doors opened, releasing men in dark suits and ties. They hurried to secure the area around the vehicles, each looking out across the dimly lit streets and yards. One of the men gave a curt nod, and another flung open the back door to the middle sedan. A tall gentleman stepped out. He wore a navy blue suit with a black tie and white pinstripes. His thick, blond hair swept over his left eyebrow. Calculating blue eyes the color of an iceberg scanned the scene, doing his best to imitate the security team.

Bo watched the parade with smug disapproval. Amateurs, he thought. Not everyone in the private security game was incompetent. He knew several companies that ran more than adequate outfits. This group, however, looked the part. They acted the part. But they were clueless. Bo's team wasn't invisible. Collier was pretty close. A good unit would have noticed Luis in the car up the block, but these guys didn't seem to even notice the occupied vehicle. Billy was mostly out of sight, though the silhouette of a human head and shoulder protruding from the side of the giant bell should have been a dead giveaway. Carson's window blinds were closed except for one or two in the middle, a clear sign someone was looking out. Bo would have to have a chat with his team. Then again, why bother? After this, they were going their separate ways.

The first two guards appeared in the archway and stepped inside, each checking their respective corners before moving down the aisles toward the end of the patio where Bo waited.

The contact appeared with two more guards at the archway. The man smoothed his suit jacket and inclined his chin, then strolled into the biergarten with his shoulders broad and head held high.

The two guards on either side of him split off and took up positions in the center of the patio while the last two protected the exit.

The entire show made Bo want to laugh, but he didn't dare.

The black briefcase in his hand barely swung as he strode through the biergarten. The contact stopped abruptly at the head of the table, assessing his seller the way a shrewd businessman would. His tanned skin betrayed many days on beaches or yachts. Though, Bo didn't sense the man was soft.

"Please have a seat," Bo said.

"Thank you," the man said and pulled out one of the white chairs circling the matching table. His accent was blunted, a sign he'd spent many years abroad, probably in the UK or the US, though it was still strong enough that no one would mistake him as anything but German.

"Yes, sir," Bo said.

"I hope you don't mind the venue," the German said, waving a hand around the biergarten.

"Not at all. I'm impressed you could pay them enough to shut down for an evening, although there isn't much going on in the village right now."

"Holiday," the man explained. "Many of the locals are out of town for a week or two. Those who aren't are closing down their businesses earlier than normal. This establishment's owner was more than happy to make a little extra money to allow us to have our meeting."

Bo appreciated the man's savvy. "Some money is better than no money."

"Exactly." The man raised a finger and made a dot in the air. "And while we are on the subject of money, here is yours."

He hefted the briefcase onto the table and set it down with a clunk, flipped it open and spun it around.

"This is more than enough, I believe, for what you've brought me. I assume the treasures you discovered are somewhere close by."

The German pulled open the lid to the briefcase. Bo's eyes blinked rapidly for a few seconds as he gazed at one of the most beautiful things he'd ever seen in his life.

"We never even negotiated a price," Bo said with an edge to his tone. "You haven't seen the goods."

"Yes, well, let's just say I know a good buy when I see one. This case contains five million. I hope you don't mind, I took the trouble of bringing American dollars for your convenience."

"Five million," Bo said, trying to sound unimpressed. His heart pounded. That was a million dollars a man. More than enough to jump-start his new life.

"Yes," the German confirmed. "There are four more cases just like it in the car."

"Four more?" Bo blurted. It was rare for him to be thrown off his game, but he found himself nearly gasping for air. He quickly recovered, steeling his excitement into a hardened exterior. With a clenched jaw, he asked, "So, your offer is twenty-five?"

"Correct."

"And you haven't seen the product."

"As I said, I know a good buy when I see one. And I've seen enough. I trust my offer is adequate."

Bo's head slowly nodded. "Yes. Adequate."

"So, we have a deal?"

Bo smirked. "Absolutely, old friend. Pleasure doing business with you."

He stood and extended his hand toward the German. The man took it as he stood and then pushed the case toward Bo.

He turned to one of the guards and ordered him and the others to bring the four additional briefcases, speaking in German as he issued the command.

The two guards in the middle of the biergarten immediately stepped to the center of the room and trotted out of the patio to retrieve the items.

"Bring the goods," Bo said into his radio.

The car up the street revved to life, and within a minute, Luis swung around to the entrance of the biergarten.

The German looked back over his shoulder at the sound of the vehicle's engine and the tires grinding on the asphalt. "Didn't trust me?" the man asked.

"No, it's not that," Bo confessed. "It's just easier to transport that way."

The businessman didn't let on that he believed or disbelieved the explanation. "Let's have a look then, shall we?"

"After you," Bo said, extending a hand toward the aisle as he stood.

The two men walked back to the front of the biergarten and through the archway. Luis stood outside the car with his hands over his waist, doing his best to look professional. The truth was, Luis was ten times the pro compared to the German's guards.

"Luis, the trunk, please," Bo said.

Luis nodded and reached into the car. He pressed a button near the bottom of the seat and the trunk popped open.

Bo took a step closer and eased the trunk's lid up. Sitting atop the carpeted interior were five gear bags.

"Please inspect them as much as you like," Bo offered. "For the price you're paying, you can roll around in it for all I care."

The German grunted a laugh and moved toward the trunk. He unzipped the first bag and ran his fingers over a collection of necklaces, gems, and golden coins. He repeated the search with the second and third bags. When he came to the fourth bag, though, he stopped midway through his sifting when he found a large, unusual gem.

He pulled it out and held it up to the streetlight. The ruby was the size of his fist, but it had been cut in a way unlike anything Bo had ever seen before. He'd thought as much when he retrieved the jewel from the cave.

The ruby had the same conical shape as most, with beveled edges and a flattened top, but in the center of the top portion, it had been bored out to mirror the shape of the bottom.

Bo hoped that wouldn't lower the value of the gem, but he figured the rest of the collection would still fetch a generous price. He would never have imagined twenty-five million, though.

He watched as the German inspected the jewel, unwilling to comment despite the rush of defensive thoughts intruding into his mind.

"A most unusual piece," the German said, still analyzing the gem in the streetlight. "Incredible."

Bo hid his relief at the man's comment. "Yes. I'm not an expert in precious stones, but I've never seen anything quite like it."

The German drew a breath. "I imagine you haven't."

Was that derision in his voice? Bo wasn't sure, and he couldn't imagine why there would be. "So, it's good?" Bo asked, trying not to sound insecure.

"It's perfect." The German gently set the stone back into the bag and zipped it closed. He motioned to two of the guards nearby. The men immediately rushed to the trunk and lifted the four bags out, one in each hand, then carried them over to the convoy to begin loading.

The German swiveled and extended his hand to Bo. "I have to say, Mr. Taylor, this has been one of the easiest negotiations I've ever been a part of. I wish they were all this way." He twirled a finger around in the air and two other guards produced four matching brief-cases. The men walked over to where Bo was standing and set them down at his feet.

"The feeling is mutual," Bo said. "Pleasure doing business with you."

"The same."

The German walked away, stalking toward his sedan. Bo kept his eyes open and his hands ready, just in case the businessman issued an order to kill. That command never came. Instead, the German climbed into the open back door of his car and slammed it shut while the guards finished stowing the bags into the trunk of the middle car.

With the bags secure and the guards back in the vehicles, the convoy drove off and disappeared around the corner, leaving nothing but the fading sounds of their engines groaning in the night.

Bo nodded and looked down at the four briefcases at his feet and the one in his hands.

He had more than enough money to disappear now. The whole team did.

"Mission accomplished, gentlemen," Bo said into his radio. "Time for us to begin our new lives."

He pulled out the radio earpiece and let it dangle on his neck amid a series of shouts and joyful hollers.

Bo felt their emotions, but he also felt the tug of paranoia. After all, Dak Harper was still out there somewhere. And while that man had air in his lungs, there were few safe places to hide.

FIVE
ISTANBUL

Dak stood in the shower for an eternity, letting the hot water soak over his tired muscles. The soothing warmth reached deep into his bones and gave him a sense of relief he hadn't felt in days, though it seemed much longer. When he finished, he stepped out of the shower and grabbed a towel from off the nearby rack, dried himself off, and tied it around his waist.

He padded over to the mirror and slicked his hair back, then used a hand towel to finish drying his beard.

While he stood there at the sink, a knock came from the door. "You decent?" Nicole asked, cracking the door open an inch.

"Yeah, I have a towel on," he said.

She pushed it all the way open and stepped in. Nicole caught herself accidentally appreciating the man's form, the broad shoulders and back, the muscles in his arms and chest.

"My eyes are up here," Dak joked, motioning to his face.

She shook her head quickly and recovered. "I have no idea what you're talking about. But your clothes will be dry in a half hour."

"Thank you," he said sincerely. "Any luck finding my friend Will?"

"Actually, yes. Turns out he wasn't that difficult to locate."

"That's a bit of a surprise," Dak said as he turned around to face her, planting his palms on the edge of the sink as he leaned back.

Again, she caught herself admiring his form, but he said nothing this time.

"Yes, well. It surprised me too, since you seemed to think it would be much more difficult. If your friend is trying to keep a low profile, he's not doing a very good job of it."

Dak offered a snorted laugh and bobbed his head.

That much was true.

Will wasn't good at keeping a low profile. He had too much pride for that. The man known as the quartermaster had always been happy to share tales of action and adventure with friends, even some stories that were supposed to remain classified. He omitted names and locations, of course, but the stories were there just the same. The funny thing was, Will almost never took part in any of the missions he discussed, though no listening ear could discern that. He was an armorer, a guy who could get things, but a killer? Maybe in a life Dak didn't know about, but as far as he knew, Will had never even been in a bar fight.

"Where?" Dak asked pointedly.

She crossed her arms. "You're welcome, by the way. I said it wasn't hard, but I'm good. For an ordinary person, maybe it would be."

"Thank you," Dak offered. "I do appreciate it. Seriously."

"Good. And you're welcome." She cleared her throat. "He's in a small Portuguese fishing town called Nazare. It's famous for some of the largest waves in the world. Once that word got out, surfers from around the world started coming to visit or buy condos there. Your friend Will has a place on the beach."

"You're amazing," Dak said with a smile. "Thank you again."

"Don't mention it. I'll leave you to yourâ€¦ um, drying off. You'll hear the alarm on the dryer when your clothes are ready."

She abruptly left the bathroom and closed the door behind, leaving Dak alone to his thoughts and speculation.

Nazare, he thought. It was just like Will to find some obscure European beach to settle down. It was also the last place anyone would look for an ironmonger like him. There wasn't a huge market for weapons on the Iberian Peninsula, not that Dak knew of, but from there Will could connect to buyers in France, England, and beyond. Then again, it wasn't really Will's style to work with those types, which meant Dak's friend may have changed his business a little. In the past, he was happy to sell certain kinds of weapons to citizens in the US, weapons that were deemed illegal.

He still ran background checks on them, making sure he wasn't selling these guns to psychopaths. Will had strict standards for that sort of thing, considering what he was doing was illegal.

That was another reason Dak trusted the man. Will had a code of ethics and stuck by it. Even when breaking the law.

A thought occurred to Dak. He tried to keep it from slipping out, but he couldn't fight off his curiosity. He pushed away from the sink and stepped around the corner to find Nicole standing over a glass of red wine at the kitchen counter. He couldn't tell if she was crying, but it sure looked that way from the side.

The pain from years before sunk into his chest like a rusty knife. He knew another apology wouldn't change anything. Maybe a little flattery could.

"I gave you nothing but the man's first and last name. How in the world could you have possibly located him in less than ten minutes with that minimal information?"

Nicole's lips creased, easing up her right cheek. "First of all, you were in the shower for twenty minutes. Five more and you would've run out of hot water. Second, a girl has to have her secrets, doesn't she?"

He inclined his head, peering at her over the tops of his lower eyelids. He surrendered a nod. "I suppose so."

"Although," she added, "since you gave up the fact he was in the military before and maybe had a few run-ins with authority in one form or another, that helped a bit. I also don't think your friend is trying very hard to keep a low profile. Not like I would if I was in his shoes. Honestly, I expected it to take hours, maybe even a day or so to find him. And I'm good."

"He's on Instagram. Isn't he?"

"Yep." She emphasized the word with a pop. "Didn't even bother changing his name to an alias."

"Well, in his defense, he's not super creative with things like that. Circumventing the law? Definitely."

Nicole sighed. She delicately picked up the stemless wine glass and tipped back the drink, taking in a huge gulp.

"I thought you were a whiskey girl."

She cocked her head to the side and twisted it to face him. "Yeah, I am. Sometimes you got to mix things up."

"I never heard of a saying about whiskey before wine. Plenty about beer and liquor, though."

A feeble laugh leaped from her lips. "Yeah, I think we all know that one." She took another sip, this time less aggressively, then set the glass down. "You can sleep on the couch tonight. Then go find your friend in the morning."

"No," he said, shaking his head. "I can't do that."

"Well, you're not sleeping in the bed with me."

After he snorted, he corrected his statement. "I meant I can't stay here tonight with you. I don't want to put you in danger, any more than I may already have. I have to keep moving until I get to Will."

"One night won't put me in danger. I know how to take care of myself."

She was right. Nicole could handle herself in most kinds of fights. Plus, with him there, they'd be a formidable adversary for any assassins or bounty hunters the colonel could have sent.

"That's true," he said. "You can. But I won't be able to sleep if I stay here."

"Where are you going to stay, Dak? Got a hotel on the outskirts of town or something?" She turned to face him, leaning on an elbow atop the counter.

He rolled his shoulders. "I'll figure it out."

"No. You're staying here. If this colonel sent people to find you and they knew you were here, they would have already busted down the door."

That part wasn't entirely true. If he was one of the hunters, he'd wait until dark. Fewer eyes to witness anything suspicious. Maybe he was being overly cautious. He usually erred on the side of caution more often than not.

Nicole's safety wasn't the only reason he didn't want to stay. He wanted to stay there with her, more than anything. He wanted to scoop her up in his arms and kiss her until the sun rose over the eastern horizon the next morning.

That wasn't on the docket, though, and he knew it probably never would be.

"Look," she said, pointing at the couch. It was a beige chaise with thick, soft cushions. "It's not a sleeper sofa, but it's more comfortable than any couch I've ever slept on. I pass out on in some nights while I'm up late watching television. I have sheets and a pillow you can use."

He lowered his eyes to the floor again, humbled by her generosity, generosity he didn't deserve. Not in a million years.

"Okay," he grunted.

"I'm sorry, what?" she teased.

"Thank you," he corrected as he lifted his eyes to connect with hers. "For everything."

"Yeah, well, you're welcome." She turned and raised the glass, then dumped the remaining contents into her mouth. She swallowed hard. Nodding as she apprised the container, she looked back at him. "Yeah, you're right. Whiskey is better."

"Mind if I have another?"

She permitted a grin to cross her face. "May as well. Probably the only way either of us will get any sleep tonight."

SIX

NAZARE, PORTUGAL

Dak woke up to see Nicole's face lying on the pillow next to him. She smiled dreamily as he allowed gravity to keep him trapped in the sheets and comforter.

"It's time to wake up, Dak," she said, her voice carried by an unusually heavy reverb. It sounded blurry in his ears.

"I don't want to wake up," he slurred. "I'm tired. And I'm comfortable."

The same grin he'd fallen for over and over again creased her lips and she shook her head at him. "No, sleepy boy. You have work to do. And I can't stay."

"Just five more minutes," he growled. He reached his arm out to wrap it around her waist, but it passed through her covered figure and the apparition vanished.

"Nicky?" he said, suddenly overcome with panic. "Nicky?"

His head snapped up from the pillow, and he looked around the room. Dark blue curtains at the far window blocked the rising sun's rays. One of the windows, cracked the night before, allowed the sound of waves crashing against the shore to dance through the room.

The ambient sound helped him to sleep and had done wonders for his poor nocturnal habits.

He swallowed and looked down at the bed sheets covering his legs. He planted his hands firmly on the mattress to keep him upright while his brain caught up with reality.

The same blasted dream, he thought.

It was at least the tenth time he'd experienced it. He wished he could make it go away, but Dak knew that particular nightmare would likely haunt him the rest of his days.

With a sigh, he swung his legs over the edge of the bed and stuck his feet on the bamboo floor. Another breath and he stood, albeit with a slight wobble, and meandered over to the window ten feet away.

The room wasn't large, but the primo location more than made up for the lack of space. Being alone, he didn't need much, anyway.

He pulled open the curtains and tugged the string to raise the Japanese blinds. Dak ran fingers through his hair and gazed down the hillside toward the sandy beach. Enormous waves crashed onto the shore, bringing with them a cool breeze from the ocean. The salty air mixed with the faint scent of seafood wafting up from a grill down the street. Several surfers were already on the beach, wading into the frothy churn while fishing boats bobbed in the gentler swells farther off the coast.

Dak had lived here for six months. And for six months, he had no complaints, except one; he couldn't locate the other five members of his former team.

After leaving Nicole's place in Istanbul, he took a series of trains to Portugal and eventually landed at Will's doorstep.

It felt like yesterday.

Will had opened his door and stared at Dak as if he was the ghost of someone he'd wronged long ago. Will was almost the same height and build as Dak. The two friends had joked in the past that they could have been brothers if their ancestries weren't so opposite. Will's history traced back to Cameroon and Ivory Coast, while Dak's was all over the place, mostly in Europe.

"Look what the cat dragged in," Will had said upon Dak's arrival.

"Bad clichés?" Dak asked.

Will snorted at the snarky remark and then gave his old friend a welcoming hug. After being invited in, the two went through the usual catch up kind of conversation for half an hour before Dak dragged Will into more recent events.

To his credit, Will never flinched, never balked at any of it. He knew only too well what it was like to be wrongfully accused, though he didn't complain about it.

Dak explained what he wanted—needed — to do, how he planned to track down the men who'd taken everything from him. Will was happy to help with that. Maybe a little too happy. The fuel of vengeance seemed to course through him, as if he was getting a little vicarious payback for his own misfortunes.

More than just offering to help, Will set Dak up in a cozy apartment next door to his own, complete with a coastal view. Dak wondered how many of these apartments Will owned, but didn't ask.

Will also hooked Dak up with new ID and paperwork too, including a brand new passport that would have slipped through any customs agent's inspection.

His new name was Dan Bronson, which Dak was fine with. He was still Dak. The name was only for getting through security checkpoints, wherever they might be. His driver's license was a work of art too; it even included the holograms for the state ID of Tennessee that few people could replicate.

Now, six months later, little had changed.

Dak wasn't one to mooch, though, and refused a job with Will to make his own way. That resulted in a low paying gig at a local restaurant as a dishwasher. He didn't mind the work. It was honest, and it took care of his basic needs. His life was on hold until he tracked down the five men who betrayed him. Luxuries or comforts could wait.

However, this life certainly had its perks—the view of the beach being one of them.

He turned around and walked softly across the floor, mindful of the neighbors below. He felt certain that they never heard him moving about, but he tried to be a good tenant and not disturb the others.

Dak stopped at his black IKEA dresser and pulled out the top drawer. He'd found many Europeans preferred the inexpensive yet efficient Swedish furniture, especially in smaller flats like this one.

He took out a Led Zeppelin T-shirt and pulled it down over his torso, then slipped into a pair of khaki cargo shorts and flip-flops. After a yawn and a long stretch nearly to the ceiling, he walked out into the hall toward the kitchen and living room.

The apartment's 500 square feet didn't offer much in the way of room, but it was more than adequate. He'd set up a desk in the corner near the balcony overlooking the coast and the village to the left so he could enjoy the views with his coffee, and while he checked the computer for any information about the five men he hunted.

Each day the routine was the same. If it changed, the difference was miniscule. He'd learned to surf to kill time between shifts since there was only so much he could do in his online search.

He knew that Will was doing his best, too, and had recently made a few less-than-ethical updates to his software that allowed him access to cameras in some of the larger cities around the world. The number of feeds he could access were finite, and he'd been clear just how tiny a needle they were trying to locate in a planet-sized haystack.

Dak compared it to fishing. Not the kind done in the sea off the coast of Nazare, but the way he used to fish back in the States on the lakes and rivers of the southeast.

He flipped open the laptop, a hand-me-down from Will—one of the few gifts Dak accepted from his friend—and entered his password.

His right index finger ran along the track pad to move the arrow on the screen and then clicked the email icon at the bottom. It was the same morning routine he'd grown accustomed to over the months of waiting, hoping. Every time doubt crept into his mind, telling him he'd never find the other five, he beat those thoughts away with a steel hammer and forced himself to hold out faith he would find the men who did this and bring them to justice, his own brand of justice.

They were probably living on sandy beaches, sipping fancy drinks, going to nightclubs, living in small mansions. Maybe they weren't that stupid. Dak knew Bo would have given them instructions on how to spend their ill-gotten fortunes, if they'd even been able to find a buyer for the horde.

This entire time he'd operated on the assumption that the five Judases had made a ton of money from their heist. That assertion was proven likely when none of them turned up in their former homes, or anywhere.

They'd made their money and gone dark. That much was clear.

The only lead Dak had in his back pocket was a conversation he once had with Carson about the city of Miami.

Carson had a thing for it, the Art déco buildings, the Cuban food and cigars, the nightlife, and most of all, the beaches. He talked about it like it was the greatest city in the world. After that conversation, he never brought it up again. When Will asked which cities, he should target for traffic feeds first, Dak told him Miami.

That lure had produced nothing for six months, but neither had any of the others.

Dak entered the password for his email account and it bloomed onto the screen. He scanned through some of the usual stuff, mostly promotional mail from various retailers he ordered everyday goods from.

Halfway down the page, he stopped. His eyes opened like a time-lapse of a flower opening its petals.

Possible match.

He read the words again. And again. Then he clicked the email and opened it.

Will's software had automatically generated the email upon facial recognition of one of the targets. Will warned that there could be dozens, maybe hundreds of false positives throughout the search, but so far the software hadn't sent them any bad leads, or any good ones for that matter.

Dak felt his heat pulsing as he clicked the black and white video clip from a street camera near South Beach.

The video began with nothing unusual, just tourists and beach-goers enjoying a stroll in the hot sun. Then a face appeared in the middle of the screen and a shiver ran through Dak's body. His skin pebbled at the visual.

It was Carson Williams. There was no question in his mind. He'd recognize the man anywhere.

He was wearing a white Polo and gray cargo shorts with a phone held to his ear. The image resolution even allowed Dak to identify the model and version of the smart phone his ex-teammate used.

Dak nearly shot out of his seat when his phone vibrated in his pocket. He took it out and looked down at the caller ID, though only one person in the world had this particular phone number.

He pressed the answer button and raised it to his ear.

"Did you see?" Will asked.

"I did," Dak said. "You know, your apartment is next door. You could just come over."

"Good point." Will ended the call, and three knocks came from the front door.

Dak rolled his eyes with a laugh and walked over to the entrance. Out of habit, he peeked through the eyehole and saw his friend's head drooped over his shoulder as if the act of waiting for ten seconds was the most inconvenient thing he'd ever experienced.

Dak unlocked the deadbolt and pulled the door open. "I didn't ask for turn down service."

"Yet," Will quipped.

Dak stuck out his hand sideways and Will clapped it hard, shaking it for a second.

He let go and stepped inside as Dak shifted out of the way.

"So, looks like your boy is in Miami, huh?"

"Looks that way." Dak closed the door and locked it behind him.

"What's your plan?" Will asked, spinning around slowly and crossing his arms. "Going to head back to the states and hunt him down?"

"Something like that."

"I thought you'd say that." Will gave a nod and wandered over to the door that led out onto the balcony. "It's been nice having you around. Offer still stands if you ever want to come back and do some work with me. You can make some good money in this gig."

Dak figured his old friend would make the offer at least one more time.

"I'm good," Dak said. "Once this is over, I'll find something."

Will nodded and reached into his pocket. He fished out a wad of Euros wrapped in a rubber band and dropped it onto the coffee table.

"This should help you get whatever you need." He held up a hand, sensing Dak's forthcoming protest. "No, you don't get to turn this down. I have more than I need, brother. You're going to need a plane ticket, too. I'll cover that. And when you get to the states, I know a guy who can get you armed."

Dak thought about arguing with the man, but he needed the money. The dishwashing gig didn't pay great, and he was going to need enough to get settled in while he tracked down Carson. "I have guns and other supplies in a shed back home. Bo and his guys don't know about it. It'll be safe to go there." He paused. "Thank you. I appreciate everything you've done for me."

"Don't mention it. You'd do the same for me."

That was true. Dak hoped the need never came, but he would relish the chance to return his friend's kindness if it did.

"You want me to bring you some cigars?" Dak asked off-handedly.

"Maybe," Will said with a chuckle. "But I can get those too."

"Of course you can."

"When you going to leave?"

Dak stared at the image on the screen, fury raging like a furnace inside him. "As soon as I can."

SEVEN

MIAMI

Dak watched the opposite sidewalk from behind a newspaper, sunglasses, and an Atlanta Braves baseball cap pulled down low to cover most of his face. All that remained of the dark, thick beard he'd kept during his time in the Middle East and in Portugal was a thin stubble that peppered his skin. The sun radiated on his arms, legs, and neck, reminding him how hot it got on the southern tip of Florida.

He'd only visited the city of Miami a few times in his life, but the weather never seemed to change. Hot and humid was always on tap, except next to the beach where a lukewarm breeze offered relief to those in bathing suits—or not.

Will had provided him with some money—against all Dak's protests—so he could purchase a one-way plane ticket to Miami, and enough cash to hold him over for as long as he needed.

Dak told his friend he'd pay him back, but Will swore off the promises. Will wasn't hurting for money, but that didn't mean Dak was okay with the charity. Even though he relented, he planned on paying Will back.

A bus rolled by, kicking out a puff of diesel fuel in its wake. The brakes screeched up the block as it came to a stop. The sights, smells, and sounds of Miami assaulted the senses. On one corner, a cluster of four old men in various colors of flower-patterned button-up shirts smoked thick cigars around a domino table. Across the street from that, a mojito bar offered cool drinks to its scantily clad, reveling patrons who sat on the patio under red umbrellas, laughing drunkenly behind sunglasses. A Cuban sandwich shop next-door sent smells of meats, onions, and toasty bread into the mix. While Dak had never been much for eating ham, he had to admit the scents wafting out of the sandwich place possessed a siren's call of sorts.

He only allowed the distraction for a second or two before returning his focus to the bar next to the cigar shop.

The joint was a legitimate business—mostly. Dak had been watching the place for the last week since arriving from Portugal. The bar kept a steady flow of traffic in and out, people looking to quench their thirst with fruity alcoholic beverages or crisp beers while watching baseball or soccer. He was tempted to get a better feel of the establishment's layout, but he'd been holding back until today.

He'd seen Carson go by three times in the six days he'd staked out the bar. Each time, Carson looked like he was in a hurry or stressed out, or both. He wore a look of nonchalance on his face, though Dak recognized it as a facade. Based on Carson's previous schedule, it was a good bet he wouldn't be coming in today.

Carson, Dak thought with loathing. The man had changed his name to Baker Tomason. The name change was no surprise, though the choice was certainly interesting. Dak assumed all his ex-teammates were now operating under false identities. Maybe they'd changed them legally, unlike himself. It didn't matter.

Carson, Baker, Vicky, it was all the same to him. When he finished with them, their names would be irrelevant. Dak meant to erase them from existence.

Carson, like the others, hadn't been stupid. Not completely. But he, like most people, had his vices. Dak recalled Carson talking about sports betting more than once during their time together. Usually, he brought it up when they were in the base, killing time. He'd look at the lines for upcoming games and rattle on about how some odds were wrong, the over/unders too high or too low, and other gambling stuff Dak didn't care about.

Even though he had yet to venture into the bar, Dak had a feeling he knew what went on in there. The place was a cover for a sports book. He just needed to get a few more details.

Fortunately, the perfect target was one of the bar's regulars. And today, the guy was right on time.

The man was probably 300 lbs and five feet, nine inches tall. He wore a purple cotton Polo that barely clung to the man's skin by a thread. Khaki shorts and white sneakers with tall white socks completed the ensemble.

His business done, the man carelessly walked out of the bar counting a wad of bills out in the open. Dak folded his paper and tucked it under his arm, carefully checking the pistol on his hip—a weapon he'd purchased through Will's Miami connection.

Dak crossed the street between slow-moving cars and fell in line behind the man as he waddled down the sidewalk. Dak watched him closely, knowing the pasty, hulking man had no clue he was being followed. The guy stuffed the money into his pocket and made a call on his phone.

The conversation provided Dak with everything he needed to justify an interrogation. The gambler bragged to a friend about how much money he made over the weekend and how he was playing with house money.

When the man reached his car around the next corner, parked on a side street two blocks away, he used his key fob to unlock it and reached out for the door handle.

Dak stepped quickly toward him, and as the guy pulled the door open, Dak stopped it with a steady hand.

The man turned his head, fear and anger erupting in his eyes. He swore and reached for his belt.

"No need for that," Dak said, his own weapon already in hand, concealed from view by the car and the wall next to him. He twisted his body slightly to make sure no one passing would notice, though this part of the city block remained nearly vacant except for a few random pedestrians strolling by on the other side of the street every so often.

The man's anger left his face and transformed to pure fear. "What do you want?" he blathered, the loose fat under his chin jiggling as he spoke. "Money? You can have it. Take it? It's yours. Just don't shoot me. Please. I have a family."

"No, you don't," Dak said cooly. "You live alone in an apartment in South Miami, over a bar where you go every night for drinks and to take shots at any lady you deem desperate enough to consider letting you talk to them. You have no wife, no children. And you gamble. From what I can tell, you're pretty good at it."

Confusion filled the man's eyes. His head darted back and forth, a desperate search for someone who could help him.

"What are you, a cop? I haven't broken any laws."

Dak shrugged at the comment. "No. I'm not a cop. And the lawbreaker would be the bookie at the bar, not some lowlife like you. You're just a customer."

"Look, man, I don't know who you are, but please, just let me go. Here, take the money. I have more where that came from." He instantly regretted the confession.

"I don't want your money," Dak said. "I want information."

The gambler's fear eased slightly, his jaw sagging. "Information? About what?"

"I need to know who runs that establishment. What's the bookie's name?"

The man's eyebrows knit together. Deep lines formed on his forehead. "Bert. His name is Bert."

"What does he look like?"

"He's big," the man babbled. "Big Puerto Rican guy. Taller than me."

"He taking new clients?"

More confusion filled the gambler's face. "What?"

"Is he taking new clients?" Dak asked more pointedly, deliberate with every syllable.

"I... I don't know." The man stammered the words. "I guess so. Probably. You want me to introduce you?"

"No. I can introduce myself. I don't want you involved in this conversation. Do you understand?"

The man nodded. Flesh around his neck jiggled again.

"I'm going to let you leave now. If you call Bert and tell him I'm coming or that I asked about his operation, I will find you. Am I making myself clear?"

Another eager nod.

"Good. Now go home. Place your bets. Don't do anything different. Got it?"

"Got it. Yes, sir. Thank you."

"Get in your car."

"Yes. Of course."

The gambler nervously pulled the door open and slumped into the driver's seat. Dak stepped back and watched the man turn on the ignition and hurriedly drive away. The gambler probably wondered how Dak knew so much about him. Getting information like that with unsuspecting, normal folks was easy. The first time Dak laid eyes on the guy, he knew the man was a regular for the bar and whatever seedy underground operation was going on there.

He tailed him back to his apartment and then put the rest of the pieces together. The family thing was a guess, but probably an accurate one. Based on the lack of protest when Dak asserted as much, he figured he'd hit the nail on the proverbial head.

Things were falling into place. Carson hadn't seen him yet, and if he had, the man didn't make a move on. Maybe he'd seen Dak and simply not recognized him. Probably not. Dak's change of appearance and meager disguise would—at best—cause a second glance from someone who really knew him, but so far it seemed to work.

When the gambler's car was out of sight, Dak spun on his heels and stalked back toward the bar.

He needed to have a little chat with its proprietor, Bert, and he hoped the man was in the mood to talk.

EIGHT

MIAMI

Carson sat down on his black leather couch and turned on the television. The 72-inch flat screen TV blinked to life, displaying Samsung in white letters on the black backdrop.

He sighed impatiently and cracked open a can of beer he'd retrieved from the fridge.

"Come on," he urged.

Finally, the television switched to the last channel he'd been viewing—ESPN. He pressed the channel up button on the remote several times until he found the obscure horse racing channel way down on the list. Selecting it, he eased back into his soft couch and took a sip of lager.

It had been a bad week, a bad month, actually. In the months prior, he'd been ahead a significant amount of money, nearly thirty percent of his five million dollar take from the deal Bo set up in Germany.

Four million gone in just under four weeks, though much of that was from his previous winnings.

Not a good weekly win rate by any gambler's standards.

He still had plenty left and Carson knew there were swings like this, ups and downs that plagued a betting man from time to time. He'd get it back, of that he was certain.

After paying cash for his home in Homestead, Florida, and two high-end luxury cars, he still had more than a million or so left in the vault hidden within the confines of his basement.

He couldn't trust banks. Investing was also out of the question. Carson viewed gambling as a kind of investing. The risks were similar, and so were the payouts. The difference between the two was that neither the government nor Dak Harper could track the flow of money—if Harper was still alive.

Carson believed the man died out in the desert somewhere. It was possible his ex-teammate was hanging out in some sheep village in Northern Iraq. Maybe he'd crossed the border into Turkey, as the colonel believed. It didn't matter. Harper was in his past. Carson had a new name and no way of being discovered by anyone from his past life, not even Bo and the other guys.

That was one rule Bo insisted upon. No contact between the five of them had seemed a little paranoid at first, but Carson accepted it, happy to begin his new life out of the military.

The announcer for the race broadcast a rundown of the participants and the odds for the favorites and long shots. Carson watched as the horses were led into the numbered stalls, colorfully clad jockeys riding atop the steeds.

Carson shifted in his seat, anxiously awaiting the start of the race.

A shot rang out, and the horses took off, their legs and hooves churning in a furious blizzard of motion, dirt flying in their wake.

"Come on, Mounty," Carson said. He'd placed a significant wager on a horse called Canadian Mounty to win. The horse wasn't the favorite, but it had strung together several good races and recently won two of them.

The payout was 4 to 1 and a win would get Carson back up to nearly break-even for the month. It helped he had a connection in the horse racing industry, a former trainer at Lake's Bend Farms north of Orlando. His guy claimed that Canadian Mounty was a sure thing for this race, especially given the track conditions, the weather, and the competition.

The favorite didn't run as well on days when thunderstorms were in the area—so the trainer claimed—and as with so many afternoons in South Florida, there just so happened to be several storms to the southwest.

Carson watched with rapt interest, eyes locked on the television as the horses rounded the first turn and entered the backstretch. He'd only recently gotten into betting on horses, usually preferring to bet baseball. But baseball gains were slow and his tastes expensive.

Halfway through the backstretch, Canadian Mounty pulled into the lead, the horse taking long, powerful strides ahead of the pack.

"Come on, Mounty! There you go!" Carson cheered, inching forward to the edge of his couch. "You're not taking my money today, Bert," he muttered under his breath.

The bookie irritated him, but he was a means to an end, the conduit to more cash, and at the very least a way to filter his money through various channels so it came out clean on the other end.

Carson's laundering plan was solid at first, but as the losses mounted, he grew more and more impatient, desperate to get back what had slipped through his fingers.

This race, however, would put things right, and maybe, he hoped, start a roll of good fortune.

The announcer's voice escalated as the horses rounded the final turn and galloped onto the home stretch. Canadian Mounty held the lead by two lengths with the finish line in sight.

"Yes! Go, Mounty! Get it!"

Halfway down the home stretch, another horse emerged from the pack, breaking away from the others and ducking to the outside. The jockey and saddle were draped in red with black polka dots. The brown thoroughbred stormed away from the others, charging toward the front where Canadian Mounty held on to a tenuous advantage.

That gap closed rapidly, and Carson could see it. The finish line loomed so close, just on the edge of the right side of the screen. Carson stood from his seat, still clutching the beer can. He leaned forward, mumbling, as if able to will the horse to victory.

He sensed the lead slipping away. His horse had broken too soon, and now the animal was running out of steam. The favorite closed the space between them to just half a length while the upstart in red and black roared past on the outside, easily taking the second position with fifty yards to go.

The jockeys bobbed in rhythm with their horses. The announcer's voice climbed to an enthralled crescendo. "And now they're neck and neck! It's going to be a photo finish, folks!"

"Go, you stupid horse!" Carson roared.

But it was too late.

The horse in red and black—dubbed Peyton's Rally—poked its head out in front and never looked back. It crossed the finish line half a length ahead of the favorite, leaving Canadian Mounty in third.

"No!" Carson shouted and threw his beer at the television. Luckily, he missed, and the can smashed into the wall just beside the screen, splashing lager onto the drywall and hardwood floor around the entertainment center.

Fury pulsed through him. He rubbed his shaved head with both hands, digging his fingers deep into his skull.

He strung together a slew of obscenities—how in the world could the horse have blown it.

A phone on the coffee table vibrated twice and then went silent. He didn't have to look to know who it was. Bert was probably texting him to gloat.

Carson clenched his jaw and bent over to look at the message.

"Tough break, bro. See you tomorrow."

Pressing his lips together, Carson nodded. He ran fingers over his smooth, shaved head. He blew air out of his nostrils like the horses on the television after their long sprint. "Tomorrow?" he mumbled, adding a few more choice adjectives to the statement. "What do you mean, tomorrow? You collect at the end of a week. I just paid you yesterday?"

"Yeah, well, funny thing about that is, we have a new policy. My associates and I are concerned about your ability to pay."

"What's that supposed to mean? I always pay. And on time."

"True," the Bordicuan said. "But like I said, new policy."

"This is bull and you know it, Bert. You can't just do that."

"You think you can tell me how to run my business? No one. No one tells me how to run my business. You understand? You're lucky I don't put the juice on what you owe right now. I took your huge bet. I doubt many bookies in Miami would have. Now you're going to insult me?"

Carson had overstepped. He wasn't afraid of Bert and his group of collectors. Even if they tracked him down to his house in Homestead, they were hardly the battle-hardened soldier he was. If Bert was foolish enough to send his goons after Carson, it would not end well for the bookie's operation.

Yet here he was, making threats, or at least the insinuation of a threat merely by asking about being insulted.

Carson knew he could kill the man if he wanted, along with all the guys on his payroll, but that would bring with it an entire slew of problems, not to mention he wouldn't be able to get any of his money back.

For now, Carson decided the only thing to do was play along, kiss the ring, and make things good with Bert. In the back of his mind, though, Carson began formulating a plan.

Bert had to keep his money somewhere, and most of it couldn't be in a bank. He likely had multiple cash operations going, filtering and scrubbing his dirty, untaxed money until it was cleaner than a general's shoes.

"I'll be there," Carson said.

"I knew you were good for it. I'll see you tomorrow."

The call ended abruptly with Carson still hanging onto the device.

He'd just lost a significant portion of his remaining money. And only one thought kept knocking at the back door of Carson's mind. I can get it back. One way or another.

NINE
MIAMI

Dak listened to the conversation through the wall from his seat in the back of the bar. One of the few devices he'd picked up from his stash in Tennessee was an audio amplification device that could pick up details of sound from sixty yards away. There was more powerful tech out there, but this one was portable and could fit under the folds of a jacket or the pockets of cargo shorts, as was the case when he walked into the bar. The half-domed unit was a smaller version of what could be seen any Sunday on the sidelines of football games.

Walking into the bar twenty minutes before, Dak seated himself at an empty table in the back.

There were only five other patrons in the bar at the time, which wasn't a surprise since it was the middle of a workday. As such, the bartender handled all the serving and pouring duties for the entire establishment. Dak imagined two or three servers would show up in the next hour or two before the end of the business day began dumping weary, thirsty customers through the doors.

Dak had arrived in time to hear Bert talking to at least one of his goons in the back office. The gray door into the room was marked with a placard that read "Manager." The table Dak chose shared the wall with the office, which made it the perfect place for listening to any conversations held within.

Dak lowered the radio earpiece to his pocket and took a sip of the golden lager he'd been nursing. He enjoyed the beer and would have already downed it and at least one more in the time he'd been there if he weren't working, but he had to keep his wits.

Dak watched the young bartender with the handlebar mustache making his rounds to check on other patrons, the brown apron hanging from his neck flapping in the breeze. The bar looked like a million others Dak had seen in his life. Dark wood panels covered the façade of the main counter. Bottles of every liquor variety festooned the shelves behind it. To the left of the mirrored shelves, ten taps jutted out from the wall to provide patrons with draft beer varying from IPAs to a locally made coffee stout, and a few ales and lagers in between.

Unlike most bars with that design and layout, this one allowed a decent amount of sunlight through the windows. Even with the mesh blinds pulled down to keep the interior temperatures lower, it was probably the most well-lit saloon Dak had ever visited.

The young bartender approached after checking on the other drinkers and stopped at Dak's table.

His wavy, black hair matched the mustache against a backdrop of bronze skin. Dak figured he probably went straight to the beach across the street after every shift.

"Can I get you anything or are you good?" the young man asked.

"No, I'm good," Dak said. "Although," he added, "I do have a question."

"Sure."

Dak cocked his head to the side and took a swig of beer, a larger gulp than the previous. He swallowed and set the glass down.

"I'm looking for someone."

"Okay." The bartender looked confused. "Can you elaborate?"

"I'm looking for a Puerto Rican guy named Bert. I hear he runs this place. Is there any chance I could talk to him?"

The bartender shifted uneasily. "I'm sorry, what's this about? Bert is usually pretty busy."

Dak's eyes panned the room and then landed on the brown orbs belonging to the younger man. "Yeah, I'm sure he's overwhelmed with running the business." He gave the sarcastic remark a second to register with the barkeep.

Before the guy could protest, Dak went on. "I'm looking for a job. Was hoping I could speak to the manager. That's all."

The bartender shifted nervously. The name tag clinging to his apron jiggled.

Dak noticed the name for the second time.

"I don't think we're hiring, sir."

"Josh. That's your name?"

"Yes, sir."

"Would you mind just asking for me? If Bert says no, I'll be on my way." Dak produced a hundred-dollar bill and slid it across the table. "Just walk over there," he pointed at the management office door, "give it a knock, and ask if he can see someone about a job. If he says no, you keep this money. If he says yes, you keep this money. Either way, you win a hundred bucks for taking five steps to that door and asking your boss a simple question."

Dak's eyes scanned the room again and then met Josh's once more. "I doubt any of these scamps are going to tip that well."

Josh licked his lips and then chewed on the bottom one, contemplating the offer. His eyes filled with the things he could do with an extra hundred.

"Okay," he said and reached out for the money.

Dak pulled it back temporarily. "You're not going to run off with this, are you?"

"What?" Josh asked, sincerely curious.

"I'm kidding," Dak said. He slid the money across the table and leaned back, hefting the beer glass to his mouth again.

Josh nodded and scooped the money into his hand and stuffed it into his pocket. He glanced around the room as if he'd just broken some law, then ambled over to the manager's office.

He hesitated at the doorway and looked over to Dak, who urged him on with a raise of the glass. "Go on," Dak mouthed.

Josh licked his lips again and then raised a fist. He rapped on the door three times and took a step back.

Ten seconds passed before the doorknob twisted. The hinges creaked as someone inside pulled it open.

"What?" a gruff voice asked. This one had a New York City accent, though Dak couldn't place which borough.

"Sorry to bother you," Josh said. "There's a guy here who said he's looking for a job. Wanted to talk to Bert."

"What are you talking about?" the man said.

"He's over there if you'd like to see him." Josh pointed to Dak and a second later, a man in his thirties with a dark tan leaned out. He was wearing a black tank top that revealed several tattoos stretched across his muscular arms and up the sides of his neck.

"We're not hiring," the guy said. "You can check one of the other bars."

Dak nodded and looked down at the beer in his hand. "I'm sorry," he offered. "I thought Josh told you I was asking for Bert. You're obviously not him."

The man stepped out of the doorway and into the bar. He wore white shorts with his blacktop, along with black sneakers. It was a strange look for an enforcer, though Dak wasn't surprised—things were different in Miami. This guy was clearly a transplant, though how he came to work for Bert probably had an interesting backstory.

"What was that?" the guard said.

Dak took another sip of the beer and set the glass on the table. "I said, I wanted to talk to Bert about a job. You're not him. Bert's a Bordicuan," Dak said, using the native term for Puerto Rican he knew the bar's owner would recognize. He even said the word with an authentic accent from the town of Rincon, a place he'd visited several times before.

"For someone looking for a job, you got a lot of nerve, punk," the grunt said. He took a threatening step toward Dak with the obvious intention of attempting to cause physical harm, or at the very least, toss him out of the establishment.

Dak didn't move. His heartbeat remained steady.

"That's fine," he said. "I didn't realize you made the managerial decisions here. I guess I'll just be on my way."

"That's probably a good idea," Tank Top replied. "And I'll be happy to show you out."

The man reached down to grab Dak by the arm. Within a split second, Dak snatched the man's wrist and jerked the muscular arm down while picking up a fork and driving it straight at a vulnerable throat. He stopped at the precise moment the prongs touched flesh.

The guard's eyes erupted with fury, but he couldn't move, he didn't dare.

Dak felt the man's strength. The guy looked the type who spent hours every day at the gym, lifting the heaviest weights possible. Keeping him from backing away took every ounce of strength Dak could muster, but the fork at the man's neck certainly helped.

"I just wanted to ask Bert about a job," Dak said. "There's no reason anyone should get hurt."

"Let him go," a new voice spoke from the doorway. It was the same accented voice from before.

Dak turned his head and looked at the man standing between him and the retreating bartender. His long, black hair was pulled back into a ponytail that lapped over the top of his back. Streaks of gray in it and his matching beard betrayed an age probably in his mid to late fifties. Bert wore a light blue button-up shirt and faded beige linen pants with brown leather flip-flops.

"You're looking for a job?" Bert asked. "You don't look like the kind of guy who wants to wash dishes."

Dak chuckled. "You'd be surprised." He let go of the guard and the man stumbled back. Rage burned in his eyes.

"Deno," Bert said. "Get a couple of drinks for us. I'm curious to hear what kind of work this man is looking for."

Deno's right eye twitched. A vein pulsed on his tanned forehead and two more raised under the skin of his neck. "Yes, sir."

The guard turned reluctantly and walked over to the bar.

Bert smiled at Dak. It was a humble gesture, but also one a boa constrictor might give a mouse just before wrapping its body around the unsuspecting prey.

He motioned to the open door. "By all means, please come in. We shouldn't disturb my customers."

Dak nodded, downed the rest of his beer, and stood. "Much obliged."

TEN

MIAMI

Dak followed Bert into his office. The mere fact the bookie turned his back to Dak either showed a lack of awareness or the absence of fear.

Deno followed them in with two tumblers, each with a couple of fingers of whiskey sloshing around.

"Please, have a seat." Bert motioned to a vinyl chair with metal arms. There was a second one just like it a few feet away. They were the kind of chairs you'd see in a used car dealership or the waiting room of a doctor's office.

The office looked as Dak expected; a gray leather couch against the back wall, facing a television hanging from the opposite corner. An open door led into a small, private bathroom. To the right, a metal relic from the 1980s served as a desk.

Bert slumped down into a deep red, high back leather chair. It was the only furniture in the room that possessed the slightest hint of taste.

Deno set the drinks down on the desk, one in front of his boss and the other on the edge closest to Dak. He didn't say anything, but the twisted scowl on his face expressed his displeasure at having to serve the stranger. He backed away and slinked into the other chair like a pouting child.

"So," Bert said, throwing his hands up in the air, "what kind of work are you looking for? I assume you're not inquiring about a dishwashing position."

"Not exactly," Dak said. "I've already done that gig."

Bert let out a short chortle. "You don't strike me as the dishwasher type."

"A guy has to do whatever he can to get by."

The boss sized him up, eyeing him for several seconds before speaking again. "Indeed. So, what is it you want? I don't need bartenders or servers either if that's what you were thinking. But something tells me it isn't. You looking to gamble?"

"Not quite."

"Yeah, I thought that wasn't the case either. But you know about my operation." It wasn't a question.

"I do."

Bert nodded, "I don't suppose you'll tell me how you know about it. So, if you're not going to place a bet and you're not here to do regular work, am I to assume you're looking for a job as part of my security?"

"You're getting closer. But I'm not here for a job." Dak put the confession out on the table and waited to see how the man would respond. He could easily take it as a threat, but no fear streaked through Bert's eyes, no confusion cluttered his lips.

"There it is," he said. "But if you were a cop, you'd already be taking me outside or maybe trying to make a deal with me."

"Definitely not a cop," Dak offered. "I'm here to help you."

The Puerto Rican laughed again, this time a huge bellow. He looked over at Deno as he continued to laugh and the New Yorker joined in with an uncomfortable chuckle.

"Help me?" Bert said amid the laughter. "What are you going to help me with?"

"I'm going to keep someone from robbing and killing you."

The display slowly died as Bert stared at the visitor. The room descended into silence and the boss wiped his eyes with the back of his hands, drying tears that dribbled down his cheeks.

"Who is going to try to kill me? I'm not sure if you noticed, but that's what I have Deno for. Not to mention a crew of guys who watch my back."

Dak merely nodded at the information. "I'm sure you do. None of them, Deno included, are going to be able to save you when this guy comes for you. He's former Special Forces. He's killed more men than you can imagine, in ways you can't and don't want to fathom." He turned to Deno. "No offense. You seem more than capable."

Deno responded with an offer for Dak to go do something lewd.

"Thank you for that," Dak said. He returned his gaze to the boss behind the desk. "You just got off the phone with him a few minutes ago. I imagine he placed a large wager with you, one that you normally wouldn't take. But you couldn't help yourself, could you, Bert?"

For the first time since meeting him, Bert's face cracked slightly. The tough, fearless exterior melted, and curiosity and fear dripped into his eyes.

"How do you know that? How the—"

"I know because I know your client, Bert. I served with him in Iraq."

The concern deepened on Bert's face and he shifted uncomfortably in his chair. "You served with Baker? In Special Forces?"

"Delta Force, actually," Dak corrected. "Yes. And his name isn't Baker Tomason. It's Carson Williams. You just told him he needed to come in tomorrow to settle that big debt he just piled up on you."

Deno shifted backward and stood up out of his chair. He drew a pistol from his hip and pointed it at Dak, aiming for the visitor's temple.

"He's a cop," Deno accused.

"If I'm a cop," Dak said, keeping his eyes locked on Bert, "then I wouldn't be telling you this. I would be here for you, not Carson. Let me assure you, Bert, I am here for one person. And it's not either of you."

Bert rubbed his beard, contemplating whether to have the intruder executed or to let him live.

"Why should I believe you?" he asked. "How do you have that kind of information if you're not a cop?"

"We can sit here all day as I try to explain to you that I'm not a cop. Just know this, Carson will come to see you tomorrow. I doubt he's going to come to pay his debt. How much does he owe you right now?"

"A few million," Bert said after a slight hesitation. Something about this visitor's line of questioning piqued the Puerto Rican's interest.

"Sounds about right," Dak said. "He's addicted to the rush. I've seen it before when we were on missions. His adrenaline would get going and he couldn't stop himself sometimes. He needs the excitement, the risk. He feeds off it."

"What's your point?"

Dak tilted his head to the side and shrugged. "He's probably going to try to rob you."

Bert replied with an uneasy laugh. "Rob me? How would he do that?"

"A couple of million bucks is a lot of money, Bert. If I was a betting man, I'd wager Carson is going to call you back in a few minutes and ask if he can bring the money directly to your home instead of this place. He'll say something along the lines of feeling unsafe about bringing such a large sum downtown or to a bar. Your house, he'll say, will be a safer place to do the exchange."

"He doesn't know where I live."

"That you're aware," Dak corrected. "Carson probably knows the name of your cat."

Bert scowled at the insinuation.

"I know you have a cat, Bert. I can see the traces of fur on your shirt."

The man looked down abruptly and brushed the fabric with his hands. Then he looked over at Deno and motioned for him to lower the weapon.

Dak continued. "Carson probably still has plenty of money, Bert. But he hates losing. Especially large sums. He's probably starting to get a little nervous. Most gamblers would just keep betting until their well ran dry. Not Carson. Now that he senses things are spiraling out of control, he's going to make a play. Tell me, do you keep a safe at your home, perhaps where you stash a bunch of cash, maybe some precious metals?"

Bert shifted in his chair, a dead giveaway of the truth. "Okay, you know what?" He drew his pistol and pointed it at Dak's head. The gun was impractical, a .44 Magnum that could have blown a hole through the wall behind Dak after the bullet obliterated his skull. Not a great weapon for concealment or for moving around.

Dak never flinched.

"That's the fifth-largest weapon I've had pointed at me this year," he said coolly. "Just wait, Bert. Carson will call you soon and when he does, he will ask if he can bring the money to your place. If he doesn't say that, then you can shoot me right here. I won't put up a fight. But if he does make that request, you will need my help."

"Oh, yeah? And what's in it for you? You some kind of guardian angel wandering the streets of Miami?"

Dak shook his head. "No. I'm here to right a wrong Carson did to me. What's in it for you is if you let me have him, I'll let you have whatever he has left in his coffers. My guess is, it's probably at least a million."

Bert's face tightened with doubt, jaw clenching and releasing as he pondered the offer and its legitimacy. "And how would you know about his... coffers?"

"Let's just say I know where Carson got his fortune. Anything beyond that is classified." He paused for a second and then cracked a mischievous grin.

Bert snorted. Then nodded. "Classified," he said, looking at Deno.

Bert wiped his nose with his free hand. "You know, I've never seen a guy with two guns pointed at him act so calm. Usually, people are begging for their lives right about now."

"Do you normally put two guns on someone when they come to do business with you?" He didn't wait for an answer. "I don't owe you money, Bert. I'm here to give you money. And the only catch is, you play along and let me have Carson."

The Puerto Rican stroked his beard again with his free hand, the other rested on the desk still clutching the hand cannon. A minute ticked by, though it felt more like an hour in a defensive driving class.

His phone suddenly vibrated in his pocket. Perturbed, Bert reached into his pants and pulled out the phone. He looked at the number and his brow tensed.

"Do me a favor," Dak said. "Don't tell him I'm here."

Bert answered the phone. "What is it... Baker? I hope you aren't going to try to skip out of town on me."

Dak heard a forced laugh and then some inaudible noise. He waited patiently, listening to Bert's end of the exchange. The boss finally ended the discussion with a "Sure, you can come by my place. That sounds like a good plan. I'll text you the address."

When Bert ended the call, he stared at Dak with bewildered eyes.

"Told you," Dak said dryly.

"Okay," Bert replied after a short deliberation. He uncocked the weapon and set it to the side. He motioned to Deno, and the body-builder wannabe reluctantly lowered his pistol. "I'm normally the one who deals with gamblers, but I'm willing to take a chance on you. But before I hear your plan, I'm going to need to know your name."

"My name is Dak. That's all you need to know."

"All right, Dak. What are we going to do?"

ELEVEN

MIAMI

Carson woke early the next morning to begin preparations.

He pulled most of his firearms from their concealed locations in his home: a few from the gun safe in the study, one from a desk, and another two from behind a secret RFID activated panel that doubled as a bookshelf. He stuffed the guns into a bag along with eight spare magazines.

He doubted he would need that many rounds, but it was better to have too much than too little.

Carson did a drive-by of Bert's palatial home the night before. He pulled up to the curb a half block away to admire the two-story mansion. He envied all of it: the red-tiled roof, the white stucco wall surrounding the property that matched the home's exterior, and the lush palm trees sprouting up to the height of the rooftops. It was the picture of pure luxury in every sense of the word.

Not that Carson was doing badly. His home was more than enough for him, with over four thousand square feet of space and all the luxury he could ever want. The location, though, wasn't ideal. It was situated in Homestead, nearer to the Everglades. While Homestead was a great place, he longed to be closer to the nightlife he craved; he feasted on. The bars, nightclubs, beaches, and the entire scene around the islands and South Beach beckoned to him.

While Bert's place wasn't in the hub of the party zone, Carson knew that if he were to acquire a home such as Bert's, the party would come to him—and be much more inviting than his current residence.

He didn't risk getting out of the car during his recon mission, instead driving by at normal speed once he'd taken a look from a few hundred feet away.

With a tertiary understanding of the home's layout and no sign of any exterior security forces, he drove to the end of the street, turned around, and sped home.

Now, with the bag full of everything he figured he needed, Carson zipped it up and lugged it into the kitchen where a full pot of coffee waited.

The earthy, nutty smell of the brew called to him as it filled his home. It was already half-past ten in the morning and he was way overdue for a second cup of joe, having already had his first before his routine morning workout.

He set the rucksack down next to the front door, ambled over to the coffeepot, and poured the steaming brown liquid into a to-go mug. With the lid secure, he walked back to the door and hefted the bag over one shoulder.

The drive at this time of day offered little in the way of traffic. In three or four hours, however, the roads would be packed with commuters. Carson planned on being in and out of Bert's in less than thirty minutes, though he believed he could pull off the heist in less than half that time.

In his mind, he went over the exterior of the house. That wouldn't matter much since there had been no guards by the gate or at the front door. He concluded that Bert kept most of his men inside with only a superficial offering of security outside.

The plan was simple. Bert expected Carson to show up to pay his debt. That meant getting in would be easy enough. Once inside, Bert would probably invite him into his study or maybe the living room for a drink to exchange the money. Bert was a bookie, but he wasn't an animal. The man possessed at least a modicum of civility.

Carson would set down the bag, letting Bert and his men assume it was the money. If any of them got close to it, Carson would take that person out first, then kill any other guards in the room.

All of his weapons were equipped with suppressors, but even with the muted effect of the silencers, any other guards in the building would probably hear what was happening.

They would rush to help their boss, and Carson would be ready to cut down. Then he would ransack the place. He'd take Bert for every nickel he had hidden. Carson was certain there would be a horde of cash stuffed in vaults or safes free for the taking.

He'd let Bert live, though Carson knew the Puerto Rican would probably have to be shot in the shoulder or leg. After all his men were dead, Bert would give up the combinations or codes to any security box or safe he had in the building. Only then would Carson give him the mercy of a bullet through the head.

The plan played out in Carson's mind as he crossed the bridge onto Allison Island and made a left onto the avenue leading to Bert's place.

He pulled the Aston Martin up to the gate and rolled down the window. His high-end luxury car would have fit in anywhere Miami elites preferred to be, and this neighborhood was no different.

He looked out the window at a tiny fisheye camera set in a four-foot-high concrete pillar with a keypad beneath it. For a second, he wondered if he had to dial a number or something, but then the gate raised from the right side.

Carson drove through and parked the car in a guest parking area off to the right of the driveway. The red and gray paving stones continued farther, passing under an archway where a guest house or perhaps a maintenance building was attached to the main house by a covered walkway.

A quick check at his ankle told him the extra firearm concealed under his gray slacks was still intact.

He got out of the car, walked to the back, and pulled the rucksack out of the trunk before turning and heading toward the front door.

Still no security. No guards stepped out of the building to welcome or threaten him. It was odd, but not everyone was as careful or borderline paranoid as him.

He looked back at the gate as it lowered into place and then walked purposefully to the arched entryway of the mansion. He climbed the four steps and paused at the massive oak door. It featured reliefs of angels and demons carved into its surface and a boxed wrought iron cage in the middle near the top where anyone inside could look out to check who dared visit.

Carson reached over and pressed the doorbell button and waited.

An intercom speaker over the button crackled and then Bert's voice came through, "Thank you for coming, Baker. I appreciate it. The door is open, come on in. I'm in my study. Straight ahead and then make a right through the living room. It's the open door past the grand piano."

That was odd, Carson thought. Then again, Bert was odd, and unaware of any danger that might be lurking just outside his home, specifically in the form of Carson Williams.

Carson nodded and pressed the latch, pushed open the heavy door, and stepped inside.

TWELVE

MIAMI

Standing inside the mansion's foyer, Carson looked around, rapidly taking in the interior's layout. Bert's laziness in not greeting him at the door, or the very least, sending one of his goons to let the guest in, could prove to be a grave error.

Twin staircases on either side of the atrium twisted up to the second level. The oak banister atop a wrought iron railing matched the door. Red Spanish tiles covered the floor and ran toward the back of the house, passing under an archway where the two staircases met. Plants adorned the windows and alcoves.

No pictures lined the walls, which was no surprise. Bert didn't have a wife or children, and posting pictures of himself on vacations would be vain even for a man like him.

Carson checked to make sure his untucked shirt hung over the pistol at his side. The gun was tucked into the inner portion of his pants, but he welcomed any extra concealment he could utilize.

A guard stepped out from a doorway with a grin on his face. Carson immediately recognized the grinning, muscular man.

"What's up, Deno?" Carson said, casually. "Where's the boss?" He tried to act as normal as possible for someone who was supposedly about to give up a fortune on a gambling debt. Act too happy, and Deno might suspect something was up. Act too abrasive, and there could be trouble before Carson wanted. Everything needed to follow a specific set of plans before any violence took place. Most importantly, Carson had to be the one to initiate it. Being on the defensive was fine, but in this situation, he wanted to be the one who shot first.

"Here to pay up?" Deno asked in a gloating tone.

"Yeah," Carson said. "You could say that." He didn't want to overplay his hand, but he wasn't going to give this idiot any satisfaction. He looked like he was a reject from one of those New Jersey Shore reality shows. His T-shirt was too small, probably intentionally to show off his bulging muscles. He struck Carson as the kind of tool who'd hit the gym just before a date so he could look as muscular as possible.

"Big hit you took yesterday, bro. I hope you got more where that came from." He held a toothpick between his fingers and twirled it for a few seconds before slipping it into his mouth. He spied the bag on Carson's shoulder. "The money in there?"

"Yep."

"Hand it over and I'll take it to the boss." Deno took a step toward the visitor.

"No," Carson said. "I'll take it to him myself."

"Whoa," Deno said, putting his hands up innocently. "I was just trying to help, but be my guest. Straight ahead, amigo. Make a right. You'll find the man in his study."

"Yeah, I know. Past the grand piano."

Deno nodded. "I'll be here if you need anything," he said and turned to go back into the kitchen.

Idiot, Carson thought. I will definitely kill him.

He briefly considered shooting him in the back right then and there, but doing so would tip off the entire fortress and send an alarm to every nook and cranny in the compound.

Still, Carson hadn't seen any other guards. With all the resources at Bert's disposal, how could he be so careless?

Carson tossed aside the questions and sauntered through the archway into the great room at the rear of the building. Giant windows reached to the vaulted ceiling, making the entire back wall look like it was made of glass. Through the extravagant windows, a long pool stretched away from the house, surrounded by lounge chairs and sofas, drink tables, and two round tables shaded by dark green umbrellas.

Beyond the pool, waves crashed onto a private strip of the coast where a skiff was moored to a dock. Out beyond that, a white sixty-foot yacht bobbed in the ocean.

I'm on the wrong side of the gambling business, Carson realized.

He turned and noted the grand piano to his right. The glossy black finish glistened in the light of a Swarovski chandelier hanging in the center of the room.

Bert certainly enjoyed opulence. Well, he did.

The Puerto Rican had no idea he was about to die. If he did have a clue, Carson was certain he would have taken drastic measures. His mind momentarily drifted to the final scene of the film Scarface and the assault on the drug lord's mansion.

Carson shook off the daydream and made his way past the piano to a doorway leading into a darkened room. The only light came from the windows along the far wall and a wall to his left.

When he reached the threshold, he rapped on the door four times. "Bert? You in here?"

"In here, Baker," the Puerto Rican said. "Come in."

Carson stepped into the study and found himself in a world Ernest Hemingway would have loved. The smell of cigar smoke hung in the air, drifting up from a thick cigar pinched between Bert's fingers. The man sat in a deep leather club chair to the right. An empty one waited next to him. A gas fireplace behind the seats flickered with yellow flames, certainly more for ambiance than the necessity for heat.

More windows filled the back wall, and dozens of bookshelves filled with tomes surrounded the fireplace. A white leather couch sat in front of the windows to the left with matching side chairs and a coffee table with an oak top and legs wrapped in wicker reeds.

"I didn't know you were such an avid reader," Carson commented coolly as he stepped deeper into the room.

"I enjoy a bit of good fiction now and then," Bert confessed. "Though most of these are collectibles, rare first editions."

His eyes wandered to the bag on Carson's shoulder. "That's a lot of cash to carry around. Weren't you worried about someone trying to steal it?"

Carson offered a snort. "Not at all." He heard his deep voice echo throughout the room.

"I know I would."

"You aren't me."

Bert took a puff of the cigar and blew smoke out of his lips. Tight rings swelled and floated into the air, then dispersed after hovering for a few seconds.

"True." He looked at the cigar box. "Would you like a smoke?"

"I don't smoke," Carson said. "Thank you." He lowered the bag to his hand. "Where would you like me to put this?"

Bert twitched slightly. Over there on that couch is fine," he said, pointing to the leather sofa along the far wall.

"Suit yourself."

Carson turned to head over to the couch, his mind already setting the plan in motion. He'd altered it in the few minutes since arriving. Without any guards except for Deno in sight, Carson would shoot Bert first and let the muted gunshot and the man's screams for help call for anyone else in the mansion. They would rush through the open door without realizing they were running headlong into a trap. They'd be cut down before they realized what happened. One by one, Bert's men would die on the floor of his study and then, Bert would die too, but only after he gave up the information Carson wanted about where he kept his treasures. Although, right off the top of his head, Carson realized those first editions might fetch a handsome price. His brain darted to the mysterious German who'd bought the artifacts and treasure horde.

"Over here?" Carson asked, pointing to the white couch.

Bert rolled his eyes. "Is there another white sofa there? Yes, that one." He sounded irritated and went back to puffing on his cigar.

Carson was going to enjoy this. He hadn't killed anyone in a while. Honestly, he hadn't missed it, but now he was starting to.

He walked silently over to the couch and set down the bag. He started to unzip it, but Bert's voice stopped him.

"That's good," he said. The voice was much closer than it should have been.

Carson twisted his head and looked over his shoulder. Bert was standing halfway across the room, holding a .44 Magnum.

"What are you doing, Bert?" Carson asked with a tenuous laugh.

Bert's eyes filled with nervous tension. "Step away from the bag and put your hands up, slowly."

Carson put on his best confused-face as he gradually raised his left hand.

"Both of them," Deno said from the doorway, also brandishing a weapon. His was a gaudy, gold plated number. If Carson had to guess, he'd say it was a Desert Eagle, though it was unlike any he'd seen before. These two preferred show guns."

Carson sighed and raised his right hand into the air.

"Step away from the bag," Bert repeated.

"Fine," Carson agreed. "But I don't know what you think you're doing. I brought the money like you asked."

"Yeah, I doubt it. Move over there, toward the side door."

Carson frowned and risked a glance at the proffered door. It led to a garden, surrounded by a hedgerow that towered at least seven feet high. A birdbath outside one of the windows played host to a collection of red and yellow songbirds. Flowers of several colors lined a small yard that ran behind a concrete pool deck.

"What's your plan here, Bert?" Carson said, the serpent inside him finally revealing its true colors. "You going to kill me? If you think that, you're making a big mistake."

"No," Bert said. "I'm not going to kill you."

Two more guards stepped into the room and surrounded Carson on both sides. One removed the sidearm from his right hip. The other searched his legs and found the .38 on his ankle.

How did they know?

One of the guards unzipped the bag and found the stash of extra weapons and magazines.

He looked over at the bookie and nodded.

Bert shook his head. "You were going to kill me. Such a shame. You were a good customer. You know, I don't want to be the guy who killed the golden goose."

"You said you're not going to kill me," Carson pressed.

The two guards pointed their weapons at him, taking a cautious step back.

"Through the door, please," Bert said.

He walked over to it and pushed it open. Hot, muggy South Florida air rushed into the study.

Carson exhaled and trudged across the room. His mind raced with ideas of how to get out of this, but the guards, the bookie, even Deno, were playing it safe, keeping their distance from the former Delta Force operator's deadly reach. Bert led the way, backing out through the door, keeping his barrel pointed straight at Carson's chest.

When everyone was outside, the last guard through the door closed it shut and stepped to the side.

"Now what?" Carson asked, throwing his hands out wide. "You took my guns. You gonna shoot me here in your garden? Your neighbors will hear that, Bert. Cops will come. Federal investigators too. You should have killed me in your house, called it self-defense. You can't shoot a man outside."

Bert's head turned from side to side in a deliberate, slow movement. The grim look in his eyes betrayed no fear, no concern.

"Like I said, Carson. I'm not going to kill you."

Carson flinched at the sound of his real name. There was no way the Puerto Rican could know that.

"What did you call me?" he asked, fear suddenly trickling into his throat.

"He called you Carson, Carson." A new voice entered the conversation from behind the row of bushes.

Then an apparition stepped out of the maze, a ghost that had haunted Carson's mind in his most paranoid of moments.

"Dak?" he said, bewilderment cracking his tone.

Dak nodded. "Yeah, Carson. It's me. And Bert wasn't lying to you. He's not going to kill you." He paused, cocking his head to the side and meeting Carson's gaze with his own icy glare. "I am."

THIRTEEN
MIAMI

Carson stared at his former friend with a mixture of loathing and disbelief. The last time he'd seen him was just before Bo ordered the cave exit sealed, and they'd left Dak inside to die.

Of course, Carson knew about Dak's return to base in Hamrin after his inexplicable escape.

"How did you get out of that cave?" Carson asked, stretching his neck muscles with a twitch of the head to each side.

Bert and his men shifted backward, keeping their weapons at their sides, but ready to whip them into action if necessary. As the men moved, they formed a wide circle around the two opponents.

Dak cocked his head to one side and flipped his hands up like a magician showing there were no tricks up his sleeves. "Does it matter?"

Carson took a suspicious glance at Bert and the others. "So, what? You're going to fight me? Is that it? These guys aren't going to interfere?"

Dak's head turned dramatically back and forth. "Nope. In fact, I told them that if you beat me, they're to let you go free. I'll have to trust Bert's word on that one."

Carson snorted at the notion.

"But that's not going to happen," Dak added. "You left me to die in that cave, Carson. You and the others. You were my brother. All of you were my brothers. And you stabbed me in the back. For what? Thirty pieces of silver?"

A warm breeze flowed through the yard, rustling the bushes and tossing the palm leaves overhead. The long tree trunks bent and swayed. A few of them creaked under the strain, though they'd certainly seen much worse in tropical storms and hurricanes.

"That what you think, Dak?" Carson spat. He shifted his feet, moving slightly to the right. "You think you're some kind of martyr for turning down that money? No one knows about it, Dak. No one will. It was free money, and you turned it down for what? Huh? Some ridiculous, ill-placed morals?"

"It's not about the money now, Carson. No price is worth killing a brother."

"Oh, yeah?" Carson inclined his head. "But you're not dead, are you? You're alive and well, free to live your life."

"Hardly," Dak corrected. "I'm a wanted man, in case you forgot. The colonel won't stop until he finds me or I clear my name. I don't see much chance for the latter, so I'm going to have to take you all down one at a time."

Carson snuffed at that one. "You think you can get to all of us?"

Dak put his hands out wide. The gesture gave his answer.

"Well, I don't know where the rest of them are, but you're welcome to go after the colonel if you want to. You'll have to get through an entire base, though, so good luck with that. Then again, you're not going to leave this lawn alive today."

"That may be," Dak conceded. "Maybe you do beat me. You're stronger than me. No doubt about that. I guess that's a risk I'm willing to take."

"You should have had Bert and his goons shoot me when you had the chance."

"Maybe I should have stayed in that cave too, huh? But here I am.

So, if you're done talking, I've been wanting to hit you for six months now. I'm curious if it will feel as good as I imagined."

In his mind, the dance had already begun and the longer he could draw things out, the better he could plan his attack. Not that he had to do much planning. He'd served with Carson for years, fought alongside him in firefights, and hand-to-hand combat. He knew Carson's moves. Maybe Carson knew his too. He had to assume that was the case.

Bert and his guards took additional steps back to give the two fighters plenty of room to operate.

Carson shook his head like a horse, tossing it back and forth to try to reinforce what a mistake Dak was making.

Dak didn't show a blink of emotion. His vapid eyes glowered at his opponent like only the eyes of a man who'd already seen death could.

Carson stepped in closer, shifting his feet as he twisted to the side. His preferred style was boxing. Dak had seen his skills in the ring during training sessions and in the gym when the team worked out together. He knew exactly how Carson would attack and what signs to look for. That wasn't to say he couldn't use his feet. Guys who leaned on boxing skills often did so to conceal a disabling strike from a kick when an enemy least expected it.

Dak considered letting his ex-teammate take the lead in the dance, but he knew that's what Carson expected. So he stepped in, closing the gap between them. He let anger streak across his face to allow Carson to believe he'd lost all sense of strategy and tactics, replacing them with fury.

He charged ahead and turned to throw a powerful cross punch. Carson dipped and raised his hands to protect his face, then let his back foot drop laterally to counter. He ducked the strike from Dak and jabbed hard, but Dak knew it was coming. He jumped and snapped his foot straight up into Carson's chin, flipping over backward in one motion. Dak landed on his feet with a bended knee, bracing the landing with one fist on the ground.

Carson staggered backward, his vision blurred. The world tilted to one side, and try as he did, he couldn't get it to steady.

Deno swore at the abrupt and powerful martial arts move. Bert said something in Spanish that Dak was certain to be profanity.

Dak moved in to end the fight with a second blow, but in his daze, Carson managed to sidestep a snap kick to the chest. He jabbed again as Dak lunged by and his fist caught the attacker on the jaw.

Dak's head whipped to the side. He felt a dull pain course through the bone. It was a good punch, but not good enough to knock him out or give him a concussion. He spun around in a circle, anticipating another cross punch to follow.

His guess proved correct. Carson launched his right fist forward, but he missed badly, still dazed from the kick to the chin. Dak jabbed back after the wild miss, his fist smacking into Carson's right cheek. He jabbed again and again, throttling the man with his fists until they were rubbed raw.

With each punch, Carson stumbled backward toward the hedgerow, like a boxer in a ring.

When he felt his back hit the brush, he knew there was nowhere left to go. Carson put up his hands and desperately blocked. Then Dak made a mistake.

In his fervor to end the fight quickly, he'd expelled tremendous energy throwing punch after punch, most of which landed with devastating accuracy.

But none of them had felled Carson, and now the big man fought back.

He wrapped his arms around Dak's neck as the punches grew weaker and pulled him close. Then came a surprise attack. Carson raised his knee hard into Dak's midsection.

Dak felt the air sucked out of his lungs in an instant. He doubled over, but that only made him more vulnerable.

Carson chopped down on the back of his neck with the side of his hand. If he hadn't been so beat up, the strike would have likely ended things then and there. As it was, Dak dropped to all fours and nearly blacked out. He crawled forward to grab at Carson's ankles, desperately hoping to trip him up and spill him onto his back.

Still, in a slight haze, face swollen and one eye shut, Carson saw the feeble attempt and brought his foot up fast, sending the bone crashing into the side of Dak's face.

Dak flopped over onto his side. Pain screamed at him from several points in his body, and he still couldn't find air for his lungs.

He tried to cough to clear a passage, but it didn't come.

Bert and his men merely watched.

"You think you can just track me down like I'm some animal?" Carson groused. "Huh?" He kicked Dak in the ribs. "You think I'm a chump you can pick a fight with? Is that it, Dak?"

No response came from Dak's lips. His lungs burned for lack of air, and he couldn't force a single word out of his throat.

"I don't hear you," Carson taunted. He reached down and grabbed Dak by the hair, raising his head so their eyes met. "You were stupid not to come with us, bro. You were stupid to come here. And you were stupid to leave that cave. Now you're going to die, just like you should have six months ago." He threw his head down and kicked Dak in the gut for good measure.

The blow unexpectedly reversed whatever damage the initial one had done. Dak felt air flood his lungs, and he gasped deeply, repeatedly, relief filling his entire body.

Carson stepped around behind Dak, who clawed at the ground to get some kind of distance.

"Nah, Dak," Carson said. "Where do you think you're going?"

He bent down to grab Dak's head. It was a move Dak had seen his teammate use on enemies in close quarters combat before. He recalled the first time he saw Carson snap someone's neck, and he knew that was what the man intended now.

Carson's thick fingers grabbed Dak's jaw on one side and the top of his head with the other. In two seconds, Dak would be dead.

He mustered every ounce of strength and wit he could as the muscular man pulled him up to his knees.

"Bye-bye, Dak. I think you've seen this one before."

Dak abruptly let his legs give out and his head slipped through Carson's sweaty fingers. While he fell forward, Dak kicked his right leg out hard and struck his opponent in the gut.

The blow drove Carson backward. It was his turn to feel the air leave his lungs. He hunched over, hoping gravity would help him, but Dak wasted no time.

He clambered to his feet and staggered over to the enemy. He raised his fist over his shoulder and whipped his hips around like a pro golfer, using every bit of strength he could muster. The hammer fist smashed into Carson's cheek, shattering the bone within. His head snapped hard to one side, and he staggered like a heavyweight fighter in the last round, barely able to stand.

Dak reached out and raised his old friend's chin, then threw another cross, then a hook, a jab, another hook. Each blow sent Carson reeling, the garden swirling in his vision and the man before him blurred more with each shot.

Carson tried to defend himself, tried to throw a punch, but they may as well have been thrown by the blades of grass at their feet.

When Carson was near to the opposite hedgerow, Dak reared back and threw a devastating uppercut.

Carson's head whipped back for a second, his eyes staring blankly into the sky. Then he toppled over onto the grass. His chest raised and lowered, the air finally flowing into the man's lungs.

The breaths would be his last.

Dak stepped over him and looked down into his ex-teammate's eyes. "You were my brother," he said with infinite sadness in his voice. "And you left me to die."

Carson didn't respond. His head lolled back and forth on the grass, only half-controlled.

"I could ask you where the others are, but I doubt you know. It doesn't matter. I'm going to find them. I'm going to find them all. And I'm going to kill them. Starting with you."

Dak bent his knees and leaped into the air. Time slowed as his body descended. Carson may have only been half-aware of what was said or what was happening. Then Dak's knee plowed into the man's throat, crushing it through to the spine.

Dak stood up and took a step back, watching the body twitch for several seconds as the lungs tried to fill in vain. Arms and legs flopped around. Then the movement slowed. Then there was none.

Birds squawked in the distance. Bert and his men stared with wide, dread-filled eyes at the grisly scene.

Dak breathed heavily for a moment. He stared down at the body of his former friend. His knuckles hurt and he was certain he'd cracked a rib, but he would live.

He staggered toward the door into the house after a moment of silent contemplation.

"Hey," Bert said.

Dak stopped and slowly turned. "Yeah?"

Bert still held the hand cannon loosely in one fist. "What do you want us to do with him?"

Dak rolled his shoulders. "I don't care. Take him out in your boat. Tie some weights to him. Let the fish have him."

The Puerto Rican pouted his lips and nodded. "Old school. I like it. But what about the money? You said he has money."

"Take his keys. You can figure out where he lives. I'm sure there's a safe there or something. Nothing a drill can't fix for someone who knows how to use it."

Dak stepped over the threshold into the house.

"What about you? Where are you going?"

Dak paused, then looked over his shoulder. "To find the others."

THANK YOU

Thank you for taking the time to read this story. We can always make more money, but time is a finite resource for all of us, so the fact you took the time to read my work means the world to me and I truly appreciate it. I hope you enjoyed it as much as I enjoyed sharing it, and I look forward to bringing you more fun adventures in the future. If you this story kept you up late, on the edge of your seat, or burning your fingers as you swiped or turned the pages, swing by Amazon and leave a review. I'd appreciate it and so would other readers.

See you in the next one,

Ernest

OTHER BOOKS BY ERNEST DEMPSEY

Dak Harper Origin Stories:

Out of the Fire

You Only Die Once

Tequila Sunset

Purgatory

Scorched Earth

The Heart of Vengeance

Sean Wyatt Adventures:

The Secret of the Stones

The Cleric's Vault

The Last Chamber

The Grecian Manifesto

The Norse Directive

Game of Shadows

The Jerusalem Creed

The Samurai Cipher

The Cairo Vendetta

The Uluru Code

The Excalibur Key

The Denali Deception

The Sahara Legacy

The Fourth Prophecy

The Templar Curse

The Forbidden Temple

The Omega Project

The Napoleon Affair

The Second Sign

Adriana Villa Adventures:

War of Thieves Box Set

When Shadows Call

Shadows Rising

Shadow Hour

The Adventure Guild:

The Caesar Secret: Books 1-3

The Carolina Caper

Beta Force:

Operation Zulu

London Calling

Paranormal Archaeology Division:

Hell's Gate

For the other Ernie

ACKNOWLEDGMENTS

Special thanks go out to my super fans. We ride together. I appreciate and love you all. And a huge thank you to Anne Storer, Ray Braun, Denyse Léonard, and James Slater for your extra effort in helping make this story a better reading experience.

TEQUILA SUNSET

A DAK HARPER THRILLER

ERNEST DEMPSEY

ONE

SEQUATCHIE COUNTY, TENNESSEE

Dak sensed the movement before he heard a twig snap and leaves rustle. He turned his head, slowly, cautiously, peering through the forest with piercing jade eyes. Covered head-to-toe in forest camouflage, he blended perfectly against the tree trunk to his back. Twenty feet up in his tree stand, he had a clear 180-degree view of the forest below and anything that might approach.

His ears pricked when he heard the sound of more leaves rustling. The abstruse noise came from his right. He kept his eyes locked on the area while he covertly raised his hunting bow and drew back the string. He pulled only halfway, keeping three fingers on the tightly wound cord.

The deer emerged from a thicket of privet and stepped into the open. Dak had seen the buck before, an eight pointer with a healthy, light brown coat. He knew the animal would return to this spot as he'd seen it, as well as several does in the last month since hunkering down in his mountain cabin.

Dak waited until the buck fully exposed his flank before drawing the bowstring back, his fingers brushing lightly against his cheek. He breathed slowly, half through his nostrils and half through his mouth to remain utterly silent. The razor-sharp point on the arrow aligned perfectly with the target.

With a slow blink, Dak gradually allowed the string to retract until it was back in a neutral position.

"Not today, young fella," he whispered. He didn't speak loud enough for the deer to hear him, but the animal's head shot up and looked around, spooked by something.

It took a few steps forward and then resumed foraging for food in the forest undergrowth.

Dak smiled.

He didn't enjoy killing animals. Hated it, in fact. Animals naturally acclimated to their environment, doing their instinctive best to live in harmony with nature and the planet. People, on the other hand, stripped the land of its resources in their all-consuming hunt for more, more, more.

Dak had hunted since he was young, his late uncle Ben taking him on trips into the mountains for wild turkey, deer, and pheasant. The most important thing about hunting Dak ever learned from his uncle, was to never kill what you don't need. That was one of the greatest sins of humanity against the earth, taking more than people needed.

Back at the cabin, Dak had a freezer full of food that would last him several months. On top of that, he had an emergency supply of MRE-style meals that could stretch a year or more if needed.

He'd considered the irony of not taking more than he needed when comparing it to his long-term food supply, but that was different. Being ready to sustain himself for a while wasn't greedy or hoarding. It was good planning. Killing this buck right now, when he had plenty to eat, was another matter.

The animal looked up again, this time locking eyes with him. The creature blinked, its dark orbs flashing behind wide eyelids. Dak felt overwhelmed by the moment. It was spiritual, serene, surreal, as if looking into the eyes of a ghost reincarnated into this beautiful creature.

Dak watched the buck, observing its movements as it continued grazing. Then, when the animal had exhausted the easily gleaned supply of food on the ground, it trotted deeper into the forest, flicking its cotton tail as it retreated from view.

Dak took a deep breath and exhaled, realizing his breathing had grown shallow while he watched the beast, almost as if he'd forgotten to breathe at all.

The moment over, he shifted in his seat and reached down for the thermos of coffee to his right. He pushed back the magnetic seal on the lid and took a sip. Two hours later, the rich coffee still steamed like it did when he first poured it.

This was what Dak loved most about hunting. Not the kill, but the peace of being in nature without so much as a scratch of humanity to interrupt his thoughts. A few birds chirped and sang in the treetops. The trickle of the mountain spring near his cabin barely reached his ears. Other than that, the location was utterly peaceful.

The smell of dried leaves, pine, and coffee were the only other interruptions the morning provided.

Until he felt the phone in his pocket vibrate against his thigh.

He let out another sigh. Irritated and curious, he pulled the device out of his pocket and looked at the message preview on the screen. Only one person had this number, though he wished he could share it with another. That, however, would be too dangerous. Nicky had helped him get back on his feet. He couldn't risk contacting her again, not with Bo Taylor and the others still out there.

Carson Williams was dead, either still sitting at the bottom of the ocean off the coast of Miami, or in the bellies of a hundred sea creatures. But four threats still remained, and Dak didn't dare contact Nicole until they were gone.

Four more, he thought. Dak still wasn't convinced the colonel could be swayed with evidence of his innocence in the events that took place in Iraq more than seven months before. He hoped that could be the case, that he could return to his life as Dak Harper and not some alias hiding out in the mountains. He would do that as long as it took, years even, so long as the men who betrayed him paid for what they'd done.

He tried not to dwell on vengeance, but it was nearly impossible. The only way he truly justified it was knowing that if those men had stabbed him in the back, there was no limit to the sins they would continue to commit against others.

Dak's green eyes fell to the phone again. He pulled his baseball cap off and ran his fingers through thick, almost black hair, reading the message again.

His irritation melted.

"I found Luis. Call me."

The text was from his friend Will in Portugal.

Will had been scouring the globe, going above and beyond what Dak could have ever requested. For the last month, though, he'd come up empty, finding no sign of Luis or the others.

Deep down, Dak hoped Luis would be the next one he found. The Mexican-American had been the softest of their group, the one who—if interrogated—would prove most likely to give up information about the others, assuming he had any. That last part was improbable, but Dak had to try.

He'd known Carson would never share any details about the locations of the others if he had them at all. Carson's overconfidence led to his downfall, but it would never have wavered.

Dak took another swig of coffee, set down the thermos, and pressed the green button to call Will.

The phone only rang once before his friend answered. "Found him," Will said.

"So I saw. Where?"

"Good morning to you too. And you're welcome."

Dak merely twisted his head slightly back and forth. "I'll thank you when you tell me where he is."

"Mexico. And you're not going to believe what he's been up to."

TWO

URUAPAN, MEXICO

Marco Espinal watched the road through the windshield of the black Ford Explorer. For the last two hours, his focus never wavered, eyes always locked on the cracked, undulating pavement that stretched down the hill toward the flats of Tiamba.

Every few minutes, a gentle breeze rolled through the hills and passed through his open window, providing some relief from the sun's warmth. He allowed himself the distraction of a sip of water now and then to keep hydrated, though he didn't dare drink too much. The last thing he needed was to be relieving himself when the convoy passed.

If that happened, there would be no mercy from his employer. And he knew too well the methods his key enforcer would use—he'd witnessed them firsthand more times than he could count. It was that man's plan that Marco was here to execute.

A rival cartel—El Nuevo Guerreros—was rumored to be sending a convoy down this route. It was more than a rumor, though, and Marco knew it. The Guerreros were sending a shipment of guns to one of their factories to the north of Tiamba, a small village on the outskirts of Uruapan.

The village itself was irrelevant. With only a few hundred inhabitants, however, it made the perfect cover for the operations of one of the largest cartels. With the Mexican government under pressure for the last couple of years, they'd been pushing harder and harder in the war against the drug cartels.

Marco knew that much of it was show. Most of the cartel members knew it too. They played their part, sending the most expendable of their ranks into open gunfights against police and military personnel. For the heads of the cartels, it was a win-win scenario.

If the government's gunmen won a fight here or there, killed a few dozen men, it would be plastered in all of the papers. The cartels would look weakened to the public, and the war on illicit drugs would appear to be working. Whenever that happened, profits went up because the authorities had a bad habit of resting on their laurels.

It helped that some of their ranks were paid by the cartels.

On the other hand, if the cartels took out some cops, some government agents, their stranglehold on the region would grow that much more. Some people trusted the cartels more than they trusted the government, which was easy to understand given some of the recent displays of incompetence.

A shootout near a school one week ago resulted in several civilian casualties, including one teacher who died as a result.

The government was vilified in the papers and on social media. The mayor's ability to keep people safe hung on the minds and mouths of thousands. The governor, too, was unable to curtail the violence, though many believed he was also heavily influenced by the cartels.

It was impossible to say which one or ones, though Marco knew the truth.

His organization was currently one of the largest in the country, rivaled by few. As it happened, their most notorious rival was located in the same region, making Uruapan the epicenter of much of the violence.

Marco didn't feel bad for the civilians. If they wanted to take an active role, they could take a side. Dying innocently in the war was still dying. He'd rather have a gun in his hand and go down fighting than die as collateral damage.

He reached down to his cup holder and plucked the bottle, raised it to his lips, and took a sip. As he put the container back in its place, he looked down the road. A few thousand feet away, three more SUVs waited, concealed by dense outcroppings of trees along the route. The convoy would never see them coming, just as they wouldn't see Marco and the vehicle across the road.

He noticed the driver of the other SUV looking down toward his lap. Even from thirty yards away, Marco could tell what the man was doing.

Marco touched the button on the radio piece in his ear. "Juan, stop looking at your phone. They could be here any minute."

Marco's driver, a muscular man with a shaved head and a thin beard, looked over with a humored chuckle. "He's going to get killed one of these days."

"Only a matter of time," Marco said. While Marco kept his appearance mostly clean with only a few hidden tattoos, his driver was a canvas of body art. Flames licked up the sides of the man's neck. A skull stared out from his throat. Dozens of other tattoos covered his arms, and probably the rest of his body, Marco imagined, though he didn't care to let his mind wander into too much detail.

The sound of motors moaning and tires rolling along asphalt interrupted his thoughts.

He touched his earpiece again. "All teams be ready. Here they come."

Marco checked the AR-15 in his lap, twisting it over to inspect it for at least the sixth time since he'd been sitting there. He pulled on the charging handle and notched a round into the chamber, then flipped the cover off the red dot sight mounted on the rail.

Two more men in the back of the SUV did the same and shifted in their seats as adrenaline began seeping through their veins.

The first enemy vehicle zoomed by, a silver Chevy Tahoe. Three more vehicles followed; two minivans and an old Toyota Landcruiser.

They weren't the usual vehicles the Guerreros used, but that was probably by design. Most of the time, vehicles running shipments of drugs or weapons utilized a variety of transportation modes to disguise their operations.

Marco waited for ten seconds after the last vehicle passed before giving the order.

"Team one, move into position."

The SUV across the road pulled out from its hiding spot and turned right, heading up the hill until it reached the top, while Marco's driver stepped on the gas and veered toward the convoy.

The other SUV turned and stopped in the middle, blocking both lanes so no other traffic could get through.

"Team two, set the trap."

Marco watched the road ahead, and within seconds the other three SUVs emerged from their cover. They drove out onto the asphalt and blockaded the road, along with the shoulders. The only way any of the enemy transports could get by was to drive into the forest, and that would be a short trip ending in a collision with a tree.

The convoy's Tahoe slammed on its brakes and skidded to a stop. The two minivans did the same, both steering into the other lane to avoid hitting the car in front. The last SUV trailed a few car lengths behind and stopped less abruptly.

Team two flung open their doors and stepped out of their SUVs, leveling their guns at the first truck. The men fanned out, surrounding all four vehicles as Marco's driver sped to the rear, hit the brakes, and spun the wheel to block both lanes—sealing off the enemy's only potential exit.

Marco was the first out, a true general willing to step into battle with his men at a moment's notice. He leveled his weapon, aiming at the back of the last SUV while his driver and the two other men from his ride spread out to encircle the vehicle.

The people in the convoy barely moved, except to look around at the circle of death surrounding them. They never got a chance to put up their hands or even step out and offer to surrender.

"Kill them," Marco ordered.

The sound of gunfire rolled up and down the highway, echoing through the forests. The deadly hail of metal punctured the convoy's vehicles, shattering glass and tearing through metal, riddling the bodies that occupied them.

When every magazine ran dry, all that remained of the massacre was the cloud of bitter smoke that hung in the air from the mass discharge of powder.

Marco lowered his weapon and stalked toward the last vehicle—what was left of it. He stopped at the rear door and pulled on the handle. To his surprise, it wasn't locked. The door swung open and a pale-skinned woman's body slumped over, the seatbelt around her lap and shoulder keeping her from falling out onto the road. The woman wasn't dead, but she soon would be. Her body bled from at least ten bullet wounds in the legs, torso, and arms. She breathed heavily, but each breath brought more blood into her lungs and sent her into coughing fits.

Marco frowned at the sight and immediately peered deeper into the vehicle to the other side. "Gringos?" he muttered.

Something was wrong. These weren't the men they were after. He stepped to the back of the SUV and flung open the rear door.

Instead of guns, he found boxes of food, medicine, and shoes.

He swore in Spanish and closed the rear door, then walked back to the open passenger-side door and the dying woman. He drew the pistol from his hip, pointed it at the top of the woman's head, and squeezed the trigger.

The American woman's coughing ceased, and she went still.

Marco stuffed the pistol back in its holster, took a phone out of his pocket, and called the first contact on his recents list.

"Bueno," a man answered.

"Luis," Marco said. "We have a problem."

THREE

SEQUATCHIE COUNTY, TENNESSEE

"You're sure about this?" Dak asked. He immediately regretted slinging the question.

"Sure?" Will said, doing his best to sound offended. "Of course I'm sure. I wouldn't call you if I just had a hunch. It's him."

"Sorry," Dak said, ducking under a low hanging tree branch.

He trudged through the forest toward the cabin, paying no attention to how much noise he made. Disturbing the wildlife didn't matter now. A far more pressing concern riddled his thoughts.

"It's fine," Will laughed. "I'm just messing with you, but yeah, don't think I'm going to call you with information that might be correct."

"I'll try to do better in the future," Dak panted.

"What are you doing, anyway? Sounds like you're a little out of breath."

Dak exhaled as he reached the top of a small knoll. The Swedish timber-style cabin sat perched in a clearing just ahead. A hundred feet of meadow surrounded the mountain retreat on all sides. He'd tilled some of the cleared area for a micro-farm and planted a few varieties of vegetables. It was too late to plant corn, but he'd considered constructing a greenhouse for year-round growing.

"I'm hiking back to my cabin," Dak answered. "I was up in a tree stand."

"Tree stand? It's not hunting season yet. Or is it? I can't ever keep that stuff straight. I'm not much of a hunter and being out of the States for so long, it's hard to remember."

"No, it's not hunting season yet. I was just enjoying the serenity of it all."

"Oh," Will said, then paused. "I hope you got all the serenity you wanted because if you're going after Luis Martinez, it's going to be anything but tranquil."

"I still can't believe he's with a Mexican drug cartel. That doesn't sound like Luis."

"Based on what you told me, none of those guys from your team are who you thought they were."

Dak reached the cabin and clomped up the three steps onto the wraparound deck. He turned the latch, opened the door, and stepped inside. "That's an understatement."

"There's more," Will hinted. "Luis didn't just join a cartel. He's with one of the biggest in the region and there's a bloody war going on between his organization and a few other rivals."

"That's not unusual. The cartels are constantly fighting for supremacy down there." Dak set his coffee thermos on the counter to the left, slipped off his boots at the door, and ambled over to a wooden writing desk in the right corner. The workstation's position between windows on either side allowed for a wide view of the forest. The peaceful view of nature was only one of the motivators for choosing that spot for his laptop. The other reason was that it allowed Dak to see if anyone approached his property from the trail that led down to the road.

"Yeah, and Uruapan is notorious for the violence. It regularly spills into the streets and sucks in civilians."

Dak didn't know as much about that particular city as some of the others. Juarez, Guadalajara, and other larger cities received more press in the American mainstream media, but behind those headlines, dozens of other towns and villages teemed with violence.

Many of the details Dak had seen were worse than anything he'd ever witnessed during his service with the military. Beheadings, dismembered body parts, public hangings, and worse, were all standard methods utilized by the cartels.

The barbaric display of butchery the cartels used was intended to get people in line, to choose a side, or to let everyone know who was on top—at least for now. With his peripheral view of the Mexican drug wars, Dak didn't know all the ins and outs, but he noticed how it seemed like a seesaw in the way that cartels rose and fell. Few had been around for more than a decade, with new and ambitious leaders climbing through the ranks or building their own operations to rival others.

Some tactics in the power struggle smacked of Romanesque methods with covert assassinations, sabotaging supply chains, and plying corrupt government officials and police for assistance in a multitude of avenues.

It was a zero-sum game. There would be no winners, only temporary leaders atop a board that constantly changed, evolved, and stripped down even the mightiest king, elevating new pawns to a monarchy built on powder. Cocaine had always been a part of the cartels' commodities, but with marijuana legalization on the rise in the United States, the organizations had to make a pivot.

They were businesses, after all, and when a product became less profitable, the leaders knew it was time to push something else with higher margins.

Enter the return of heroin.

A dangerous narcotic that had all but played itself out in America returned to the streets with new vigor. The cartels flooded American drug houses with the stuff, and with it, the number of overdose deaths had skyrocketed in recent years. On top of that, many of the drug lords blended fentanyl into their heroin, which caused the number of deaths to surge even higher.

Dak sat down at his computer station and flipped open the laptop. "So, what is Luis doing with a cartel?" he asked as the screen bloomed to life. An image of El Capitan in Yosemite filled the monitor with a few blue folders and documents populating the right-hand side.

"From what my intel says, he's the right-hand man to Giovani Mendoza—the head of the Dorado Aguila cartel."

"Golden Eagle," Dak said. "Interesting name. Someone thinks highly of themselves." Dak masked his bewilderment at the information for a moment, then spilled it. "Did you say he's the right-hand guy?"

"Yeah. It seems he's head of security and a key enforcer. From what I've gathered, he's pretty ruthless. Cops won't touch him. And American agencies won't try. They have too many other fish they're working on, higher-profile targets."

Luis, ruthless? The thought shook Dak to his gut. He'd seen Luis operate in combat. He did his job with careful efficiency. He'd killed in battle, everyone on the team had. But ruthless? That didn't sound like Luis. Then again, siding with Bo and the others to leave Dak for dead went against everything he thought he knew about the man as well as the rest of the crew.

It seemed Luis Martinez had completed his journey to the dark side.

Will interrupted Dak's silent contemplation. "I don't think I have to tell you how dangerous it will be to go after your boy on this one, Dak. He's protected. Not just by guns and a small army of cartel soldiers, but by the local law enforcement too. You won't get much help on this one if you decide to do it."

"I didn't have help on the last one either, except for your intel."

"Yeah, but this is different. Car—" He caught himself and stopped before he said Carson's name. "Your last target was on his own. I wouldn't advise an entire team of spec ops guys from any branch going into this hornets' nest. It's suicide."

"Thanks for the advice," Dak said. "I'm not taking a team. So, I should be fine."

"I had a bad feeling you'd say that."

Dak ignored him. "You said I won't get much help. Does that mean I'll get some?"

"Yeah," Will confirmed. "I have a contact in Guadalajara not too far from there. She can help you with anything you might need: weapons, supplies, whatever. I told her you'd be in contact."

"She?"

Will snorted. "You got a problem working with a woman?"

Dak chuckled. "No. Just wondering if it's one of your old girl-friends, because if so, maybe she won't help me as much as you think."

"You're funny," Will said flatly. "No, nothing ever happened with me and her. I'll send you her contact info when we get off the phone. Her name is Carina Perez. She's a tough one. Used to work for an anti-drug task force with the Federales. Now she runs a cantina outside Guadalajara."

"She's a bartender?" Dak's doubts were obvious in his voice.

"I didn't say she was pouring the drinks, although maybe she is. I recall she made a pretty good margarita. But the cantina is a cover. She helps equip locals with weapons so they can defend themselves. Keeps it real hush. Only works with double-checked referrals and always uses trusted third parties to make her deliveries. She's smart."

"I wouldn't say being a gun runner is smart if you're going against the cartels, but I like her moxie. I'll say that."

"I'm sure you do. I'll send over the information now. Good luck, Dak. Don't get yourself killed. Or worse."

Dak snorted. "I make no promises."

He ended the call and focused on the news headline he'd pulled up during the conversation. His finger dragged the article down beyond the fold as he read the details about a convoy of Methodist missionaries who'd been slaughtered in the crossfire of a local drug war. The location of the killing was Uruapan.

According to the reports, a cartel called El Nuevo Guerrero was being blamed for the massacre. Dak figured that was one of the rivals of Luis' organization. Why would they attack missionaries?

That question would have to wait until later. His phone buzzed on the desk. He took his eyes off the computer and looked down at the text from Will.

"Carina Perez," Dak said. "Looks like I'm in for some tequila."

FOUR

URUAPAN

Luis stepped into the dark basement. The sound of water dripping from a leaky faucet in the corner echoed through the room like a slow, persistent hammer. He quickly surveyed the room as he always did, taking in every detail. Even as one of the top men in the organization, Luis knew things could change quickly. A man who was an ally one minute could be the one to stick the knife in your back the next.

His senses always remained on high alert, whether he was eating a bowl of cereal or dolling out punishment on behalf of Mendoza.

Not counting himself, the headcount in the room was five: two of his security men on the right and two on the left, the fifth man sat in a metal chair, hands bound behind him and his feet clamped together with zip ties. Duct tape was wrapped around his belly and lower ribs to keep him firmly attached to the chair.

More duct tape stretched across his mouth, sealing his lips shut. His swollen, bulbous eyes barely allowed the man to see. Luis' men had been thorough in their beatings. If he had to guess, the prisoner probably had a few broken ribs, too.

The man's head sagged so low his chin nearly touched the top of his chest. His black hair was caked in sweat and blood.

Luis moved deeper into the room like a ghost floating above the floor. He stopped a few feet from the chair, hovering menacingly until the man raised his head, staring out through narrow slits.

"Why, Eduardo?" Luis asked.

The gangly man stared back blankly. His white shirt and blue jeans were stained with dirt, sweat, and splotches of blood—the poster child for torture.

Eduardo's breath came in heavy, labored gasps. Exhaustion had set in. Over the last 24 hours, Luis instructed he not be allowed to sleep, knowing that would weaken the man's will to resist the truth.

"I... I didn't—" Eduardo muttered. Spittle and blood spewed out from his lips.

"Yes, you did," Luis interrupted. "Yes, you did." He stepped closer to the prisoner and grabbed him by the back of the skull, propping the man's head up so he could look nowhere else but into Luis' probing brown eyes.

"I swear, Luis. It wasn't me."

Luis cocked his head to the side, feigning sympathy. "Oh? But you were the one who gave us the intel about the convoy. You were the one who told us when they would be passing through that route. You gave us the exact time and location, Eduardo."

He shook the man's head, clutching a fistful of hair, then shoved it down. Luis stood up and cracked his neck in both directions, dusting off his hands at the same time as if that would get the congealed blood off his skin.

"See what you did, Eduardo? You got blood on my hand."

One of the guards stepped forward immediately with a wet rag, extending it out to their general.

Luis accepted the proffered cloth with a nod and worked meticulously at getting his skin squeaky clean before handing it back to the guard.

"Gracias," he said.

The man accepted the gratitude and stepped back into the

shadows near a sink to the right. A bucket sat on the floor next to him.

"Do you know what that is?" Luis asked, pointing to a plank five feet away in the middle of the room. It was propped up by cinder blocks, a metal drain cover underneath an ominous clue.

Eduardo barely had the strength to look to his right, but he managed and then brought his gaze back to Luis. "No," he said, weakly turning his head.

Luis squatted down so he looked at eye level. "You see, Eduardo, Senior Mendoza doesn't like traitors." He pouted his lips and bobbed his head as if making a concession. "I realize that in our line of work, that sort of thing is common." He raised a finger. "That doesn't mean we have to accept it."

"I didn't—"

"I wasn't finished," Luis said, raising the back of his hand to threaten further punishment. Eduardo's chest heaved as sobs climbed up into his chest and spat out of his mouth. "I want to know why. I want to know who put you up to this. Give me every detail, Eduardo."

"I swear, Luis. Please!"

Luis drew a long breath through his nostrils and stood up straight again. He flattened his black, button-up shirt and matching pants. "Okay, Eduardo."

He looked over to the guard who had brought the rag and nodded.

The man picked up the bucket at his feet and brought it over. Water sloshed over the sides and splattered on the floor. The other three guards immediately moved to the center of the room and picked up the chair holding Eduardo.

"What... what are you doing?" the prisoner asked, panic suddenly giving him a short burst of energy.

The men positioned the chair legs over the plank and then tilted it until Eduardo was on his back, staring up at the ceiling, head resting on the wooden board.

Luis shifted his feet and looked down at the man. "Have you ever wondered what it feels like to drown, Eduardo? Did you know you can experience this wretched feeling on dry land?"

Eduardo knew then what was about to happen. Dread filled his swollen face and his head rolled back and forth as if that would somehow keep his inevitable fate from knocking.

"No," he blathered. "Please, don't do this, Luis. I've always been loyal."

Luis leaned forward menacingly. He hovered over the man's face for a moment. The smell of sweat, the acrid scent of blood, and the pungent odor of desperate fear hung in the air. "Loyal to who, Eduardito?"

Luis turned to the man with the rag and gave a nod.

Eduardo shouted his protests, twisting his head violently back and forth as the guard placed the bloody rag over the prisoner's face, then pushed down with both hands to keep the victim still.

"No!" Eduardo's muted screams filled the room, his voice bouncing off the concrete walls and going no farther. No one would hear him. Not even upstairs in the mansion where Giovani Mendoza conducted business as usual.

One of the other guards, a man with a shaved head and matching crosses tattooed on both cheeks, picked up the plastic bucket and held it over Eduardo's head.

Luis waited for a second, and then said, "Who put you up to this, Eduardo?"

"Please! I didn't—"

His voice cut off as the guard dumped a stream of water onto the rag. Eduardo choked and gagged. The man with the bucket righted the container for a moment while the prisoner coughed.

"Who?"

After another ten seconds of gurgled coughing, Eduardo tried to speak. "Please, Luis. Please!"

Luis ignored the pleas and nodded again at the guard. Once more, the bucket tilted. The liquid poured onto the rag. Eduardo shook violently, jerking his head in every conceivable direction, but he couldn't escape. Water seeped into his mouth and lungs. The coughing returned as his body tried to reject the liquid. Eduardo's chest burned and squeezed in terrible agony.

The guard tipped the bucket back to its upright state and waited again.

"Tell me, Eduardo. Tell me who put you up to this. I want to know where the guns went. Give me everything and I will make this end."

Eduardo hesitated. Luis hadn't been certain of the man's guilt. It was entirely possible they were torturing an innocent person. That, however, came with the job. Sometimes the innocent were punished, but that was how control was maintained. That hesitation, though, told Luis he'd been right about Eduardo.

"Guerreros," Eduardo yelped. "Nuevos Guerreros." He sobbed openly now from under the soaked rag. His body convulsed with ever choking tears. "They said they would kill my family, Luis. My parents, my wife. They said they would execute all of them."

Luis inclined his head at the information. He'd suspected the Guerreros were responsible. They were the only organization clever enough to pull a stunt like that, in this part of the country, anyway.

The intention, Luis believed, was to make it look like Dorado Aguila had taken to butchering American missionaries. The plan would have worked if not for Marco's quick decision and Luis' ability to manipulate the media.

He'd spun the story on its head, turning it against the Guerreros before they could take further action. Now, they were a target for both the Mexican government and the Americans. The latter wouldn't do anything official. They would send in covert ops, teams of them, to mete out their own brand of justice.

One thing Eduardo said, however, needled at Luis. His heart—for the briefest of seconds—tensed at the prisoner's comment about his family.

Luis swept the emotions under a resolute, grim façade. "Thank you, Eduardo. I knew it was them. I'm glad to see you have confirmed my suspicions."

The man holding the rag pulled it back and revealed Eduardo's face again. "Please, Luis," he begged between feeble coughing fits. "I'm sorry. I won't do it again. I sw—"

Luis raised a pistol in his right hand and fired. The suppressor muffled the sound to just above a click, like someone flicking their fingernail on a desk.

Eduardo's head fell back against the wooden board and slumped to the side, a blackened crimson hole in his forehead.

"Get rid of him," Luis ordered his men. "Leave his body at one of the known Guerreros pickup locations. It's time to send them a message."

He turned and stormed out of the room and up the stairs, never once looking back.

FIVE

GUADALAJARA

Dak scrolled through his phone, reading an article about the terrible massacre that happened on the road between Uruapan and the village of Tiamba. His heart ached for the victims and their families. Yet all he could see from the incident was an ongoing argument between the local cartels. The government, for their part, also helped gloss over the tragedy by continuing to put out statements about how the investigation was ongoing and they weren't certain who was responsible.

Could Luis have been behind the killings? The possibility was 50/50 at this point.

Dak sat at a corner booth so he could keep an eye on everything and everyone in the place. The cantina harkened back to the days of old Mexico, when outlaws roamed freely, kicking in doors and settling matters with pistols instead of law and order. Ironically, it seemed much of the country still embraced those antiquated customs. At least here, in this part of the big city, the cartels' grasp wasn't as firm. Expensive high rise condos and apartment buildings reached to the sky over the rolling plains of Guadalajara. He'd passed Ferrari, Aston Martin, and Maserati dealerships on his way to the bar—a telling contrast between the lives of the wealthy and those who kept the country running from the depths of blue collar mediocrity.

To her credit, Will's contact had picked a place between the two. The location of the bar on one of the many side streets Guadalajara had to offer gave it enough business to look legitimate, but not enough to bring in any significant revenue.

That, Dak knew, came from somewhere else.

The bar was nearly empty, only playing host to three other patrons. To be fair, it was still early in the day, but he estimated the busiest time would only produced six or seven more customers. The books probably reflected that, showing just enough profit to keep the lights on and the cops away.

He set the phone down on the table and picked up the glass of light gold tequila. He raised it to his lips and took a sip, letting the peppery liquid sit on his tongue before swallowing it.

He exhaled as the smooth burn slipped down his throat.

A black-haired woman in a white v-neck button down and faded blue jeans emerged through the manager's door to his left. She stalked over to him, crossing the twenty feet with long strides. The door closed slowly behind her as she approached. The untucked shirt, flapped at her hips. The long v at the neck stretched down to the very top of her breasts, revealing nothing, and promising the same.

She stopped short of Dak's table and crossed her arms. "Enjoying the reposado?" she asked in a heavy, exotic accent.

He looked down at the glass, letting his gaze linger on it for a few dramatic seconds, then diverted his eyes to meet hers. They pulled him in like twin vortexes, their gravity stronger than a thousand black holes. He wondered if her soul was as dark, but didn't push himself to find out.

The stunning young cantina owner stood out in the dusty bar like an orchid in the Sahara, an impossible bloom in an otherwise desolate wasteland.

Stupid pickup lines bubbled to mind. *Not as much as I'm enjoying the view,* he thought, but he knew better than to say something so trite. She was a businesswoman. Attractive, no question, but she wasn't here to be hit on or complimented. If they'd been two strangers at someone else's bar, he might have taken a chance, though he knew deep down it could go nowhere. His heart was still in Istanbul with a woman who would never take him back.

"It's excellent," he said, opting for focused honesty on the drink.

"I should hope so. I make it."

He tilted his head to the side and questioned her with raised eyebrows. "Yeah?"

"Yep," she said with a twitch of the head. "Family secret."

She slid into the seat across from him and folded her hands atop the table.

"Well, your secret is certainly safe with me," he offered.

"I hope so. I wouldn't want it slipping out."

Was she flirting? He was off his game. It had been a long time since he'd flirted with anyone. Nicky was the last woman he'd engaged with romantically. A few memories flittered in and out of his mind, but only sparse recollections of flirting appeared.

"I don't have any friends and I can't speak to my family. So, I'd say it's safer with me than in Fort Knox."

There was the cliche he was trying to avoid.

"Why do you think I agreed to meet you?" she asked. "My clients are one hundred percent referral only. Will vouched for you. While he didn't give me many details about your situation, he did say you were on your own and trying to keep a low profile." She held up a dismissive hand. "Don't bother telling me your story. I don't want to know. Will said you're good. That means you're good. So, what brings you to Guadalajara to my," she twirled a hand in the air, "fine establishment?"

Dak reached under the table toward his pocket. She shifted cautiously at the suspicious movement.

"Just a picture," he said, and produced an image slightly larger than a business card. He slid the picture across the table and spun it around, then withdrew his hand. "Luis Martinez," he said. "I need to find him."

She looked at the image for all of three seconds. When she lifted her head, she looked aghast.

A tentative chuckle escaped her lungs. "You need to find Luis Martinez? Why? You got a death wish or something?"

"No," Dak said. "I have something for him."

Surprise stretched across her face. Her wide, disbelieving eyes glowered back at him. "You're not a drug dealer. And you're not with the American government. What could you possibly have for Luis?"

"How do you know I'm not a Federale?" Dak joked.

She snorted. "Right."

"You're correct. I'm not a drug dealer. Luis Martinez tried to kill me. He and some of my...coworkers left me for dead in a cave on the other side of the world. I intend to repay that kindness."

The astonishment melted from her expression, replaced by incredulity. "You think you're going to kill Luis Martinez?" She said it as if he was trying to fly a cardboard box to the moon. "If you're a friend of Will, I assume that means you're skilled in some form of combat. Maybe you're ex-military."

He gave no hint of truth to the last.

"The fact is, it doesn't matter." She leaned in close. She didn't need to look over her shoulder. If someone was listening, her newest patron would have cautioned her. "Luis Martinez is the head of security for Giovani Mendoza. You know who he is?"

Dak nodded. "Head of the Dorado Aguila cartel."

"That's right," she confirmed. "And do you know who they are?"

"You don't have to fill me in on the danger," Dak informed. "I know who they are, what they are, and how they deal with enemies. The way they deal with innocents, apparently, isn't much different. I'm here for Luis. He owes a debt and he's going to pay it in blood. If they kill me, so be it." He slumped back, twisting the the tequila glass with forefinger and thumb. His eyes glazed over as he stared at the contents. "Doesn't matter. I'm dead anyway."

A stout man walked through the front door and sauntered over to the bar. His belly protruded over his belt, barely held back by a dirty red T-shirt that was easily one size too small. His jeans bore patches of dust and his cowboy boots should have been replaced years ago. Somehow, he still had money for booze.

The bartender, a skinny young man with a black handlebar mustache, stepped to the counter to serve the newcomer.

Dak watched the exchange for a second and then returned to the conversation. "All I need from you is his location. I can handle the rest."

"You can't. That much I can promise you. But if you're looking to die, who am I to stop you?" She stood up and pushed the picture across the table, stopping near the glass.

He wasn't sure what that meant. Was she going to help him or was that the end of the conversation?"

"So, does that mean you'll help me?"

She took a deep breath. "If you have money, I'll get you whatever you need. Maybe a little more since you apparently think you're a one man-army ready to take on the Mendoza clan."

"I have money," he said.

Her head tilted back. She appraised him with analytical eyes and then lowered her chin. "Be back here tonight. We close at eleven. We'll do business then."

"Thank you," Dak said, pulling the image back under the table and out of sight.

"Don't mention it. To anyone."

He nodded. "Of course."

She turned and started walking back to her office.

"Name's Dak, by the way," he said.

She paused, barely twisted her head toward her left shoulder, and said, "I know." Then she disappeared through the door and into the confines of her office.

Dak looked down at the glass again and raised it. "Well, Carina Perez," he whispered to himself, "nice to meet you too."

SIX

URUAPAN

Luis stepped out of the great room on the second floor and onto the veranda. He took a deep breath of the warm, dry air and planted his hands atop the porch's railing. The Mendoza estate sprawled out before him. Trees sporadically popped up along the rolling hills, with a dense forest to the right that hosted a variety of wildlife, including wild game for Mendoza's hunting hobby.

The man prided himself on being an avid hunter and even boasted about his expertise when he hosted parties for his allies. He'd killed an impressive number of animals, but all in a controlled environment with elevated safety measures in place. Luis looked back over his shoulder into the great room at the mounted quarry the cartel's leader had slain over the years.

Luis had no desire to kill animals. He detested the idea. Problematic humans, on the other hand....

Another breath and his frustrations were gone, though a lingering needle still pricked at his brain. Eduardo had been a good soldier. Loyal—at least for a while. Maybe he never really had been. On the outside, the man had played the part perfectly. It caused Luis to wonder how many others might have infiltrated the organization, the organization he was tasked with protecting. If he failed, he knew what would happen.

Eduardo claimed he was protecting the ones he loved most. Luis could identify. It was why he was here, in this situation. In a million years, he never would have guessed he'd return to his familial homeland to work for one of the most dangerous cartels in the country.

Luis detested the situation, but there was no other way.

His parents were stubborn. Owners of a small textile business in Uruapan, they'd been approached for years by the cartels about using their facility as a front for running drugs. The couple always turned them away, despite the growing number of threats.

After the events in Iraq, Luis decided disappearing to Mexico would be the best course of action. There he could drop off the grid and watch over his parents at the same time.

Eventually, Mendoza upped the ante, sending four of his men to burn down the textile shop.

It just so happened Luis was there, working late that night.

The men were armed, but that did little to save them against a seasoned, battle-hardened soldier like Luis, who kept a small arsenal both in his home and at the shop—just in case.

He'd seen the men approaching in their SUV and knew immediately they were there to wreak havoc.

In the end, Luis killed all of them with brutal, tactical efficiency. In the early evening darkness, he loaded each of the bodies into the SUV and drove them to Mendoza's estate, this estate where he now stood watch.

Luis dropped the bodies outside the gate at the bottom of the hill and waited, knowing that cameras were on him at all times. He'd held his hands out wide, unarmed, shouting at the mansion, "Mendoza! I have a gift for you!"

Within minutes, a dozen armed men in trucks arrived at the base of the estate. They surrounded Luis, who still brandished no weapon.

He thought about the moment, just seven months before, and

leaned forward on his elbows and watched the sun setting to the west. Streaks of orange and pink spanned the sky, melting into darker shades as the burning sun descended.

Sounds of nature cut through the air now and then, mostly led by various birds chirping, squawking, and whistling in the forest or the garden below.

"It's a beautiful view, no?" a familiar voice interrupted the peaceful silence. "They call this a tequila sunset. In the old days, the workers would toil late into the day on days like this, when the sky was clear and the air warm. And when they were done, they sipped tequila together as the sun set in the west."

Luis didn't turn around, instead keeping his gaze on the sprawling garden below, full of roses, neatly trimmed hedges, and a concrete fountain in the center of the square-shaped courtyard. The fountain displayed a sculpted angel holding a dying man with robes draped loosely over him. The figure lay across the angel's lap while the holy creature poured an endless stream of water from a jar in one hand. The water spilled over the dying man, a symbol of healing by the divine.

"Yes," Luis answered in Spanish. "It's gorgeous here." He did his best to hide the disgust oozing out of his soul. This man threatened his parents. It would have leaked over to his sister, who lived here. Luis was grateful his brother had remained in the States. Their parents were American citizens, as were his brother and sister, but when Luis' grandparents passed, no one was left to run the family business. Luis begged his parents not to leave the United States, the country they loved and that had given them so much, but they felt there was no choice.

"Roots," his father said, "are as important as anything else."

Mendoza approached and slapped his hand on Luis' back. The old man was shorter than Luis by an inch. His rotund belly stuck out over his belt, stretching the short-sleeve button-up shirt out so that the fabric at the bottom hung over his feet. His thick black mustache matched half of the thinning hair on his head. The front of his scalp glistened in the dying daylight.

"I remember," Mendoza said, "it was an evening much like this one when we finally met face to face."

Luis nodded, reflecting again on the events of that day.

"You killed four of my men and dropped them at my gate, still bleeding and mangled." Mendoza chuckled.

"Took your men two days to get the interior of that SUV clean."

Another laugh erupted. "Yes," Mendoza concurred. "It was quite the mess."

Luis took a deep breath. "I thought you would have been angrier."

The cartel boss shrugged. "They were good men. The fact that you killed all four of them by yourself told me we needed to make some changes."

"I thought the same," Luis said, forcing a laugh of his own.

When the laughter died, Mendoza took on a serious expression. "I was going to kill you that day," he confessed.

Luis replied with a snort. "You were going to try."

"Perhaps." He paused and looked out at the sunset, taking in its beauty. Even a man so full of evil could enjoy one of the simple, but spectacular pleasures in life. He breathed it in, appreciating every second. Then he turned to his security advisor and leaned on one shoulder. "Did you find out who it was?"

Luis acknowledged with a nod. "Eduardo Diaz."

Shock splashed across Mendoza's face. It was quickly melted by steeled nerves and sheer will. "He was one of my most trusted scouts. I'm not a fool, Luis. You know that."

"I do."

"While I'm not stupid enough to think no one will stab me in the back, Eduardo would have been one of my last guesses."

"Heavy lies the crown," Luis quipped.

"Indeed, my friend."

It always bothered Luis when the man referred to him as a friend.

Either he didn't truly understand the meaning of the word, or it was merely a skewed view that had warped over time as he'd callously watched lives disintegrate around him.

Luis shifted his thoughts. "That's why you pay me, no? Perhaps not as much as you should." He offered the older man a wink. Mendoza rewarded him with a low chortle.

"Perhaps not." He turned and looked out over the estate once more. "Where is Eduardo now?"

Luis checked the expensive watch on his wrist. "By now, I'd say six feet under, somewhere on the estate."

"Good." Mendoza exhaled slowly. "You handled the situation with the Guerreros well. You moved quickly on that one, beat them to the press, the authorities, it's made things difficult for them."

"Yes."

"Maybe I should pay you as both security adviser and as public relations." He turned his head and offered a grin. The expression melted away quickly. "It's going to come back against us, you know?"

"I do."

Mendoza went on. "Their business is already suffering setbacks in production and shipping." He chuckled tentatively. "I fear their loss of profits and the increased scrutiny from the locals is going to push them to the brink."

"You're concerned they're going to launch an all-out attack on us." It wasn't a question.

"Yes," Mendoza breathed.

"Your men are far better trained than they were seven months ago, Giovani. They could fight with some of the best in the world now. The Guerreros don't stand a chance if they throw everything they have at us. We will cut them down. This place," he motioned around at the walls and the hills, "is a fortress. The cops won't help them anymore. I say let them come. Once we've wiped them off the face of the earth, we will run the entire region uncontested."

The cartel boss listened quietly, envisioning the battle to come. "There will be bloodshed. Some of it will be from our men."

"You almost sound like you care about them."

Mendoza pouted his lips and shook his head. "I care as I would care for a pet. I love them, sure, but they are expendable."

Luis absorbed the harsh comment. He certainly didn't feel that way about pets. To him, they weren't expendable, which was why he didn't have any. Getting close to someone or something only led to more pain when they were lost.

He shoved aside the moment of softness brought on by his past when he was a better man than now. Being soft in a place like this, in a position such as this, would get a person killed.

"We will lose some men," Luis said flatly. "But we have many. And they're all better than what the Guerreros have. If they come, they'll do it under cover of darkness. I've made all the necessary preparations. We have multiple sensors and cameras across the entire perimeter. There isn't a place they can approach we won't see them."

Mendoza nodded. "Good." He lowered his head in thought. "I knew, the day I met you, that you had guts. Not only that, you had a plan. You offered right there at my gate to be my security advisor and to oversee the training of my men."

"And you held a gun to my head as I made the offer."

"True," Mendoza said with a laugh. "I thought you'd piss your pants." He laughed again.

Luis nodded, not joining the laughter this time. "And that's why you knew I was the right guy for the job. Because I didn't."

"Yes," Mendoza agreed. He looked out toward the horizon again as the final piece of the sun dipped below the mountains. "It certainly is a beautiful sunset," he said.

SEVEN

GUADALAJARA

Dak waited until he saw the last customer stumble out of the cantina and into the dim streetlights before he made his move.

He'd been watching the building for the last hour from a bench on the other side of the street. It would have been more comfortable to just find a seat at the bar or his "usual" table, have a drink or two and wait until Carina closed the place, but he wanted to get an idea of what went on outside the bar once the sun went down.

After speaking to her before, he returned to the cheap hotel room he'd rented for cash three blocks away. He took a quick shower and changed clothes, then got ready to go back and reconnect with the intriguing woman.

He'd taken a headcount of the people coming and going, though through the darkened windows it was difficult to tell who else might have been in there from previous hours.

Dak was about to get up when he saw Carina appear at the door. She flipped a sign around in the window to say cerrado and then stared across the street at him.

He stood up and strolled over as she held the door open, looking at him with an accusatory glare.

"You want to be a little more conspicuous, gringo?" she asked. "Doesn't at all look like you're staking out the place."

Dak absorbed the jab. "Yeah, well, I thought about coming in for a drink, but the bartender doesn't pour heavy enough for me."

He stopped at the threshold and waited for a second.

She glowered at him. Then her concrete facade broke and she allowed a mischievous smile to crack through her lips. "I like your style," she said with a nod. "Come in. I have something for you."

He stepped through and she locked the door behind, then led him over to the counter where she stopped and ordered two more tequilas from the bartender who was hanging clean mugs over the back bar.

The young man grinned, grabbed a bottle from under the counter, and set it on the surface, then plucked three tumblers from a shelf and arranged them in a row. To call it a bottle would be generous. The pale, golden liquid sloshed around in what looked like an old Hawaiian Punch jug.

"I thought you said two," Dak said, hoping his Spanish hadn't slipped that far in the last few years.

"You think I'm not going to have one too?" the bartender asked with a snicker.

"Homemade, huh?"

The bartender nodded.

"Juan makes excellent tequila," Carina said as the barkeep poured three fingers into each glass.

Dak's eyes widened at the generous pour. "Is this what I had earlier?" he asked.

A smirk and a shake of the head from the bartender gave him his answer.

"This is more like what you would call moonshine back in Tennessee," Carina said. "It's not exactly legal, but no one's going to stop us from making it. The authorities have too many other problems to deal with right now."

"Like the cartels?"

"Among other things," she said. She lifted her glass and raised it toward the two men. They joined her and clinked their drinks together. "Salud."

"Salud," Dak and the bartender joined.

Carina downed the entire glass in one shot. Dak arched an eyebrow at the impressive display, then took a little sip. The barkeep finished his in one go as well and looked at their guest with curiosity in his eyes.

"Too hot for you?" the young man asked.

"Nope," Dak said. "It's perfect. Incredibly smooth. But where I come from, we sip good whiskey. Seems like the right thing to do with your tequila. It should be appreciated."

Carina eyed him suspiciously, then nodded. "I don't usually have time for such things, but I like your style."

She tapped her glass on the counter, signaling for another round. The barkeep splashed another pour into the vessel, and this time when she picked it up, she only took a slow sip.

"Come," she said with a flick of her head. "We have business to attend to."

"Thanks for the drink," Dak said to the bartender. "Quite the talent you have there." He raised the glass to the young man who took the compliment with a humble grin and a bow.

Carina led the way back to the manager's office door. When she opened it, he was greeted by a tiny room barely 150 square feet, if that. An antiquated metal desk sat to the right with a computer monitor atop it with cords running to a tower on the floor to the right. A lamp with a canvas lampshade on the left side of the desk illuminated the room with a dim, yellowish glow. A black plastic wastebasket in the corner and a vinyl-upholstered chair were the only other furnishings in the minimalist space.

She closed the door behind him and locked two deadbolts and the latch. He took another sip of tequila as he watched, surprised at the number of locks she utilized on an office door.

For a place this small, he knew there had to be more than met the eye.

"I'm guessing this isn't your real office," he suggested.

She looked up at him, momentarily losing herself in his emerald eyes. Her mind didn't wander for long.

"You'd guess right." She motioned to a closet door in the back of the room, then glided over to it with an elegant speed.

She pulled open the wooden door to expose exactly what it looked like—a closet. Inside, a few windbreakers, shirts, and slacks hung from hangars. Cardboard boxes full of paperwork, receipts, and invoices littered the floor. She bent over and dragged one of the boxes out. Dak quickly averted his eyes at the spectacle until she'd moved the container out of the way.

Carina spun and looked at him. "What's the matter with you?"

He pulled his focus away from the uninteresting ceiling. "Sorry, I just didn't want to... um...."

Her eyebrows lifted, her face relaxing with amusement. "Wow. A gentleman and a killer. Interesting." She paused as if contemplating the enigma standing before her. Then the moment was over and she motioned for him to follow her. She stepped back into the closet, drawing back the hung clothing to reveal a keypad on the wall. Dak noted how both corners displayed the thinnest of seams. They were barely visible in the darkly lit room.

She entered a code on the keypad, but before she finished, turned to him and said, "If you're going to avert your eyes, I'd rather you do it now than when I'm bent over a stack of boxes."

He blushed. "Yes, ma'am," he said, turning his head to the side.

The panel beeped, and a green light glowed. As he suspected, the wall slid backward exposing an entryway to the left interior.

"Very cool," Dak offered.

"I like it. Gives me real privacy. And the cartel goons are too stupid to look beyond the boxes and clothes. Also helps that I'm a woman."

He followed her through the narrow opening into a room that was three times the size of the previous.

"Why's that?"

She looked at him like ants covered his face. "You don't know much about the cartels, do you?"

"Only a little. I don't believe what I read in the papers or on the news."

"At least you have that going for you." She walked across the room to a stand-up desk midway down the right-hand wall. A flatscreen monitor sat on it. The computer on the floor next to the desk glowed with several sapphire LEDs. A steel table in the center of the room reminded Dak of a butcher shop he'd seen once, except there was nothing on it. Except for a white leather desk chair near the elevated desk, and a sparse few other necessities, the room was empty. She put her hand on the optical mouse and clicked it.

The screen bloomed to life with dozens of images. Some featured a massive estate with a mansion atop a rise in the center. The gray stucco and terra-cotta roof stood like a fortress against the natural backdrop of the hills, forests, and mountains in the distance.

"When was the last time you heard of a woman running a cartel?" Carina asked, continuing her line of thought.

Dak lifted his shoulders and bobbed his head. "I guess I haven't."

"And why do you think that is?"

He shifted. "I don't know, but I feel like the answer isn't a complimentary one."

"You'd be right. None of them suspect me of much because I'm a woman, incapable of running an operation like this."

Dak scanned the room, bewildered. "An empty room with a computer in it?"

She sighed in derision and clicked the mouse again. Without looking, her fingers tapped across the numbers on the keyboard and then dramatically hit the enter key.

Within a second, the sounds of locks clicking filled the room. The floors in front of each wall began moving, all rising from the ground. When the hydraulic motors stopped, Dak found himself in a completely different space.

"Now this is a gun cave."

She looked at him, befuddled. "Never heard that before."

"Just made it up." He looked at her with squinting mischief in his eyes. "Man cave sounded wrong, on account of you being a woman."

She blushed. "Thank you."

The hidden walls held racks of weapons from small, compact revolvers up to a few .50-cal sniper rifles complete with tripod and long-range scopes. Some racks on the back wall held rucksacks and metal boxes marked with a symbol indicating explosives.

"Try not to get too excited, soldier," she said. She reached out and touched his face, pulling it back toward her.

For a second he thought, no feared, she might try to kiss him. He was both relieved and disappointed when she turned his head to the computer screen. There, in several boxes, was a face Dak had imagined finding for the last seven months.

"Luis," Dak muttered.

"Yes," she said. "And before you play with those," she indicated the weapons stash with a finger, "you need to learn all you can about his organization."

"Good call," he said. "By the way, I'm Dak. I know you know that, but I thought a formal—"

"Carina. A pleasure," she said, forcing her eyes to stay locked on the screen and not the powerful, rugged man next to her. "But we both know who each other is. Actually, I'm surprised you didn't ask how I know so much about you already."

"You're a professional," he said. "I would expect nothing less."

Another blush reddened her faintly tanned cheeks. "Well, I appreciate that."

He leaned forward, placing one hand on her desk as he peered at the images. She could feel his warmth near her and caught her breath for a second.

"So," he said, quickly steering back to business. "Tell me everything I need to know about this cartel."

EIGHT

GUADALAJARA

Carina clicked on a minimized window and the screen's main image changed to a white background with grid lines.

"A spreadsheet?" Dak wondered.

"A list," she corrected. "It lists nearly every point in Mendoza's supply chain. Each one of these businesses is used as a front to move drugs, money, and weapons. His system is elaborate, but the concept is simple enough. He uses legitimate businesses: supermarkets, shoe stores, coffee shops—any business you can imagine. And he doesn't own any of them, not on paper, anyway."

"He coerced the owners into helping him."

"Coerced is putting it mildly. Mendoza only knows one way of negotiating."

Dak knew exactly what she meant. While his experience in the drug trade was limited, he'd seen enough organized crime to know how it worked. If you owned a business, either you cooperated and got to keep your livelihood, or you didn't and you would end up in a ditch.

Back in the United States, the exploits of the Italian, Irish, and Russian mafias were well known. If you didn't work with them, you'd be out of business or at the bottom of the ocean. The cartels weren't much different, although their schemes differed.

In the States, businesses in the larger cities paid for protection from other organizations. Racketeering was truly one of the country's oldest professions. They used their businesses for other purposes, certainly money laundering, but not to the level the cartels operated. And Mendoza's system was impressive, to say the least.

"Most of his allies are taken care of," Carina went on. "He pays well because he understands their value in the grand scheme. It also helps him move more money around to keep both the United States and Mexican governments off the money trail. And yes, he runs similar operations in the US."

"Doesn't surprise me." Dak's eyes rolled down the list. There were dozens of businesses in Uruapan alone, but there were others with different towns or cities listed next to them. "What are these?" He pointed his finger at the monitor, indicating the anomalies.

"Expansion," she answered simply. "Mendoza is pushing all the way to the Pacific. He's also making a move toward Central Mexico and the Gulf. If I had to guess, he wants to set up a regional empire where he can go virtually unchallenged by anyone."

"With that kind of power, he'll be untouchable," Dak echoed her sentiment. "Neither government could get to him."

"Correct."

He leaned closer to the screen, studying it intently. His focus, however, was sucked away by the distracting scent of rose and lilac from Carina's perfume. She'd been working all day and still smelled like a meadow of blooming wildflowers.

He cracked the whip in his mind and got back to business, pulling his wandering eyes from their attempt to admire her.

"Can you show me a map of this area?" he asked, clearing his throat.

"Sure." She clicked a button, tapped several keys, and then hit enter.

A map of the region blinked on the monitor.

"Zoom out," he directed.

She pulled the wheel on the mouse and the image of the area narrowed as the camera view withdrew.

"That's good," he said. The entire nation of Mexico was in full view. A red pin indicated Uruapan on the map.

"He's not just trying to establish a long-term foothold in the region," Dak said, realization hitting him like the glove of a heavy-weight boxer.

Carina twisted her head and looked up at him. Dak felt her gaze but didn't meet it with his own.

"Look at what's on either side of this," he said.

It was her turn to corral her impulses. She looked at the monitor once more. "Water," she answered. "Like I said, he wants to stretch from the Pacific to the Gulf."

"Yeah," Dak said, "but men like Mendoza have egos. They don't just look to set up a safe place where they can operate unimpeded. Do you think he's going to stop expanding once he reaches both seas?"

She studied the map for several breaths before she realized what Dak was saying. "You think he wants to go farther?"

Dak nodded. "I think Mendoza is looking to build a vast empire. He can't take on all the cartels in Mexico."

"No single organization is capable of that," Carina offered. "Even though they're at war with each other, there is a sort of unwritten understanding that no one group should get all the pie. They squabble over territory, but in the end, things usually come out the same. Some cartels have more than others, but all always have some-thing. Unless, of course, they break the rules. When that happens, the organization is wiped off the face of the earth."

"Interesting sub-culture," he commented.

"So, what's your point?" Carina asked.

He liked the blunt way she went about her business. She was no nonsense. He appreciated that. In his life, he'd seen plenty of the other. It was refreshing to meet someone who operated more like him.

"My point," he said, "is when Mendoza secures territory on both shores he'll be able to export his goods to a wider customer base. All of South America will be open for business. Not to mention Canada and the Caribbean. From there, my guess is he'll establish bases on some of the islands. When that happens, the Eastern Hemisphere will be in reach."

Carina looked up at him again, this time with disbelief. "No cartel has ever tried to get that big," she said. "It's too broad for any of them. The logistics alone would consume them and spit them out."

"You know that. I know that. It's the classic cautionary tale from every major empire that's ever existed, from Babylon to Persia to Rome, all the way down to Great Britain. Sooner or later, your resources are stretched too thin. Even so, that lesson has been ignored more often than not, most recently by Adolf Hitler."

He let the words loom over her.

Carina considered what Dak was saying. Deep down, she knew he was right. She could see it now, though she wondered why she hadn't before. She'd spent so much time working on undermining the cartels; piecing together an understanding of how their systems and processes operated—maybe that was the problem. She'd been close to it for so long, she'd become blind to other possibilities, other schemes the cartels might use to expand their businesses to feed their hunger for more power, more money.

"You've been tracking Mendoza's expansion," Dak said, "how soon until he has businesses and property along the Pacific shore?"

"Could be weeks," Carina said. "He's closer to the Pacific than the Gulf, though I'd say within a month's time we could see him running some operations there as well."

Dak stood up straight and bobbed his head. "Okay, then. I guess I should get to it."

"Get to what?" She swirled around in her chair.

"Mendoza's rival is the Guerreros' cartel, right?"

"Yes."

"I think it's time I make them a little business proposition."

Lines cut into her forehead as she frowned. "What?"

"You know where they're based. You can point me to them."

She laughed at the absurdity of his request. "Sure, but it's not like I can set up an appointment for you. If you try to go talk to the Guerreros, they'll murder you with the same thought they would give to swatting a fly."

He cocked his head to one side and shrugged. "You got to go sometime, right? This is the only play I can see that makes sense, Carina. Can you point me to them or not?"

She stared at him with both wonder and fear in her eyes. "This is crazy. You know that, right?"

"Yep."

She tossed her head, resigned to the fact his mind was made up. "Okay, it's your funeral. What exactly is your business proposition for them, just out of curiosity?"

A wicked grin crossed Dak's face. "I'm going to sell them some real estate."

NINE

URUAPAN

Luis stood in the grandiose boardroom Mendoza had built in the basement of his mansion. It was the cartel leader's personal NORAD. Surrounded by four feet of poured, reinforced concrete, it could withstand almost any type of attack. While Mendoza's preparations would keep him and his most trusted men safe from rival cartels, the situation room wasn't only built as a safe harbor from other cartels.

He'd seen what the United States government could do when they really wanted to eliminate a target. They could do it covertly with a small team of operatives, and while that posed a threat, his greater fear was of an aerial assault. The United States military had, at their disposal, an arsenal of silent bombs that could hit with laser precision if given the order.

He recalled seeing such weaponry blasted over the media in the 1990s when President Bush sent his troops into Kuwait, then again after the events of 9/11. The American military capabilities were put on full display for everyone to see. Mendoza wasn't foolish enough to believe they would only launch such attacks at foreign militaries.

In the late 1990s, a mysterious explosion killed a cartel boss in

Colombia, along with his entire entourage and security detail. Their compound was reduced to a rubble-filled crater. Precariously, a similar fate met the cartel's main cocaine processing plant.

The American media didn't mention it, and the Mexican outlets barely caught wind of the story.

Every cartel boss from Juarez to Montevideo in Uruguay spent several months on edge, wondering if they would be the next target.

Further attacks never came, and many of the leaders fell into their usual routines, once more getting comfortable in their day-to-day operations.

When Mendoza took over Dorado Aguilas, his first order of business was to build this place, along with a half-mile-long subterranean escape tunnel that exited in the jungle. He kept a getaway vehicle there, always fueled and ready in a makeshift garage constructed out of an old barn.

A projection screen at the back end of the room displayed a map of the region, with Uruapan highlighted. Two other areas were highlighted in a different color, with a light green, semi-transparent hue.

"We are still on schedule, sir," Luis said. "We currently have operatives along both shorelines evaluating the best locations."

Mendoza grunted, but it wasn't entirely of approval.

Luis noted the irritation and continued. "We've selected two potential warehouses along the gulf and three on the Pacific side. All of them are owned by struggling shipping business, which gives us strong leverage."

"Leverage?" Mendoza asked.

As prepared as he was, and as savvy as the man's business sense proved time and time again, he sometimes baffled Luis with his nativity.

"Yes, sir. Now that we have a good choice of locations and the shipping lanes are nearly open, we can begin with the next phase of operations."

Mendoza's lower lip lifted slightly, as if impressed, but Luis knew that wasn't what the man felt. He was impatient, always wanting results yesterday. Luis understood. The life of a cartel boss didn't exactly have a long expectancy unless, of course, they could make enough money to eventually drop off the radar. Luis could count on one hand how many had been able to pull off that trick, and he'd still have a finger or two left.

The leader took a deep, dramatic breath through his nostrils and rubbed his nose. The gesture put Luis on edge. Even as good as he was, there was no way he could take out the other four men in the room, along with Mendoza, if the man ordered his execution.

Luis had a plan in mind for such an event, as that sort of thing was common in the sinister world of drug lords and minions. He'd draw his weapon and shoot Mendoza, knowing that while the other men in the room cut him down, at least he took out the leader.

It was a zero-sum game that Luis knew Mendoza didn't want to play, and one the boss knew his security general wasn't afraid of using.

"Our enemies plot against us," Mendoza said with another flair of the dramatic. "With every passing second, they grow, their operations expand. We should be outrunning them, overrunning them, and yet you speak of preparations and phases as if we're some kind of corporation looking at businesses to buy."

Luis suppressed his anger and offered a smirk. "Absolutely."

Mendoza's eyebrows dropped, in both confusion and disbelief. "We're wasting time," his voice thundered. He slapped his hand on the long, glossy wooden table to emphasize the point.

One of the guards to the man's right startled.

Luis never flinched.

"We are being strategic, sir. It's important that we select the best locations for your venture. We can't exactly walk in, call the lawyers of a shipping company, and make them an offer."

Mendoza stewed, so Luis kept going. "You're a smart businessman, Gio. You are on the cusp of doing something than no cartel leader has ever done before. Something that big takes time."

"We're out of time," Mendoza spat. "You," he pointed a thick finger at Luis, "are out of time. You are my general. This expansion idea will crush the Guerreros and make us the biggest player in all of Mexico. Pick a company on both sides, and send them a message."

He leaned back in his chair and crossed his arms, the anger that overshadowed him seeming to slide off like a sheet of melting ice.

"You...want me to pick the locations?" Luis allowed the man to see and hear his confusion.

"Of course," Mendoza said, unfolding his arms to flash his hands in front of him. "You're my right hand, Luis. Or did you forget?"

Luis shook his head. "No, sir. I didn't."

"Good, then. Make the decision and move forward with the plan. I expect to have two properties on the coast in the next seventy-two hours."

Seventy-two hours? The man wanted the impossible, or, at the very least, the improbable.

Luis knew which two properties were probably the best suited for their needs, but they were both owned by long-time family businesses. It would take something drastic to get them to sell. He couldn't simply take the properties by force, though he knew Mendoza would be fine with that. Such action would bring suspicion, investigation, and more trouble than any of them needed. He was going to have to hurry things along, and Luis hated to rush. Careful planning was his MO.

"Seventy-two hours," he said, confirming Mendoza's order.

The boss gave a single nod, stood, and walked out of the room with his four guards in tow. Luis stood alone in the room for nearly a minute before Marco entered from just outside.

"What are we going to do?" Marco asked.

Luis didn't want to say it, but he knew it was the only way. This gig grew more nauseating by the minute and it sickened him to think of what he'd become, what he'd done, what he was going to do to keep his family safe. But how long would that truly last? There was no way of knowing.

He stared at the table, ignoring the question until Marco pressed him by saying, "Luis?"

Luis raised his eyes and met the man's questioning gaze. "We're going to have to blow up some boats."

TEN

URUAPAN

Dak hunched over the bar at the Caballo Oscuro Cantina, his fingers loosely wrapped around a glass of tequila. When in Rome, he thought. His normal drink of choice, a neat whiskey from Kentucky or Tennessee, was his preference, but he figured he should probably do everything he could to fit in.

Being a gringo in most Mexican towns wasn't so bad. Few people paid any notice, especially since he dressed like an ex-pat who'd been there for years on a meager salary. Those who moved to Mexico and dressed extravagantly drove expensive cars, they were the people who made easy targets and drew too much attention, the wrong kind of attention.

Ironically, attention was exactly what Dak wanted at this bar. And he was after the worst kind.

The bartender stood at the edge of the counter in the corner, leaning on one elbow as he watched a soccer game on a television behind the bar. Leon and Club America were fighting it out in a 2-2 thriller with twenty minutes to play.

Most of the people in the bar were likewise glued to the match, including the one female at a booth with two other men.

Four guys at the bar sat together, watching with keen interest. With every foul, every near-miss, their emotions rose like a tidal wave and crashed onto the rocky shore of disappointment.

Dak knew immediately they were part of the organization he sought, along with the bartender. The other three at the booth, he wasn't sure.

One of the players in a white, green, and yellow Leon uniform fired a shot into the top right corner of the goal, sending the occupants of the bar into a frenzy. The four men down the counter from Dak leaped out of their seats, slapped each other on the back, and chanted songs. They high-fived the bartender who joined in the jubilation with his own brand of celebration, pumping both fists over his shoulders.

The man was older than the rest of the people in the cantina by at least twenty years. A thin ring of black hair clung to his scalp, just above the ears, and his head gleamed from the overhead lights. A dense mustache stretched out over his lips and draped down past the corners of his mouth until they nearly reached his jaw. His potbelly betrayed a sedentary life, probably much like the one Dak currently witnessed.

The raucous celebration died down as the ball was returned to midfield and play resumed.

The tension, however, was even higher than before, reaching to Himalayan heights at the thought of their team pulling off an upset that, no doubt, also involved some pretty heavy wagers.

"Could I get another tequila?" Dak asked, keeping his eyes on the counter.

The bartender didn't budge. His eyes remained fixed on the flatscreen.

Dak nodded at the poor service and dumped the last bit of Reposado tequila down his throat. He slammed the glass down on the counter loud enough that it startled the bartender and the four men at the bar. He didn't bother to look back at the group sitting around the booth.

"I said, can I get another tequila," Dak repeated, this time with feigned irritation.

The bartender fired him an irritated glare, then reluctantly walked over to the shelves behind the cash register, grabbed the bottle he'd poured from before, and spilled another shot into Dak's glass.

The barkeep locked eyes with the American, glowering at him until the glass was full. "Drink that and don't bother me again until the game is over."

He set the bottle next to the glass and turned back toward the television. He was about to amble back to his standing spot in the corner when Dak stopped him.

"That's not good business," he said. "Pretty sure your boss wouldn't appreciate you giving away free drinks."

The bartender froze in mid-stride and turned slowly. "What did you say?"

The four men at the counter also perked up, each spinning around to see who dared mention the bartender's boss.

It was one of those moments that Dak had seen in the movies, where the music stops and everyone freezes, time slows down, and then all eyes shift to the offending party.

He raised the glass and took a sip. The warm liquid washed over this tongue and eased down his throat with a slow burn.

"Although, with tequila like this, I can see why you'd give it away. Who made this anyway?"

Dak saw the four men to his right ease out of their seats and plant their feet on the ground. He already knew they were armed, each carrying a pistol on their right hip, tucked into the back of their jeans. Their untucked button-up shirts did almost nothing to hide the weapons from plain sight. But when you worked for the Guerreros, you weren't worried about petty laws.

It was easy to assume the bartender was armed too, probably with a shotgun hanging from a couple of hooks under the counter. If Dak had to guess, it would be positioned directly under the cash register.

Carina had informed Dak that this place was one of the fronts the

Guerreros ran. A bar was an excellent choice when it came to moving both money and product. Enough cash changed hands to avoid raising any red flags, and bars all over the world were frequently used as transaction stations for moving small and sometimes medium amounts of drugs from cocaine to heroin.

The Guerreros cartel boss, Carlito Esparanza, was known to frequent the place, and they carried a special tequila that few other bars in the state could get. It just so happened, Dak was drinking that very tequila. He knew, of course, about Esparanza's affection for the drink, which was why he'd added on that last little dash of venom to his comments.

The first of the four men at the bar drew his weapon and held it at his side. The other three soon followed suit.

The bartender stuck to only flinging daggers from his eyes as he spoke. "You should leave, gringo. It's not polite to insult a barkeeper's tequila in Mexico."

Dak nodded, gave a sniff at the liquor, then took another sip. He swallowed, somewhat enjoying the sip, but not giving the bartender the satisfaction. He scowled at the drink and set it back down.

"You know what, I'm sorry I asked for another one." His words came out in a slur. "It's one of those things like when you taste something you know is probably good, but it isn't, and you think maybe it's because you just brushed your teeth. You know what I mean?"

"Callate!" the bartender blurted.

"He's right, gringo," the nearest man to Dak said. He hovered dangerously close. Dak kept up the drunken charade. "But it's too late for that. You should have shut up."

"He should have gone to another bar," another one said in Spanish.

"Yeah," the first agreed.

"I didn't like the other bars," Dak muttered.

"Doesn't sound like you like this one either, ese."

The four men surrounded Dak. The bartender crossed his arms as if he'd seen this play out a hundred times.

Dak looked at the first guy who took up a spot to his left. The gun hung loosely at the man's side. He was probably in his early twenties, maybe a year or two older. The others looked to be about the same.

"Is that a gun?" Dak asked. "It's so shiny." He did his best to sound completely hammered.

"Yeah. It is. And I think we're going to take you out back and use it on you."

The referee blew the whistle on the screen and issued a yellow card to one of the players for Club America.

"But then you'd miss the game," Dak groused.

He reached for the tequila glass again.

"We'll catch the highlights."

The man to his left reached out to grab Dak by the arm. That was a mistake.

Dak abruptly snatched the man's wrist, jerked him forward, and drove his elbow into the guy's throat. Still holding the tequila tumbler, he whirled around, ready for the attacker behind him to make his move.

The man didn't disappoint. He raised his weapon, but Dak spun and shattered the glass against the guy's skull.

A gash opened over the man's right eye and he staggered backward. Dak jerked the gun out of his hand, released the magazines, and ejected the round in the chamber within a second, then tossed the pistol to the other end of the room. The next two were slower, though still armed. Dak rushed them both as they pulled their pistols and readied to fire. He lunged at them, dropped to the ground, and slid between them, driving his fists into their groins like twin hammers.

The two men doubled over, groaning.

Dak popped up off the floor, grabbed each by the collar, and jumped down to the floor again, driving the back of the men's skulls into the hardened tile. They instantly lost consciousness and went limp, their weapons falling just as lifelessly at their sides.

Dak stood up straight as the first attacker continued to struggle to breathe. The other dabbed at the bleeding wound on the side of his head.

The bartender looked conflicted, his eyes darting from the cash register to Dak and back again.

Meanwhile, the three patrons at the booth merely sat in abject silence, as if watching a movie.

"You thinking about going for the shotgun under the register?" Dak asked.

The man licked his lips.

"Don't," Dak advised. "I'm not here for you. I'm not here for them, either. In fact, your tequila isn't all that bad. But I had to make sure I was in the right place."

The bartender seethed, breath coming out of his nostrils like an angry horse. "Right place?"

Dak nodded. "I'm looking for Carlito Esperanza. I have something he wants."

"And what would a vagabond American like you have to offer Carlito Esperanza?"

The voice came from behind him, at the booth.

Dak turned slowly and faced two more guns, one held by the woman, and the other by the guy across from her.

The man who'd issued the question sat with one arm around her shoulders, but he brandished no weapon.

"A way to get ahead of Dorado Aguilas."

ELEVEN

URUAPAN

The man in the booth stared at Dak. Questions seeped out of his eyes.

He glanced around at his guards. Three of them were starting to recover. The one who'd been unconscious sat on his rear, eyes glazed over in a fog. The guy Dak punched in the neck had managed to loosen his airway. He breathed in desperate, relieved gasps, finally able to fill his lungs with precious air.

"You took out four of my men," the man said, "in less than thirty seconds."

Dak breathed easily as if he'd just walked to the kitchen for a cup of coffee. "To be fair," Dak said, looking around at the guards, "they're not very good."

The man blinked slowly. "Or perhaps you are better than most."

"Quisas," Dak said, agreeing in Spanish.

The man smirked and nodded slowly. "And you speak Spanish." He turned and took a sip of tequila from a glass on the table. He let out an appreciative "mmm" and set the glass back down.

"So, what is this? You looking for a job? I have to say, you do quite the interview."

"I'm not looking for a job. I'm looking for a man named Carlito Esperanza."

"Yes, I heard," the man said. "You also said you had a way to get ahead of the Aguilas. I imagine, with a man like you in my organization, we would definitely have an edge."

"I'm not looking for a job," Dak repeated, this time more firmly.

"So you say." His eyes wandered to the weapons the woman and the other guy at the booth aimed at the American. "You know, I could make this simple and tell them to kill you if you don't want to work for me."

"Then you wouldn't get what you want."

"Which is?"

"May I sit?" Dak asked, motioning to the henchman to his right who still held the gun firmly in one hand.

"I'd prefer you stand."

"I'd prefer to be on a beach somewhere, sipping your tequila—preferably on the rocks with margarita mix. Yet, here we are."

The man leaned back, letting his left arm stretch out over the back of the booth, the other still behind the woman's shoulders to his right.

"So, why are you here?" the man asked. His left hand flipped up. "I mean, other than your proposal. I know you say you have a way for me to level the playing field against the Aguilas. But why are you really here? There must be some reason you'd be foolish enough to walk into a known hangout of Esperanza and his men."

"Esperanza and I have a common enemy. I don't think I need to remind you of the old saying about the enemy of my enemy."

The man analyzed Dak for several seconds before responding. "So, friends, then? I wonder, though, who this enemy is? Giovani Mendoza has many, but I'm curious how he would have drawn the ire of such a dangerous man like you."

"Mendoza isn't my target. I'm after his new general, Luis Martinez."

The guy in the booth blinked slowly, then he motioned to the other two. They immediately lowered their weapons. The guy on the right slid out of the booth and patted Dak down. When the guard was certain the American was unarmed, he gave a nod to the man calling the shots.

"Please," the man said, motioning again with his left hand, this time at the seat across from him and the woman.

Dak stepped near and then eased into the seat. He folded his hands on the table as a show of good faith.

"So," the man said, "what is it you have against Mendoza's new pet?"

"We used to work together," Dak confessed. "He betrayed me. Stabbed me in the back, so to speak."

"Ah," the man said, wagging a finger. "Now it makes sense. You're out for revenge."

"I'm out for justice."

"Funny how those two are often intertwined, isn't it?" He looked to the bartender and raised two fingers. "Two more glasses, please, Pedro."

The barkeeper hesitated, still looking as if he was trying to decide whether to grab the shotgun and go to town on the intruder, or do as he was told.

"Yes, sir," he said finally. "Right away."

The bartender hastily poured two more rounds of tequila, scurried around the end of the bar, and delivered to the table as requested.

"Thank you, Pedro. Go back to watching the game. Looks like there are still ten minutes left."

"Yes, sir." The bartender humbly bowed and made his way back around the counter, behind the bar, and reluctantly returned his attention to the game.

"When were you going to tell me your name is Carlito Esperanza?" Dak wondered.

The man let out a snort, then grinned mischievously. "When you asked. Yours?"

"Dak. Let's leave it at that."

"Okay, Dak. Like the quarterback for the Dallas Cowboys. Should be easy to remember."

"I get that a lot."

"I'm sure." Esperanza raised his glass, and Dak took his, lifting it toward Esperanza. "Salud."

"Salud," Esperanza echoed.

The two men took a sip and set the glasses back on the table.

"I like a man who can appreciate good tequila," Esperanza said. "Now, I would love to hear this plan of yours."

Dak leaned forward, planting his elbows on the table. He steepled his fingers and tilted his head. "Do you always trust a stranger this quickly?"

Esperanza shrugged. "You took out some of my best guards in no time."

"They'd been drinking."

"And you keep trying to blow off your efficiency. Most men, if any, who were able to do that, would probably be boasting about it right now, demanding I make them my second-in-command. Which means you aren't here with some egotistical demand. You have a plan. And you have cojones. You've earned my ear."

Dak appreciated the man's assessment. Esperanza was no fool. For a moment, Dak wondered how the man hadn't been able to take his organization ahead of the Aguilas.

"Mendoza isn't satisfied with this region. Or with Mexico. He wants to expand beyond the borders."

Esperanza let his head tilt back and he blinked a few times while he looked at the ceiling. Then he brought his head down and leveled his gaze with Dak's. "I'm not sure how much you know about what we do, but we're all beyond the borders of Mexico, amigo."

"Oh, I'm well aware. I wasn't talking about the United States." He paused until Esperanza's eyes gave away the fact that he was interested. "Mendoza wants the rest of the world."

Esperanza's cheeks tightened, eyelids narrowing to dark slits.

"He wants to have ports on either side of the country. Having those will make him the unrivaled leader in the drug trade for years to come."

"Ports?" He shifted uncomfortably and reeled in both arms, resting his hands on the table around the tequila glass.

"My guess is Mendoza is figuring out which ones he wants. Once he decides, he'll use the usual tactics—sabotage a boat, burn down a warehouse, whatever it takes to lower the value of the business he wishes to buy. Once that happens, he'll have easy access to the Gulf, and to the Pacific. Shipping lanes to the east and west, the Caribbean, South America, Africa, you name it."

Esperanza let out a scoffing exhale. "Every marketable nation has a coast guard, radar, it would be impossible to move that many ships out of Mexico alone, much less land them safely in other ports around the globe. Moving product by boat isn't a new idea, amigo. We've been doing it for years. Everyone has." He flashed his hands. "We don't do it much anymore. Too many profits lost to the patrol boats on both sides of the shipping lanes."

"I know," Dak said, leaning back. He stopped when he felt his shoulder blades touch the seat, then stretched out his arms across the upper edge. "That's why I think he's going to choose two companies that both run medical supplies to several countries."

Esperanza cocked his head to the side. "Medical supplies?"

Dak confirmed the question with a nod. "Medical supply ships will get first priority to ports, especially in times of crisis. They'll be ushered through the usual channels with fewer checkpoints, fewer questions." Dak knew that was only partially true, but he also knew that the argument made so much sense that Esperanza would almost certainly bite.

"Medical supply ships?"

"Yep," Dak said.

Esperanza pondered the idea for a moment. Dak knew the man was intrigued, and not just by the idea of Mendoza utilizing it. His eyes betrayed his own designs on such a grand scheme.

"Tell me, Dak," Esperanza said quietly. "If what you say is true, how does this information help me get ahead of Mendoza?"

Dak smiled. "You make an offer to both companies that Mendoza can't beat."

The cartel boss scoffed audibly, blowing air through his lips. "That's not possible. Not yet."

"Perhaps you underestimate Mendoza's penchant for a deal. Like I said, he's going to try to drive down the price."

"You don't know that."

"It's what I would do," Dak admitted. "It's what you would do."

Another chuckle. "So, why don't I just step in before his men can do it?"

"You don't have that kind of time. Besides, you don't have to buy the properties. Not yet. Just get the owners to agree in principle. Once you have a verbal agreement in place, it will block Mendoza. Then nothing he does will matter. If he comes after your ships, your warehouses, it still keeps him from building out his empire. And it gives you cause to go into his back yard and raise hell."

"You're leaving out something." Esperanza didn't wait for Dak to ask, and he had a feeling he already knew the answer. "What's your role in all of this?"

"As I stated, I'm going after Luis Martinez. With Mendoza focused on the coasts, I'll make my move and eliminate the man I'm sure has become a bane of your existence."

"Mm," Esperanza agreed. "Yes, he's made things much more diffi-cult. His men are better trained than they were before. I fear we would be annihilated if we risked an all-out assault on their compound." His eyes played around the room to his fallen guards, still nursing their wounds.

"I'm going in alone," Dak said. "It'll be easier for one man to get in than an army."

"That's suicide," Esperanza said.

"That's my problem." He slid out of the booth and flipped a few pesos on the table to cover the drinks.

"You don't have to pay for that," the cartel boss stated.

"I like to leave a good tip."

He turned and made for the door.

"Dak," Esperanza stopped him when he neared the exit. Dak turned around and locked eyes with the man. "When should I make this... offer?"

"Immediately. I'm sure you have an accountant or real estate person who can run the numbers and put in a bid. Make it over the top. And do it soon. Mendoza might already be sending his goons there."

He pushed through the exit and stepped out onto the street, letting the door creak to a close behind him.

Inside, Esperanza stewed with thoughts of cutting off Mendoza's grand scheme. He looked over at the woman next to him. "Make it happen," he said. "And find out who this Dak person is."

"You want me to kill him?"

Esperanza considered the question. "No." He glanced around at his fallen guards one more time. "I have a strange feeling that man might actually be able to pull off his plan."

TWELVE

URUAPAN

Mendoza stormed through his castle like a tyrant king. His navy blue button-up shirt fluttered in the breeze. The brown, Italian leather shoes on his feet clicked hard with every step, causing the sound to echo throughout the corridors. Two guards hurried to keep up with him on either side, but staggered just behind.

Anyone within earshot knew the boss was angry, though most of the people in the compound were working security detail, patrolling the main building, or the perimeter of the grounds.

He tore around a corner into a wide foyer with arched windows and a matching door that lead out into the courtyard. Through the glass, he saw Luis approaching with a phone pressed to his ear. He wore a look of utter disbelief mingled with a hint of panic.

Mendoza flung open the door, unwilling to wait on one of his guards to do it for him.

When he stepped out into the warm evening air, he drew the gold-plated pistol from a holster on his right hip and pointed it at Luis. Quetzalcoatl, a feathered flying serpent similar to a dragon, adorned the shiny yellow metal, engraved into the side with its tongue ending near the muzzle. The beast represented a deity in ancient Aztec mythology, one of the key players in the creation of mankind.

Luis had been uncertain if the man thought himself to be some kind of messenger of the ancient deity or if he merely liked the way it looked. Either way, with the gun pointed at his head by a man with zero reservations about killing anyone, he knew he was going to have to talk fast.

"What happened to the plan?" Mendoza demanded.

"I'll call you back," Luis said and pressed the red button on his phone to end the call.

"Who was that?"

"One of our men on the Pacific coast."

"You mean one of my men." Mendoza offered the correction as he shook his weapon threateningly.

"Yes," Luis agreed. "One of your men." He was unshaken by the sight of the gun. Having stared down the barrel of men every bit as nasty as Mendoza, Luis felt almost accustomed to the gesture.

"What happened?"

Luis exhaled in irritation. "You told me to pick two locations. I did. They are the two that best fit all of our needs, and both are medical supply companies. I've done my best to keep you in the loop for all of this."

"Do you think me a fool, Luis?" Mendoza growled.

"No. If I did, I wouldn't be working for you. Do you think me a fool?"

The boss tightened the muscles in his face, clenching his jaw at the absurd question.

"Only a fool would hire one, Gio," Luis said calmly. "And you're no fool."

He saw the man's face relax. It wasn't much, but Luis knew his point was made.

"Tell me what happened," Mendoza rumbled.

"Only a small group of people knew about our plan," Luis offered. "So, if you think someone in your organization had something to do with it, you'd be right. Except that we have been extreme-ly careful about all of this. Everything was planned out in fine detail."

"Perhaps the details weren't fine enough, no?"

Luis tightened his jaw, doing his best not to be insulted. He wanted to tell the man that if there were any leaks; they were with the men he'd hired, the ones that Mendoza had brought on. Insulting the cartel leader's vetting skills, however, would prove unproductive and dangerous.

"I don't think anyone in the organization did this," Luis stated. He said it with a confidence that hinted at a greater conspiracy.

"What is that supposed to mean?"

The two guards behind Mendoza waited patiently. They were both armed, but hadn't drawn their weapons. Mendoza lowered his, probably not because he was willing to let go of his outrage, but due to his arm growing tired from being extended for so long.

"Someone figured out our plan," Luis said. "I don't know how, but they did. Maybe they noticed how we were expanding and told the Guerreros."

Mendoza rubbed his left temple as if the action would somehow massage the stress from his mind.

"Why would they be interested in those ports, Luis? Huh?" He wagged the gun at his hip. "They don't have the infrastructure. And we control the routes they would need to use."

"Which is all the more reason why I believe this came from outside. I just don't know who yet."

"Americans? The Mexican government won't touch us right now."

"No, I don't think it was the Americans," Luis hedged, "though we have to be open to that possibility."

Something about this reeked, and he couldn't put his finger on it. Luis wanted to tell his boss to just outbid the Guerreros, but they'd offered such an insane amount of money, there was no way Mendoza would go for it. As extravagant as he was with his home and lifestyle, he proved to be extremely frugal when acquiring assets that could benefit his business.

Luis had been surprised to find out how much the Guerreros offered for the properties. It was more than he thought they had on hand, and they'd used no subterfuge to lower the values.

When Mendoza's men arrived on site, they immediately withdrew, recognizing dozens of Guerreros guarding the gates into the ports.

Luis had only sent a handful to both locations, so they were right to retreat. Now, however, their plan was crumbling. Another option, however, popped into his head. It was a strategy he'd used before when with the military.

"The Guerreros are over committed," he blurted.

"What?" Mendoza asked, eyebrows furrowing.

"They sent too many men to the coast," Luis explained. "They're weak in their own compound." He could feel the adrenaline of excitement pumping through his veins. "This could present an excellent opportunity for us, Gio."

"How so?"

"Carlito sent many of his men out to handle the deals. With them gone, we could overrun their compound and eliminate the Guerreros in one swift strike. With Carlito dead, we will be free to pursue our plan, and we will be unrivaled in the entire region."

"What are you saying?" Mendoza's eyelids closed to slits.

"You know what I'm saying."

"You think we should attack them." It wasn't a question.

"Now is the time to strike. I realize this isn't typically how things play out here. No one goes after the other guy in his own house." Luis inclined his head. "Maybe it's time to change the rules."

Mendoza considered the proposal, rubbing his chin as he often did when contemplating something serious. And as a cartel boss, almost everything was serious.

"How quickly can you put the plan together?"

"It's already done."

If Mendoza was surprised, he hid it under a stoic mask. "Good. Tell Marco to lead the men."

Luis puzzled at the order. "You don't want me to go with them?"

"I need you here," he said.

He turned abruptly and stalked back into the mansion, leaving Luis with a bag full of questions.

One answer glared at him, and he realized it was probably correct. If his plan failed, Mendoza would have him executed.

His thoughts wandered to his family again, the parents he wanted desperately to protect. As long as Mendoza was alive, they would never be safe. Perhaps, he thought, that was the solution to it all.

THIRTEEN

URUAPAN

Dak held the binoculars against his face, watching the flurry of activity from his perch in the tree across the street.

Twenty vehicles had converged on the circular driveway in front of the mansion. All around the Mendoza compound, men rushed to SUVs, checking their weapons, and storing more in the rear compartments. When the trucks were loaded with their cargo, the men climbed in and took off. The convoy snaked its way down the long, winding driveway, through the front gate, and out onto the road.

The roar of the engines reached Dak's ears as they sped toward Esperanza's.

Dak felt his heart skip one, and only one, beat when he saw the face he'd been fixated on for the last several days, although in his thoughts for much longer. Luis directed the men like a general sending his soldiers off to war.

It had been a gamble to lay out the plan this way. The strong possibility that Luis went along with his men to take out Esperanza certainly loomed. In Dak's mind, it was 50/50. But he'd set things in motion in such a way that he felt confident Mendoza would ask him to stick around—for more than one reason.

Mendoza would be suspicious of how everything fell apart, how Esperanza had somehow managed to acquire the two key pieces of property that Luis was tasked with selecting.

Several assumptions went into the plan, but Dak knew one way or the other, Luis would get his.

If Mendoza sent him along with the troops to Esperanza's complex, he would likely be cut down in the ambush that waited.

Esperanza made quite the show of his offer to purchase the ship-ping businesses. He'd dressed up workers from his manufacturing locations to look like his security detail, sending them to both loca-tions simultaneously. To Luis, it would look like the ultimate invita-tion to wipe out the rival cartel once and for all. And it was a temptation Dak knew his old friend couldn't resist, nor could Mendoza.

Dak figured it didn't take much to convince the Aguilas boss to take action. And the man's choice to keep Luis at the mansion showed—at least to some degree—the man wasn't foolish enough to put all his eggs in one basket. He kept a skeleton crew on hand for personal protection, including Luis.

Now, however, the odds were tilted. Infiltrating the compound would still be a challenging endeavor, but with more than half of Mendoza's men gone, Dak liked his odds.

He climbed down from the tree and approached the outer wall in a section between where two security cameras hung along the exte-rior. He carried a lightweight, aluminum ladder, careful not to let it rattle as he moved. Carina had also equipped him with two concus-sion grenades, two flash-bang grenades, four 9mm pistols—one on each hip and one strapped to the outside of both legs—a hunting knife, and an AR-15 with a 10-inch barrel for easier maneuverability. A black, Kevlar utility vest carried extra magazines for the weapons.

Even though it appeared Dak was armed to take out a small army, he knew the resources were finite, and he couldn't just recklessly sprint into the compound with guns blazing.

Carina had also provided the best layout of the mansion she

could obtain. Dak had studied the blueprints for hours, making certain he memorized it forward and back.

He stayed low, sticking to the remnants of shadows that faded ever darker as the sun dipped over the hills to the west. In the hours since he'd arrived, Dak hadn't seen any guards walk along the narrow ledge atop the wall. He also saw none patrolling the exterior along a beaten path that wound around the perimeter. Mendoza leaned heavily on his encompassing camera system, which proved to be one of the few weaknesses Dak could find in the man's security array.

He crouched when he reached the base of the wall and gently raised the ladder, extending it until the top rung was nearly even with the upper edge, and the rails overlapped by several inches.

Dak looked to his left and right, scanning the path. No threat approached. Confident he wouldn't be easy pickings, he scaled the ladder, careful with every step not to make even the slightest sound. Once at the top, he slithered over the other inner edge, clinging to it with his fingertips, then let go and safely dropped to the ground on the other side.

Again, keeping low, he swept the immediate area with the AR-15, checking both with the naked eye and through the red-dot sight Carina equipped on the sight rail. He lowered the weapon and raised the compact binoculars to get a better view of the area.

The enormous yard—if it could be called that—stretched across a field in two directions, while the third rolled up a slight incline toward the mansion where a courtyard sat atop the plateau. He'd seen the images of the property at Carina's office. Whoever said crime didn't pay had clearly not been to this place. It was a poster child of opulence, a blatant slap in the face to the governments of two nations that whoever controlled the drugs could get away with almost anything.

Dak didn't notice any guards patrolling the interior wall. He figured Mendoza must have pulled back the remnant of his security forces to the main house, forsaking the perimeter as he'd suspected when he saw no threat during his observation in the tree.

The drug lord was throwing everything he could at Esperanza, looking to end the feud quickly and barbarically.

With a clear path to the mansion, Dak sprinted across the field to a patch of shrubs next to a rock outcropping. There, he hid behind a boulder and raised the binoculars again. From the closer vantage point, he made out three guards around the near side of the mansion. Two stood next to an arched doorway that appeared to be the rear entrance into the building, the other paced a wraparound balcony on the second floor. From that vantage point, the balcony guard had a 180-degree view of the property's backside. Dak imagined a second was similarly stationed on the other side to watch over the front that led down to the road.

Carina's intel had been stellar, including drone footage of the compound, the timing of the guards' rotations when their shifts changed, and even when Mendoza typically went to sleep.

At the moment, the fortress was operating at thirty percent.

When the balcony guard turned the other way and began his long walk in the opposite direction, Dak left his hiding spot. Keeping as low as he could without sacrificing speed, he circled the rise until he reached a giant tree. He stopped for a second behind the wide trunk, stole a look up at the building again, and darted toward the wall.

The run was only fifty yards, but it felt like a thousand. Every second ticked by like a hammer blow. Dak feared someone in the building would see him, or that maybe the guard from the front balcony would—for some reason—appear at the nearest corner as he looped around.

None of that happened and Dak skidded to a stop on the tile walkway surrounding the building.

He pressed his back against the wall and shuffled his feet to the corner on the eastern side of the house toward the entrance. His approach had come from the northern side, allowing him to get a good view of the front and the back, though up to the point the assault team left, he hadn't seen any guards on the front side.

Dak knew that wasn't going to last, and that it was only a matter of time until more men were deployed to keep watch of the entrance.

Leaning into the wall, Dak waited for a moment, listening. He heard a silent click, the tap of a shoe on hard stone. Just as he'd suspected. A guard approached. Dak retreated to the side and waited.

The guard appeared within two seconds. The man's head was turned to the left, looking out over the property. He didn't notice Dak until his periphery caught movement.

By then it was too late.

Dak plunged the hunting knife up through the man's throat and into his head. He twisted the tip slightly, killing the guard instantly, and then yanked the blade out. The guard fell to the ground with a quiet thump. Dak pulled the body to the side to hide it from anyone in the front of the mansion. Then he stripped the man's radio out of his ear and put it in his right ear. After he wiped the blade clean on the dead guard's shirt, he circled back to the rear of the building, satisfied—at least for the moment—that he wouldn't face an attack from the front.

He sheathed the blade when he reached the second corner and raised his AR-15. The suppressor attached to the barrel would conceal most of the sound, though not all. It would have to do.

Calling on his memory of where the two guards were stationed by the door, he stepped out with the AR-15 already braced against his shoulder. The red dot lined up with the farthest guard's head. Dak moved forward, his knees absorbing the shock of each step to keep his aim steady. He squeezed the trigger. The click preceded a pink mist exploding from the side of the guard's head.

As the man toppled sideways, the nearest guard turned his head to see what happened to his partner. Before he could turn to face the unseen threat, a second bullet bore through the back of his skull near the base of his neck.

He fell next to his partner as if someone had shoved him in the back.

Dak picked up his speed and rushed toward the doors, skirting under the view of huge windows along the way.

When he reached the rear entrance, he paused, double-checked the two guards with a nudge of his right boot, and pulled on the latch.

The door swung open easily, and he stepped inside.

Dak swept the room with his weapon. A couch to the right near a fireplace, a grand piano to the left, and a staircase winding up to the next level exposed no new threat. That wouldn't last long. The next patrol could be seconds away.

He eased the door shut and hurried to the left, past the piano and into a study.

Dak stopped at the threshold where two dark wooden doors led into the room. He checked the left first where shelves filled with books wrapped around a sitting area. He continued his scan, whipping the weapon around to the right.

He froze.

There, behind an ornate desk, sat Mendoza. The drug lord's head drooped onto his right shoulder, a bullet hole through his temple.

Standing next to him, Luis held a pistol with a suppressor attached to the barrel.

FOURTEEN

URUAPAN

Luis sensed the intruder and snapped his pistol up, aiming it at a lethal pair of jade eyes that he'd seen so many times before.

Dak kept the red dot squarely over Luis' heart.

"Dak?" Luis spoke the word, befuddled. "What are you doing here?"

"We both know what I'm doing here, Luis."

The bitter scent of smoke lingered in the room, hovering near Luis and the dead man, then gradually made its way across the room to where Dak stood.

Luis inclined his head. "Ah. You came to kill me? Is that it?"

"Very astute of you."

The red dot in the sight never wavered from the white button-up shirt his old friend wore. The rest of the ensemble looked exactly like what you would expect a drug lord's lackey to wear—beige linen pants and expensive, brown leather shoes.

"How did you get in here?" Luis asked.

Dak cocked his head to the side. "Do you really have to ask, Luis? How many years did we serve together?"

"True." Luis lowered his weapon; resignation filled his face.

Hesitation crept into Dak's mind, and he didn't know why. "That Mendoza?" He knew the answer, but he wanted to keep Luis talking.

"Yes."

"Why did you kill him? You taking over the cartel? Have you really turned so far to the dark side that this is who you've become?"

"No," Luis said quickly, almost too quickly. He shook his head and repeated the answer. "No. I don't want to have anything to do with it anymore."

Dak searched Luis for the truth. It covered the man's long-drawn face, eyes full of regret, and a hint of deep sadness.

"It was the only way," Luis continued, "to keep my parents safe, my relatives. My cooperation with Mendoza meant they wouldn't be in danger."

"Doesn't sound like you thought that through," Dak said.

"Maybe. Maybe not. But he's dead now. They'll be safe."

Dak turned his head left and right. "I don't think that's how it works, Luis. Unless you had designs on taking over the cartel yourself. Is that your plan?"

Luis paused for a second, considering the question. "I don't want to be the head of a cartel, Dak. I never wanted any of this. And I didn't want to leave you in that cave."

"Ah. But you did it anyway."

"Bo would have killed me. You know that."

"Yeah," Dak said with a nod. "So, to save your own neck, you were willing to cut mine."

"No," Luis said, shaking his head vigorously. "When they buried you in that cave, leaving you for dead, I hoped you would get out. Then I heard about how you returned to base, how the colonel tried to arrest you."

"I suppose you tried to tell him I was innocent, that Bo and the others... that you were the ones who betrayed me?"

Luis dropped his head. His chin nearly rested on his chest. "No. I didn't." He lifted his head to meet Dak's piercing gaze again. "I wish I had, but I didn't. I can't go back and change that now."

"Nope."

"But I can help you find the others," Luis insisted.

For a split second, Dak let down his guard and felt a pang of hope flutter in his chest. "What did you say?"

"Williams, Collier, and Trask. I know where they are."

"Williams is dead," Dak informed as if mentioning he'd squashed a bug.

Luis looked surprised. "Dead?"

"I suspect he's at the bottom of the ocean right now off the coast of Miami. I wasn't the only person he owed a debt."

"I see."

Dak let him stew before he spoke again. "Why? Why do you know where they went, Luis?"

Luis sighed. "Because I knew that one day you would find me."

"And you thought helping me would save you?" Dak spoke with cold steel in his voice.

"No," Luis said dejectedly. "I did it because it was the only thing I could think of to right the wrong. I should have stood up to Bo and the others. I made a mistake, a big one. I know that. I knew it all along and was too afraid to do the right thing."

Dak considered the irony. He'd witnessed Luis in battle. The man was a fierce warrior, as strong and courageous as any he'd seen, yet he cowered to Bo, not just in the cave, but all the time. Dak wondered what it was about the man that Luis feared, but now wasn't the time to ask.

"You don't know where Bo is?" Dak pressed.

Luis shook his head. "No. I'm sorry, Dak. I did try to find him, but he's dropped off the map. Collier and Trask did too, for a while. They were difficult to locate. But Mendoza's resources are... were considerable." He regarded the dead man to his right with a tilt of the head. "Trask is in Colorado. Bought property on a mountain. I figure he probably built a cabin there, went off-grid."

"That didn't help him, though, did it?"

"Collier was trickier," Luis said, ignoring the question. "Last I heard, he was in Kentucky in a—" Luis stopped abruptly and pressed his earpiece.

Dak heard it too.

A man's voice spoke frantically in Spanish. Within seconds, another voice joined the first. Soon after, shouts came from various points outside the mansion.

"They know you're here," Luis said.

"Thanks," Dak said, his response smothered in sarcasm. "My Spanish isn't that bad."

Dak took his eyes off Luis and turned as he heard footsteps rushing toward him. A guard ran recklessly around the corner and Dak squeezed the trigger. The round caught the man squarely in the chest and dropped him to the ground in mid-stride. The guy slid to a halt near the grand piano.

More voices filled the radio, ordering men to secure Mendoza. They didn't know it was too late for that, or that their head of security was the one who'd killed him.

Dak slammed the heavy doors shut and bolted them. There were still the windows along the outer wall, though, and that would make them easy targets.

"How many men are still here?" Dak demanded, stalking over to the desk where Luis still stood.

"We only left sixteen in reserve," Luis said. "The rest went to pay Esperanza a visit."

"I figured."

Luis looked puzzled, then realization washed over him. "It was you," he said. "You were the one who set up the deal to screw over Mendoza. But... how did you know?"

"Not the time, Luis. Please hold your questions until the end of the gun battle." Dak stepped around behind the desk and grabbed the back of Mendoza's chair. He glanced at his ex-teammate. "But yes, it was me."

He shoved the chair out of the way, sliding it around to the front of the desk.

"What are you doing?" Luis wondered. Still holding his pistol, he considered pointing it at the back of Dak's head and executing him in cold blood. It would be easy. The intruder had let his guard down. Luis could kill him, then blame the American for the assassination of their leader. With Mendoza out of the way, Luis would make the obvious successor to the throne. He felt his fingers tightening on the pistol.

He exhaled and loosened his grip.

"Putting Mendoza between us and anyone else who might be coming. A gunshot popped from somewhere outside the building. A window shattered to the right, near the far corner of the room.

"Here they come," Dak said. He ducked down behind the desk once more, using it as a barricade.

Luis did the same, taking cover next to his former friend as they'd done in combat so many times before.

"So, what's the plan?" Luis asked. "We wait here and shoot our way out?"

"Something like that." Dak stole a peek over the top of the desk and noted the shooter's location outside. Darkness descended onto the estate, but with it came the bright glow of floodlights that switched on automatically.

The gunman fired again, this time letting loose a flurry of automatic gunfire. Rounds obliterated the window's jagged remains and smashed into the desk. Several peppered the wall behind it, destroying a brass clock on a shelf, and punching holes through expensive artwork.

Dak slid to the corner of the desk and raised his weapon. He put the red dot on the target and squeezed the trigger three times.

The gunman's body shook as he absorbed two of the rounds before falling to his knees, then out of sight.

More shouting ensued from all around Luis and Dak's position. Then new voices came through the radios.

Luis' face turned crestfallen as Dak looked to him with questions in his eyes. He already knew the answer. He'd heard the same orders.

The men in the SUVs were turning back to help squelch the sudden attack on Mendoza's compound.

"It's Marco," Luis said. "He's bringing back the assault team."

FIFTEEN

URUAPAN

Dak and Luis managed to survive the initial onslaught from Mendoza's men. They had surrounded the room and fired copious amounts of bullets into the study. The front of the oak desk looked like it had been through a tornado, with holes and jagged pieces of wood splintering off from its façade.

The desk held, though, leaving Dak and Luis unscathed.

They knew that wouldn't last.

The two former Delta Force operators knew that when the reinforcements arrived, they would be overrun, and that was minutes away.

"You think this Marco character is willing to throw everything at us?" Dak asked as he sat on the floor with his back against the right-hand filing drawers.

"Definitely," Luis answered. "Marco is savage. I'm pretty sure he's never liked me, either. I think he wants to take over the cartel."

Dak lowered his AR-15 and grabbed one of the pistols from his hip. He leaned around the corner and fired another three shots through a window at a silhouette beyond.

The target jerked and then withdrew, taking a round to the shoulder. Dak immediately retreated to the safety of the desk's cover as another volley followed the outburst.

Within seconds, the shooting ceased again.

The men firing at them would run out of rounds at some point, or at least Dak hoped that was the case. He figured that was the reason for their conservative approach thus far as they waited for reinforcements to arrive.

"Is there another way out of here?" Dak asked.

"Out of the study?" Luis met his gaze. "No."

Dak swore to himself.

"But there is a secret passage leading out of the compound. It's in the basement, attached to Mendoza's war room."

An eyebrow arched over Dak's right eye. "War room? He has a war room?"

Luis shrugged. "The guy was a planner. I'm not sure if you noticed, but these cartels are engaged in a war."

"You don't say."

Another smatter of gunfire roared from outside the building. The ravaged drywall behind the desk puffed clouds of white dust, the tattered remains of the surface ripped with each bullet.

When the cacophony died down again, Dak exhaled. "So, secret passage, huh?"

"Yeah. But the door will be covered on the other side by Mendoza's men. We'll be easy targets for the guys outside. We won't even get close."

Dak looked down at the two grenades and the flash-bang attached to his vest. He could take the chance and throw one through a window, but he could miss and the thing might take a bad bounce. They'd be safe behind the desk and there was an outside chance the shrapnel would take out some of the men close to the windows, but that was doubtful.

Then Dak remembered seeing a fireplace in a sitting area near the bookshelves on the other side of the room.

"That fireplace is gas, yeah?" he asked, a flicker of hope rising in his chest.

"Yeah," Luis said. "Why?"

Dak glanced over at his friend and handed him the pistol. "Cover me," he said.

"What?" Confusion filled Luis' eyes.

"On three, we open fire. Aim for the two farthest windows. I'll take the two closest."

"Why do I have to take the farther targets?"

Dak sighed. "Because I'm on this side. It doesn't matter if you hit them. We just have to get Mendoza's men to back off for a second."

"What are you going to do?" Luis searched his old friend for answers.

Dak met his eyes. "Something crazy."

Luis snickered the way only a man with nothing left to lose could.

"Does this mean I'm forgiven?"

"No," Dak said. "You still have a beating coming."

"That's fair," Luis nodded.

"You ready?"

"Yeah."

Dak readied the AR-15 again, gripping it firmly in his hands. "One. Two." He stole one last glance at Luis. "Three."

The two popped up from behind their cover and opened fire. Luis stood with both pistols extended, reminiscent of outlaws from the Old West, guns firing, ready to go out in a blaze of glory.

Dak fired two strategic shots through the first window, then two more through the next before he bent down, using the table as a brace for the shot that mattered. He looked through the scope with Luis hovering over him, still unloading his magazines. Dak lined up the red dot on the pilot flame inside the fireplace, then lowered it by a couple of inches until he found the metal hose where it connected to the valve.

He heard one of the magazines eject from the pistol in Luis' right hand, and it clattered on the desk to Dak's left. Dak didn't budge, didn't flinch. His breath came slow, deliberate, as he tensed his trigger finger and squeezed.

The silenced weapon let out a muted pop. The bullet zipped through the air and clipped the valve. The pilot went out instantly, its supply of fuel cut off. The damaged valve housing, however, spilled natural gas out into the room.

"Get down," Dak ordered as his friend fired the last round of his magazine.

Another reply came from the gunmen outside. As Luis ducked back down, a bullet caught him in the chest. Another caught him in the gut. A third struck his right arm.

He fell to the floor with his back to the desk drawers. His chest rose and fell rapidly, desperate to fill his lungs with air. The heavy breaths, though, also brought blood with them.

Dak looked to his friend and saw the wounds.

"Luis?" Dak said.

"I'm fine, Dak," Luis replied. "I'll be okay."

Dak's face tightened against the flood of emotion. He came here to kill this man, to right the wrong done to him. Now, all he could feel was sadness and regret.

"Don't look at me like that," Luis said. "It's okay. I'm getting what I deserve."

"We can get you to a hospital," Dak said, trying to convince himself as much as the man next to him.

Luis coughed a laugh and turned his head. "You always were stubborn, Dak. It's one of the things I liked about you." He swallowed hard and his eyes started to roll back, but he fought off the darkness for a few more breaths. "Find Billy and Nathaniel. You get them for what they did to you. Okay? One of them might know where Bo is." The words came stammering out as the mortal wounds continued to do their deadly work.

"Billy is in... Colorado."

"You told me," Dak said.

Luis coughed again. "Get to the... to the escape tunnel. You... you can make it."

"We can make it," Dak insisted.

The dying man shook his head. "Tell me what your... crazy plan was."

Dak looked down at the grenade on his vest and plucked it from its nest.

"I shot out the gas valve on the fireplace," he answered.

Realization glimmered in his friend's dark eyes. "That's a good plan." His eyes lingered on the grenade. "Let me do it."

"No," Dak said. "I can't—"

"Shut up, Dak. We both know I'm a goner. I'd rather go out fighting than lying here like a coward."

Dak hadn't been prepared for this. Again, the plan ran through his mind of coming here to avenge the wrong Luis helped perpetrate. Now, he wished he could save the man's life. That wish could never come to fruition.

He nodded and placed the grenade into his friend's palm.

"Thank you," Dak said.

Luis offered a feeble smile and coughed. "Does that mean you forgive me?"

Dak snorted weakly. "Yeah, amigo. You're forgiven."

"Cool." Luis pulled the pin and gripped the explosive device to prevent it from detonating too soon. He struggled to turn around and then gave one last look at Dak. "See you on the other side, amigo."

Dak nodded. "See you on the other side."

Luis struggled to stand. Using a chair off to the side as both a brace and a shield, he turned and started toward the door. The gunmen outside fired again, dumping hot metal into the study. Bullets sailed by, whizzing past Luis' ears. Several struck the back of the chair. A few made it through and struck him in the torso. He shuddered at the impact but kept going, sliding the chair forward as he made for the door.

Dak slid under the desk and stayed as low as he could, knowing what was coming. He jerked one of the drawers out and used it to cover his head. Then... he waited.

The gunfire slowed as the shooters changed out their empty magazines for full ones. Another bullet struck Luis in the leg and he yelped. The new wound slowed him, but Luis wouldn't be denied this last effort at salvation. He tasted iron in his mouth from the blood he coughed up.

When he was fifteen feet from the door, another shot echoed through the study. The round hit him in the shin, shattering the bone. He fell forward, his leg screaming in agonizing pain. The world around him moved in dizzying slow motion. He was so close. As he toppled forward, Luis summoned every scrap of energy he had left and shoved his left hand forward, shuffling the grenade toward the door.

He slumped down onto the seat, watching the explosive hit the floor and tumble toward the doorway. It rolled to a stop mere feet from the threshold. Luis exhaled one last time and smiled in satisfaction.

The hard shell of the grenade erupted in fire and shrapnel, blasting the doors to shreds and seriously injuring two guards beyond. That was just the appetizer. The blast shook the entire mansion as it ignited the gas that now filled the room and flowed out of the tattered windows.

A ball of fire seared through the open doorway, scorching two more guards who'd been standing by the wall in ambush. The flames leaped out of the windows and blinded several more guards. Shards of glass and chunks of debris smashed into the gunmen, injuring some, killing two with blunt force trauma to the head.

Dak huddled under the desk as the explosion rocked the study. He pressed his forearms against his ears with the drawer pinched tight in his fingers. Flames coursed over the desk and climbed to the ceiling for all of two seconds. The searing heat licked at the drawer over his head, but didn't touch his skin. The front side of the desk absorbed the concussion from the blast as well as the deadly debris it flung across the room.

Then everything went eerily still.

Strips of torn paper and ash fluttered to the floor. Dak dropped the drawer and scrambled to his feet. He peered through the smoke and dust. Much of the outer wall was gone, reduced to rubble. Half of the ceiling had collapsed. The doors to the left, leading back into the mansion, looked little more than chunks of charred, splintered wood somehow still clinging to their hinges.

Dak's eyes fell to a pile near the door. Huge pieces of ceiling covered the chair Luis had used, but Dak could see the man's legs protruding from under the debris. The rest of his body was covered. Dak actually appreciated that. He came here to kill Luis, one of the five who'd betrayed him. Now that Luis was dead, Dak felt conflicted.

That emotion would have to be sorted at another time.

SIXTEEN

URUAPAN

Dak detected movement through one of the wide openings in the exterior wall created by the explosion. Turning, he hurried over the piles of hulking pieces of the demolished study. He paused at the doorway, drew one of his pistols, and looked out into the next room.

Four dead guards lay strewn on the floor.

A man shouted from the top of a staircase dead ahead. The guard was only able to raise his weapon a few inches before a charging Dak unleashed three rapid shots, two striking the man in the chest. The guard lurched forward and tipped over the railing. He hit the floor with a smack and didn't move.

Dak rushed around the next corner, heading for the stairs that led down to the basement; his escape route. Headlights shone into the room through the front doors, and Dak knew that Marco and his men had arrived.

Slowing to a stop, Dak waited at the corner, knowing that the thirty feet to the stairs would give the cartel thugs an easy line of sight. He peeked around and noted the two alcoves along the right-hand wall. The stairs were along the left wall, halfway to the foyer. It wasn't much, but they would give him a chance to take cover as he advanced.

The front door opened, and footfalls followed by the dozens.

Colorado, Dak thought. I have to get to Colorado.

He waited until the last second, drawing one of the two remaining pistols strapped to his left side, and stepped out.

The charging men didn't have time to stop. They unwittingly sprinted into a death funnel with Dak Harper at the nozzle.

He unloaded on them at a deadly close range. His fingers twitched. The suppressor barrels puffed bursts of smoke. Bullets tore through flesh and skull as Dak took no prisoners, going for headshots to every one of the cartel soldiers. Few missed the target, even fewer missed at least a part of a henchman.

The bodies hit the floor all around him and none of the attackers even reacted until the fourth wave. Even they were too slow as Dak finished the contents of one magazine and drew the last loaded pistol. Ten more men fell as they ran ahead into the deadly hail.

By the sixth wave, the cartel soldiers realized they were being cut down, and they retreated to the foyer to take cover behind the walls on either side. Thirty men lay in several heaps on the floor, leaving a trail of death to the entrance.

Dak felt no remorse, no emotion at the grisly sight. These men had killed innocent people, killed others like them, all without regard. They'd tortured and maimed, helped run deadly drugs to untold thousands, perhaps more.

Their lives, in his mind, were forfeit.

He looked out through the open doorway at a man in a black shirt and matching cargo pants. He stood like a king among pawns, and Dak knew it had to be Marco. He could see the confusion on Marco's face, the lack of recognition at this stranger who had killed so many of his men with such ruthless efficiency.

Dak dropped the empty pistol in his right hand and moved it to support the left, which held his remaining handgun. The AR-15 still had some rounds in the magazine, and he had spares for that, along with more rounds for the pistol.

Marco was barely within range, and Dak knew hitting a target precisely from that far away would be difficult.

The stairs were ten feet away to his left. He could rush to them, but Marco would send his men after him. And because he worked for Mendoza, it was likely Marco could go around and cut him off.

Dak made a quick decision. He fired the pistol at Marco, who abruptly lost the stupid grin on his face and dove to the side of the entrance. Marco's men popped out from cover and opened fire. Dak leaped into the alcove to his right, knocking over a vase in the process. The expensive blue and white pottery shattered on the floor at his feet.

"Oops," he muttered.

He shoved his empty pistol back into its holster and grabbed the flash-bang from his vest. He pulled the pin and waited for the gunfire to cease. When it did, he whipped his arm around the corner and tossed the device down the corridor.

It slid to a stop just a few feet into the foyer and then exploded.

The searing white light flashed through the hallway. It blinded every gunman in the entryway. Dak stepped out into the open and saw the henchmen staggering around, rubbing their eyes. Marco stumbled through the doorway and tripped on the threshold. He fell clumsily to the floor and clawed at the tiles to get up.

Dak plucked the last grenade from his vest and pulled the pin as he stepped over the bodies and headed toward the stairs. Sirens echoed from the valley beyond the open doorway, and he knew the fire department was on their way, along with a few curious—and probably corrupt—cops.

Dak lobbed the grenade down the hallway and rushed into the stairwell. He didn't see the explosive as it rolled to a stop in front of Marco just as the man's eyes began to clear from the blinding light. Dak only heard a split-second "Ah" before the blast killed the cartel enforcer and sent deadly shrapnel through the bodies of the remaining forces.

When he reached the bottom of the stairs, Dak looked in both directions, keeping his AR-15 ahead of him, and searched the corridor until he found the boardroom Luis had described.

Dak ran around to the head of the conference table where he assumed Mendoza usually sat and ran his fingers under the heavy wood. He found the button exactly where he would put it if he were a drug lord in need of a quick exit. He pressed the button and the wall behind him slid open, rotating away from the table and into a dark tunnel. Lights flickered on along the cinderblock walls.

He stepped inside and found another button on the wall near the doorway. When he pressed it, the secret door swung closed again.

Dak took a deep breath and swallowed hard. More heavy breaths followed as the series of events caught up to his body. His legs felt like lead and his balance wavered.

After ten seconds, he steeled his nerves again and started running down the tunnel. He could rest when he was out of Uruapan.

SEVENTEEN

GUADALAJARA

Dak looked down the sidewalk to his right, then to his left, before pushing open the cantina door.

He took a step in and glanced over to the booth on the left where he'd sat the first time he came here to meet Carina. The young bartender immediately recognized him, offering a curt nod in welcome.

"Tequila, amigo?" the man asked as he finished wiping down the counter. His right hand reached for a glass before Dak could say yes.

"Gracias," Dak offered as the man poured a generous dose of the hazy liquid.

The barkeep slid the glass across the counter to Dak, who raised it, then made his way over to the corner booth.

He sipped on the drink for several minutes before the stunning Mexican woman emerged from the office.

Her eyes fell to him immediately, ignoring the other patrons hunched over the counter or sitting in the other booths.

She sauntered over to him, her navy blue blouse fluttering. The cream-colored slacks flapped over black high-heels. Carina stopped at the table and motioned to the seat opposite Dak.

"This one taken?" she asked.

His lips cracked a smile. "One of the most cliché pickup lines of all time, and this is the first instance it's ever been used on me."

She offered a flirtatious grin. Her dark hair, nearly black, draped down one side, pulled around to expose the left side of her face, her neck, and a hint of her shoulder.

He lost himself in her deep brown eyes, the red lips accented by a maraschino cherry lipstick.

"That's a shame," she said. "Maybe American girls don't know a good thing when they see it."

Dak chuckled and nodded, then took another sip. "Maybe. Or maybe I was always too busy."

She said nothing, but her quiet gaze told him she understood. She'd lived that life, the path led by a government agency always telling her where to be, what to do, and often putting her in dangerous scenarios. That life wasn't conducive to dating or relationships. The danger aspect made it almost necessary not to get close to anyone.

He felt like she still clung to that paranoia, that concern over an assassin hiding in the shadows, the sounds in the night that kept decent sleep at bay. He certainly held onto the same worries.

His mind wandered to Istanbul. He hoped Nicole was safe, that the colonel hadn't learned about her, about their connection. He doubted he would. They'd never been married, and the colonel didn't know much about his personal life. He could find Dak's parents, sure, but Nicole was about as off the map as a person could be in regards to the depths of his reach.

He missed her.

For much of the last few years, he'd forced that emotion away, stuffing those feelings down deep in his gut where they were constantly squashed by the high-alert nature of war.

Carina stared back at him, her eyes unquestionably longing. Part of him wished he could move on, to let go of the past. This woman wanted him. If he was honest, he felt the same way.

Was it just a physical attraction, the need for physical touch and companionship after so many nights alone?

He couldn't bring himself to go there. Not yet. Despite the things she'd said, the way Nicole had acted toward him, Dak didn't feel that chapter had yet reached its end. He needed closure before he could turn the page.

"I came here to say thank you," Dak spoke, his voice devoid of emotion. "You didn't have to help me, but you did. And I appreciate it."

"Happy to do it," she said, tossing her head to the side as though she'd just tossed a coin to a child. "Mendoza and all of his lieutenants are dead. Most of his men, too."

"Esperanza is still out there."

"True." She shrugged. "There will always be another."

He felt those words for a different reason.

"Esperanza is weak, though. He won't survive another two months, I'll make certain of that. If Uruapan can be liberated from the cartels' grasp, perhaps other cities can as well. In time, we may be able to push them out completely."

He knew it was an unrealistic dream and he could tell she knew it, too. Far be it for him, though, to tell her not to hope.

"So, you're leaving?" she asked, emotion cracking her voice for the first time since they met.

"Yeah." He let his eyes fall to the table where the tequila glass rested. "I have a few more stops to make on my journey."

She nodded her understanding. "Well, Dak Harper. It's been a pleasure. I hope our paths cross again." A feeble smile parted her lips.

"Me, too," he said. Then he tossed back the tequila and watched her get up. She strolled back to the office too quickly, and he knew it was because if she remained any longer, she would demand he stay.

When she was gone, he looked down at the empty glass and sighed.

"What are you doing, Harper?" he asked himself.

He shook off the question, dropped double what he owed for the drink on the table, and walked out of the cantina.

Outside, the warm sunshine radiated on his face and arms. He let it wash over him for a few breaths. Then he turned and raised his hand to hail a cab.

Dak had a date with a sniper in Colorado.

THANK YOU

Thank you for taking the time to read this story. We can always make more money, but time is a finite resource for all of us, so the fact you took the time to read my work means the world to me and I truly appreciate it. I hope you enjoyed it as much as I enjoyed sharing it, and I look forward to bringing you more fun adventures in the future. If you this story kept you up late, on the edge of your seat, or burning your fingers as you swiped or turned the pages, swing by Amazon and leave a review. I'd appreciate it and so would other readers.

See you in the next one,

Ernest

OTHER BOOKS BY ERNEST DEMPSEY

Dak Harper Origin Stories:

Out of the Fire

You Only Die Once

Tequila Sunset

Purgatory

Scorched Earth

The Heart of Vengeance

Sean Wyatt Adventures:

The Secret of the Stones

The Cleric's Vault

The Last Chamber

The Grecian Manifesto

The Norse Directive

Game of Shadows

The Jerusalem Creed

The Samurai Cipher

The Cairo Vendetta

The Uluru Code

The Excalibur Key

The Denali Deception

The Sahara Legacy

The Fourth Prophecy

The Templar Curse

The Forbidden Temple

The Omega Project

The Napoleon Affair

The Second Sign

Adriana Villa Adventures:

War of Thieves Box Set

When Shadows Call

Shadows Rising

Shadow Hour

The Adventure Guild:

The Caesar Secret: Books 1-3

The Carolina Caper

Beta Force:

Operation Zulu

London Calling

Paranormal Archaeology Division:

Hell's Gate

For Russell

ACKNOWLEDGMENTS

Special thanks go out to my super fans. We ride together. I appreciate and love you all. And a huge thank you to Anne Storer, Ray Braun, Denyse Léonard, and James Slater for your extra effort in helping make this story a better reading experience.

PURGATORY

A DAK HARPER THRILLER

ERNEST DEMPSEY

ONE

DENVER, COLORADO

Dak had been waiting on this call for nearly two months. During that time, the warm embrace of late summer had rapidly given way to the chill of fall and the coming winter.

After the events in Mexico and the death of Luis, Dak Harper made his way back to the United States, circumventing the Border Patrol with the documents his friend Will had created for him back in Portugal.

It was the second time he'd been forced to sneak back into his own country, the country he fought and sacrificed for. The irony wasn't lost on him, but he did his best not to dwell on that. Those kinds of thoughts and feelings weren't productive.

He'd come to Denver, Colorado, immediately after re-entering the country. Luis told Dak that Billy Trask—one of the five men who'd left him for dead in Iraq—was holed up on a mountain somewhere in Colorado. Luis had failed to mention precisely where before he died in the firefight at the Mendoza cartel compound. Maybe he didn't know. Telling himself that made Dak feel a little better about the state of the unknown, but just barely.

Billy was a sniper and an excellent one at that. The obvious conclusion to Billy's selection of a mountain location was that he'd have a clear line of sight to any approaching threat. It was possible, of course, that Billy simply loved the mountains—a fact that Dak recalled from one of their conversations when they first met. If the sniper could have the best of both worlds, then that was just an added bonus.

Dak looked out the window of his seventh-story apartment. The downtown Denver skyline spread out across the plains leading into the Rocky Mountains. The city had witnessed a population explosion in recent years that resulted in rapid expansion both to the south and to the north toward Fort Collins.

He pressed the answer button and held the device to his ear.

"I've been waiting for your call," Dak said, half cryptically, half-jokingly.

"I bet you have," Will responded. "I hope you've picked up a hobby or two during all of this."

Dak snickered. He had picked up a hobby. Since arriving in Denver, he'd been learning more about drones—specifically racing and freestyle models capable of reaching speeds beyond 90 mph while taking incredibly crisp video via GoPro-mounted cameras. He'd built four drones in the last two months. He lost one high up in the mountains when it crashed into a rocky crag. He crashed another one, but that unit managed to survive—for the most part. It needed some new propellers, two new motors, and two new cameras, but the aircraft proved to be far more durable than he would have believed.

Flying the drones gave him the feeling of being on a motorcycle with wings. It was fast, adrenaline-fueled, and filled a need for excitement he didn't realize he had. Being in one of the more picturesque, breathtaking places in the world didn't hurt, either.

"I've been doing some photography and videography," Dak said, downplaying the new hobby.

Will burst out laughing. "Not weddings and birthdays, I hope."

"Not really."

"Well, that's a relief. I couldn't imagine you standing around one of those events, taking pictures and video. Besides, you're supposed to be keeping a low profile."

"I am."

Will huffed. "Man of few words today, I see."

"Simple questions deserve simple answers."

"Fair enough."

"So, you have something for me, or you just calling to check on my routine?" Dak leaned forward to look out the window to his right. Dark clouds rolled in from the north and a few flecks of snow fluttered through the air around his building.

That was the downside of Denver. Winters were hard. That wasn't a problem for the people who loved to head into the mountains to hit the slopes. He fit into the other category, though he hoped that one day he might be able to return and visit Vail again. He'd been there once before and loved the little mountain village. It felt like being in Germany or Switzerland, two places he enjoyed visiting on his travels. For now, though, he had work to do.

"Your friend Billy Trask," Will said, "he's definitely in Colorado."

Dak felt a wave of relief crash over him, followed by an injection of adrenaline pumping through his veins.

"That's good to hear. Would be unfortunate if he was in Australia."

"No doubt," Will chuckled. "He's down in the south, in the Sangre de Cristo mountains area. It was difficult to track him down. Based on what you told me before, I wouldn't have thought this one to be as resourceful, but he clearly tried to work every angle he could to disappear."

"I assume he has an alias."

"Now, you and I both know what happens when we assume." Will let the statement linger for a few seconds before going on. "But yes, he goes by the name of Tyler Mumford."

"He looks like a Mumford."

Dak turned away from the window and walked over to the kitchen counter, where he perpetually kept a pen and paper waiting just for this call. He took the pen and pinched it between his fingers and thumb, then jotted down the information.

"I don't know what that means, but whatever. He bought an abandoned ski resort just outside the town of Cuchara."

Dak froze for a second, wondering if he'd heard correctly. "Did you just say he bought an abandoned ski resort?"

"Yeah, I did a double-take on that one too. Apparently, that area has a few of them. Not sure why. I guess it wasn't the destination that some of the more popular resorts are. Whatever the reason, there was one available and your boy scooped it up. Has a sweet chalet at the top of one of the peaks, too. I bet the view up there is one in a million."

"I'm sure it is," Dak said begrudgingly. A view like that would make it easy for Billy to see someone coming. He also knew Billy couldn't be on watch 24/7, which meant he likely had a couple of security personnel watching for him, or at the very least cameras and sensors.

"I sent the address to your secure email. You need anything else?"

"No," Dak said, shaking his head. "This is good. Thanks again, Will."

"Not a problem. Two more after this one, right?"

"Right. Talk to you soon."

"I hope you do."

The call ended and Dak stared at the name and location he'd scribbled on the piece of paper.

"Okay, Tyler," Dak whispered. "You're up."

TWO
CUCHARA, COLORADO

Tyler raised the rifle and then lowered it down onto the wooden fence rail. He felt the familiar nudge of the stock in his armpit, cradled against his shoulder. The target lined up in the crosshairs as he centered the scope in his line of sight. A gentle breeze rolled across the field. He compensated, easing the weapon just a fraction of an inch to the right to compensate.

"Well? Go on then?" a voice behind him prodded. "What are you waiting for?"

Tyler didn't answer immediately. He kept his breath steady, a monotonous rhythm he always employed when taking down a target.

"Being an expert sniper takes patience, Tripp," Tyler said without so much as a sideways glance at the pest.

"Uh huh," Tripp mocked. Standing a few feet behind Tyler, he watched with his arms crossed, a skeptical smirk on his face, and a bottle of beer in one hand.

"Leave him alone," Steve said. "He's trying to focus." He took a swig of beer and tilted his head up. "Don't pay any attention to him, Tyler."

"Thanks for the tip," Tyler responded unappreciatively.

Steve was the shortest of the group, but built like a rock. He'd played Division II college football at one point in his life, but knee injuries and a lack of height caused coaches to pass on him going any further. He still worked out hard, though, and bore the look of a starting collegiate fullback.

To his right, John Collinsworth was the polar opposite. The giant towered over the other men at six feet five inches. He played college basketball, and like Steve, had suffered injuries that kept him from pursuing a career in it, though he admitted on more than one occasion that professional basketball was probably never in the cards for him. He sipped his beer while the others were happy to chug theirs.

"You just want to win our money," John commented to Steve's intrusion.

"Yeah," Tripp agreed. "Besides, if you're a good shooter, you have to be able to do it under pressure."

Tyler didn't say anything, instead letting the statement blow away on the cool, late fall breeze.

He kept his eye on the target—a beer bottle sitting on a fence post at the other end of the field, nearly five hundred yards away. Tyler—Billy Trask in his former life—had picked off moving targets from farther away when he was in the military. These buffoon friends of his had no idea how good he was or the things he'd done. That, he knew, would always have to remain the case. He couldn't take the chance of them catching on to his true identity. If they caught wind of that, he doubted they would cause any trouble, but he couldn't risk it. Dak Harper was still out there, as far as he knew, and all it would take would be a single slip up. Then there would be trouble.

Billy had been careful, keeping his backstory in line as a former ROTC guy who attended Virginia Tech in Blacksburg. His new crew accepted the explanation without dispute. The fact that he was a deadeye with a rifle attested to at least some kind of military training. Since none of the guys had ever spent as much as a second in the military, they had no foundation to question anything he said.

As far as Billy's money was concerned, he told "the boys" he ran an e-commerce website that he claimed took off—even went as far as buying the domain and throwing up some merchandise to make it look like the real thing. That story kept his new friends off his back, as well as any newcomers that found their way across his path.

It didn't hurt that he was almost always happy to pay for everything when the group went out to the bars or even up to one of the larger cities, such as Colorado Springs or Denver. Coincidental bribes were always an easy way to throw people off the trail.

He felt himself ease into a familiar groove. Even with the alcohol pumping through his veins, Billy was cooler than the other side of the pillow when it came to shooting.

He squeezed the trigger, and the rifle discharged. The thunderous boom echoed through the valley, rolled up into the mountains, and dissipated.

The bottle atop the fence post exploded into a hundred pieces. For a moment, the other three could only stare in disbelief.

John was the first to say anything. "Bam! Looks like you two owe us a hundred bucks a piece," he exclaimed. The usually stoic giant let the thrill of victory overcome him.

Tripp merely stood there speechless. Steve shared his sentiment, staring slack jawed across the vast field at the fence post. He raised the binoculars he held in his right hand and peered through them just to make sure he wasn't seeing things.

Satisfied with his workmanship, the shooter stood up straight, grabbed his bottle of beer from the ground at his feet, and took a swig. He swallowed and clicked his tongue. "You can look through those all day, Steve. You won't find much of that bottle left."

Steve lowered the binoculars, shaking his head. He looked over at his pal and swore. "I ain't never seen anyone shoot like that before, Tyler. I mean, I knew you were good, but that's insane. And with a breeze, too."

"You have to compensate for that," Tyler confessed. "Little trick they taught us when we went out to the sniper range."

"I went to the wrong college," Tripp said, finally able to find the ability to speak.

"Maybe."

"Nah, I've never seen anything like that. None of us even came close."

That part was true. The other three took two turns each at the bottle before Tyler stepped up to the plate. The empty shell casings littering the ground at their feet reminded the other three of their failure, though John didn't seem to mind. He'd put his money on the winning horse.

Tyler shrugged. "You boys want to go double or nothing?"

He gauged Tripp's interest, though Steve appeared to know when to tuck tail and run. Tripp was about to respond when they heard the crunch of tires on gravel and the accompanying sound of a patrol car's engine.

The men spun around in time to see the county deputy's car pull up. The driver blipped the siren for a half second to get their attention, as if he didn't already have it, then parked near Tyler's, concrete-gray four-door Jeep Wrangler.

"Great," Steve spat.

The deputy cut off the engine, stepped out of the vehicle, and put his police-issue hat on. He slammed the door and sauntered around the hood with one hand resting on his belt near the pistol.

"Got a call about some gunfire coming from out here at the old Huxley place," the deputy said, stopping twenty feet from the four men. "Now, I don't suppose you four would know anything about that. Would you?"

"If it ain't Deputy Andy," Tripp groused. "Why don't you just scurry on back into town and see if you can't catch some speeders? I'm sure someone's going four or five miles an hour over the speed limit."

Steve snorted at the comment. "Yeah, Andy. We're not hurting anyone. And no one lives here anymore."

"Makes me wonder who called it in," John added.

Tyler inclined his head and leaned the rifle against the fence rail. "I'm surprised you're working today, Officer Eller," he said casually. "I thought Mathews was on duty."

"Glad to see you're keeping tabs on the county's business," Andy said. "Officer Mathews called in sick. I'm covering for him."

"That's a shame. Be sure to tell him I said I hope he gets to feelin' better soon." Tyler's words oozed with venom, full of unspoken warnings.

Andy didn't say anything at first. He knew Tyler and his cronies had Brad Mathews in their back pocket. Brad was too easy on them; let them get away with pretty much everything. Rumor had it the newcomer, Tyler Mumford, had been slipping little rewards now and then—sometimes cash, sometimes other, more subtle bribes of a more feminine persuasion.

"I'm sorry, Tyler," Andy said, his words catching in his throat. "I'm going to have to confiscate that rifle. And your beers."

"My rifle?" Tyler sounded hurt.

Andy did everything he could to stand strong, to not let Tyler and the others intimidate him.

"And the beers?"

The deputy gave an exaggerated nod. And with the threat, he inched his thumb closer to the pistol. The men couldn't see the move since his body was turned slightly.

"Yep," Andy said. "The beers too. That's what I said."

Andy stood as tall as Tyler, maybe a half inch taller. Their lanky frames mirrored each other, though Tyler's arms rippled with veins and sinew from his years in the military. He clearly kept up at least a semblance of his former training regimen. The deputy, on the other hand, appeared slimmer, though not weak in his own right.

Tyler nodded, pouting his lips in a sort of mocking surrender. "Well, all right then." He lifted the beer and drained its contents down his throat in less than three seconds, then tossed the empty bottle at the deputy's feet. It hit the ground with a clank and rolled to a stop when it hit the tip of Andy's boot. Tyler looked at his friends. "You heard him, boys. Give him your beers."

The others followed suit and chugged their drinks until the bottles were empty. They rolled them to the officer and then stood defiantly, waiting to see what he would do next.

Andy swallowed and nodded. "Rifle," he said, his voice only half-full of resolve. "You fellas step away from it. Nice and slow."

Tyler's eyebrows descended, feigning offense. "Now, Andy, you afraid I'm going to do something with that rifle? I wouldn't think of it."

"Just step away, Tyler. All of you."

Tyler licked his lips. This cop had no idea who he was dealing with. He'd seen the deputy alter his stance, which meant he was prepared to draw that pistol if the need arose. What Andy didn't know was that he'd cornered a venomous snake, fully coiled and capable of flipping that rifle over and blowing his head clean off before the deputy's pistol was above his waist.

That wouldn't do, though, and Tyler knew it. Murdering a police officer would be difficult even for him to cover up. This deputy, however, was a thorn in his side. He'd have to think of another way to get rid of him. An accident, perhaps.

Tyler put up his hands and eased to the right. "Step aside, boys," he ordered. "Let this lawman do his job. We were breaking the rules, after all."

"Thank you," Andy said, though suspicion still filled his veins.

When the four men were a good fifteen feet from the weapon, Andy shuffled over to it and lifted it off the ground.

"You can come get this at the office later," he said. He removed the magazine and checked the weapon to make sure there were no more rounds chambered.

Satisfied, he backed over to the patrol car and laid the rifle in the trunk.

"That it, deputy?" Tripp asked. "Or are you going to arrest us?"

Andy knew he couldn't do that. Tripp was the sheriff's son. He should have taken the keys to their jeep, called in for backup to arrest all of them. But none of that could happen.

"Let's call it a warning," Andy offered.

"That what this is? You warning me?"

Andy opened his door and put one foot inside. He locked eyes with Tripp for a long breath, then exhaled. "Yeah. It is."

The four men watched as the deputy drove away, not taking their eyes off the vehicle until it disappeared around the bend, behind a patch of spruce trees.

Tyler sighed, his breath coming out of his mouth in a chilly cloud.

"He's got a lot of nerve," Steve said. "Sometimes I think he forgets his place."

"My dad will make sure he remembers," Tripp threatened.

"No harm, boys," Tyler said, his voice as cold as the snow on the ground. "Like he said, I can get the rifle back later. Let's finish these beers and head to the bar. Might be a few early snow bunnies in town from the city."

THREE

CUCHARA

Dak peered around at the surrounding forest, full of aspens and Piñon pines. The silent serenity overwhelmed him and for a moment, he felt at total peace.

The unfamiliar, strange feeling unnerved him in a way. He could ill-afford to let down his guard at any time, especially when on the hunt—and he was certainly hunting.

He climbed the wooden steps to the cabin and crossed the creaky porch planks to the door. Stopping, he entered the prescribed code on a keypad next to the doorknob.

An electronic beep, followed by a mechanical whir, unlocked the deadbolt. He stepped inside and closed the door behind, keeping his rucksack snug against his shoulder.

Dak surveyed the cabin from the narrow foyer. An open door led into a bedroom to the left. To his right, key hooks hung from the wall next to a coat hanger made out of faux antlers. At least he thought they were fake.

He continued farther into the kitchen on the right that merged with the living room. Deep, brown leather couches surrounded a thick rug topped with a rustic, wooden coffee table. The gas fireplace beyond was framed with mountain stone and a timber mantle that matched the beams supporting the cathedral ceiling overhead.

"This'll do," Dak muttered.

It was way more than he needed in terms of space and amenities —though the hot tub on the front porch overlooking the valley beckoned to his sore muscles. Travel had taken a toll on him and he yearned to relax.

Perhaps he could take a soak after doing a little recon in town.

He didn't dare to hope. In fact, Dak couldn't recall the last time he—yes, he could. That annoying tug at his heart jerked painfully at his chest. Before he went away to join the army, Dak and Nicole took a ski trip up to Snowshoe, West Virginia. Their chalet was much smaller than this one, and far more modest, but it had a hot tub—as seemed standard with all cabins.

That was the last time he'd been in one.

He sighed at the memory and let his gear bag slump onto the couch. He patted the concealed subcompact pistol on his hip—an old habit he'd forged long ago. With his outer shell jacket over a hoodie, no one would notice the weapon. And as long as he didn't run face to face into Billy—or Tyler—no one in the little mountain town would know who he was. To them, Dak would be just another traveler coming through in search of adventure or some peace and quiet.

Dak wandered over to the island in the kitchen and found a welcome basket with a couple of bottles of water, some candy, chips, and tips on some of the local things to do. He looked through the list and found a couple of places he knew he'd need to visit. One was the general store. He would pick up some additional supplies in case his stay would last more than a few days. Dak was certain it would.

The only bar in the town looked like an interesting place on the list. In the summer, people were welcome to bring their dogs there to hang out on the patio. Dak had seen a place like that in St. Pete Beach, Florida, once, though it was late at night and only one person was sober enough to bring their dog out at that hour. Or maybe they were drunk enough. He figured the local bartender would have at least a little information that might prove helpful, though he knew he'd have to play it cool.

Small towns like this one could have allies or enemies mere inches away, and it was always difficult to tell which was which.

Dak walked around the rest of the cabin, inspecting the upstairs bedroom, the loft, and the deck out front. He rested his hands on the newly fallen snow along the rail, letting the cold stab into his fingers. He looked down into the valley, his gaze sweeping over the slopes. To the average observer, they may have believed he was simply enjoying the view. He was, but more than that, Dak's mind ran through potential approach points in case somehow Billy brought the fight to him.

It was unlikely, but Dak always prepared for any contingency.

He turned, sweeping the powdery snow from the rail, and returned inside.

After locking the doors and securing his rucksack in the upstairs bedroom closet, he went back out to the Isuzu Trooper he'd purchased in Denver, and headed back down the mountain.

He had to drive slowly along the twisting, winding road. Though the snow was still thin in most spots, it could still be slick. After ten minutes, he was back on the main road. The clear asphalt was a welcome relief to a guy from the southeast who'd grown up almost never having to drive on snow of any kind—save for that once-a-year winter storm that sprinkled two or three meager inches of accumulation.

From the mountain road, the drive into the little town of Cuchara only took another seven minutes.

Dak slowed down as he passed a welcome sign where one of the local police cars sat partially hidden behind it. A speed trap.

He rolled his eyes and continued into the little town.

Calling it a town was generous. It looked more like a village with only a few buildings on the left and right, most appearing like structures that were built during the times of the Wild West when outlaws roamed the land. A liquor store, gift shop, general store, and a few other wooden buildings stood on the right. Up ahead, he noted the bar and grill he'd spotted on the list at the cabin and steered into the parking lot off to the left in front of a wooden rail.

Five other vehicles occupied spots outside the bar. It was getting late in the afternoon, and Dak expected more people to show up in the next hour or so. The more the merrier as far as he was concerned, so long as none of them was Billy.

He walked up the clean-swept wooden steps to the wraparound deck and pulled open the door. Inside, the bar looked pretty much exactly as he'd expected. Rough-hewn, dark-stained panels covered the walls. A litany of various beer-brand neon lights hung sporadically around the room. The U-shaped bar occupied the center, directly across from the entrance. A female bartender and a male bar back worked next to each other, one pouring drinks, the other wiping down the counter and carrying beverages to the patrons scattered across the room.

The bartender tipped her head up at him the way she must have greeted every person who walked through the door.

"Seating's open," she said. "If you want a table, Merrick will take care of you."

"Thanks," Dak said. He spotted a table in the back corner of the room that would give him a full view of everything and ambled over to it.

Merrick, who was apparently both a server and the bar back, hustled over to him with a glass of water and a laminated one-page menu. The young man was skinny with a thin, black mustache under his nose that matched the dense clump of hair on his head.

The bartender—probably in her mid-twenties—was an attractive, outdoorsy type with a black tank top that revealed a collection of tattoos that adorned her arms and one at the top of her chest just below the neck. Her light brown hair was pulled back in a ponytail that whipped around as she worked feverishly to keep the drinks coming.

Dak didn't know what her hurry was with so few patrons in the building. He guessed she was trying to stay ahead before the afternoon rush, if there was one.

"Can I get you anything stronger than water?" Merrick asked.

"A local lager would be good," Dak said.

"We have a few of those as well as some good IPAs if that's your thing," the young man offered.

"Nah, the lager is fine," Dak said. "If I wanted to taste a pine tree, I'd go outside and lick one."

The server snorted a laugh at the unexpected comment. "Haven't heard it put like that before. And now I don't know if I can ever drink another IPA." He laughed as he started to turn away. "Oh, did you want something to eat?"

"How are the burgers here?" Dak asked, perusing the menu with analytical eyes.

"They're really good, though we have an excellent bison burger."

"Let's do that with fries," Dak said.

"You got it. I'll be right back with your drink." Merrick didn't even bother writing down the order as he scurried over to a computer panel affixed to the bar and began tapping on the screen.

Dak leaned back against the seat and scanned the room, taking note of each of the customers. Most of them were unremarkable. There were at least two sets of visitors, men and women probably in their forties. One of the couples had a kid with them, a little boy in an orange coat. The bar was toasty warm and seeing the kid unnecessarily clad in the outerwear reminded Dak that he still had his on. He slipped out of it and hung the coat on the back of the chair, watching as the bartender filled up a glass from one of the beer taps.

A female server burst out of a light blue kitchen door to Dak's immediate left. She carried a food-laden tray in her right hand—the plates cradling burgers, fries, onion rings, and a grilled chicken breast.

Dak watched the woman carry the food over to the table with the small family of three and expertly unload the burden onto the table before giving them a pleasant smile and asking if they needed anything else.

The people declined and the waitress spun on her heels and returned through the blue door with a whoosh.

Dak managed to catch sigh of her name tag as she passed. "Tanya," he said unemotionally under his breath.

Merrick returned a minute later with the lager and set the brimming pint glass down on the table atop a coaster he slid across the surface at the last second.

"That burger should be out in a couple of minutes," the waiter said.

"Thanks." Dak pulled the glass a little closer.

"Can I get you anything else while you're waiting?"

"Actually," Dak said. "I was curious. I'm from out of town."

Merrick chuckled. "Most people who come through here are. Not sure if you noticed, but this isn't a big town."

Dak allowed a grin to part his lips. "Yeah, but I like it. It's quiet here, not too many people around. And this valley is breathtaking."

Merrick looked around at the walls as if he could see through them at the natural beauty surrounding the building. "Yeah," he said proudly, "it's the reason I live here. Not many people to bother you if you know how to keep your head down."

That last addition caused Dak's ears to prick.

"What do you mean?"

The server backtracked, twitching his nose as he shook his head. "Oh, nothing."

"Ah. Well," Dak shrugged it off. "I'm actually curious about a couple of the abandoned ski resorts around here. I heard about them when I was in Denver and thought it might be fun to take a look around—if that sort of thing is permitted."

Merrick nodded. "Yeah, I mean, you can visit one of them. If you're wanting to hit the slopes you'd have to get permission from the organization that bought it, but the other one was purchased several months back."

"Purchased?" Dak feigned being impressed. "That had to be an expensive buy." He drew a sip of beer from his glass, keeping his eyes on the server's reaction.

"You'd be right to assume that. I don't recall the amount, but it wasn't cheap." He shifted uncomfortably.

"Local person or someone from out of the area?"

The young man's face blushed, and he looked around over his shoulders, growing more uneasy by the second. "Out-of-town guy." He lowered his voice. "His name is Tyler Mumford. Just... forget about that place. If you want to see the old abandoned resort, it's just up the road. You can't miss it. The runs are still there, big trails through the trees you can see for miles."

"Thanks for the tip," Dak said, his own cheeks burning—for an entirely different reason.

"Sure thing. I'll go check on that bison burger for you."

Merrick turned to leave, and Dak stopped him.

"Just out of curiosity," he said, holding the beer close to his lips again. "What was the name of the place the stranger bought?"

Merrick glanced over at the bartender. She busily poured a whiskey into a tumbler on the other side of the counter, well outside of earshot. Merrick leaned subtly and spoke with uncertainty. "It's called Purgatory Peak."

FOUR

CUCHARA

Tyler shoved the door open and stepped into the county police department building. He ignored the receptionist to his left and kept walking, leaving the woman licking her lips as she wondered what she should do.

"Um, Mr. Mumford?"

"The sheriff knows I'm coming, Amy," Tyler said without so much as a backward glance over his shoulder.

Amy pressed her lips together and nodded before returning to her computer work.

Tyler passed a couple of offices and a corridor leading into the holding tank, then stopped at a wooden door with a reinforced glass window in the center. A placard just below the window was imprinted with the name Sheriff Craig Sanders. The door was cracked open. Tyler took that as an invitation to enter.

He eased the door forward and tilted his head inside.

Sheriff Sanders was hunched over his desk, writing something with a black ink pen on what looked like an official form.

"You're not exactly making things easy for me, Tyler," he said without looking up from the desk.

He finished scribbling on the page and slid it to the side. Tyler stepped into the room and closed the door shut with a click. He shifted sideways to one of the twenty-five-year-old vinyl chairs opposite the cop and plopped into it.

"We weren't doing anything wrong, Sheriff," Tyler defended. "Just having a few beers, killing some bottles."

"With a rifle that some people would deem an assault weapon."

Tyler snorted and rolled his eyes. "You and I know better than that. It's a hunting rifle, Sheriff. Plain and simple."

Sanders leaned back and laced his fingers together atop the desk. "Sure it is, Tyler. But perception counts for a lot these days. Always has, but more now than ever. You know that."

"I do." Tyler slouched in the chair with his hands folded in his lap. Back in his military days, he never would have considered sitting that way. But these people didn't know his past. No one in Cuchara did. The best they knew, he was some rich guy who hit it big with an online business and decided he wanted to buy a mountain for himself.

Along with not knowing his real identity, the townsfolk also had no clue about what he'd been up to for the last eight months—accruing a vast amount of wealth with some well-played investments in the stock market. He doubted any of his other Delta Force teammates fared so well with their share, not that they needed to. The amount of money they made from the German's purchase of the Iraqi loot was more than enough to sustain someone for life. Billy, however, had always known that if he really wanted to be safe, he'd have to grow that initial cash pile into something more substantial.

When he arrived in Cuchara under the alias of Tyler Mumford, his net worth was a whopping thirty million, far more than any individual in the entire county as far as he knew. With such a hefty collection of assets behind him, Tyler set things in motion to get the cops on his side, along with a new set of friends he could ply for everything from information to enforcers.

He'd been surprised at how easily they all caved. Though, to be fair, he'd never been rich before.

Billy grew up in a small town with poor parents. The military had been the best chance for him to do anything with his life. Now that he had more than he could have ever imagined, he found it odd how people simply fell in line around his desires—even law enforcement.

"Then why do you insist on continuing to make trouble for me?" Sanders' leathery face sagged with a condemning scowl. He shook his head, barely moving the short, thinning grayish brown hair on top. Calculating blue eyes glared back at Tyler, full of unspoken accusations.

"I don't insist, Sheriff. Me and the boys were just having some fun. No one got hurt."

"How long until that happens, Tyler? What you were doing was irresponsible."

Tyler wanted to jump across the desk, grab the sheriff by the collar, and pound his face into the hard metal surface until he blacked out—or worse. Who was this idiot local to tell him what was irresponsible? If Sanders knew what he'd done, the people he'd killed, the way he'd killed them, he would think twice before offering a rebuke of any kind.

The cop may as well have been talking to a venomous snake sitting in that chair, trying to convince it to be a cuddly teddy bear.

Irresponsible. What a joke.

"Thanks for the tip, dad," he scoffed. "Now give me my rifle so I can get out of here."

The sheriff swallowed and shifted in his chair. "I'm the law around here, Tyler. Don't you forget that. What I say goes."

Tyler sat up a little straighter and leaned forward. "That's right, Sheriff. You are the law around here. You got yourself a cushy job." He played his hands out wide at the modest office. "A good paycheck. People respect you. What you say goes. But it would be a shame if word got out that you were taking money to turn a blind eye to certain things. Wouldn't it?"

Sanders' breathing quickened. "Are you threatening me, son?"

"We both know I am, Sheriff." Tyler's voice brimmed with rage, like a charging bull staring at a red cloak. "Like you said, perception means a lot these days."

He stood up and inclined his head. "Get a leash on your deputy before something bad happens to him. You understand?"

The sheriff nodded reluctantly, though he never locked eyes with the visitor. "Yeah."

"Good. Now give me my rifle."

FIVE

CUCHARA

Dak did his best to not ravenously consume the bison burger and fries he'd ordered. His military background begged him to down the entire plate in a few minutes, as he'd grown accustomed to doing during basic. That habit had been reinforced during his various deployments.

Eating slowly gave him cause to linger at the restaurant and bar for longer without facing too many questions, though he knew he'd have to keep ordering beers now and then to prevent Merrick from getting annoyed. Servers depended on their tables for a constant influx of money during their shifts and there was nothing worse than a group of people sitting around chatting it up for an hour or more while new customers were sat at other servers' tables. Dak knew as long as he kept spending money, Merrick wouldn't mind. Plus, he'd leave a big tip—especially if he could ply the young man for more information.

After sitting there for thirty minutes, the waiter came by a third time and asked if he could get him dessert or another beer.

"This is good lager," Dak said. "I'll definitely have another one. Sorry if I'm drinking them slow. Don't want to catch a buzz."

"Well, if you like we can get you a cab back to wherever you're staying." Merrick risked asking the obvious question. "You at a cabin in the area?"

"Yeah," Dak said with a single nod. "Not far from here. Took about eighteen minutes, but I don't think it's more than three or four miles away. Had to take it slow with the dusting of snow y'all got."

"Smart," Merrick offered.

"Don't worry," Dak said, tilting the nearly empty beer glass. "I won't hang around too long." He looked out over the room, noting how it was beginning to fill with more patrons. "I'll just have one more and be on my way. I know you guys need these tables."

Merrick twisted his head around, looking out over the bar. "I'm not too worried about it. You take as long as you want. And you did say you want another lager, right?"

"Please."

"I'll get that right away for you."

He made a beeline back to the bar and asked the bartender for another lager. Dak noted that this time, the young man didn't enter the drink in the computer before he retrieved the full glass and brought it back.

"This one's on me," Merrick said.

Dak furrowed his brow, surprised. "For what?"

The server rolled his shoulders nonchalantly. "For understanding. And being cool. Most people would sit around and take up a table for an hour or more and not think twice about it. You're considerate and I appreciate that."

"Likewise," Dak said. He tipped the glass to the young man.

The front door barged open and swung around so hard it nearly slammed into the doorstop. The dim light of dusk poured into the bar as three young men, probably in their late twenties at best, sauntered in.

Merrick swiveled around. His head drooped visibly upon seeing them. "Oh great," he mumbled.

"Friends of yours?" Dak pried.

The server retreated a little with his downtrodden attitude, knowing that it was inappropriate to show such emotion in front of a customer. "No, they're just... locals. That's all."

"I see." Dak didn't need to get the full story. He could fill in the blanks from the newcomers' body language—the way they walked in as if they owned the place, snickering and making snide comments about some of the customers as they made their way to one of the tables on Dak's side of the room.

They plopped down in the booth and started looking through the menu. One of them—the average-sized one of the group—slapped his hand on the table and waved his hand, calling out for Tanya.

"Not your table, huh?"

"No, fortunately for me. Not so fortunate for Tanya."

Dak took a long sip of the remnants in his glass, then slid the empty container off to the edge of the table.

The woman he'd seen before appeared through the blue door and stalked over to the guys at the booth.

Dak saw everything: the annoyed look on the bartender's face, the fear on Merrick's, and the anger on Tanya's as she passed, loosely carrying a notepad in one hand with a pen tucked behind her right ear.

"Do you idiots always have to be so loud when you come in here?" Dak heard the woman ask.

He winced, knowing already that her question would spark further belligerence.

"You sure got a lot of attitude for a plate slinger," the instigator said. If he made an effort to keep his voice down, it was minimal.

"What do you want, Tripp?" she asked.

The man eyed her up and down and licked his lips. "I think you know."

She huffed. "To drink, moron. What do you want to drink?"

"Just because your husband is a cop doesn't mean you have to play hard to get with me. We both know he can't take care of you the way I could."

She tilted her head to the right and put her left hand on her hip. "If, by take care of, you mean annoy and disappoint me, you're right."

The other two men at the table snickered at the comeback.

The one called Tripp blushed, but quickly recovered. "Shut up, you two. It's all part of the chase. Ain't that right?" He started to reach out his hand to touch her other hip but she swatted it away.

"Don't you ever touch me," she warned.

His playful idiocy turned to embarrassment, then rage. Dak could see it in his eyes from his side of the room. He'd witnessed that same look a dozen times back in the days he frequented bars with his buddies. It was a look that always came calling when someone had had too much to drink and was too easily offended.

"Okay," he relented, but the venom in his voice said otherwise. "Bring me a beer. And a round for my friends, too."

"Maybe you've had too many already, Tripp."

"We would have," the tallest one said from across the table. "But your husband interrupted our fun."

"Yeah," the runt of the group agreed. He was stocky, built like a football or rugby player. "So, in a way, you only have him to blame for us being here."

"Exactly," Tripp finished the thought.

"Three beers coming up," Tanya surrendered. She turned to head over to the bar when Tripp stopped her.

"Hey. Aren't you going to ask what kind of beer we'd like?"

Dak saw her eyes roll as she exhaled, exhausting every ounce of patience left in her reserves. She wheeled around on her heels and ambled back to the booth.

"What kind of beer would you like?"

"What have you got?" Tripp antagonized.

"You know exactly what we have. Same as we always do. Stop being an idiot. Just because your daddy is the sheriff doesn't mean you have the right to be stupid."

The two friends cackled again, adding in some ooo's and ahh's.

"What kinds?" Tripp demanded, choosing to ignore the barb.

A few of the other patrons hastily collected their things and started making their way out of the bar. The few who still had food on their plates ate faster, sensing either something bad was about to happen, or just too uncomfortable to deal with the scene.

"We have an IPA, a lager, and a pale ale from local breweries," Tanya recited. "All major domestics, both on draft and in bottles."

"Three IPA's on draft then," Tripp said. "And bring us fresh ones every ten minutes."

She spared the energy of fighting the demand and spun around. She reached the computer station with a sigh of relief and started entering their orders.

The bartender slid over to Tanya, looking at her apologetically. "I'm sorry," she said, quiet enough for only Tanya to hear, though Dak caught it too. "They'll have a few beers and be on their way."

"I know," Tanya said, forcing herself to be strong.

Dak admired her immediately for not letting them see any weakness.

"Sorry about all that," Merrick said under his breath, leaning over the table. "Those guys, they think they own the town."

Dak hefted the fresh glass of beer and took a sip. "Do they?"

"Yeah. They definitely think that."

"No," Dak corrected. "Do they own the town?"

Merrick's right eye twitched at the question, and he shook his head. "No. I mean, I don't think so."

"Who does?"

The server blinked rapidly. "I mean... no one questions what they do." He lowered his voice out of caution. "Tripp is the sheriff's son."

"And who does the sheriff answer to?"

Merrick swallowed, suddenly aware that he'd been standing at the table for far too long.

"I know you have other tables to take care of," Dak said, attempting to ease the young man's mind.

Merrick glanced over his shoulder. "Actually, one just left and one looks like they're about to."

Dak reached into his pocket and pulled out a silver money clip. He pulled back two slides on either side and pressed them together, loosening the fold. He produced a hundred-dollar bill and slid it across the table. There was at least another that Merrick could see, along with several more bills of unknown denominations.

"I'm going to keep this table for a while," Dak said. "This is for your trouble."

Merrick eyed the money hungrily. It was more than he'd make in his entire shift, or at least close to it.

"And I'll give you another one if you let me sit here until you close down."

The server stared at the bill for several seconds, then met Dak's intense gaze. "Seriously?"

"Seriously. All I ask is you keep bringing me drinks every twenty minutes or so. Make it look like I'm drinking them. I have no intention of getting hammered tonight, so if you don't fill them up that's fine by me. Understood?"

"I think so, sure."

"Good." Dak nudged the hundred an inch closer to the server. "Go on. Take it. And another one at closing."

"Okay. Thank you."

"You're welcome. And thank you."

Merrick started to turn and check on his other remaining table, then he paused, and shifted closer, hovering over the edge of Dak's nearly empty plate. "You asked me who the sheriff answers to."

Dak neither confirmed nor denied. He merely answered with a blank stare.

"Before... he didn't answer to anyone. Then Tyler Mumford showed up. Thick as thieves, those two. If I didn't know better—and you didn't hear this from me—I'd say the sheriff is in Mr. Mumford's back pocket."

Dak inclined his head and gave an understanding nod. "Thanks, Merrick. Go check on those other people. I have a feeling they don't want to hang around much longer."

The young server hurried away while Dak kept a close watch on the booth at the other end of the room and the three hoodlums who occupied it.

SIX

CUCHARA

Dak sat at the table for the next three hours, only getting up now and then to go to the restroom. Merrick continued to do as requested, dropping off a beer every twenty minutes or so to keep up appearances.

The troublemakers at the booth hung around for a little over two hours before paying their bill—albeit with demands that they be given the meal and drinks on the house.

When they were gone, Dak gave it another thirty minutes before he decided to get up and leave as well.

When Merrick came around, Dak thanked him and slid a second hundred across the table. "I appreciate you letting me hang here," he said.

"Not a problem at all, man," Merrick stuttered. "But I thought you were going to stay till closing."

Dak looked around the room and twitched his left shoulder in a shrug. "Looks like things are dying down now. Think I'll head on back to the cabin and get some rest."

"All right. Well, thanks again. You get home safe."

"Will do."

Dak ambled slowly toward the door, eyes sweeping the room for the hundredth time to make sure he wasn't missing anything, or anyone. Once outside, he padded down the steps, wary that ice could have formed during the time he'd been inside. At the bottom, he zipped up his coat and exhaled into the chilly night air.

His gaze drifted up toward the sky. Stars speckled the black canvas above like diamonds in a tar field. The only light pollution keeping it from being a pristine view came from the lights in the parking lot and the one over the porch at the entrance. The other shops across the street were closed and their lights dimmed for the evening.

Dak longed for a few minutes in the cabin hot tub even more, but noticed something out of the corner of his left eye that told him he'd get no such luxury tonight—at least not soon.

A black Ford Explorer sat across the parking lot under a collection of four pine trees. Dak only allowed his vision to pan across the vehicle so the occupants wouldn't think he'd noticed. But he did.

The silhouettes of the three men inside the SUV stood out against the clear moonlight in the valley behind them. Their faces remained shrouded in shadows, but Dak could feel their vapid gaze fixed on the entrance to the bar, perhaps only momentarily flashing at him as the lone point of change in their view.

Dak knew they were there before he saw their outlines. It was why he'd decided to hang around for the last three plus hours. He'd seen it before. Pretty young woman gets hit on by the village idiots, then they wait to harass her when she gets off work because she denied their advances.

Harassment would be the mildest version of how it could go down. He hoped that's all it would be.

Dak continued shuffling toward his car, swerving a little in one direction and the other to make it appear he might be a little too buzzed to drive home. If Tripp and his two friends were paying attention, they'd deem Dak a harmless drunk and continue watching the bar's front door.

He fumbled with his keys when he arrived at the driver's side door and then made a show of inserting it in the keyhole, then dropping the keys to the ground. As he bent down to pick them up, he peered through the windows of the Isuzu and noted the men's forms shaking a little. In the utter silence of the Rocky Mountains, Dak thought he could even hear a little laughter.

Perfect, he thought. They were paying attention to him and now making fun of his perceived drunken state.

Dak managed to unlock the SUV on the second try and climbed in, then slumped back in the seat and used the button on the side to decline it toward the rear.

He imagined Tripp's crew believed him to be getting ready to sleep off a tough night of drinking in the parking lot. That was the goal, though it was possible they weren't that gullible.

Dak allowed enough space for his eyes to see over the edge of the window toward the bar's porch so he would know when the next person left.

Thirty minutes went by and no one from the Explorer came over to pester him. They clearly had one goal in mind for the night. And Tanya was the target.

Dak wondered where her husband could be, why he wouldn't be sitting here in the parking lot to wait for her shift to end. He'd overheard that the man was a deputy in the local police force. Had Tanya not called her husband? Maybe she wasn't concerned about the earlier altercation.

That had to be it.

Civilians—most anyway—didn't think about things like that. They weren't always on alert like Dak, perpetually considering every ripple along the water's surface from the slightest disturbance.

He didn't want to call it naivety, but he knew that was the right word. It was why he was sitting there in his Isuzu, waiting for the building to clear out. A side door opened and Merrick stepped out of the building with the bartender. They each went to their respective cars, a white Subaru Outback and an old pickup truck. The lights inside the bar flickered off as the other two started their engines and pulled out of the lot.

Dak refocused his attention on the entrance. He didn't have to wait long for what he feared. Tanya emerged through the front door with a set of keys in one hand and a paper cup in another. She locked the door and spun around nonchalantly, waving to Merrick and the bartender as they drove off.

She took a sip from a red straw and made her way down the steps, veering toward a black Toyota Land Cruiser at the back of the lot near the road.

It was a twenty-five yard walk to her car. Dak was somewhere between, with the threat behind her.

He remained low and out of sight until he saw the headlights of the Explorer turn on, their beams shining brightly through the lot. The engine roared a second later, followed by tires scratching against the lot, kicking gravel and dust out behind them.

Tripp wheeled the SUV around, nearly sliding sideways in the process, and steered the vehicle straight at Tanya. All she could do was turn her head into the blinding light of the oncoming threat.

SEVEN

CUCHARA

Tanya cringed as the SUV ground to a halt. Clouds of gravel dust plumed out from the tires and billowed dramatically in front of the headlights. The high beams seared her eyes, and she put up her left hand to shield them from the blinding light. She stepped back, shifting away from the focus of the headlights, and lowered her hand, peering into the cab as the doors slammed shut.

She swore under her breath. "Tripp, you idiot. What are you doing? You could have hit me."

Tripp sauntered toward her as the sound of two more doors slamming shut accompanied his approach. His shoulders slumped a little and his legs wobbled. "Idiot? That's not a nice thing to say, Tanya."

"You're drunk, Tripp. You need to call a cab."

"I'm not calling anyone. And I'm not drunk." He stepped toward her. Lust oozed from the devil's gaze that filled his eyes. His friends, John and Steve, loomed a few feet away to her left, just out of the headlights' glow, their eyes locked on her.

"Fine," she said nervously. "Suit yourself. Drive home if you want to, but I don't think your daddy will appreciate that."

He surged forward in an instant and grabbed her arm. Gripping it tightly, he glowered at her, his eyes rampant with alcohol-fueled desire.

"Let me go, Tripp," Tanya demanded. There was no hiding the fear in her voice. "You're hurting me."

"You should have been nicer to me," he said, spittle flying with each word. "But no worries. I always get what I want in the end."

He grabbed her other arm even as she tried to wrestle free. His grip was too strong and she couldn't get loose, so she did the only thing she knew how to do. Tanya kicked as hard as she could with her knee, driving it deep into his groin.

Tripp's eyes bulged, and he doubled over, groaning in agony. His fingers let go of her arms and went to his wounded area as he dropped to his knees.

He let out a string of obscenities. More than a few of the adjectives described her in a less than complimentary way.

Tanya turned and started to run toward her truck.

"Get her," Tripp ordered, his voice still lathered in nauseating pain.

His cronies jumped at the command and took off after her. Tanya barely reached the truck in time. She fumbled with the keys in her panic, seeming to take minutes to get the one to her vehicle. As she inserted the correct key into the door, she felt four hands grab her by the shoulders and arms.

"Where you think you're going?" Steve said, his thick digits digging deep into her skin.

"No!" Tanya shrieked. "Let me go! Stop it!"

Tripp had recovered—mostly—and made his way toward her as his friends held her on both sides. She struggled as best she could, like a wild animal wriggling and jerking around to get free. Tripp was still hunched over as he stalked toward her, one hand over his groin, signaling the pain was still racking him.

He stopped a few feet short of her and shook his head, looking into her eyes with disgust. "That was stupid," he said. He slapped her across the face with the back of his hand.

The cheek reddened almost instantly, though barely noticeable in the dimly lit parking lot.

"I was going to let you know what it felt like to be with a real man. You would have liked it. But now?" He shook his head. "Now I'm going to make sure you don't."

"No," she said, pleading with her eyes. "Tripp, don't do this. You're drunk. You can't do this."

"I can," he said. "My dad is the sheriff. I can do whatever I want."

Her head twisted back and forth. "No. Please."

"That's good," he said. "Keep begging. That'll make it even more fun." He looked at John. "Open up the back of her truck."

"No!" she shouted. "Please, someone! Help me!"

John took the keys out of the door where they still hung and walked around to the back of the SUV.

"You can't do this," Tanya went on. "I will press charges, Tripp. I'll tell everyone about this."

He shuffled closer as she struggled against Steve's strong grip. He reached up with a finger and touched her chin. She snapped her head away, unwilling to look into his eyes another second.

"Well, I guess it would be your word against ours now, wouldn't it? I mean, me and the boys left the bar a long time ago. Everyone saw that. After we took off, we decided to head over to Tyler's place and hang out. I'm sure Tyler will vouch for that."

"No," she tried to deny it. "You can't get away with this."

He ignored her. "I'm sure you'd try to tell someone what happened. So I guess we're just going to have to make sure that doesn't happen. Will be easier for all of us if you're dead."

Her head whipped around again at the new threat and she met his eyes. "Tripp, please. Don't. Don't."

"Oh, I'm still going to have my fun with you. All of us will. Right, boys?" He cast the words over her shoulder.

The other two snickered amid a series of oh, yeahs.

John opened the back of the SUV and stepped back into view.

"Take her around to the back," Tripp said, noting the scene of the crime was ready.

"Hey!" a new voice cut in.

Tripp spun around and saw the drunk from before. The man was around six feet tall, give or take. He staggered through the explorer's headlight beams in a serpentine fashion, zigzagging his way across the parking lot.

"Can you morons keep it down over there?" the man slurred. "I'm trying to get some sleep."

He stopped fifteen feet away, his body tilting to the left. Then the man felt his balance waning and over corrected, suddenly shifting to the right in a dramatic show of intoxication.

"This is none of your concern, stranger," Tripp said. The pain in his groin had finally subsided, eased by the work of gravity. "Go on back to your truck and sleep it off."

"That's what I'm sayin'," the stranger said, throwing his hands up in the air as if a long-made point was finally understood. "I musta had ten or fourteen beers and you are in no condition to drive me home."

Tripp's eyebrows lowered at the man's nonsensical comment. He'd had a few drinks, but he was far from blown out the way this guy was.

"Look, stranger," Tripp continued, "we don't want any trouble. So, just stumble back over to your vehicle and close your eyes. We'll be leaving here soon enough."

Dak's upper body wobbled in orbit over his waist. He shuffled forward, closing the gap between him and Tripp by another six feet before stopping and nearly tipping over onto his face.

"Trouble? Am I in trouble? You guys aren't cops, are you?" The slurred words continued, accentuated with peaks and valleys in pitch that continued to drive home the notion he was inebriated beyond comprehension.

Tripp snorted and looked back at Steve, who continued to hold the struggling woman.

"Yeah, that's it, buddy. We're cops. And this woman is under arrest."

"They're not cops!" Tanya shouted. "My husband is a county deputy. Please, sir, call the police. Don't let them do this!"

Dak stumbled another five feet forward, teetering on the edge of falling flat on his face or tipping over backward.

He leaned forward, eyelids narrowed to slits as he peered into Tripp's face. "Listen, occifer," he spat, body still wavering. "I need to report a crime."

Tripp almost couldn't keep himself from laughing, briefly forgetting about his wicked intentions.

"Tell you what," Tripp offered, "go back over to your vehicle and rest for a bit. When we're done with her, I'll make sure to take care of you."

"You promise?" Dak blathered.

"Definitely. We'll handle it as soon as we're done with her."

Dak rocked back onto his heels. He hiccupped once and nodded. "All right, then. Just hurry up, would you? I really need to get some sleep."

Tripp nodded. "Yeah, you go back over there to your truck and do that. We'll wake you up when we're ready to hear your complaint."

"No!" Tanya yelled. "Don't listen to him!"

Steve clamped his left hand over her mouth, wrapping his arm around her torso with the right and squeezing hard. She tried to scream, but the muted sounds didn't go far.

Dak started to turn around, then paused. He scuffed his feet forward again, closing the distance between him and Tripp to less than five feet. "Hey. Isn't that the waitress from the bar?"

Tripp took a threatening step toward Dak, irritation brimming in his eyes. His face tensed with anger. "Listen, stranger. Don't make me ask you again. You need to go back to your vehicle and mind your business. We'll take care of your problem as soon as we're done with her."

The sheriff's son didn't realize the danger. He'd stepped well within striking distance, assuming that this drunkard was no threat.

"What are y'all going to do with her?" Dak asked. He already knew the answer. He'd seen their plan unfolding, heard what they said. They were going to use her for their own perverted needs and then kill her. In his eyes, that meant their lives were forfeit.

He'd hoped Tanya's husband would show up, or that the bartender or even Merrick would return to collect something they'd forgotten. Not that either of them would be of use. Since he'd been out here, though, Dak hadn't seen a single car go by.

Sure, he could beat these guys up, hope to teach them a lesson. But they wouldn't learn. Men like this would simply find another target, another woman, or even the same one at a later time. The sheriff wouldn't help with an investigation if charges were pressed. She would be shamed as a liar, and her husband would look even weaker in her eyes.

Her world would crumble and these scumbags would get to keep on keeping on as if nothing had ever happened. And Tyler would help with the coverup.

Dak had wanted to be more calculated in drawing out his old Delta Force teammate. Those fanciful plans, however, were tossed by the wayside.

"You going to have a little fun with her before you arrest her?" Dak asked, his words still slurred, but only slightly.

"I told you to mind your business, stranger. Don't make me use force."

Dak looked around, as if searching the parking lot for something. "You know," he said. "I don't see your patrol car around here? You three in unmarked vehicles or something? Is that explorer an undercover thing?"

Tripp had heard enough. He took one last step toward Dak.

Menace flamed in his eyes. "I'm telling you for the last time, stranger. Go back to your vehicle. This is none of your concern."

Dak's spine stiffened. The wobble vanished and his legs steadied. The distant, glazed look in his eyes disappeared, replaced by fierce and righteous indignation.

"Unfortunately, Tripp, I'm making it my concern."

EIGHT

CUCHARA

Confusion shone in Tripp's eyes for a second, but only for a second. Dak's fist smashed into his jaw. Tripp's head snapped to the right, and he stumbled backward onto his butt, barely able to catch himself with his hands as he hit the ground.

Steve still held the struggling woman, but when he saw the stranger hit his friend, his grip loosened. Tanya jerked her elbow back into his gut and felt his arm drop away. The blow wasn't much, but it was enough, and she darted away from him, retreating behind the stranger and pulling her phone out of her pocket.

"You've made a big mistake, stranger," John said, stalking toward Dak from the shadows behind Tanya's SUV. "You have any idea who you just hit?"

"A punk who probably wasn't spanked enough by his daddy when he was little," Dak answered.

"That right?"

"Seems to be."

Tripp scrambled to his feet, feeling the wounded jaw with his fingers. He grimaced at the pain throbbing through his face.

Steve circled around to the left, Tripp to the right, as the towering Collinsworth approached straight ahead.

"Looks like we have ourselves a hero," Tripp said. His voice tightened with pain. "You're going to pay for that one, Mr. Hero."

Dak heard Tanya on the phone behind him, telling her husband to get there as fast as he could, rapidly explaining what was happening.

"You shouldn't have done that," Tripp went on. "We were just having some fun with her."

"That's not what I heard and saw," Dak countered. "You were going to rape her and then kill her."

"I guess it's your word against ours, then, Mr. Hero."

"Yeah, Mr. Hero," Steve prodded. He was the consummate bully sidekick, making up for a lifetime of shortcomings.

"I'm not a hero, but I've seen your kind before," Dak said, his eyes locked on Tripp, keeping a watch on the other two in his peripheral vision. "You'd throw an innocent life away just so you can get your jollies. You don't know where to draw the line. So, I guess someone's got to draw it for you."

Tripp shook his head. "I don't think so. And when we're done with you, we'll finish what we started with her sooner or later. You hear me, Tanya? This is not over."

He and the other two closed in on Dak. Tripp raised his hands in bad boxing form. Dak sensed the other two moving quickly at him from either side, just behind his field of view. It was a typical strategy for people who didn't know much about hand-to-hand combat. The two thugs would try to grab him and hold him so their buddy could pummel away.

Dak heard the gravel scuff to his side and drop stepped back, bringing both of the assailants into full view. He dropped down nearly to his knee and swept his right leg at the taller of the two. His heel caught John on the shin, hitting it hard enough to hurt, but more importantly, knock the big man off his balance. He stumbled forward and collided with the much shorter guy on the left. The two nearly fell, but Steve managed to catch his partner and steady himself.

That recovery didn't stop the next attack from coming.

Dak sprang up once more and lunged forward. Steve saw him coming and shoved John away to brace for what he thought would be a tackling impact.

Instead, Dak faked to one side and dipped to the other, raised his arm, and clothes lined the shorter man in the nook between his forearm and biceps. The blow crushed Steve's windpipe a split second before he felt his feet lift off the ground. Time seemed to slow as the air beneath him left nothing but wonder as to when he would hit the ground.

His tailbone struck gravel with a crunch, but his immediate concern went to his closed airway. He grasped at it while John steadied his balance and drew a switchblade from his right pocket.

The gangly man pressed the button and the sharp point shot out of the handle, the shiny metal glimmering in the residual light of the Explorer's headlights.

John charged Dak, intent on gutting him like a fish. The man had no real training, that much was evident. He lunged wildly, stabbing straight at Dak's abdomen.

Dak deftly twisted left, allowing the blade to pass, then grabbed the tall man's forearm, jerked him forward using his own momentum against him. At the last second, Dak twisted the man's wrist upward and plunged the knife through his throat.

He yanked the bloodstained blade out of the wound just in time to meet another reckless attack from Steve. The grunt rushed at Dak, shoulders squared to tackle him and drive him to the ground.

Dak ducked and stabbed up into the attacker's chest. The assailant's forward movement dragged the blade through flesh until it sunk deep into his belly. He howled in pain and fell to the ground beside his dead friend.

Steve curled into a fetal position as blood leaked through his fingers, soaking into the gravel.

Tripp finally sensed the very real danger and used the only advantage he could. He slipped into the shadows and hurried around behind the fight, slipping up on Tanya who'd been focused on the one-sided battle.

She was still on the phone with her husband when Tripp snaked his arm around her waist and pressed the sharp edge of a hunting knife against her neck. In a second of startled panic, she dropped the phone to the ground and the screen cracked against the gravel.

Tripp's wide eyes blazed with fury. The fact that one of his friends was dead and the other soon would be hadn't fully set in, but the sight of them on the ground quickly worked to correct that.

"Johnny?" he said, looking at the long, still form on the ground. "Johnny, you okay?"

Dak let the bloody switchblade slip down to his fingertips. Pinching the flat sides of the knife, he carefully calculated the distance between him and the man holding the woman hostage.

"He's dead, Tripp," Dak said, speaking the words as if they held no consequence, the way he would after stepping on an insect. "The other one will be soon."

Tripp's eyes flashed to Steve who lay curled up, a dark patch of crimson covering the ground under him. His movement had slowed, the severed artery in his gut pumping his life through his fingers.

"You killed them," Tripp muttered through a flood of confusion and anger. "You murdered them!"

"You murdered them, Tripp," Dak said. "Your decision to try to rape and then murder this woman to cover it up sentenced them to death."

Tripp's nostrils flared. His breathing quickened. He swallowed and pressed the edge of the knife against his captive's throat. Andy Eller's voice kept coming through the phone at her feet, just loud enough to hear him attempting to calm the situation down.

"They were my friends," Tripp said as sobs filled his voice. "And you murdered them in cold blood." The words fluttered through trembling lips.

"I think you need to reassess what your definition of cold blood means," Dak said. "Now, let her go. Put the knife down."

Tripp shook his head. "No. That's not how this is going to end, stranger. I'll slit her throat and then I'll kill you."

Dak's target stood less than twenty feet away.

"Let her go, Tripp," Dak said. "This ends one of two ways: you in the back of a squad car, or dead here in a bar parking lot with your friends. Choice is yours."

A sick laugh escaped Tripp's lips, and he shook his head in denial. "You think that's how this is going to go? Do you have any idea who you're talking to? Do you know who my dad is?"

"Local sheriff?" Dak answered. "I'm sure he holds a great deal of sway over the... thousand or so people who live in this area, but I don't think there's much he can do here. You tried to rape that woman. And I overheard you talking about killing her after the fact. So you can either let her go right now, put down the knife, and let her husband arrest you, or you can be stupid and die right now. To be honest, I don't care either way. I'm not here for you."

Tripp narrowed his eyes at the last part. His eyelids could have pinched a gnat they were so close. "What's that supposed to mean?"

"That's none of your concern. Your only concern is that you don't have to die tonight like your friends. They made their choice. You can go to prison for a while, serve your time, and get out—hopefully a better person."

"No," Tripp said, his head twisting again. "You killed my friends."

Tanya shook in his grip, too afraid to move lest the knife sink into her throat and slit the artery. A thin trickle of blood oozed out from under the blade's edge.

"If anyone is going to prison, it's you. For murder! My daddy will make sure of that! I promise you!"

Dak sighed, knowing the man had made his decision.

"And the first thing I'm going to do is cut this—" he started to use a derogatory slur regarding Tanya, but the word never came.

In the blink of an eye, Dak's right hand snapped up and forward.

The fingers pinching the blade released, and the knife cartwheeled though the air with blinding speed, the sharp point sinking into Tripp's right eye.

His grip on Tanya weakened instantly as he wavered and then fell backward onto the ground, his own blade clanking on the surrounding rocks.

Tanya dared to look back at the dead man and then shrieked. Her screams echoed through the valley as she doubled over, expelling a wave of terror, confusion, and anger.

Dak glanced over at the shortest of Tripp's crew. He didn't move, and Dak figured he'd succumbed to his injuries. He lingered for a second, giving Tanya a minute to collect herself before he spoke. When he did, it was in a matter-of-fact tone with only a sprinkling of empathy.

"You okay?" he asked.

She'd stopped screaming, but her breaths still came quickly. She rounded on him and nodded. "You saved my life," she said, tears welling in her eyes.

"I was lucky to be in the right place," he said. "That's all."

She shook her head vehemently. "No. What you just did." Her eyes played out over the grisly scene. "No normal person can do that. You some kind of killer or something?"

"No." A partial lie. "I'm trained. That's all you need to know. And don't bother asking who I am." He turned halfway to his vehicle. "Please, do me a favor, don't try to find me. Okay?" His eyes wandered to the phone at her feet.

"You said you weren't here for them," she realized, the words coming out half consciously.

"I'm not," he admitted. "And I'm not here for the sheriff or your husband, either. Someone owes me a debt. I'm here to collect. When I'm done, you won't see me again. Ever. Understand?"

She nodded, not truly understanding.

"Tanya?" Andy's voice crackled through the speaker on the phone. "Tanya, are you there? I'm en route. Please, baby, answer me!"

"You should get that," Dak said. "Your husband sounds like a good man. He'll know what to do with all this."

She abruptly remembered her husband on the phone and bent down to pick it up. She pressed it to her ear and looked back to the spot where the stranger stood. He'd already made it back to his SUV and climbed in. The engine groaned to life, and the man sped out onto the road. She watched the red taillights disappear around the bend as the sound of sirens pierced the silent valley from the other direction.

NINE

CUCHARA

Sheriff Craig Sanders slammed the door to his police car and stormed across the gravel to the yellow police line. One of the officers standing guard saw him coming and raised the tape without needing to be told.

Floodlights dumped bright hues across the crime scene; most focused on the three bodies lying in close proximity to one another. Sheriff Sanders stopped short the second he recognized the long body of John Collinsworth. Close by, Steve McGill's crumpled corpse lay on its side.

Sanders' heart dropped into his gut. A tsunami of nausea swept over him as his eyes trailed from the two men over to his son Tripp's body. One of the forensic investigators, in a white jumpsuit with blue gloves and a mask covering their face, crouched over the corpse. Another stood nearby, holding an evidence bag in the light as they inspected the contents.

"Tripp?" Sanders said. He spoke so loud, the two dozen people working the scene all stopped what they were doing and looked over at the man.

"No," Sanders blubbered when he neared his dead son, the knife still protruding from the right eye. The sheriff shook his head vehemently in denial. "No. Tripp. No!"

He felt his knees buckle, and an arm swooped in at the last second to brace him under the armpit.

"Easy, Sheriff," Andy said. "Take it easy. Come on, now."

"My son," Sanders blathered. "They killed my son."

While tears brimmed in the sheriff's eyes, they never broke through. Instead, righteous anger burst forth. He breathed hard for several seconds, letting the deputy balance him. Then strength returned to his legs and he stiffened and pushed away.

His eyes locked with Andy's. "Who did this, Deputy? You said your wife was leaving the bar and found them out here like this."

Andy never flinched. "Yes, sir."

The sheriff looked over at the back of an ambulance. The bright sterile lights from inside glowed over Tanya Eller, wrapped in a blanket—her coat zipped up and a scarf around her neck.

Puffs of mist spewed out of the angry sheriff's mouth and nostrils like a bull on the prairie in the middle of winter.

"She's pretty shaken up," Andy went on. "Said she was the last one out of the building. Merrick and Natalie had already gone and went out the side door where they were parked. I guess they didn't see." The deputy hung his head empathetically.

"Sheriff?" A familiar voice sliced through the chilly late night air.

Sanders and the deputy spun around to see Tyler Mumford standing at the yellow tape where an officer was blocking the way.

Sanders motioned with a wave, and the officer raised the tape and allowed Mumford to pass.

Tyler walked over to the two men and stopped short. He looked down at the bodies and drew in a long, deliberate breath. Instead of an explosion of grief, Tyler's face hardened to stone.

"Who?" he asked.

"We don't know," Andy answered. "The CSI team is doing their job right now."

"No," Tyler said, grabbing the deputy and spinning him around. "I want to know who did it and I want to know ten seconds ago."

Andy resisted the urge to rebuke the man for laying his hands on him. He was in an emotional state and not thinking clearly.

"We have to let the CSIs do their job, Tyler."

"And what? Wait for weeks while they analyze the DNA evidence? No," Mumford shook his head. "Someone saw something. I want to know who did this."

"No one saw anything, Tyler," Sanders offered. "The bar closed. Andy's wife came out after locking up and found them this way."

Tyler's eyebrows furrowed low, and he rounded on the deputy. "Your wife? Where is she?"

"Now, Tyler. Take it easy. I know they were your friends, but this was pretty traumatic for Tanya. She's never seen anything like this before."

"Your wife got something to hide?" Tyler ventured.

"What did you just say?" Andy's voice suddenly went from the usual pushover everyone was accustomed to, to an angry bear.

Tyler shuffled closer to the cop until they were almost toe to toe. Andy could feel the man's breath washing across his face as they stood nose to nose.

They were nearly the same height and roughly the same build. If a fight broke out, most would bet on a stalemate.

"Did I stutter?"

Andy's face reddened as he held back the reins of the furious stallions in his mind.

"Now, Tyler," Sheriff Sanders stepped between the two. "This isn't helpful. Andy's wife had nothing to do with this. You hear?" The sheriff looked up into the newcomer's steel gaze that remained locked on the deputy. "I'm just as torn up as you. That's my son over there," Sanders fumed. He used his anger to push away the grief that he feared would overwhelm him and send him into a crumpled heap on the gravel lot.

Tyler sensed he was overstepping his bounds and forced himself to calm down, at least on the surface.

"Sorry, Sheriff—Deputy." He took several deep breaths. "Those boys are... were my friends," he corrected. "I just think that anyone who was here today should be questioned. That's all."

"We know how to do our jobs," Sanders said in a stern voice. He sighed and let his eyes wander again to his dead son. "And we will catch this murderer. I promise you that."

Andy suppressed the urge to look up. It was an instinct, a flinch he knew would give away information he hid from the two men. Fortunately, his awareness was stronger.

"He's right," the Deputy said solemnly. "We will find whoever did this. I promise you that."

Tyler glowered at Andy, but said nothing, allowing the fire in his eyes to do the talking for him.

Sanders patted Tyler on the shoulder and looked up at him. "Everyone who was here this afternoon when the boys were here will be questioned. Okay? First thing in the morning, we'll call the wait staff and start figuring out if there were any customers who came through who might have looked like they could have done this. If we don't get anywhere with that, we'll check receipts and look at any travelers who passed through. We will find the killer, Tyler. I swear it."

Tyler swallowed his pride and then nodded. "Okay, Sheriff. Okay." Then he cast one last glance over at Tanya who sat in the back of the ambulance. The EMT was saying something to her. Tanya shook her head to whatever questions were being asked.

"When you find out who is responsible. I want to be the first to know."

TEN

CUCHARA

Dak stepped into the cabin and marched to the back porch. He stuffed the keys to the SUV in his pocket, knowing that at any second he may have to get back in and drive.

He turned the latch to the door leading onto the porch and stepped out, returning to the cold evening air. He gripped the railing and leaned over to watch the winding road leading up the mountain from the valley.

Headlights would be easy to see all the way down to the bottom, but getting away would be next to impossible. The road was little more than a trail. Two vehicles passing on either side would fill it entirely. Still, Dak had to watch. He glanced off to the slopes on his right, considering an escape on foot. The left was just as good in that regard, but any law enforcement pursuing him would catch up sooner or later, whether he tried to escape in a vehicle or without.

His head raced with a slew of options, none of which he really liked, and several that ended with him dead.

Dak grunted in anger and shoved the rail. It didn't budge, even under his strength. He could have complained about Tripp and his friends getting in the way of the grand plan, but Dak knew his plan of revenge didn't hold a candle to what almost happened there tonight.

A twinge of guilt needled his heart.

Had he stepped in too soon? It was a philosophical question he'd pondered before, and it revolved around the idea of taking out an enemy before they'd committed an atrocity.

The sword bore two edges. On the one side, you could prevent a crime, but you'd never really know if it would have for sure happened or not. On the other, if you let the crime happen, then people got hurt, sometimes killed because of it.

The decision was never truly a win, but Dak settled his doubts by reminding himself that those men were caught in the act, not before or after. If he'd waited another minute, it would have been much, much worse.

They got what they deserved. He knew that was the truth. Dak had a feeling her husband would say the same thing.

He stood there for ten minutes, twenty, thirty. The sound of sirens never came. No blue lights flashed through the forest along the slopes below.

The chill started to take over his will to remain vigilant, and Dak returned to the warmth of the cabin.

He turned on the fireplace and the gas logs whooshed to life, radiating warmth from the lapping flames. He lingered there for several minutes, allowing the heat to wash over him.

A look at the clock on the wall to his left told him it wasn't yet midnight. The bar closed around ten, but he'd felt like more than two hours had passed since the incident.

His head swiveled to the right, and he stared at the hot tub for a long couple of seconds.

"Might as well while I watch the road," he said to himself.

Three minutes later, Dak sat in the bubbling waters with steam wafting up around his face. He watched the road below as he let the hot water soak his muscles.

The sheriff would probably be at the scene of the crime, learning about his son's demise. From what Dak gathered, the apple didn't fall too far from the tree.

The father would be angry. He'd be striving toward his own vendetta, payback for whoever did this.

Dak had no doubts that Tanya would keep his identity safe. She knew the gravity of what just happened. He didn't think she was afraid of him. She had no reason to be, though sometimes people could experience strange thoughts or feelings over an extreme circumstance.

He wondered what she told her husband, what they told the cops. The husband had been on the phone during a portion of the altercation. Dak was curious about what the deputy heard. It was a near certainty he'd heard most of Dak's end of the conversation, and likely Tripp's responses.

But would they tell the sheriff?

Dak believed they wouldn't. Something along the lines of Tanya locking up and finding the bodies in the parking lot seemed more like her style. Could the lawman lie about what happened?

There'd be no way Andy could accuse the sheriff's son of what he'd tried to do. The sheriff wouldn't go for it, and Dak hoped the deputy was smart enough to see that something like this could end with a tragic cover up that left him and his bride dead somewhere in the hills.

Dak had to believe they'd be smart about it.

He let go of that thought and took a sip from one of the bottles of water left by the cabin host. What would be the next play for the sheriff and for his sugar daddy, Tyler Mumford?

Would Tyler... or Billy recognize the handiwork? Had Dak blown the element of surprise?

That was doubtful. Or was it?

Billy might well recognize the skill that went into killing the three men. If he was let into the crime scene, he'd see the bodies—assuming they were still where Dak left them. The manner in which each of the men died would be obvious to Billy, and not just by a knife wound. The precision, Billy would recognize it. If Dak's former teammate already concerned himself with being a target, the triple homicide of his close friends would put Billy over the top. He'd be on high alert in his cabin up on the mountain.

Dak had to consider several next moves on the elaborate chessboard, too.

The sheriff would get few if any leads out of tonight's investigation, which meant they would start asking the bar staff about any new customers that may have been acting strange the night before, or perhaps took issue with the three dead men.

Merrick and the bartender both could mention Dak, but he hadn't done anything to cause any trouble. Paying Merrick a couple of hundred dollars might make the young server think Dak was up to no good, but he doubted it. If anything, the young man would likely deny even mentioning he was there. Unless he was pressured.

Dak let his concerns melt away with the heated liquid around him. There was no reason he couldn't get a good night's sleep. He'd wake up early in the morning and head toward Purgatory Peak. That was why he'd come to Cuchara, to take out Billy and maybe—if he was lucky—find out where Nate went.

His mind set, Dak leaned back and rested his head against the seat back until the water came up to his earlobes. He looked up through the opening in the canopy surrounding the cabin and stared into the cloudless sky at the stars twinkling in their black canvas.

Dak blinked slowly, enjoying the moment. Then he forced himself out of the water, dried off, and went back into the cabin. He had to be up early in the morning and sleep would come at a premium.

He spent the next thirty minutes setting traps at every entry point, including the door onto the porch. The alarm system was a trick he'd learned in his childhood, using common kitchen utensils and dishes to alert him if an intruder entered.

If someone were to try to slide up a window or crack open a door, he would know it by the sound of a crashing plate, bowl, or drinking glass.

When he was finished setting his traps, he rinsed off in the shower and climbed into bed. Dak's confidence in his alarm system was so high, he fell asleep within two minutes, his mind wandering to a café in Istanbul.

ELEVEN

CUCHARA

Tyler paced back and forth across the span of his living room, occasionally stopping to look out through the massive windows that spanned much of the front wall that faced toward the valley.

The clock on his microwave told him it was a few minutes after midnight.

He stopped pacing and turned toward the door leading out to the huge deck that wrapped around three sides of the cabin. He pushed the door open and stepped into the chill, thinking he'd heard a sound coming from the valley below.

After a few misty breaths, he managed to convince himself it was just his imagination. The sound of the breeze blowing through branches, howling at certain points along the slopes beneath him, was the only sound that reached the top of the mountain.

Tyler chose this spot for a reason.

He had a wide field of view from up here and could see or hear pretty much anything approaching. An electronic gate blocked the driveway leading up to the cabin. The driveway itself was nothing more than a gravel trail that wound up the mountain slopes. Cameras around the gate also alerted Tyler to anyone curious enough to wander too close. Even if a trespasser decided to circumvent the gate and go it on foot, they would face a long uphill journey. In a vehicle, it would take nearly fifteen minutes to reach the summit.

That was more than enough time for him to prepare.

Still, anxiety racked his mind.

"How did he find me?" Tyler asked out loud. His voice died in the cool darkness, sucked up by the trees. "I was careful. I took every precaution." Anger and frustration overshadowed each word.

He had been careful.

The other men from the team didn't even know he was here, as far as he was aware. He'd been able to keep tabs on Collier for the simple reason that the man was a loose cannon, a true sociopath in every sense of the word. Nathan Collier always rubbed him the wrong way. The guy enjoyed killing; took a sick sort of pleasure in watching his enemies perish, and often in gruesome ways.

When parting ways with the others—all agreeing never to make contact again—Billy did everything he could to track Collier, if for no other reason than to make sure the man never tried to hunt him down and take his share. Billy always had suspicions that one of the others would do that, make a play for a larger chunk of the fortune they'd gleaned from their discovery in Iraq.

Even with most of his money secured in various accounts and shelters under his new identity as Tyler Mumford, there was still a good amount of it in the safe in the cabin's basement. He'd always believed that bullion was a commodity that needed to be kept on hand, and so Tyler invested heavily in it.

Gold and silver could be exchanged anywhere in the world, so he kept nearly a quarter of his remaining funds on site in case he had to bug out and drop off the grid.

He spun around and stormed back into the cabin with no answers and more questions than he had when he stepped outside.

If it was Dak who'd killed his new friends, Tyler needed a plan. Would he stay and fight? Or should he take his resources, load up, and leave? He'd disappeared once. He could do it again.

Or could he?

If Dak had tracked him down once, he could do it again.

Paranoia gripped Tyler as he stalked into the kitchen and stopped at the corner where a collection of bourbon bottles occupied the marble countertop. He reached for a bottle of Blade and Bow and simultaneously slid a tumbler closer to the edge, away from the backsplash. He poured a couple of fingers into the glass, set the bottle down, and took a big gulp.

The smooth burn tickled his throat as he swallowed. He let out a relieved sigh and poured a second drink, then capped the bottle. Tyler turned with his glass, content to sip this one, and made his way over to the couch where the fire crackled in the hearth.

He ran through the crime scene again in his head—the bodies laid out on the gravel, each killed with expert precision. Was it the work of Dak? Or was there someone else capable of such killing?

His thoughts wandered back to the equally sinister possibility that Collier could have found him. Was it Nate who did this?

If so, he would be calculating the best way to take Tyler out. He'd map the entire mountain, figure out the best approach, and strike at the opportune moment.

Tyler had placed enough sensors around the perimeter of the cabin to give him plenty of notice if someone was approaching on foot. He had to remind himself of that so he could get some sleep, but he already knew that was going to be tenuous at best.

He took another swig of the bourbon and eased back into the thick leather couch. A pistol sat on the cushion next to him. One of his AR-15s rested on the coffee table with two spare magazines beside it.

Whoever was behind the killings, Tyler convinced himself that they wouldn't attack him tonight. They would wait and plan their next move.

For now, he needed to get some rest. The local cops were doing all they could, which wasn't much, but the killer would lie low for a little while. It's what Tyler would do. When he put himself in the shoes of Dak or Nate, he figured that's what they would do, too.

Moderately satisfied with his rationale, Tyler finished the rest of his bourbon and lazily watched the fire flicker and crackle as his eyelids grew heavy and he surrendered to sleep.

TWELVE
CUCHARA

Sheriff Sanders burst through the front door of the building before the first rays of sunlight streamed over the horizon to the east. The smell of cheap, burnt coffee barely registered as he passed the front desk.

"Sheriff?" said the woman on duty.

For a second, her call to his attention passed him by in the haze of thoughts and emotions running chaotically through his head.

He paused and then turned to face her. "Yes?"

"I'm sorry, sir. I know you have... a lot going on."

"Spit it out, Amy. I'm conducting an investigation of my son's murder. In case you hadn't noticed."

She blushed, her rotund cheeks burning the color of ripe plums. "I know, sir, and I'm sorry. It's just that—" She hesitated for fear of attracting more of his anger.

"Well?"

She gasped and let it out. "There's a man here to see you," she said. At the sight of his vague confusion, she continued. "He said it's about the investigation, sir. He claims to have information about the... um, killer."

The sheriff blinked. "Where is he?"

"He's in your office, sir."

"My office? You just let him walk into my office?"

"No, sir. Well, sort of. He was very insistent."

"Insistent?" Sanders looked as if his head might blow off and fly into orbit. "Amy, this is a police building. We don't just let strangers have access to any room they want, and especially not my private office." His voice built until it ended in a shout.

He spun and continued down the hall at a faster pace than he'd begun with until he reached the open door and looked inside.

A man, probably in his early or mid-thirties sat in one of the chairs across from the desk. He had one leg crossed over a knee and hands folded in his lap, the picture of someone trying to mind their own business.

Sanders' head bobbed in all directions as he threw his hands up in the air. "Can I help you?"

He marched into his office, leaving the door cracked open, and plopped down in the chair behind his desk.

"Well, are you just going to sit there or are you going to explain yourself? Amy said you claim to have information about who might have killed my son."

The words stung coming out of his mouth. Sanders hadn't slept the night before. His son had been brutally slain in a bar parking lot along with his two closest friends. A range of emotions constantly swept over him throughout the night, rousing him every brief moment it seemed slumber would finally take him.

The man across from him didn't respond at first. He stared back at Sanders with steel blue eyes that could have cut through stone.

"I do," the man said finally, seconds before the sheriff could ask again.

Sanders' temper eased and he slumped back into the chair. Here we go, he mused. The first of probably dozens of claims.

Anytime something like this happened, law enforcement had to pore over piles of claims from people swearing they had legitimate information regarding a crime. The worse the crime, the more people typically came forward with "information."

Most of the time, it was little more than rumor or guesswork.

Sanders hadn't seen much of it in his time in Cuchara, but he'd heard from his buddies with the State Troopers and in other cities. It was always the same and there was a high correlation between the higher rewards offered and the number of people claiming to have helpful information.

The sheriff had to admit this guy didn't look like the freeloader type, trying to get a few grand with a lucky guess about the suspect's location.

He was strong, with broad shoulders and a striking tan that belied years of outdoor work. His gray jacket over a casual dress, navy blue sweater and dark blue jeans also portrayed a guy who had experienced some moderate success in life. Sanders guessed he was an amateur real estate investor whose actual job was probably in one of the cities—Denver or Colorado Springs—by proximity. He might have been a financial advisor or perhaps one of those startup guys looking to be the next Elon Musk or Bill Gates.

"I'm listening," Sanders said nonchalantly.

"The way those young men died," the stranger began, "would have taken someone who knows what they're doing, wouldn't it?"

The sheriff choked back his grief and gave a single nod. "I suppose so."

"Your son, his friends, did they have any formal combat or martial arts training?"

Sanders' irritation burned on his skin. "You have a point to all this, sir? Because right now I don't see where this is going."

"My apologies, Sheriff," the man said with just a little too much coolness in his voice. "I was only trying to connect a few dots. That's all."

"What dots?" Sanders snorted.

"Seems to me that you have a troublemaker in your midst. Quiet little town like this probably doesn't see many homicides. I'm guessing you haven't during your entire tenure."

Sanders stood and planted his palms on the desk. He leaned over, his face sizzling. If he were a cartoon, smoke would have been spilling out of his ears.

"You better make your point and make it fast, stranger."

"Yes, sir," the man said. "How well do you know Tyler Mumford?"

The question startled the sheriff, but he answered honestly. "Not too well, I suppose. He moved here several months back. Bought one of the old abandoned ski resorts just outside of town. He's done a little philanthropy in the area since he got here. People seem to like him."

No need to mention that most of the "philanthropy" had ended up in the sheriff's pockets.

"I'm sure he has," the visitor hissed. "I'm not going to bother you about how Tyler Mumford came by his fortune. I honestly don't care. What I do know is that he isn't who he says he is."

The irritation on the sheriff's face melted into a frown. "What's that supposed to mean?"

"Exactly what it sounds like, Sheriff. You're a smart man." He let those last words hang with a bit of sarcasm.

"What? Are you suggesting Tyler is someone else? As in, he's using an alias or something?"

"I realize it must sound ludicrous to you. So, tell me. Was he friends with your son?"

The knot returned to the sheriff's throat. He sucked in air through his nostrils and let it out gradually. "They had recently become acquainted, yes."

"Did you notice any animosity between your son and Mumford? Any issues at all?"

Sanders' patience waned, desperate to get to the point. "Sir, I'm going to need you to either tell me what it is you think you know or let me go about my day. I'm very busy and as I'm sure you can imagine, this is an extremely difficult time."

"I understand," the stranger sympathized. "You want to find who did this. I'm telling you who is responsible."

The sheriff lifted and dropped his shoulders. "So, you're saying Tyler Mumford killed my boy and his two friends? That's your big reveal?"

The visitor reached into his jacket, and the sheriff drew back instinctively. The man eased his concern with a twist of the head and the slightest, albeit devilish, grin.

"Just a file, Sheriff. I'm unarmed."

The man pulled a manila folder out and set it on the desk, sliding it toward the lawman.

"What is this?" Sanders asked, confused and curious at the same time.

The visitor said nothing, merely staring at the sheriff with the cool gaze of a world champion poker player.

The sheriff took his cue and opened the file. He passed over the pictures of the man he knew as Tyler Mumford, but in a different guise. He was wearing military fatigues. In one of the pictures, Mumford cradled a sniper rifle against his shoulder as he peered through a scope.

"Is this a—"

"Dossier?" the visitor finished. "Yes. You'll see in the file that Tyler's name is actually Billy Trask. He's a former Delta Force operative gone rogue. I'm here to bring him in."

"Bring him in?" The sheriff's confusion mounted.

"I work for a special agency with the DOD, Sheriff. It's my job to locate and arrest particularly dangerous people, people we previously employed. He changed his name and moved here to avoid justice. I'm tasked with the duty of making sure he's brought in. I'm sorry to say that I got here too late to save your boy, Sheriff, but if you help me get to Billy, I can keep it from happening to anyone else."

The sheriff considered the story, sorting through the details of the file in his hands. It was all there in black and white. The truth about the mysterious Tyler Mumford was at his fingertips.

"I can't believe I didn't see through it," the sheriff admitted. "We all just accepted his story without question."

"I assume he was... persuasive, Sheriff. I would tell you not to beat yourself up, but I know you must feel somewhat responsible for what happened last night. You have to let that go for now. There will be a time for grieving, but it isn't now. I need you to take me to Billy's place. I understand he built a cabin on the top of Purgatory Mountain."

The sheriff nodded absently. "Yes, but if you know where he is, why do you need me?"

"He's a marksman, Sheriff, a killer of the highest order. He's taken out targets thousands of yards away. His cabin is perfectly situated to take out anyone foolish enough to come after him. He trusts you. You can get me up there. Once you're in the cabin, I'll make my move."

"He won't suspect anything?"

"Why would he? You're conducting an investigation into the murder of his friends. He doesn't know you know the truth now. Tell him you have some new information on the case."

Sanders thought about it. "He did say he wanted to be the first to know if I got any leads."

The visitor opened his hands wide. "There's your in, then."

The sheriff nodded, anger filling his veins once more. "Okay. Let's do it."

"We have to make it look like you're going alone, Sheriff. No other cars or deputies. Just you. I'll hide out in your car until you're in the cabin. Then I'll move in. Understood?"

"Why no backup?" Sanders wondered.

"That'll spook him. Believe me when I say the last thing you want to do is spook this guy. He could take out your entire department in twenty seconds. You go in alone. I'll have your back."

The sheriff pondered the plan for thirty seconds before he nodded. "Okay. Let's load up and go after him." He stood and then realized he didn't know the visitor's name.

"I'm sorry," Sanders said. "I didn't get your name."

"I didn't give it, Sheriff. And if it's the same to you, I'd like to keep it that way. I'm sure you can understand. But, if you need my credentials, I have them right here."

The visitor reached into the other side of his jacket, but the sheriff stopped him. "No, I don't think I want to know. You've given me more than enough." He looked down again at the man he'd trusted so quickly, the man he now believed killed his son.

THIRTEEN

CUCHARA

Sheriff Sanders steered the county police vehicle off the road and onto the gravel driveway leading up the mountain. The empty runs of the old Purgatory Mountain ski resort traced wide, white lines down the slopes, winding through dense stretches of trees.

Sanders stopped at the security gate that sat thirty yards off the road, surrounded by pine and spruce. A metal speaker box with a numbered panel stood to the left, held up by a black metal post. The sheriff reached out and touched the call button, then waited as the heat escaped his car into the cold morning air.

The phone connected to the key panel rang three times before someone answered.

"Sheriff? What brings you here so early? You have information about the killer?"

"Good morning, Tyler," he managed. "And yes, I do."

"That was fast," the voice through the box said, surprised more than skeptical. "Did you arrest him?"

"We're tracking him down," Sanders said, stumbling through the words. He immediately worried he'd given away the fact he was lying. "I think we'll have him soon, probably within the hour. I have some questions, though," he added quickly. "I want to make sure we get the right guy."

A pause on the intercom furthered the sheriff's concern. Had the ruse worked? Or was he going to have to call for backup and go in guns blazing? He didn't like the second option. If the dossier on Trask was as legit as this mysterious stranger suggested, cops could be hurt or killed. Trask would probably hold out in his mountain fortress, picking off approaching officers one by one until an all-out assault took place. National news would cover the siege and subsequent battle. None of that sounded like something Sanders wanted. He did his best not to glance into the back of the county SUV where the stranger hid from sight. Even the slightest look might give away what the sheriff was up to.

"Okay, Sheriff," the voice said through the speaker. "Come on up. Sorry it took me a second. I was making some eggs."

"No problem, Tyler. Be right up."

The iron gate slowly retracted to one side. The chain pulling it bounced along until the path was clear and the motor automatically shut off.

Sanders continued through the opening and watched in his mirror as the gate began to close behind.

"Good job, Sheriff," the stranger said in a deep voice from behind the seat.

Sanders didn't acknowledge the comment. Instead, he remained focused on the twisting road leading up around the backside of the mountain.

The forest engulfed the SUV on all sides with pine, aspen, and spruce. The lush evergreen had always given Sanders a sense of safety and serenity in a chaotic world. Since his wife Lorita left him over a decade ago, he'd always found comfort in the mountains and woods around Cuchara. She'd had her reasons for leaving. He wasn't around enough, and when he was, Sanders didn't always give her enough attention. It was doomed from the start, he supposed, and he was less than shocked when she ran off with another man, a rancher from Wyoming who she met while he was passing through town on business.

In some ways, Sanders had been relieved when she left. But it had been hard on Tripp. The boy was sixteen, so at least it hadn't happened when he was young, but the sheriff often wondered how much his son blamed him for what happened.

Now Tripp was dead, and Sanders had nothing left but his job and the lonely mountains around him.

At the moment, however, he had something else in his possession: revenge.

In his mind, he prettied it up by calling it justice. He'd run through the footage in his imagination of how he wanted this to play out at least a dozen times during the night and again that morning.

His favorite was walking into Tyler's... Billy's cabin and shooting him in the back of the head. But that would be messy, difficult to clean up. He knew people who could handle that kind of work, but he resisted using them. Loose ends were problematic and the more eyeballs that fell on a crime scene, the more lips tended to flap later on down the line.

Sanders had settled on a single plan, one that would be simpler to cover up. He would go in, perhaps have a cup of coffee with Billy, then lure him outside where blood would soak into the ground after the sheriff executed the man who killed his son in cold blood.

A quick wrap up in the black plastic tarp Sanders had stowed in the back of his SUV that morning, a little wash with the hose on the driveway or dirt, and the scene would be pristine—just as if Billy Trask had simply been erased.

Of course, Sanders would have to deal with the man in the back, which is why he brought two pieces of plastic. The stranger was dangerous, there was no doubt about that. But with his attention focused on either arresting Trask or whatever the man's intent might be, Sanders could take out both of them.

The stranger had suggested that he was some kind of government agent, but Sanders knew better. He was no fool. The man would have presented some kind of identification as soon as he introduced himself. That hadn't happened, though he'd offered at the end of their initial meeting.

The sheriff had declined to play the role of the dumb country bumpkin cop who trusted people too easily.

It was a simple role for him to play since that's exactly how he'd lost his wife.

As long as the stranger believed that Sanders bought his story, he wouldn't be a threat.

He knew the man was armed. Maybe he hadn't been when he came to the office the previous afternoon. He claimed he was unarmed. That would have been smart. Entering a police station with a firearm... not so much.

None of that mattered. The man in the back would get the first bullet. Billy would get the second, although Sanders planned on letting the man who killed his son get more than one. He'd probably start with a knee, then the top of a foot, the groin, and work his way up until the final round went through Trask's head.

He would suffer for what he did to his son. That much was already decided.

The sheriff guided the vehicle around the last bend, and the cabin came into view. The modern design featured a single roof that slanted down toward the driveway, covering a porch that wrapped around to the front. A matching work shed stood off to the right.

The sheriff had been to the cabin before, right after Tyler... Billy had finished construction. Sanders preferred the older style log cabins to these modern ones, but he had to appreciate the location. The view was incredible, and in the back of his mind, the sheriff started considering how he might acquire the property when the owner was gone. That would be months down the line, but the daydream prodded at his mind as he pulled up to the building and shifted the transmission into park.

"Stay in here and keep a lookout," Sanders ordered. "When you see us come out the front door, you can get out."

There was no protocol for this. Sanders hinged everything on the belief that the stranger would do as told. But why wouldn't he? The sheriff was helping the man catch his quarry in a subtle, legal manner.

"Whatever you say, Sheriff. I'm a lawman too. I know how to play by the rules."

Sanders didn't buy it for a second, but he gave a curt nod to acknowledge the man's statement, and climbed out of the car.

The air had cooled more overnight and a fresh layer of thin powder coated the gravel driveway underfoot. It squished and crunched beneath the sheriff's boots as he approached the cabin.

As he neared the steps, the wooden, windowless door opened.

Billy stood inside, holding a white coffee mug.

"Come on in, Sheriff. I'll finish up my breakfast and we can head out. Got a fresh pot of coffee if you'd like a cup."

"Sure," Sanders said reluctantly. The ache in his heart still throbbed from the loss of his son. That feeling only swelled as he climbed the steps, drawing close to the man who had befriended and then killed him. "Good morning for a hot cup of joe."

"It sure is," Billy said. He closed the door once Sanders was inside and led the way to the kitchen.

He set down his mug next to a nearly empty plate of eggs, toast, and cottage cheese, and made his way over to the coffeepot in the corner.

Billy took down a mug with the Colorado state flag imprinted on the side and proceeded to fill it with the remains of the pot. He turned around, holding the mug at waist level. When Billy saw the sheriff holding his pistol he abruptly halted, spilling steaming liquid onto the floor near his boot.

"Sheriff?" Billy asked. "What are you doing?"

"I know who you are, Billy," he said, slandering the name with his tone.

"What are you talking about?" Billy kept his movements to a minimum, though he noted the heat on his jeans where some of the coffee had soaked through.

"Billy Trask?" Sanders clarified. "You came here throwing your money around, buying up friends, allies, and what you probably thought was security. Did you think you could get away with it?"

Billy inclined his head and sighed, rapidly coming to grips with what Sanders meant. "Fine, Sheriff. You got me. My name isn't Tyler Mumford. But that isn't a crime. I changed my name? So what? People do that all the time, don't they? There are certain people I would rather not find me. Okay?"

"Oh, I'm sure there are." Sanders kept the presence of the stranger in his car to himself.

"Look, Sheriff. Let's sit down and talk about this. I haven't broken any laws. Just... put the gun down and we can figure this out."

Sanders looked at the younger man as if an alien were about to pop out of his chest. He cocked his head to the side, analyzing Trask with hardened, pain-gripped eyes. "You murdered Tripp and the other two," he said finally. "Killed them in cold blood. Why? Why did you do it, Billy?"

Billy's face tightened. "Sheriff, you know me better than that. I don't know who would say such a thing, but I wasn't even at the bar last night. I was here the whole time."

"Is that right? Seems like you got there pretty fast, Billy." Sanders spat the name. "Like maybe you were close by after leaving the scene of the crime." The cop felt the trigger tighten against his finger. Every instinct in his soul told him to squeeze and end this murderer at that very moment, but that would make things tricky. Blood would get everywhere. Sanders knew he had to stick to the plan.

"Look, Craig," Billy said desperately, using the sheriff's first name. "Your son was my friend. Steve and John, too. Now, I want to find this killer as much as you do, but it wasn't me. You have to believe me."

Sanders shook his head grimly. "No, Billy. I don't. Step outside."

"What are you going to do, Sheriff? Arrest me? On what grounds?"

"Murder charges. Three of them."

"You have a warrant?" Billy clenched his jaw. He knew how things worked, or at least how they were supposed to. This guy couldn't do anything without a warrant for his arrest.

"No," Sanders admitted. A twitch of relief shot through Billy's skin. "But I have probable cause. And this pistol. So, you can either step outside right now or I will shoot you in the head and claim it was self defense. I doubt the local prosecutor will think much of it. He and I go way back."

The relief in Billy's eyes vanished. "Fine, Sheriff. Take me in. But I want an attorney."

"Move."

Sanders flicked the pistol toward the door.

Billy slowly set the coffee mugs on the counter and raised his hands. "I'm moving. Relax, Craig."

Billy eased around the kitchen island and made his way to the door with Sanders close behind. The cop kept the pistol aimed straight at his captive's spine. If he so much as twitched the wrong way, Sanders would drop him right there.

The prisoner opened the door and stepped out into the cold. "Can I at least get a coat?" he asked.

"It's warm in my ride," Sanders countered. "Get moving."

"Okay. Okay. Take it easy."

Billy descended the steps and landed on the snow-dusted gravel with a crunch. Sanders looked toward his SUV as he followed, wondering when the stranger would make his appearance.

Five steps away from the porch, Sanders heard a subtle crinkling sound behind him. He started to turn his head, but a muted pop sounded over the parking lot. The noise was little more than a click, but the bullet it accompanied zipped through the back quarter of the sheriff's head.

The sheriff dropped to the ground with a thud.

Billy heard the sound and whirled around. Surprise and fear

soured his expression as he stared into icy cold familiar eyes. His gaze fell to the barrel pointed straight at his forehead.

"Bo? How did you—?"

The muzzle puffed and sent the round through Billy's skull. For a second, the legs held, then buckled. Billy fell to the ground a few feet from the sheriff.

FOURTEEN

CUCHARA

Dak's plans were thrown out the window the second he arrived at Purgatory Mountain.

He could see the cluster of police SUVs and patrol cars gathered around the driveway entrance as he rounded a bend in the road an eighth of a mile away. He scowled at the sight, wondering what Billy was up to.

Dak rolled to a stop in front of the driveway and lowered his window. Four cops stood guard at the gate. Their casual conversation ended when Dak's SUV came to a halt.

One of the officers, a younger guy with a clean-shaven face, noticed Dak and stepped toward the vehicle.

"Gonna have to ask you to keep moving, sir," the cop said.

"Is everything okay?"

The cop cocked his head to the side, his cheek brushing against the shoulder of a thick, hunter-green coat. The expression on his face begged the question, "does it look like everything is okay?" To his credit, the officer didn't go that route. "This is a crime scene, sir, and we're conducting an investigation."

Dak didn't press the issue. He nodded, thanked the deputy, and gently pressed on the gas. As the SUV accelerated away, he kept glancing in the rearview mirror at the collection of cops loitering around the driveway.

Crime scene? What crime?

He had a strange feeling in his gut that he already knew the answer, or at least partly.

His thoughts raced. The initial plan had been to do a little recon of the mountain, get a feel for the layout by driving by it a few times, circling around as much as possible. He wouldn't make a move on Billy's cabin until he'd analyzed every approach angle and even then, he'd need a way to figure out where any security cameras were hidden in the woods that could set off an alarm or alert Billy to his presence.

All of that went out the door. Something happened at the top of Purgatory Mountain, and Dak needed to find out what.

Part of his scheme was to see if the general store had any old ski run maps from the abandoned resorts. While such a pamphlet was hardly the detailed topographical map he would prefer, it would give Dak a general idea of the mountain's layout.

He felt his heart beating faster than normal and focused on slowing his breathing as he continued into the small town. It was getting close to lunch, and he knew the bar would be open, though he did not intend to go there.

Dak needed information, and fast.

He steered the SUV into a parking spot in front of the general store and killed the engine. He stepped out of the vehicle and walked up to the front door, taking a quick look around to survey the lot. A few other cars, but no threat appeared in his view.

He pushed the door open and walked into the tiny purveyor's shop. The tightly packed aisles offered snacks, bread, cereals, cans of soup, candy, and a wide selection of other grocery goods. While the building was small, Dak marveled at how the owners were able to pack so many items inside. In the back, a refrigerator ran the length of the wall and stretched down the left side, creating an L shape. Milk, soft drinks, beer, and juices filled the chilled shelves.

To his left, an older woman worked the cash register. She was easily eight inches shorter than Dak. Her graying, curly hair dangled over huge, round glasses. Her light blue zip-up hoodie draped over her, hanging just below the waist.

"Morning," she greeted. "Anything I can help you with?"

Dak checked around to make sure she was talking to him. One other person in the room perused an assortment of beer in the back. With so many to choose from, Dak figured the guy would probably be there for several minutes. If he'd known what kind he wanted upon arrival, he would have already been standing at the checkout counter.

"Actually," Dak said as he ambled to the counter, "maybe you can. It's a pretty random request, but I was wondering if you had any old maps of the abandoned ski resorts."

His emerald eyes met hers with a sort of boyish innocence.

She licked her lips and frowned in a way that told him she was trying to recall seeing anything like that.

"No," she said finally. "Sorry, I don't think we have anything like that here. You might be able to get one at the main resort in town. It's just a park now."

"Thank you," he offered. "I heard there were two abandoned resorts. Is that right?"

She nodded. "Yeah, but Purgatory got bought up by some young fella a while back. Moved here from out of town. Bought the whole mountain. Don't know where a man his age got that kind of money, but he must have a lot of it. Built himself a cabin up there several months ago. Must be quite a view, not that he can enjoy it anymore."

Dak noticed there was no malice in her last words. "What do you mean?"

"Cops found him and the sheriff both shot dead up there earlier today."

The breath caught in Dak's chest. "Dead?"

"Yep." She crossed her arms. Her voice took on a somber tone.

"They're still investigating, but it sounds like Sheriff Sanders went up there to talk to Tyler Mumford—that was his name—about the killings that happened last night at the bar."

Dak didn't bat an eye, a statue in the face of a tempest. "Killings?"

"I know," she exhaled. "I've lived here for nearly thirty years. I don't recall anything like this happening before in our little town. It's a quiet place. Now, all of the sudden, four murders in twenty-four hours? It's all so sad. Poor Andy."

"Andy?"

Her eyes had wandered down to the countertop. She lifted them when she heard his question. "Oh, yes. Andy Eller. He was a deputy, second in charge around here in the police department. He's the new sheriff for now until the next election. He must be overwhelmed. Terrible way to take over the sheriff duties."

"I'm sure it is." Dak couldn't tear himself away from the conversation, no matter how much he wanted to. "I'm so sorry, but you said the sheriff and this... Tyler fellow, were both killed?"

She nodded. "I've only heard a little more than you, but it sounds like they were both shot. I don't know if they shot each other, but that's what it sounds like. There must have been a bad disagreement. I can't imagine why those two would kill each other. Maybe the sheriff blamed Tyler for his son's death. They were friends, after all. Still, it's very strange."

Dak decided it was time to end the conversation. He'd hung around too long already and the less memorable he could make himself, the better.

"Well, thank you. I appreciate your time."

The man in the back of the store had selected his beer and was walking toward the counter holding a twelve pack.

"Have a good day," Dak offered.

"You too, hun," she said and turned her attention to the other customer as Dak quietly left.

Outside, he casually glanced around, climbed back into the SUV, and started the engine. Several thoughts swirled in his brain as he backed out of the parking spot and eased back onto the road.

Someone had killed Billy Trask. While he was satisfied that his next target had been eliminated, more questions bubbled to the surface. Who had killed Billy and Sheriff Sanders? Had it been the deputy whose wife Dak saved the night before? Had Andy Eller learned about what happened and taken out his revenge on the elder Sanders and the man he knew as Tyler Mumford?

That was doubtful. He'd done a little digging into the local deputy and learned that the man, like his wife, was a good person. Any smidge of guilt Dak felt over killing Tripp and his two cronies in the bar parking lot vanished when he learned more about the woman he'd saved—and her husband.

Andy Eller was honest, not given to the Romanesque way of getting ahead. He'd worked hard as a cop, always doing things by the book. The lady at the general store was right about one thing: Andy Eller was going to have his hands full.

One thing was certain in Dak's mind: the two men hadn't killed each other. It made sense on the surface. The new sheriff would probably make a statement in the coming days about the double homicide, how the two men had shot the other over some sort of disagreement.

Based on the scant amount of information Dak had gleaned—some from the server, Merrick—there might even be a paper trail of money connecting the two men. From there, disagreements, arguments were easy to put together as motives.

That was fine for the town of Cuchara. As grisly as it all seemed, the townspeople could have closure and eventually move on with their lives.

For Dak, however, this twist of events had brought about more problems. As he drove down the road heading back to the cabin to collect his belongings, he was left wondering—who killed Billy, and if they could find Billy, could they find him too?

Was it Nate? Or had Bo resurfaced here in Colorado? The coincidence in timing seemed unlikely, but the evidence was written in blood soaked into Purgatory Mountain.

He had to leave town immediately.

Suddenly, Dak felt the overwhelming sensation that he'd gone from being the hunter to the hunted.

FIFTEEN
CUCHARA

The Southern Rocky Mountains cradling the small town of Cuchara gradually grew smaller in the rearview mirror as Dak headed east. He held the phone against his ear, thinking hard about the problem.

"You still there?" Will asked.

After a few seconds, Dak answered. "Yeah."

"I've been working on this one the last few days. I know that these things take time—months, maybe even years. But it could help expedite things if you gave me a little more information."

Dak made the call the second he passed the signs announcing that he was leaving Cuchara. He needed to track down Nathaniel Collier as fast as possible, in no small part because Dak feared the crazy ex-teammate might be on his trail.

Someone had killed Billy and the local sheriff. And they'd made it look like the two men killed each other in an argument.

Maybe Dak was being paranoid over rationalizing things. There was nothing wrong with being careful, though, and at that moment it felt prudent.

"I don't know," Dak said finally. "I've given you everything I can think of."

"That isn't much," Will quipped. "Is there anything else you can give me? The physical descriptions of people can change, but their habits, tastes, characters don't."

"What's the point of counseling, then?"

Will laughed. "I've wondered the same thing myself many times. My guess is that counseling isn't meant to change people, but help them deal with who they are and manage their feelings or thoughts in a productive and socially acceptable way."

Dak considered the statement. "No one ever really knew what Nathaniel was thinking, or what he felt. The man was unusually quiet, mostly kept to himself in a way that creeped out even Bo. Nothing got to Bo. He wasn't afraid of much."

"Sounds like a psycho."

"Sociopath, actually," Dak said. Then it hit him. "Wait." A memory filled his head with a vision from the past he wished wasn't there. He'd all but forgotten that stream of events, or done the best he could to purge it from his mind.

"What is it? You got something?" Will sounded hopeful.

"There was something." He paused again. "Once, when we were in Iraq, we had a mission where we were sent into a village to take out some insurgents." Regret and a tinge of pain scratched at Dak's voice. Then it grew distant. "We advanced into an old home barn on the outskirts of town. We heard that's where the group conducted their meetings to plan out attacks. When we arrived, we found the insurgents. A few of them were older men, but most of their soldiers were young men under the age of fifteen.

"I took out the two of leaders immediately. Bo eliminated one. But we both hesitated when we saw the boys. They were unarmed, watching one of the men in charge as he conducted a lesson on improvised explosives." Dak snorted derisively at the way he'd said it —a lesson.

"What happened, Dak?" Will pressed after the phone fell silent again for nearly a minute.

Dak lost himself in the memory, the sickening, wretched recollection he wished had never happened.

"Nate entered the building after us. He saw the young men, thought they were a threat, and mowed them down. He slaughtered them without mercy, as if he was demolishing an anthill."

Will didn't say anything, but the silence over the line spoke for him.

"When he was done," Dak continued, "Nate waded through the bodies. He laughed at the sight. It was one of the few times he ever laughed that I can recall. Then he made a strange comment. Strange doesn't even come close to describing it, actually."

"What? What did he say?"

"He said—" Dak sighed. "He said that he wished he could take a few of them back home as trophies, that he'd always wanted a collection like that."

Dak stopped speaking, his words falling away from trembling lips.

"Wow," Will breathed. "I've seen some messed up people in my time. Saw some stuff that I still can't shake. But that's—"

"Crazy. I know. I feel like the military was the only place that could contain Nate and who—what he really is. He was a tool when he was in the army, an instrument of death. Now that he's out, I shudder to think what he may be doing."

"Most of us were instruments of death," Will countered.

"Not like this guy. He enjoyed it." The SUV rolled over the crest of a long rise and then began its descent down the other side. "Luis said he was in Kentucky."

"That's what you told me. What are you thinking?"

Dak grimaced at the thought. The question prodded disturbing images from his mind, things he could only picture in the darkest recesses of his imagination. "Check and see if there have been an abnormal number of missing persons reports occurring in the state. If so, is there a pattern?"

"And what if that search comes up empty?"

Dak knew that question was coming. "Then the good news is Nate hasn't done what I feared. That will make it more difficult for you to find him."

"I'm okay with difficult."

"I know you are." Dak paused and looked out at the expanding prairie leading away from the Rocky Mountains. "Call me when you have something."

FROM THE AUTHOR

I appreciate you taking the time to read this story, and the others if you've been keeping up. I did take a few liberties in this one, such as using the name of the town Cuchara, which is a real place and is as close to my description as possible. There is also an abandoned ski resort there, though it has been purchased and—I believe—converted into a tourist information center. The second resort I described does not, to my knowledge, exist. Purgatory Peak is a real place, though it is spelled differently and its appearance is somewhat different than how I entailed.

Thanks again for reading the story, and I'll see you in the next one.

Ernest

OTHER BOOKS BY ERNEST DEMPSEY

Dak Harper Origin Stories:

Out of the Fire

You Only Die Once

Tequila Sunset

Purgatory

Scorched Earth

The Heart of Vengeance

Sean Wyatt Adventures:

The Secret of the Stones

The Cleric's Vault

The Last Chamber

The Grecian Manifesto

The Norse Directive

Game of Shadows

The Jerusalem Creed

The Samurai Cipher

The Cairo Vendetta

The Uluru Code

The Excalibur Key

The Denali Deception

The Sahara Legacy

The Fourth Prophecy

The Templar Curse

The Forbidden Temple

The Omega Project

The Napoleon Affair

The Second Sign

Adriana Villa Adventures:

War of Thieves Box Set

When Shadows Call

Shadows Rising

Shadow Hour

The Adventure Guild:

The Caesar Secret: Books 1-3

The Carolina Caper

Beta Force:

Operation Zulu

London Calling

Paranormal Archaeology Division:

Hell's Gate

ACKNOWLEDGMENTS

Big thanks to my editor Anne Storer and all the readers who helped out while the book was being written and posted each day on my website. I can't thank you enough. There were so many of you kind enough to send your comments. I appreciate you.

For Jim

SCORCHED EARTH

A DAK HARPER THRILLER

ERNEST DEMPSEY

ONE

BROWN'S FERRY, KENTUCKY

No one ever thinks they'll get lost in a forest. There are landmarks, noticeable differences in the wilderness that make it impossible to lose your way.

But the forest can be a serene and terrifying place. To a young boy, the danger never seems present until it is too late. One moment, you're walking along a trail, enjoying some laughs with your brother, taking in the sights. The next, you find yourself twisting around in circles among hills and trees that all look the same.

Jamie and Oliver McDowell were on a camping trip with their parents in the hills around Fall Rock, Kentucky. They'd been to this place many times since their younger days as small boys.

Jamie, the older of the two having just turned fifteen, felt adult enough to take his little brother, Oliver, out on the trails for a walk while their parents cooked lunch at the camper.

The two boys were a mix of their parents, both lightly tanned with a combination of their father's dark hair and their mother's sandy locks. Their mother often commented that the boys' blue eyes were going to cause problems for them later on in life, suggesting the girls would be powerless against them.

An hour after the brothers left the campsite, they still hadn't returned.

The food on the folding picnic table grew cooler by the minute and Martha, their mother, grew frustrated.

"I told those boys to be back in thirty minutes," she said to her husband.

Tim McDowell, ever patient with the two, tried to calm her down. "You know how boys are," he said, using the eternal argument of a father for his sons. "They're probably catching crawdads down at the creek. Just lost track of time, that's all."

She only partially accepted the answer. With hands on hips, she glowered back at him. "Well, the food is getting cold."

"It's slaw and brats. We can reheat the brats. Slaw is cold anyway, Martha." He touched her shoulder. "Let's eat. They can have theirs when they get back."

She reluctantly agreed, and the couple sat down to enjoy their meal. Martha must have looked at her watch a dozen times during their conversation. Something deep down just didn't seem right to her. The feeling continued to nag at her for twenty minutes after they finished eating.

When the plates were thrown away and the boys' food covered in plastic wrap, she began pacing, looking down the trail in the direction her sons had hiked.

"Tim, should we go look for them?"

Tim and Martha McDowell had been married for twenty years. He knew her like a secret handshake—every nuance, every wrinkle, every personality trait. He loved her, but Tim also knew that his wife tended to worry too much about things. He'd wondered now and then if she might have been different if their children were girls instead, but he doubted that would have changed a thing. In fact, she probably would have worried more.

He grinned at her, disarming her concerns the way he always did. "I'll go look for them, honey. I'm sure they're not far away. And I'll be sure to let those two knuckleheads know their food is cold and they can reheat it themselves."

She smiled back at him, accepting his offer, and watched as he trudged down the trail into the forest.

The dry, cool air smelled of crisp leaves and Tim took it in through his nose in huge, deep breaths. He loved fall, and this one had been particularly wonderful. He'd always considered this part of the country to be one of the most undervalued when it came to fall colors. As he ambled down the path, the surrounding trees assaulted his vision with an explosion of colors. It was fine with him if this place was lesser known. He preferred to keep it that way. Fewer tourists meant the camping was quieter, other than for the locals who frequented the wilderness at Fall Rock. This weekend, however, had turned out to be a good one. Tim had only seen a couple of other families since they arrived, which meant he could get some much-needed relaxation time.

He'd spent the last 22 years of his life working for the same insurance company. The work wasn't anything spectacular, but it was a steady paycheck with benefits, and over the decades he'd built up a solid 401k that would allow he and Martha to travel when they both retired. Her job as a high-school science teacher also had a strong retirement fund, though she often teased him about moving down to Tennessee at some point and double dipping—a term educators used to refer to earning a paycheck from one state's retirement fund while collecting full-time pay from a neighboring state.

He scoffed at the notion, knowing, or maybe just hoping—she was messing with him. Eight more years and they could hit the road. He had plans and lots of them. A new RV—a smaller one—would be in order. When the boys were off to college, they wouldn't need the behemoth of a camper they'd been using for the last ten years.

There were Europe plans too, and maybe a cruise he'd always wanted to take. He'd been on a casino boat once out of Cape Canaveral, but never on a real cruise ship.

Tim was glad he'd still be young enough to do all those things when he retired. He and Martha had made sound economic decisions throughout the years, saving as much as they could without skimping on important memories for the boys and a few for themselves. He'd seen some of his friends from high school and college go down different paths, spending recklessly on things that quickly devalued or making bad, short-term investments.

He sighed as he rounded a bend in the trail. The creek appeared on the right, just down a short slope. It babbled constantly—another thing he loved about this spot. At night, the sound of the flowing water mingled with a crackling fire.

It was heaven for a guy stuck a cubicle for most of his career, though he'd moved up to his own office eight years prior.

He only relished the scene for a second as he realized there was no sign of the boys.

A scowl crossed his face, and he decided to try shouting. "Boys? Jamie? Oliver? Where are you?"

His voice faced into the trees amid rays of sunlight that poked through the red, orange, and yellow canopy overhead.

His frown deepened at the lack of response.

Tim kept moving, concern growing with every few steps. After another ten minutes, he figured he'd gone as far as his sons would have, and wondered if they had—perhaps—taken another way back, maybe up over the hill and down the other side.

He stopped on the trail with his hands on his hips, turning 360 degrees as he scanned the silent forest for his sons.

"Oliver?" He yelled again. "Jamie?"

Tim waited, but no answer came. He called out again and again. Still nothing.

He was about to turn around and double back, hoping to bump into them along the way, when he noticed something down by the creek bed.

Tim cut off of the trail and hurried past the sparse undergrowth, stopping short on the sandy, rock-strewn ground next to the babbling stream.

He stared for several breaths at the disturbed earth. Rocks were dug up and moved in random directions. That wasn't what bothered him. The footprints in the soil belonged to his sons. He would have recognized the distinct indentations of their two shoe sizes anywhere.

A distant fear that resided deep in the abyss of every parent's mind began to surface as he gazed at the thing that caught his attention.

Oliver's red daypack sat on the ground next to the water.

Panic flooded Tim's chest. He called out over and over again, yelling their names as loudly as possible, but the answer remained the same as all the other times—a agonizing, hollow silence that brought the nightmare to life and gripped every fiber of his soul.

His boys were gone.

TWO

LEXINGTON, KENTUCKY

"You see that?"

Dak didn't respond to the question right away. He stared at the computer screen, analyzing the data that corresponded with the circle overlaying the map.

"Yeah, Will. I see it."

"Two more this week."

Dak nodded, barely glancing at the cell phone on the hotel desk next to him. Will was on speaker so Dak could focus all of his attention on the monitor.

It hadn't taken Will long to zero in on the pattern evolving in Kentucky. Nine people had gone missing in the Daniel Boone National Forest during the last four months. All but one were young boys under the age of fifteen. The one outlier was a young woman in her twenties, though she was suspected of being involved with a local heroin dealer.

The circle on the map shaded an area Dak had only been to twice. He'd traveled to the Cumberland Gap to meet a girl who was in college near there. The drive had taken nearly four hours, much of which was through beautiful, albeit remote, countryside.

"Seems like the town of Browns Ferry is in the middle of it all," Dak noted, zooming in on the name.

Browns Ferry was a small town of less than two thousand people spread out in the hills of Southeastern Kentucky. Dak clicked on the link and then on the images tab to look at some pictures from the area.

"Sure is pretty," he commented.

"Yeah, it definitely is," Will agreed. "Looks like a nice place to get away from it all and relax, do some camping in the woods."

"Or abduct young boys."

"Yeah," Will said reluctantly. "I've pulled the records, although it took some doing. It's amazing how these small towns are often more difficult to squeeze information from than the bigger cities. They get so uptight about giving anything away."

Dak snorted. "Dad always said that there was way more corruption in the small towns and cities than in the big ones."

"Good old boy mindset, huh?"

"Exactly." Dak continued scanning through the images for another minute and then returned to the search bar, entered Browns Ferry Kentucky, and waited for the results to populate.

Several news articles appeared at the top. The most recent was from three days before.

Two brothers had gone camping with their parents on a family excursion into the Daniel Boone National Forest. According to the report, the boys went off on a hike while their parents cooked lunch. The older boy was fifteen and in good health. That explained why the parents were okay with the two wandering off on their own. Dak recalled playing on his own when he was younger, traipsing all over the neighborhood and the adjoining forests and parks with the other kids. They never had parental supervision, and there was no telling what manner of trouble they could have gotten into.

Times were different then. The world had changed, and in the case of letting kids play outside and run wild, it wasn't for the better.

More and more parents turned into helicopters, constantly hovering over their children, watching them every second of the day.

Dak didn't blame them. With human trafficking on the rise all over the planet, and much of it happening in the United States, it was better to be safe than sorry. He wasn't sure he wouldn't keep constant watch on a child if he had one of his own.

Still, out in the forest where this family had been... it seemed pretty random.

"Will, how many people go missing in national forests each year?"

His friend huffed through the speaker. "You have a search engine the same as me, right?"

"Yes," Dak said, elongating the word. "Just thought maybe you'd already checked on it, being the thorough guy that you are."

Will sighed. "Well, you'd be right about that. I did check, actually."

Dak waited for a second, then pressed his friend. "You going to tell me or do I have to coax it out of you?"

"There isn't a clear answer, Dak. It's really strange. I've found a few resources that suggest there are around sixteen hundred missing persons in the United States who disappeared in a national park."

"Sounds like a lot." Dak struggled to fathom how that number could be so high.

"It is. And it's probably much higher. Then there are the total number of disappearances. Did you know that there are between eighty and ninety thousand active missing persons filed at any given time?"

The staggering number echoed in Dak's mind. "Ninety thousand people?"

"Yeah. Crazy, right? How do that many people just vanish? And why isn't there more news about that? I know I don't live in the States anymore, but I don't recall ever seeing anything about those numbers. It's called America's silent disaster. I pulled up some other areas where suspicious disappearances like this have been happening. I stuck to Kentucky, though, since that's where your boy Luis said this guy was hiding."

Since the double murder in Cuchara, Colorado, Dak hadn't been certain whether Nate really was in Kentucky—for the time being, at least. The more he thought about it, though, the more Dak believed someone else must have taken out Billy and the sheriff.

As the days waned on, he reinforced that belief with logic and reason. Nate had no reason to take out Billy or the sheriff. Those two must have ticked off a local, possibly someone who'd been in the military before. The execution, though, stunk of something dirtier. Dak found himself wondering what Billy had gotten into, how deep he'd burrowed into a seedy underworld.

Then again, Cuchara was a small place. How much corruption could there be?

The question returned his focus to the circle on the map. "This has to be the place," Dak said, referring to the monitor. "The rest of the disappearances in Kentucky are one offs. Not more than two occur in the same place. We have eight here, though, in Browns Ferry." He realized he'd gotten off track earlier and redirected the conversation. "Sorry, Will. You said you got in touch with the locals?"

"Yeah," Will said. "Like I was saying, tough nut to crack, but I finally got one of the real estate agents to give me what I wanted. They looked it up in the records and found that a guy came into town sometime last year and bought a huge patch of land on the edge of the national forest."

"What's this guy's name?"

"The purchase was made by a Vernon Stratford."

"I don't suppose you were able to dig up where Mr. Vernon Stratford is from, were you? Maybe some additional info?"

"Not from the real estate agent. That information, unfortunately, wasn't available to him. I was, however, able to learn that Stratford has a pretty interesting background."

"Background? I thought you said you couldn't get anything."

"I said the real estate agent isn't privy to that kind of stuff. Pay attention, Dak. After all, who do you think you're talking to?" Will pretended to be hurt, then chuckled.

"You're right. Sorry. Go on."

"Vernon Stratford has a sketchy record. I was able to dig up a birth certificate, but it was from Panama. Let's just say that some of the record keeping in certain places down there isn't accurate. The certificate claims he was born to ex-pats from Texas, Gene and Sarah Stratford. Those people are real, as far as I can tell. And they did move to Panama more than thirty years ago."

"Wonder why they did that?"

"Some places in that country are pretty nice. And they make some real good coffee. A lot of Americans move down there near the canal. Some start their own little businesses. Most probably go just to enjoy a tropical climate and do some fishing."

"I've been to Panama," Dak confessed. "Wasn't bad, except for the humidity. That was brutal."

"So I've heard."

"I'm guessing Gene and Sarah didn't have any kids."

"You'd guess right," Will confirmed. "No children, which makes the appearance of their son in Kentucky all the more suspicious."

"Sounds like whoever this guy is, he did some serious work to get his papers in line."

"Full American citizenship and all. The guy even pays his taxes and doesn't try to max out his deductions for a refund."

Everything lined up. The circle of missing persons, the file on this Vernon Stratford, all of it pointed to Dak's next target: Nate.

A chill shot across his skin at the thought, and he recalled the things Nate had said after he'd massacred all those people. He had to shake the thoughts away. The visions were too graphic, and the idea that Nate could be abducting young boys and torturing them was too much.

He had to find out more about this Vernon Stratford. The sooner the better. A mounting pressure swelled in Dak's chest and he felt a blanket of anxiety wrap around him.

Eight missing people in the last few months. Could he save any of them? Or was he already too late?

"Thanks, Will. I appreciate all the information. I'll let you know what I find."

"Do that. And Dak?"

"Yeah?"

"Be careful. I still haven't been able to find anything on Bo Taylor, which is concerning. He's still out there and if he thinks you might be a threat, it's possible he could come after you."

"He knows I'm a threat," Dak growled. "If I was in his shoes, I'd come after me, too. The last thing I'd do is sit around and wait in some bunker waiting for Armageddon to come to me."

"Yeah, I don't think I would do it that way either. Good luck. And I'll keep looking."

Dak ended the call and stared at the computer monitor. "Browns Ferry," he said. He diverted his gaze to the window and looked toward the east.

What was meant to be a payback mission had turned into a potential rescue.

THREE

BROWN'S FERRY

Jamie sat on the cold, hard floor with his back against the wall. His brother sat with his legs crossed a few feet away. Oliver's sniffles echoed in the dark room. The only light glowed dimly from somewhere outside the door and radiated through the cracks at the top and bottom. It was better than utter darkness, but not much.

Oliver wasn't a helpless kid. His instincts had been to scream and to fight off their captor with every ounce of strength he could summon. Those fanciful notions evaporated when the man produced a gun and threatened to kill them both if they so much as uttered a single word.

Then the man shoved pillowcases over their heads and marched them through the forest. They had no idea where they were being taken, with only the trail at their feet as a point of reference. After five minutes of hiking at gunpoint, they were steered off the trail and forced to continue up a hill until they reached a spot where sunshine warmed their clothes.

Jamie had spent enough time outside to know they'd probably walked into a meadow or small clearing. That knowledge did him no good. Without a way to leave a message—some kind of sign that he and Oliver had been there and were being taken—knowing where they'd been was of no consequence.

He considered pretending to trip and fall, perhaps dig into the earth with his shoes to leave prints. That desperate plan would have only angered their captor, a tall, grim-looking man with a head shaped like a brick and his dark brown hair cut to match.

Within minutes of arriving in the meadow, the boys were removed from the tall brown grass and placed in the back of a pickup truck with their hands bound behind them. The kidnapper hadn't been gentle, tightening the zip ties to the point the circulation in Jamie's fingers began to tingle. It took a good amount of wiggling his wrists on the bumpy ride to get the blood flowing correctly again.

He'd told Oliver at least ten times during the journey that everything was going to be okay, that their mom and dad would find them and the cops would arrest this guy and put him in prison for a long time.

Jamie wished he believed it.

Maybe a small part of him did—the part that still wanted to believe in Santa Claus and the tooth fairy.

He didn't know how long they'd been down in this basement or dungeon or whatever it was, but he felt like it hadn't been more than a couple of days. The oppressive darkness was broken three times a day for the boys to be fed, but that didn't do much for helping either of them get a grasp on where they were being kept.

The cinder block walls surrounding them were barricaded by a wooden door. The cell took up around sixty to eighty square feet. They'd been given a bucket and told that was their toilet, and to set it at the door each day when their food was brought.

The dim yellow light that came through the cracks temporarily brightened whenever a slot at the bottom of the door slid open for them to shove the slop bucket through or for the food plates to be given.

Jamie wasn't stupid. He knew they were being kept for something, but he didn't want to consider what that could be. And there was no way he'd share any such theories with his little brother.

There'd been stories that Jamie had heard when he was younger than Oliver—about kids who disappeared. Some tales were just that, urban legends passed down in the kid circle to scare others. Then there were others, told by his parents as a warning.

These were the ones that haunted Jamie's thoughts as he sat in the dim, musty cell.

His entire life, his parents had warned him not to talk to strangers and used examples of other missing children as examples, real-life cautionary tales. They never mentioned human trafficking by name, but Jamie knew it was something that happened. Was that what was going on here? Was this sicko keeping them down here until their slave trader came to pick them up?

Jamie would never have thought anything like this could happen to him or his brother. They lived a normal, suburban life with good, hard-working parents. Now all of that was gone.

He felt a tear lurking in the corner of his eye, threatening to break loose and dive down his cheek. He rubbed the back of his wrist against his eyelids to keep the tear from escaping. Jamie felt like he had to be strong for his brother. Crying would only make things worse.

Jamie heard a moan from somewhere else in the basement, and it shook him from his thoughts. He'd heard the sound before, but he didn't dare say anything. The man who'd taken them warned them about talking while in captivity. They were to remain quiet.

For what?

It's not like they could find a way out of this place, and even if they could, where would they go? They had no point of reference, no way of even knowing where they were. For all Jamie knew, they could be minutes away from his parents' campsite or several miles.

That was the one thing he could determine: distance.

Their kidnapper hadn't driven far. It took less than ten minutes for them to arrive here—wherever here was—once they'd been stuffed into the back of the truck. That meant they were close to the park, to their parents' camper.

The cliché throbbed in his mind. So close, yet so far away.

Jamie heard the groan of a young person's voice again. It didn't make him feel better, but he took a small measure of comfort in knowing that he and Oliver weren't the only kids down in this hole. But why, and for how long?

"I'm tired, Jamie," Oliver breathed. "I want to go home."

The words cut through the silence and stabbed straight through Jamie's heart. He turned and looked at his brother with empathy. "I know, bud. I do too. We'll get out of here. I promise."

"Are you sure?"

Jamie had never been more uncertain of anything in his life. And for the first time he could remember, he lied to his little brother. "I'm sure."

FOUR

BROWN'S FERRY

Nathaniel Collier stood erect in front of the stove, watching the sirloin steak sizzle in the frying pan. The morning sun hung over the horizon through the kitchen window to his right. Rays of light poured through and glistened over dust motes floating in the air.

Nate worked his hands deliberately back and forth in a methodical rhythm, running a kitchen knife across the honing steel. The shallow grinding sound of the blade against the rod echoed through the kitchen with only the intermittent songs of birds interrupting from the giant oak tree outside.

He took pleasure in the act, the knife soliciting a grim smile as he continued to hone it to a razor's edge.

Systems, Nate believed, were the only thing that separated civilization from chaos. He reveled in systems, fed off them. He'd approached everything he did in the military with the same precision he used with the knife in his hands.

The men on his team had called him reckless on occasion. They'd seen him cut down countless enemies with his machine gun as if he merely utilized it like a scythe. To him, it was a precision instrument more like a scalpel. He'd never argued the point with the others.

They preferred their rifles, eliminating targets with a single shot or a short burst.

When it came to clearing out a room, though, they didn't complain when he took out potential threats by the dozens.

His mind wandered to the group of young terrorist recruits he'd wiped out while deployed in the Middle East. The others thought Nate didn't hear their comments or notice their disgust at the act.

The fact was, those boys were a threat. They were extremists in training. To let them live would have been a danger.

But something else awakened in him that day, a slow burning fire that had been smoldering in the depths of his soul since he was a boy.

Nate looked over at the steak. He set down the knife on a bamboo cutting board, picked up a pair of tongs next to it, and flipped the steak over onto the uncooked side. The meat sizzled louder as the flesh touched the hot skillet. Juices bubbled all around it in the olive oil he'd sprinkled in earlier.

The smell drifted through the air and trickled through his nostrils, filling them with the intoxicating aroma.

He glanced out the window at the field beyond the gravel driveway. Rows of corn filled ten acres. Beyond, forests surrounded the entire property—a natural barrier from the outside world. He owned more than one hundred acres, much of which he'd used as his private hunting grounds.

His mind returned to the grand scheme he'd laid out, the one rooted in something he'd always been denied—except by the military.

Even as a young man, Nate was consumed by the act of taking a life. It started when he was only thirteen, when a neighbor's dogs continued to wander into their yard—barking incessantly.

His father—a drunk and a gambler—was too inept to handle the problem. And Nate's mother had left the two of them when he was only seven.

Nate found one of his father's guns, a 9mm Ruger P89, and took care of the issue on a dark night when thunderstorms rolled through town. The thunder, he rationalized, would mute the sound of the gun's discharge.

He'd been right. The neighbors never suspected a thing, though they came by once and asked if Nate had seen the animal. He lied, of course, having disposed of the evidence in a dumpster behind a local watering hole up the street.

After killing the animal, Nate felt something, something that had never graced him before. It was a strange sense of joy, but more than that, he felt powerful. He could determine the fate of a living thing. And he wanted more of that feeling.

At first, he turned to hunting as the outlet for his newfound passion. His father's old hunting rifle had been collecting dust for years while the old man sat on the couch in a drunken haze, earning money with a government paycheck for as long as Nate could remember.

With his dad plastered to the sofa, Nate started taking the pickup truck out into the hills where he could hunt small game. He was a large boy for his age and knew the local cops wouldn't pull him over if he didn't break any laws—other than driving without a license.

He'd take out squirrels and rabbits in the early days, but later he moved up to larger game. Wild turkey, deer, and hogs were among those animals he sought most, though the turkeys didn't do much for him. They were dumb animals, easy to kill. Too easy, in his mind.

Nate leaned more toward the hogs and deer for his killing preference. Most people who enjoyed deer hunting loved it for the serenity of a chilly fall morning in a tree stand, the thrill of spotting their quarry and getting off the perfect shot. Some, Nate heard, looked at it in an almost spiritual way, the way the Indigenous Tribes did long ago.

Not Nate.

His enjoyment of hunting deer derived from taking the life of something innocent and pure. But with every kill, he wanted more. On one occasion, he'd managed to kill several in a single outing, far more than was permitted by the authorities. He recalled seeing the bodies strewn out on the leaves in a forest, and how that sight had given him so much satisfaction—but hardly slaked his lust for bloodshed.

He flipped the steak again and once more the sizzle sparkled through the room.

Hogs were a joy to slaughter for other reasons. They were wild, untamed, much like the deer, but they were also capable of aggression. Dirty, vile beasts, Nate enjoyed the thrill of killing them at closer range with his father's .45 revolver. The danger of being gouged by a boar's tusks only heightened the thrill.

There had been a particularly dangerous hog on one of his hunts. The animal bore long tusks and weighed at least two hundred pounds. The hog charged at Nate, fully intending to defend its turf and rip the young man apart. Nate stood his ground, watching coolly with a pistol dangling in his hand by his right hip. He'd waited, staring into the eyes of the beast as it roared toward him, grunting with every breath.

At the last moment, Nate raised the weapon like a gunslinger from the Old West. He pulled the trigger and sent the round through the animal's skull. The boar's legs buckled under it and the creature skidded to a dead stop mere feet away from where Nate stood.

He stared into the lifeless, vapid eyes of the creature with eyes that mirrored them. He grinned, then emptied the revolver, pulling the trigger over and over until the beast's body was a mangled, bloody mess.

Nate recalled that hunt with satisfaction as he took the steak from the skillet and turned off the stove. He set the meat down on a white plate and let it rest while he bent down and took the potato he'd been baking for the last 45 minutes out of the oven.

He set the foil-wrapped tuber onto the plate next to his steak and walked over to the front room to look out the window. The forest beyond the cornfield still loitered in shadows, and he grinned with satisfaction at the plan he'd laid out.

He recalled reading fictional stories in school about strange islands where madmen hunted humans. Those hunters weren't madmen to him. They were pioneers forging a path to a forbidden and newfound ecstasy.

Nate had tried to satisfy that need, that deep-rooted desire, by joining the military. There, he thought, he could hunt other people and get paid to do it. While he'd had his share and more of confirmed kills, with every life he took he still felt something was missing.

He realized what it was when he recalled reading Lord of the Flies when he was in high school. Those young boys had taken on the characteristics of both the deer and the boar he so loved to hunt. They were innocent, yet untamed. They were clever, organized, and resourceful.

Those boys were the perfect quarry, Nate thought. And he'd felt that confirmation when he slaughtered the extremists in that room in Iraq. That day, the plan began formulating in the back of his mind. When he and his team stumbled onto the treasure in the mountains of Iraq, he knew that vision could become a reality. He could buy his own farm with more acreage than he ever dreamed—his own private hunting ground. And with the property next to a heavily visited park, he would have an unlimited supply of game.

He took in a deep breath and sighed with satisfaction, then returned to the kitchen, set down the plate on a table, and began slicing through the steak with the knife he'd sharpened so carefully earlier.

Tomorrow, he thought, the hunt begins.

FIVE

BROWN'S FERRY

Dak rolled by the police department building in Browns Ferry and let out a sigh. Two squad cars sat off to the side of the tiny brick building. The structure looked like a glorified shed. There was one door on the front with a window on either side. Faux white columns braced the overhanging triangular roof, but the place looked anything but dignified or authoritative.

There was probably one or two holding tanks inside, but if any real crimes were committed, the prisoners were likely transferred as soon as possible to a more secure county facility. Dak doubted any major crimes plagued the sleepy little town, save for the ones he was investigating.

He stepped on the gas and accelerated down the road.

Going in and talking to the local cops would be a waste of time. Not because they were inept or corrupt—although that could be the case—but Dak made certain not to judge people he'd never met.

The real reason for circumventing the police was that they had processes, protocols, methods, all of which slowed things down during an investigation. Dak had no doubts the women and men in that building or out in their patrol cars were doing everything in their power to find the eight missing boys, but unfortunately, their power was limited.

Dak briefly considered going in there and telling them he believed he'd found the location of the boys and the man who'd taken them, but he knew how that interaction would go.

The cops would file a report, take down his information—the fake stuff Will had conjured—and maybe have a look into Collier's new farm at some point in the next month, if that. They would need a warrant to search the place and going on some stranger's wild theory would hardly suffice for even probable cause, much less a legitimate warrant.

Then there was the issue of them seeing his face. Keeping a low profile was paramount.

He slowed down as he entered the Main Street square of town. A variety of shops lined the sidewalks that wrapped around the square. From parking spots along the inner portion of the street, sidewalks angled in from each corner, stopping in the center of a grassy lawn where a statue stood. The figure looked like a pioneer, with a raccoon cap and a musket in one hand. Dak figured it was either the Brown the town was named after, or possibly—and more likely—a tribute to Daniel Boone, who was a legend in this part of the country.

Dak slowly cruised through the square, noting the people and businesses along the way. Barely a minute after entering the center of town, he was through and on the other side, heading toward a motel a quarter mile down the street.

When he saw the big yellow sign with black letters—complete with the neon "vacancy" sign below it—he slowed and turned on his blinker. A few cars occupied parking spots in the crumbling asphalt lot. Two were more than a decade old and Dak assumed that one of them had to belong to the manager. The third vehicle was newer—an SUV parked next to a camper on the far right side of the L-shaped building.

Dak swung into a vacant parking spot and let the engine idle for a minute as he considered his next move.

He knew the McDowells were in the unit on the end, but approaching a couple of parents about the issue with their sons couldn't have been a more delicate matter. He had to have all the right words at the right times, or they would get suspicious and not only that, he could upset them further. Dak and their sons couldn't afford that.

He turned off the ignition and stepped out of the SUV, still wondering if he'd made the right decision in coming here. He stiffened his spine as he strode toward the door, doing his best to look confident in a rare moment of mind-racking doubt. When he stopped at the door, he paused and hesitated. After a couple of deep breaths, Dak rapped on the door and took a step back.

A woman's voice—muted by the door—reverberated from inside. After a few seconds, Dak heard it again, giving a description of him to someone else inside the room. Dak knew Martha McDowell was giving her husband Timothy the details, but at the moment those were the only definitive bits he could cling to.

The deadbolt unlocked, and the door cracked open with the chain still hanging on the rod in the frame. A tired-looking woman peered out from the dimly lit motel room.

Dark circles hung under her bloodshot eyes, and her hair dangled in haphazard strands. "Yes?"

"Mrs. McDowell?"

"Who are you?" she asked, her tone as exhausted as her features. "Another reporter? I'm done giving interviews."

"No, ma'am. I'm not a reporter. And I'm not a cop." The moment of truth built up a knot of tension inside Dak unlike anything he'd ever felt before. This woman's sons were being held by a man he'd served with, and there was simply no easy way to tell her that. "I'm here to help you find your sons."

SIX

BROWN'S FERRY

At first, Martha didn't know what to say. She merely stood there with a worn look of confusion at the statement. Then she sighed and collected her thoughts. "Is this some kind of joke?" she managed.

"No, ma'am. I wouldn't joke about something like this. I'm serious. And I believe I can find them, but we need to hurry. I don't know how much more time we have."

She puzzled over his statement, then looked him up and down. "Who are you?"

The blunt question didn't catch Dak off guard. "Let's just say I'm a private investigator and leave it at that."

"Doesn't exactly give me much of a reason to trust you now, does it?" She started to ease the door shut.

"Please," he said. "I was in the army with the guy I believe took your boys. I'd give you my name, but I don't want you to get pulled into my mess. But I will tell you this, the man who took your sons... he's as sinister as they come. I served with him a long time, and I know what he's capable of."

Tears started brimming in her tired eyes.

"But I also know how to get to him. I just need to ask you a couple of questions. That's all. I promise I won't bother you again."

"Martha?" Tim asked from somewhere inside the motel room. "What's going on?"

The man appeared behind her. His haggard face displayed the same exhaustion as his wife's, but with a hint of anger.

"This man says he is here to help us find the boys." She looked to her husband, gazing into his eyes as if her stare might pry answers from them.

He could only stare back blankly for a breath before turning to Dak. "Leave us alone. The police are doing what they can. And we've had enough fake leads for the last thirty-six hours."

He started to shut the door, but Dak set his foot in the way and blocked it, leaving nothing but the thinnest sliver between the door and frame.

"I'm not a fake lead," Dak said. "And the cops can't help your boys. I'm sure they're doing all they can, but there isn't time for red tape and bureaucracy."

"Martha," Tim said, ignoring Dak, "call the police."

She let go of the door and retreated into the room, disappearing behind the wall.

"If you call them, you will never get your boys back," Dak said. "All I ask is you give me five minutes of your time. Five minutes. I know you have no reason to trust me. But I'm going to find the man who took your sons, one way or the other. If you help me, I might be able to save them. If you don't, I could get there too late."

He could see through the crack that Tim was considering the offer. The man's eyes betrayed desperation littered among the red blood vessels streaking the whites. He was a man at his wits' end, not ready to give up the search, but with hope dangling by the most frayed of threads.

"Martha?" he said, lowering his head dejectedly. "Hold on."

Dak felt the push on the door ease and then heard the chain

unhinge from the clasp. A second later, the door swung open. The room reeked of body odor and pizza. It took less than two seconds for Dak to survey the interior. He noted the source of the second smell, two unopened pizza boxes on a desk in the corner to the left. An empty bottle of Four Roses bourbon sat next to the television, with a second half-full one nearby.

"Who are you?" Tim asked. "Some kind of private investigator?"

"Something like that," Dak said. "But I can't give you my name. I can give you a fake one if you want. I will, however, give you as much information about myself as I can, if that will help."

"A man with no name and a mysterious past?" Tim shook his head. Then he swore under his breath. "Come on in. If you're here to kill us, you'd be doing us a favor."

"Timothy," Martha protested. "For all we know, he could be the one who took—" Her voice faltered before she could finish the sentence.

Dak stepped inside the darkened room and shook his head. "No, ma'am. I didn't take your boys." He eased the door shut behind him. "But I know who did."

A weak cough escaped her lips. Tim's eyelids tightened as he searched the visitor for the truth.

"What do you mean, you know who did?" Tim begged. "Why haven't you called the police?"

Dak turned and faced the man with a calm, disarming stare. "The police are good at their jobs, Mr. McDowell. But they have to play by too many rules. I don't. If I told them who I believe took your sons, it would be days before they could get a proper warrant—if they ever did. They can't do much on hearsay or conjecture. And then there's the little issue of me not wanting them to know who I am."

"Why's that?" Martha asked bravely.

Dak twisted his head toward her. "Because the man who took your sons tried to kill me when we were in Iraq. He and the rest of my team betrayed me and left me for dead in a cave in the Hamrin Mountains. You won't see it on any news channel or website, so don't bother looking. I've been hiding out, lying low while I track their whereabouts."

"So you can kill them?" Tim guessed.

Dak didn't look over at him this time. "That's right. But right now, my revenge story takes a back seat to what's going on with your sons."

"And you think... one of the soldiers you served with took them?" Martha asked.

"I do. His name is Nathan Collier. He was spec ops and I'll leave it at that." Dak pulled a small tablet from his jacket and pressed the button to activate it. He turned the screen toward Tim and indicated the man look at it. "This is a map," he said, pointing out the obvious. "Where exactly were you camping the day your boys disappeared?"

"What?"

Dak sighed and forced patience into his mind. "The Daniel Boone National Forest is an enormous place. Lots of ways to get lost in there. But your boys didn't get lost. They were taken. That's how I'm looking at this. If that is the case, then I need to get an idea of where they were."

He didn't tell them he believed he'd already located the farm where their boys were being held. Doing so might incite them to call the police. The best-case scenario for that would be cops showing up at Collier's and making him paranoid. People who get spooked do erratic things. He might skip town, and worse, dispose of the boys before leaving.

"What makes you think you have information the cops don't?" Tim argued. "They've checked with every house within a ten mile radius of where the boys went missing. That search turned up nothing."

"I'm sure they did. Except that I have no intention of knocking on doors. My plan is to knock them down. I just need you to confirm the location of where you were camping and about where your boys disappeared. Can you point that out on the map to me?"

Tim exhaled. The breath, laden with despair and impatience,

flapped his lips as he took the tablet from the visitor and zoomed in on the area where he believed Jamie and Oliver were taken. "Not sure why you have to come here like this," he commented as he inspected the map. "The news outlets have been showing this nonstop the last few days."

"I don't exactly trust the media," Dak said. "Sometimes they get information wrong. I had to be sure."

Tim looked up from the tablet, gauging the visitor's face. Then he nodded. "Yeah, I guess you're right. One local paper spelled Oliver's name Olivier."

Dak snorted, and the tension in the room eased.

"Here is the spot," Tim said, indicating an area by the creek on the map with his finger. "That's where they—" he stopped.

"I understand."

"What do you think," Martha faltered, "what do you think this Collier is going to do to our boys?"

"I don't know, ma'am. But I'm not going to let it happen, whatever he has planned. I'll take care of him before he can harm your sons."

There was no way Dak could know that. They might already be dead. But he had to give the mother some sense of hope, even if it was false.

He turned to leave. Tim stopped him.

"That's it? You're leaving?"

Dak paused and looked back over his shoulder. "Yep. You confirmed my suspicions. That's all I needed to know. You two stay here. And please, I don't think I need to tell you not to mention my presence to the cops. That would complicate things, and I prefer to keep it simple. Understand?" It wasn't a threat, but if they took it that way Dak didn't mind.

They both nodded nervously in agreement.

"Good. See you soon."

He opened the door and stepped outside, closing it again without looking back.

His intel had been spot on. The boys disappeared within a few miles of Nate's new farm. There was no telling what his ex-teammate was up to. All Dak knew for now was that it couldn't be good. He'd have to move fast to recon the property. Luckily, he had the right tools for the job.

SEVEN

BROWN'S FERRY

The lights in the basement flickered on, casting a dim glow into the cell Jamie and Oliver shared.

"Breakfast, runts," their captor growled.

The smell of sausage and oatmeal filled the room and immediately caused Jamie's stomach to rumble hungrily.

The man holding them prisoner had been feeding them regularly since they arrived, but he had never spoken to them—not even in a demeaning tone. The fact the man decided to speak today gave Jamie a cold chill that pebbled his skin.

He could hear their warden issuing plates to the other prisoners. Jamie had already counted once before, but he did it every time they were fed just to make sure none of the other captives had... he didn't want to consider it.

He'd not risked talking to the others, but he knew there were at least six, though it was unclear if the other cells had more than one person in them as did the one where he and his brother were kept.

That meant there were at least eight people down in the basement.

Were they all boys? Or were there girls mixed in?

Again, the answer was unclear.

All Jamie knew was that something different was about to happen and he didn't like the way it made his senses tingle.

The plates for him and his brother appeared at the bottom of the door. The man nudged the food deeper into the room before the opening closed again.

"I suggest you eat up today, boys," the man's voice boomed again.

A clue, Jamie thought. He called us boys. That answers that question.

"Tomorrow, you're going to have a day out in the sun."

The sun? Jamie never thought such a simple indulgence would sound so incredible, but the mere idea of the warmth of the sun touching his face filled his soul with the slightest sliver of hope. Still, he couldn't help but sense there was a catch.

"Many of you have read books or seen movies where young people are thrown into a game where they hunt each other for sport. Only the winner survives."

Oh, no. Jamie realized where this was going. At least he thought he did. He looked over at Oliver who returned the glance with one smothered in worry.

"You have been recruited to take part in a similar game, but I have good news." Their warden paused for effect. "You won't be pitted against each other. You will have only one enemy to evade."

Jamie didn't allow the statement to give the faintest trickle of relief. He knew there was more.

"That enemy is me. I will release you and give all of you a fifteen-minute head start. After that, how long you survive is up to your ability to run, hide, and adapt. One of you might even get lucky and take me down." He huffed at the latter, clearly thinking the notion unlikely. "We will begin at noon tomorrow. So eat up and get some rest. You're going to need it."

He paused again, and for a few seconds, Jamie thought his speech was over. Then the man spoke again. "This property spreads out over one hundred acres of varying terrain. There are fields, hills, meadows, forests. If you want to survive longer, you best consider all that."

Heavy footfalls clomped up the stairs and faded as they neared the top. A door closed, signaling that the prisoners were alone again.

Jamie noted how the man said "survive longer," an insinuation that their demise was only a matter of time. He looked over at his brother again to gauge his reaction, but that tidbit seemed to sail over Oliver's head. Jamie was glad for that.

How had all of this happened? How did they end up in a place like this with a monster like the man who'd taken them?

Jamie ran over the events of that fateful day in his mind for the hundredth time. He wished he could toss away the regrets. His mother told them not to go, that lunch would be ready soon. She'd suggested their father go with them, but the boys insisted they would be okay.

How wrong he'd been.

Over the course of the last 36 to 48 hours, or however long it had been, Jamie made the same promise over and over again. He swore he would never question his parents' judgment again.

Unfortunately, he didn't see a way out.

Then again, maybe there was. He got up and took the few steps over to the plates, then scooped them up.

Oliver had remained sitting in his usual spot against the wall with his arms wrapped around his knees.

"Here you go, Oli," Jamie said, doing his best to sound cheerful. "You heard the man. Eat up. We're going to get out of here tomorrow."

"That's not what he said," Oliver disputed. "He said he's going to hunt us and kill us."

Jamie's voice soured at the comment.

"He said he's going to give us fifteen minutes head start, Oli." Jamie made sure to keep his voice low. "He also said there are a hundred acres on this property. That's lots of places to hide. Or disappear," he added quickly. "We could find a good place to hide and stay there until night. Then, when it's dark, we'll sneak out and find a way back into town."

"What town?" Oliver asked, picking at the sausage on his plate. "We don't even know where we are."

"We can't be that far from Browns Ferry," Jamie insisted. "When he put us in the back of the truck, we didn't travel far. Two or three miles, maybe four or five, but I doubt that far. He took us somewhere close to the park."

Another voice entered the conversation from somewhere else in the basement. It hissed in the darkness, barely a whisper. "Be quiet," the boy warned. "He will come back and punish us."

"Yeah," a second agreed, this one stronger, gruff.

It was the first time Jamie had heard the others since being stuffed into the cell with his kid brother. A strange comfort fluttered into his soul at hearing the other kids' voices.

"Listen," Jamie ordered. "You heard the guy. He intends to let us loose in his own private game park and hunt us down like animals."

Oliver looked up from his sausage, troubled by the statement.

Jamie quickly added, "We can get out of here if we work together."

"How do you figure?" A third new voice entered the conversation. The weak tone signaled that the boy speaking must have been there for a while. He sounded utterly weary. Jamie had heard that before, but from adults, not another kid.

Jamie held his plate, pinched between forefinger and thumb, as he shuffled over to the door. He leaned close to the opening so the others could hear better. "How many of us are in here?"

No one spoke. He waited for nearly twenty seconds before another voice, this one slightly deeper than the others he'd heard, finally answered.

"Eight, counting you two." The boy sounded like he might be Jamie's age, or maybe older. "I was the first one in here as far as I know. If there were any other boys down here, they're gone now. But

I don't think there were. I was his first." The despondency in his voice cracked, and the words faded away.

Several seconds passed before he spoke again. "The second one came in a few days later. After that, he didn't bring anyone for a couple of weeks."

"That's when I got here," the second voice said. "I was the third."

Silence resumed.

"If there are eight of us, we have a chance," Jamie said confidently. "He's only one man."

"We don't have any weapons," the first argued. "And he's not going to give us any. You heard him. Our only chance is to run and hide. I have a feeling that won't help. He's probably an expert hunter or something. He'll track us down like wild animals."

Jamie stole a sidelong glance at his brother's reaction to the comment. Oliver's eyes suddenly filled with worry. The sausage on his plate no longer seemed appealing.

"We still have a chance if we stick together," Jamie said. "We have fifteen minutes to find a way out of this place."

"It's a hundred acres," the third interjected again. "There's no way we can cover that kind of ground in fifteen minutes."

"Neither can he."

"Unless he's using an ATV or something," the first said.

"True. That's a possibility."

"We should split up," another voice said. This one was new to the conversation. The speaker sounded different from the others in that his accent was different, probably from the northeast. New York City, if Jamie recalled correctly. He'd only been there once, but met several people from that area and to him, the distinct way they spoke stuck with him through the years.

"We could," Jamie agreed, partially. "But if we do that, he could hunt us down one by one. We're stronger together."

"So, what? He can kill us all in one go? I don't think so."

"I agree," the first said. "We have a better chance if we split up.

Individually, we will be harder to track, especially if we all go in different directions. He may get one or two of us, but not all of us."

The sobering statement quieted the basement once more. Jamie hated to consider the notion that a few of them wouldn't make it out of here alive. They were right on one count, though, and he couldn't dispute that. If they moved as a herd, the boys would be easier to track—even for a novice hunter. He doubted this man was that.

"Fine," Jamie said. "We'll split up and go our separate ways."

He shook his head at the unspoken question in his brother's eyes. "Not us, Oli," Jamie mouthed. "We stick together. No matter what."

EIGHT

BROWN'S FERRY

Dak found what he was looking for on the side of the road near the forest. He'd noticed it before when circling Nate's property, but wanted to inspect every inch before returning to the spot.

He spent the last hour driving around, looking for any signs of a security system along the perimeter. All he found was the old barbed wire fence that wrapped around the farm. Nate hadn't taken the time to update the fencing yet, if he ever planned on it. There were no cameras that Dak could see, but if there were, the devices would likely be camouflaged and hung in the trees. Dak had used similar hunting cameras before to track animals that came and went in the night.

Dak steered the SUV off the road into the pull-off and continued forward until the road vanished behind the thick rows of trees and undergrowth. He'd seen the old trail on his first pass and figured it would be a good place to park. No one would know he was there unless they were really looking. Dak bet that wouldn't happen.

He stopped the vehicle and killed the engine. Peering through the windshield, Dak continued to scour the flat woods in front of him. Then he turned his attention up the hill to his right. It climbed up over a ridge and descended into what he knew was Nate's property. Will supplied the information regarding the property lines and their current boundaries. With that, Dak knew almost down to a foot where Nate's land began and ended.

It was a good start, though Dak knew he had to work fast. He'd promised the McDowells he would find their boys. There was no way to make such a guarantee. For all he knew, the boys could already be dead, along with the other six that had disappeared in the region over the last few months.

He forced that thought out of his mind. The boys were alive. He didn't know why he felt that way, but it pumped through his veins with every heartbeat. He knew it was irrational. In most instances such as this, false hope was the most crushing thing a person could cling to. The devastation that resulted from bad news would feel like falling a thousand feet with a tragic and sudden stop at the bottom.

Dak let the comparison fade away as he opened the SUV's back door and slid his gear to the edge. He pulled a black, hardshell case next to it and flipped it open.

Inside, a drone with a carbon fiber frame and gray shell rested in the foam cushioning. A white, first person viewing (FPV) headset sat a few inches away. Dak wasted no time. He unzipped the rucksack and removed a pistol and holster, attached it to his hip, and moved on to setting up the drone.

Unlike the bulkier, slower machines he'd tested, this one was built for speed. While the others were designed for shooting footage of landscapes, cities, or even weddings and real estate showings, this model was known as a racing or freestyle drone, capable of speeds up to 90 miles per hour.

Dak had been toying with various styles of drones for the last few months, growing more interested in their use for tactical situations with every passing day. He carried two of the faster versions, and one larger drone that he'd equipped with a small amount of ordnance—a chemical compound he'd come up with similar to semtec. The explosive was capable of knocking down a small building and easily killing anyone within five yards. That wasn't the purpose behind the device, though. He'd created it as diversion first—lethal weapon second.

He shoved the bag with the bigger drone back toward the rear seat and took out the racing drone. Most people who used those kinds of aircraft equipped a camera on the front next to the FPV camera so they could record their flight and post the videos to YouTube or other video hosting sites. Dak had taken a slightly different approach.

He'd need the video feed to analyze the best approach into Nate's property, but he also needed to know for sure if the boys were being held there.

So he'd added a modification to the FPV camera that made the drone a little heavier and slower than normal, but would allow him to utilize thermal scanning with the push of a button.

If the boys were being kept somewhere on the property, Dak would know. On the other hand, if there were no thermal images on his screen, he had a bad feeling it was because the kids were already dead.

After going through his preparations of getting the drone ready and adjusting the flight settings on his laptop, Dak set the drone on the ground and fit the goggles over his eyes.

He didn't like the idea of being blind to his immediate surroundings, but there was no better way for him to get the intel he so badly needed. At least in the forest, hidden in the pull-off, he was secluded.

He looked through the camera lens of the drone as the tiny aircraft's motors whirred to life, lifting the machine off the ground. Dak likened the experience to riding a motorcycle in the air. It had taken him a few months of practice to get accustomed to the controls and how to fly the thing smoothly, but once he got the hang of it, he was doing the same aerobatics as pros he'd seen on the internet.

He carefully guided the aircraft through the opening of the trail until he cleared the trees, then he pushed the machine up, sending it shooting vertically into the air.

It never got old to him, seeing the earth drop away as if he was on board a rocket. The loud whining from the motors faded as he gained altitude, climbing high over the ridge to reveal the farm on the other side.

Acres of dried corn stalks spread out over a huge field between two hills. Dak had to hand it to Nate, he could sure pick the spots. Dak imagined what the place must have looked like in the summer, when everything was green and lush.

He refocused and continued to climb until he was nearly a thousand feet above the plateau. Then Dak steered the aircraft toward the house at the other end of the field. The home was nothing special—a white, two story rancher with a porch that wrapped around half of the exterior.

Dak slowed the drone as it neared the house. The camera angle tilted forward, and Dak flipped the switch on the thermal scanner. His view of the home changed and displayed several orange and red shapes within the confines of the house's outline. One of the figures moved toward the front door. Dak's immediate assumption was that Nate was about to leave the house. If he did and looked up, Nate might see the drone.

Dak pushed the aircraft higher. The screen glitched as the scanner's sensors stretched beyond their normal operating limits. Dak flipped the switch back to normal viewing mode and continued sending the drone high into the air. He'd deliberately kept it just high enough that Nate couldn't hear it, but where the scanners would work.

Breath coming in short, tempered bursts, Dak watched, anticipating seeing his ex-teammate step down off the porch and into the front yard. He kept the machine hanging in midair for what seemed like hours. It may have been only a minute. Dak glanced at the battery indicator. The one downfall to these kinds of drones was how rapidly they burned through battery life. Dak could keep it there for a few more minutes, thanks to some modifications, but the machine couldn't linger indefinitely.

Dak decided to try something else.

He descended while retreating toward the ridge and then leveled the aircraft so he could see under the roof of the porch.

As he suspected, the towering man stood near the steps, looking out at his harvested cornfield. Dak couldn't tell what else he was doing, but he held something in one hand. A beer bottle perhaps? Dak recalled the man enjoyed a bottle of brew now and then. Not that it mattered. The only bearing that factoid might have on the situation would be impeding Nate's ability to drive—depending on how many he'd consumed.

Dak held his breath, watching as the target continued to stare out at the field. Then, after what seemed like decades, Nate turned and sauntered back through the door into the house.

The battery indicator on the screen told Dak he still had five more minutes. He'd need at least one or two to get the drone back to his location. Wasting no time, he accelerated toward the house and positioned the machine directly over the roof again.

This time, when Dak switched on the thermal scanner, he saw nine distinct shapes—all human forms. Eight were smaller than one, which Dak knew to be Nate. He counted again, slower and out loud the second time—just to be absolutely certain. "One. Two. Three. Four. Five. Six. Seven. Eight."

The boys are alive, Dak thought.

The fact shook him. It hadn't been a false hope. The boys were there, still alive in the farmhouse. But for how long?

Dak realized the drone's battery was draining fast. He flipped off the thermal scanner and tilted the nose of the aircraft back toward the ridge, then accelerated at full speed.

The meadows and cornfields whizzed by in a blur below, soon replaced by a blend of fall colors from the leaves clinging to the tree-tops. The drone skimmed the canopy atop the ridge and then descended the slope toward the road and the hidden pull-off where Dak stood.

As he steered the aircraft around the turn into the trail, he saw himself and the SUV directly ahead. The low battery warning began blinking in the corner of the goggles as he brought the drone in for a rough, but safe landing a few yards away.

Dak stripped the goggles from his head and let them dangle around his neck. He wiped his eyes with the back of his hand, staring down at the tiny aircraft. He wasn't thinking about the drone. His mind was zeroed in on the eight boys locked in Nate's farmhouse.

Now that he knew they were safe, Dak had to figure out a way to get all the boys out safely. Then he would take care of Nate.

NINE

BROWN'S FERRY

Dak stowed the racing drone in the back of the SUV without worrying to put it back in its hardshell case. Instead, he pulled out the slower, larger drone and began preparing for its flight.

He'd rigged a small winch to the bottom of it and synced it with two buttons on the controller so he could raise and lower lightweight objects. In this case, the object he attached to the long wire was a compact, highly sensitive microphone. The device was no bigger than a quarter in diameter, contained in a two-inch long plastic cylinder, and it could pick up sound through walls or from over fifty yards away.

The plan was simple enough. Would it work? There was only one way to find out.

He removed the goggles from his neck and set them next to the racing drone. The surveillance aircraft used a screen on board the controller that allowed the pilot to see everything through the camera fixed to the machine. The camera was attached via a gimbal which allowed the pilot to rotate the view on an x and y axis for better viewing coverage.

Dak picked up the drone and placed it on the ground. Satisfied he'd made all the necessary preparations, he sent the thing skyward with a push of his thumb.

The aircraft didn't shoot up like the racing drone. Instead, it climbed at a steady speed, gaining altitude until Dak could see over the ridge once more.

He eased the drone forward, pushing it higher as the machine approached the farmhouse. Hovering over the fields, Dak froze the drone in place when he saw movement around the front.

A tall figure stalked toward a red pickup truck, climbed in, and drove off down the gravel driveway, kicking up clouds of dust in its wake.

Dak tightened his eyebrows. Nate was leaving. But for how long?

He could make a move, let the drone crash, and storm the farmhouse to rescue the boys, but that would be foolish. He didn't know where Nate was going or for how long he'd be gone.

It could be a trap. If Nate felt he was being watched, it was possible he'd made it look like he was leaving to lure in a potential rescuer. Then, once inside the house, the trap would spring. Dak would be stuck inside with nowhere to run. He could always shoot his way out. That option always sat on the shelf, ready to be utilize as a last resort.

Dak ignored the irrational impulses and steered the drone ahead, pushing it to its maximum speed until it reached the farmhouse. With a quick look through the camera at the driveway to make sure Nate had gone, he bought the aircraft down rapidly toward the roof. From above, the house was shaped like a cross, with two smaller rooms jutting out toward one end. The gutter at the corner of one intersection would be the perfect place for the microphone. It would be out of sight and close enough to pick up sound in the home, possibly even in the basement—assuming that's where the boys were being kept.

He steered the aircraft toward the back corner, away from the driveway, and stopped when the machine was directly over it. The drone descended another twenty feet until it hung just below the top of the roof. Satisfied with its position, he pressed the button to activate the drone's winch.

The microphone lowered from the aircraft's body as the thin cable unspooled. Dak held his breath as the listening device neared the roof's corner. A breeze picked up and caused the microphone to sway. The drone held steady due to calibrations built into the processors for such inconsistencies. Dak nudged the machine a little to the right and continued lowering the microphone until it cradled into the corner, the sound-sensitive end pointing directly into the house.

He pressed another button, and the winch released the cable, letting it fall gently into the gutter next to the microphone.

Satisfied with the device's position, Dak maneuvered the drone down next to the house and scanned the area. He rotated the camera, inspecting the back steps leading down onto the lawn where an apple tree grew next to an old bird bath. He continued searching; moving the camera until he found what he hoped was there.

With a smug grin, Dak guided the drone over to a huge propane tank sitting behind the house a few yards from the exterior wall. He steered the machine around until it drifted into the shadows mere inches off the ground and then set it down next to one of the legs holding up the tank.

There was a chance Nate would see the drone parked there in the shadows, but that chance was slim at best. His ex-teammate had other things on his mind. What those things were, Dak wasn't sure, but with the microphone in place and the drone positioned as a backup plan, he was ready to have a listen at what was going on inside.

He set down the controller and switched it off, then picked up a black receiver box connected to a headset. He fit the headphones over his ears and turned on the receiver, pointing the top of it toward the general area he knew the farmhouse would be over the ridge.

At first, he didn't hear anything except the hum of a refrigerator inside the building.

He waited patiently for a minute, then two, hoping one of the boys would say something.

His patience paid off when, finally, someone spoke up.

"Is he gone?" the voice asked.

"It sounded like he went somewhere," another answered. "He does that now and then to get supplies. He won't be gone long."

"Not that it matters," a third voice chimed in. "There's no way to get out of these cells. He's going to keep us in here until tomorrow when he lets us out."

Out? Dak wondered.

"I still think we could do better if we stuck together," the first voice continued. "But maybe there's a way we can do both."

"Both?" This voice was new, deeper.

"If we pair up, go in twos, we can utilize the benefits of splitting up and the strength of numbers."

Silence resumed for nearly a minute.

"I like it," the second voice said. "We will pair up. That will make it more difficult for him to hunt us down, and if he happens to, maybe we could get the upper hand if we're lucky and take him out."

Dread filled Dak's heart as he heard the conversation end. Now, at last, he knew what Nate was up to. He'd set up his own private hunting ground, and the eight boys he'd captured were to be his game.

"Shut up," another voice said, snapping Dak's attention back to the radio. "He'll be back any minute. We know what to do. Tomorrow, when he lets us out, we go in twos. For now, keep your mouths shut unless you don't want to get the chance to escape."

Tomorrow, Dak thought. Nate must have told the boys his plan. The relief at discovering the boys being alive melted away like an ice cube on the Vegas Strip in July.

He had to get them out, but how?

One of the boys said Nate would be back any minute. There was no way the kid could know that, but Dak couldn't simply charge in over the mountain on foot, or attempt to drive in with his SUV.

He needed to get more intel.

With the sun heading toward the horizon in the west, time was running out. Nate wouldn't be stupid enough to make getting into his home easy. He'd have traps set and alarms. Each window and door would be covered. Nate's methodical nature insured all of that.

Dak realized that if he were going to save the eight boys, it wouldn't be by infiltrating the farmhouse. He was going to have to get to them before the hunter did.

He turned back to the truck and removed the second racing drone from its case, then replaced the battery in the first with a fresh one.

He still had a few hours before the sunset to get the lay of the land. If he had any chance of rescuing those boys, it was critical he knew every bend and rise in the property.

TEN

BROWN'S FERRY

For the eight boys, the last 24 hours dragged by like a rusty nail on a chalkboard. When night fell, sleep didn't come—not easily.

Oliver managed to fall asleep for a few hours despite the overwhelming sense of dread brimming in his thoughts. Jamie sat up most of the night, looking over at his brother as he lay on a thin mattress placed on the floor. Jamie knew he needed rest and eventually he succumbed, dozing off and waking up a dozen times throughout the night—anxiety a constant alarm with no snooze button.

The faint sound of a rooster's crow in the early morning hours roused Jamie from his thin slumber, as it had every morning since he had arrived at this place. Upon waking, he looked to his kid brother, sadness and fear filling his gaze.

Oliver still slept, though he rolled over a few times, which Jamie took as a signal the younger boy would soon wake.

He didn't know what time it was, but Jamie figured it to be around six in the morning. He remembered visiting his grandparents on a farm when they were younger. A rooster always woke them at six—dreadfully early for a child.

Jamie would have given anything to be on that farm again, with his parents and brother, safe from all of this... madness.

He'd always believed that the stories he heard of people being abducted would never happen to him. Those things happened to other kids, ones who were careless or strayed too far from their parents or weren't tough enough to take care of themselves.

Not him.

Yet, here they were, locked up in some madman's personal dungeon.

The door at the top of the stairs creaked open and the heavy footfalls of their captor's boots clomped on the steps as the man approached.

"Wakey, wakey, boys," the man's voice thundered through the basement. "Rise and shine!" His words were laced with a mocking venom.

If Jamie were stronger, he'd teach the guy a lesson, pummel him until he blacked out. Maybe going even farther. A foreign anger boiled inside him, steaming in the dark shadows of his mind that he didn't know existed.

This man didn't deserve anything less, Jamie thought. He was sick, a demented and evil being. Another look over at Oliver as he groggily woke from his slumber reinforced those feelings of rage.

"Big day for you boys," the captor said. "Breakfast will be ready in one hour. I hope you got a good night's rest. Would be a shame if you didn't make this interesting for me."

This, Jamie shuddered at the thought. The casual way the man referred to hunting human beings—innocent kids—was easily the most disturbing thing he'd heard in his life. If he and the others somehow managed to find a way to escape, he doubted he'd ever hear anyone say something more vile.

The man continued his pep talk, or whatever this was. "In five hours, I'm going to let you out of your cages. You'll be chained to each other and led up the stairs where I'll take you outside. Looks like it's going to be a nice day. Warm, too." He almost sounded as if he were about to go golfing. "For now, just relax and enjoy the morning. I'll be back down with your breakfast in a bit."

A shadow passed through the dim light shining through the doorway. The sound of the man's boots on the stairs thudded again as he ascended, followed by the creaking door slamming shut.

"Not much of a pep talk," Jamie quipped, unafraid the man would do worse to him at this point.

"Shh," one of the other boys cautioned.

"What is he going to do to us?" Jamie asked. "He's already told us he's going to hunt all of us down like wild animals."

"He makes a good point," the deep-voiced kid said. "It's not like it can get much worse."

Jamie wished the boy hadn't said that. Those words always preceded something worse, the ultimate jinx in any situation.

"Just stick to the plan," Jamie said. "Pair up from first to last. I'll stay with my brother in case we get separated in the line." He doubted that would happen. It would be more convenient to simply keep the two together in the chain gang.

He shook his head. Thinking about things like that weren't productive.

"Jamie?" Oliver said, sleep still slurring his words.

"Yeah, pal?" Jamie turned to his brother and offered a feeble smile.

"Is he really going to hunt us like animals?"

A sigh escaped Jamie's lungs, pushing through his nose for a few long seconds. "We're going to be fine," Jamie said. "Just pretend this is all a weird game. Okay?"

Oliver frowned. "I don't like this kind of game," he whimpered.

Even though the boy was twelve, nearly a teenager, the events of the week had brought out the child in him—the innocent, almost helpless, kid.

"Well, if we play it right, we'll get to see mom and dad again real soon."

Oliver stared into his brother's eyes. Jamie did all he could to hide the truth, the fear that dwelled within them. He felt as if his brother could see through him, through the empty words spilling from his lips. They weren't going to get out of this alive. Jamie felt almost certain about that. But what else could he do or say?

"Do you really believe that?" Oliver probed, the question dancing off the hard walls.

Jamie took a deep breath and sighed. "I do," he lied. "We're going to be fine. This will all be over soon. Okay? Someone will come and get us out of here."

"The cops?"

"Maybe," Jamie said. "Maybe someone else." He scooted closer to his little brother. "If we can get to the edge of the property, maybe there's a neighboring farm. Those people will help us. We just have to be smart and fast. Okay?"

Oliver searched his brother again for answers, but merely nodded. "Okay, Jamie. Smart and fast."

ELEVEN
BROWN'S FERRY

Dak needed coffee the way a mosquito needs blood. He'd only slept a few hours through the night, and those were involuntary moments at best. He had to get a little rest, though, because the next day would be demanding.

Now it was here.

The sun loomed over the horizon with only a few hours to go before Nate executed his abominable scheme.

Between brief naps in the night, Dak spent most of the time preparing. While there'd still been light the previous day, he'd used his drones to get a general idea of the lay of the land in and around Nate's property. He'd constructed a rough map with the images he'd gleaned. When night finally fell, he set out on foot to reconnoiter the area.

Dak covered dozens of acres during the night.

It was cold, but not freezing, and he'd prepared enough with a lightweight jacket and a layer of long sleeves underneath. The exertion from moving around kept him warm as he traversed the slopes and ridges.

Moving through the forest, he heard wild animals more than

once. Most were deer or wild turkey, though he heard a bobcat growl once, as well as a group of coyotes baying in the night.

With his AR-15 and night vision goggles, along with a pistol on his side, he was more of a threat to the unarmed beasts than the other way around, but that didn't keep a chill shivering down his spine at the sound of the coyotes. Their eerie calls into the darkness were one of the few things that unnerved the hardened soldier. He didn't know why. He'd heard far more terrifying things in his life that didn't affect him to nearly that extent.

Each time he heard the feral dogs howl, he clutched his rifle a little tighter, like a child gripping a soft blanket.

Dak spent the bulk of the night covering the perimeter of the property, searching the trees for cameras or other security devices that Nate might have utilized to protect his land. To his astonishment, Dak found no such measures. The rusty, barbed wire fence was the only thing he discovered, and from the looks of it, the weak barricade had been there long before Nate bought the place.

The only cameras Dak noticed were at the steel gate blocking the driveway near the main road. Since he'd already eliminated that path as a potential entry point, he disregarded the surveillance devices and kept moving along the perimeter.

While relieved to discover no real security issues to overcome, Dak's concern didn't lessen. Nate was a calculating individual. There had to be a reason for the lack of security.

Of course, there was the possibility that the man was simply over-confident in his ability to disappear, to drop off the grid and never look over his shoulder. He'd taken precautions. Perhaps he thought that was enough. Dak didn't know, but he wasn't going to take any chances.

When he arrived back at the SUV, his mind and body felt heavy from exhaustion. He stowed his gear in the floorboard of the front seat and folded the rear seat down so he could lie in the back and get a little rest. If not for the long period of strenuous mental and physical exercise in the forest, he probably wouldn't have slept at all.

At 7:40 in the morning, Dak woke abruptly to a loud, rumbling sound. Confusion swirled around him as he quickly assessed his surroundings, realizing he was in the back of his SUV after a few seconds of trepidation.

The sound grew louder, reached its climax, and then began to fade.

Harley Davidson Sportster, he thought, recognizing the familiar growl. Dak exhaled and quickly gathered his things. He climbed out of the SUV and set back to work. Noon would come fast, and he needed to be ready.

He stuffed the two racing drones into his rucksack along with the controller. The bag also contained a long-range, remote detonator. Dak had planted a few other surprises in the forest for his old team-mate, just in case.

With all his gear loaded and ready, he closed up the truck and set out on foot once more.

His legs felt heavy as he climbed to the top of the ridge, but he pressed on until he reached the crest. Then he turned east and kept moving until he arrived at a bend in the hilltop. He'd identified this location as the closest point to Nate's farm, and where he could get the best view when the hunt began.

The plan was simple, but far from perfect.

Dak knew the boys' plan—to split up in pairs and go in opposite directions. One of the pairs would, inevitably, head toward this general vicinity. If Nate happened to follow those two, Dak would take out the hunter as he pursued his quarry.

There was only a one in four chance that would happen, though, and Dak didn't count on being that lucky. More likely, Nate would go after one of the other groups first.

He had a plan for that, too.

He wished he wasn't on foot. It would be easier and faster to grab the boys and usher them to safety on an ATV. That wasn't an option, so he'd do the best he could with what he had. Right now, what he had was the element of surprise.

TWELVE

BROWN'S FERRY

Nate tromped down the steps into the basement. He'd considered using a chain and shackles to keep the boys in line, even told them that's what would happen, but he changed his mind. It wasn't necessary.

The pistol on his hip and the hunting rifle slung over his shoulder would be enough. They were, after all, just kids—easily intimidated and cast into the throes of fear.

"It's time, gentlemen," he said, using the term loosely and frosted with cynicism.

He unlocked the first door. "You've been in here the longest. I think it's only fitting you get to stretch your legs first." He spoke to the dark-haired boy with callous derision.

Then Nate set about opening the rest of the doors.

None of the boys dared move, not until they were told. There was something admirable about that, or so Nate thought. These youngsters could be taught. They could learn when to speak or not to speak, when to stand or sit on command. Perhaps, he thought, they could have been good soldiers.

Unfortunately for them, they were going to die here on his property.

"I hope you enjoyed your breakfast," Nate went on. "Now it's time for a little exercise." He motioned to the boy from the first cell, indicating the stairs with his finger. "Go on, up the stairs with you." He looked at the kid to the right, a ginger-headed fourteen-year-old with freckles and a petulant glaze in his eyes. "You too, freckles. Up you go. Everyone fall in line after those two. And don't get any ideas about running once you're up there. That would be cheating. If you cheat, you get shot before the game even begins. We wouldn't want that."

He caught another bitter, resentment-filled glare from another boy, but no one said anything.

No one except the last kid he'd taken.

The older McDowell brother stared at Nate with cold, vapid eyes as he shuffled past, ushering his younger brother to the stairwell.

"You're going to lose," the boy said.

Nate's eyebrows shot halfway up his forehead. "Oh, really? All right, then? I like your attitude, son. Best of luck to you."

The kid's eyelids shrank to slits as he followed his brother up the stairs.

"I like his spunk," Nate muttered to himself. "Misguided, but full of moxie."

He followed the young men up the stairs and found them clustered around the open front door.

"What are you doing standing here?" he growled. "Outside. Now."

They all jumped at the command and hurried out the door and down the steps and onto the grass.

Each boy put their hands up over their eyes, shielding them from the blinding light of the sun. The ones who'd been there the longest hadn't seen daylight in several weeks. Or had it been months? Nate had trouble remembering. He shrugged off the question, slipped on a pair of aviator sunglasses, and followed the boys onto the lawn between the front porch and the seemingly endless rows of harvested corn stalks.

"That's far enough," he said when the first kid reached the edge of the grass. The boy stopped, and the rest came to a halt behind him.

Most of them stood with slumped shoulders like convicts waiting to be incarcerated. All but one hung their heads, chins nearly touching their chests. The older McDowell kid kept his head high, refusing to be intimidated.

If he only knew, Nate thought.

Nate strolled around and stopped in front of the boys. He eyed each one of them, going down the row and back again. "Sun feels good, doesn't it?" He paused, knowing none would answer. "I apologize for it being a tad chilly," he said with utter insincerity. Two of the boys shivered and rubbed their arms. One of them was the younger McDowell kid.

"Not to worry, though," Nate went on. "You'll warm up once you start running. And I do suggest you run. Like I said before, you'll get a short head start. Go as fast as your young legs can carry you, because once the timer goes off, I'm coming." He turned and paced a yard to the left, spun, and stopped in front of the older McDowell boy. He locked eyes with him and wondered why this young man wasn't more afraid. He glowered back at Nate with fierce defiance.

If Nate were a betting man, he'd wager this kid would last the longest. And in a way, Nate felt a strange desire for that to be the case. He hoped this boy would be the last one standing. It would make for a better climax to the hunt, saving the best till last.

"And remember. If you make it off my land, you're free. This is your chance to escape, boys. It's what you've been dreaming of since you got here, I'm sure. Maybe one or two of you will actually make it." He chuckled and shook his head, eyes dropping to the ground in disbelief. "Anything's possible, I suppose."

He took several steps backward toward the house and stopped, putting up his hands as if in surrender. "Okay, boys. Your head start begins... now!" He covered his eyes with his hands in dramatic fashion, as if a child playing hide and seek. "One Mississippi. Two Mississippi. Three Mississippi."

He peeked through the cracks between his fingers and saw the kids still standing there, confused. "I told you to run, boys! You best go. Time's a wasting."

He partially covered his eyes again as the startled boys jumped to life, then scrambled confusedly. Within seconds, the eight divided into groups of two and sprinted in four opposite directions away from the house.

Nate nodded with satisfaction, a grim smile creeping across his lips. He watched the older McDowell boy shepherding his younger brother into the cornfield toward the driveway.

That part of the property held the longest stretch, the driveway running more than a mile down to the road. The route probably seemed like the easiest path to freedom, but that was hardly the case.

Halfway to the main road, the driveway crossed a four-foot-deep creek that ran across the property. A wooden bridge stood over the branch as the only means of crossing in a vehicle. The bridge wouldn't be an option today as Nate had removed the planks earlier that morning. One of the boys might be tempted to perform a balancing act across one of the rails, but that would be risky.

The cold front that pushed through the last several nights would make wading through the water unbearable, and would likely cause hypothermia. The creek effectively created a moat on that side of the property, which would steer the boys to either the north or south in an effort to find a way around it. Since there wasn't one, they would inevitably keep following the water in hopes of eventually reaching freedom.

They would be simple to track from the bridge. The damp soil would leave distinct footprints. Nate sighed in disappointment. At least he could still save the McDowell boy for last, knowing which way the kid was headed. He removed his hands from his eyes and watched the other three groups split off into the corn rows. He checked his watch, noting the time, and waited until the boys were out of sight before he pulled out a hunting knife and honing rod. Nate began methodically sharpening the blade, whistling some long-forgotten tune as the second hand on his watch continued to tick.

THIRTEEN

BROWN'S FERRY

Dak took the earpiece out of his right ear and let it dangle at his neck. He'd heard everything Nate said, confirmation of what he already knew.

He would hunt down the boys—two at a time—until he'd killed them all.

Dak couldn't bring his mind to grasp that kind of sickness. How had Nate come to be like this? What twisted, traumatic events happened in his youth to drive him to the point of madness that he would hunt young boys for sport?

That rabbit hole was too deep for Dak to dive into, especially at the moment.

He watched from his perch as the boys splintered into four groups, running as fast as they could through the hollow corn stalks, making their way to what they hoped was freedom.

Dak checked his watch and noted the time.

His original plan had been to try to scoop up the boys and get them somewhere safe, off the massive farm. As he watched the groups disperse, however, he realized that task would be nearly impossible—save for the two boys who were running toward him.

Dak glanced to his left, noting the direction two of the other boys took. A new scheme developed rapidly, and as the time neared the five-minute mark, he knew it was his only chance to save all eight hostages.

He snugged the rucksack against his back and skimmed down the slope toward the boys running his way. He saw them clear the edge of the cornfield and enter the forest. Then they disappeared in the dense rows of tree trunks and brush.

Dak ran hard, pounding the ground with every step. The clock was ticking and for this to work, his timing had to be perfect.

He caught a glimpse of a white shirt through the trees ahead and pumped the brakes, skidding to a stop behind a wide oak tree. He calmed his breathing so he could hear better and listened to the sound of feet bursting through dried leaves as the two boys approached.

They would make easy targets for Nate. Tracking their path into the forest would be simple, even for a novice. And Nate was no novice.

Dak had seen the man track insurgent movements in Iraq on more than one occasion. Even with all the technology and satellite imagery available, it was difficult to replace an expert, boots-on-the-ground tracker. Several instances required someone in the field.

Pressing his back to the tree trunk, Dak waited until the boys sprinted by before he stepped out. "You boys need some help?"

One of the kids shrieked as his head whipped around, but not loud enough for the sound to reach the farmhouse. The other turned a second later and stared in wide-eyed confusion at the man with the rifle across his chest.

"I'm not with him," Dak said quickly, raising his right hand. "I'm here to help you boys escape."

Doubt lingered in their eyes. They shot each other a questioning glance.

"If I was going to kill you, I'd have already done it," Dak added. "You have to trust me."

The boys simultaneously nodded.

"Okay," the dark-haired one with blue eyes said. His voice was deep and his eyes had dark circles under them. The clothes on him looked dirty, as if they hadn't been washed in weeks.

"I know you're tired. And I know your plan. You eight split up to make it harder on your kidnapper. That was a good idea, but we're going to change things up. I'm going to go after him."

"You're going to kill him?" The other boy asked. His blond hair splayed out in multiple directions.

Dak didn't want to put that on the young man. "I'm going to neutralize him. I'll handle that. But I need you two to meet up with the others." He raised a finger and pointed to the ridge in the direction of his SUV. "I have a vehicle on the other side of that ridge. You see the outcroppings of rocks sticking out at the top?" He pointed to several huge chunks of mountain rock jutting out of the hillside.

The boys looked that direction and nodded.

"If you go straight downhill from there, you'll get to my ride. The road is just beyond that."

"That'll take at least fifteen to twenty minutes to get there," the blond said.

"I know," Dak said with a nod. "You can make it." He took the keys out of his pocket and tossed them to the dark-haired boy. "Don't leave unless you see the man who took you coming your way. If you do, get out of here. I'm going to try to make sure that doesn't happen."

He adjusted his finger, circling toward the path the other two boys had taken. "Two of the others are heading toward the ridge in that direction. Shouldn't be hard to find them."

"Why do you say that?" the blond asked.

Dak arched an eyebrow. "You guys aren't exactly covering your tracks." He indicated the trail of tossed leaves and broken sticks on the ground.

"What about the others?"

"I'll take care of them. But if they veer off the path and you happen to run into them, get them to the truck."

The dark-haired kid shook his head. "He'll hunt us down. I know he will. We won't make it to the others in time."

Dak took a step forward, gripping the boy with his steel gaze. The kid looked deep into the jade eyes and saw no doubt, no misgivings. "No, he won't. He won't have the chance. You only have another seven minutes or so until he starts. In six minutes, you're going to hear a loud explosion. Do not, I repeat, do not stop running. And don't let the others stop either."

"Explosion?"

Dak nodded. "A diversion. And trust me, when it happens, he will have his hands full."

The boys searched the stranger's eyes and found all the truth they needed.

"Okay. Thank you," the blond boy said. "Mister...?"

"Don't worry about my name, kid. Probably best you don't know it for now."

"Okay, then."

"Get moving. Time is ticking, and you need every second. Find the others and get to the SUV. It's hidden in a pullout near the road on the other side of that ridge. If you don't find it, get to the road and flag down a car for help."

The boys nodded.

"Go," he barked.

He didn't have to tell them twice. The two young men turned and sprinted in the prescribed direction.

Dak watched them run. They weren't moving as fast as he would have liked, but he understood. They'd been kept here for a while, probably not given the chance to exercise or even go out for fresh air. Their weakened muscles caused a lack of balance and strength, and their lungs had grown shallow in the absence of regular activity.

He still believed they could make it. He just had to make sure Nate was taken down.

When the two boys disappeared among the trees, Dak charged down the hill once more, using the dry leaves to half run, half ski on the slope's surface until he reached the bottom where the land leveled out. Then he sprinted, the timer in his head counting down the seconds.

With one hand on his rifle, pressing it to his chest, he reached up and planted the receiver back in his ear so he could listen in on any unusual activity at the farmhouse.

An eerie sound came through the speaker, filling his head with a haunting tune. He recognized the melody, a song from long ago. He'd heard his grandfather whistle the same tune when he was a child playing with model trains in the garage while his pawpaw worked on inventions. It was an old song from simpler times.

Dak loathed hearing Nate whistle it, but he needed to make sure the man was still there at the house, not going back on his rules he'd given the kids about their head start time.

After running another sixty yards, Dak reached the edge of the forest where it met the cornfield. He only paused for a second, slowing his pace to a brisk walk as he entered the rows of skeletal stalks. In the distance, he saw the red brick chimney rising up from the end of the house. It kept him oriented now that he stood on level ground with the enemy.

Finding a landmark was always something he'd found useful in situations like this, especially in a place like a cornfield that felt more like a chaotic maze.

He checked his watch. Only a few minutes left. Dak crouched down and made his way through the dried stalks, careful not to rustle them as he moved. He knew he wasn't going to reach Nate by the time the allotted head start ended, but he didn't have to. That wasn't part of the plan. He just had to be close.

Thirty more yards and he stopped, once more checking how much time had elapsed.

As he figured, only a minute remained.

Dak got down on one knee and retrieved the radio from his backpack. He flipped the power switch and a digital readout appeared on the display. Dak pried open a plastic guard on a switch on the far right side of the black box—a personal addition to the controller. There were three other smaller switches near it, along with a red button.

He flipped the safety switch up and then glanced over at his watch for the last time.

In the distance, he heard Nate's voice scream. It carried through the corn rows and rolled up into the surrounding hills. Even as a grown, fully armed man, the sound sent a chill through Dak.

"Ready or not, here I come!"

Dak looked down at the controller, held his breath, and pressed the button.

FOURTEEN

BROWN'S FERRY

The explosion rocked the valley. A concussive wave rolled through the cornfield, knocking over several of the rows closest to the house.

Dak covered his head, letting the radio hang at his chest. Tiny chunks of debris sailed over him; a few pieces pattered the ground around his feet. When the rubble ceased raining down around him, Dak stood up straight and looked toward the farmhouse.

Black smoke billowed into the sky. The fuming column climbed higher with every passing second, and Dak knew that it was only a matter of time until someone saw it.

He doubted the blast killed Nate. Dak didn't consider himself to be that lucky. The explosion might have injured the enemy, and if that was the case, then Dak would have a strong advantage.

Careful to stay low to keep his head below the tops of the cornstalks, he crept forward. He watched where he stepped, knowing that while speed was important, it was more critical he didn't signal his location to Nate by snapping a dried stalk underfoot.

The smoke pillar loomed high in the air now, the top of it reaching a hundred feet or more. Dak had trouble gauging the actual distance, but the sight added to the surreal feeling that lingered over the property.

He kept moving, stepping gingerly on the earth as he pressed the edges of his boots into the dirt with each step. Drawing closer to the farmhouse, the crackling sound of flames filled the air, along with the smell of burning fuel and scorched grass. He noted more smoke trickling up from other areas of the cornfield to his right and left, though it wasn't the same as the black clouds roiling from the propane tank his drone had destroyed. Flaming debris must have caught hold on some dried cornstalks—collateral damage that Dak didn't anticipate, though perhaps he should have.

This part of Kentucky hadn't been in a severe drought, but there hadn't been any rain in the last few days. Based on the texture of the stalks, combined with the dried leaves in the forest, he figured it had been more than a week—plenty dry enough to make the entire field more than adequate tinder for a massive blaze.

He hurried forward with the thought, his concerns splintering to the kids who were trying to escape. They should be fine, he hoped. If a fire did start, they should be far enough away to be safe, or would keep running at the sight of it.

Dak crept to a halt at the edge of the cornfield. He peered through the last few stalks at the roaring flames lapping out of the torn remains of the destroyed propane tank. The gas had been consumed entirely in the explosion, but the grass around it and part of the house burned steadily, spreading the flames gradually across the lawn and exterior walls.

He scanned the immediate area twice from one end to the other, searching for Nate. A terrible realization descended into his mind. Nate wasn't there.

He searched again, finding no trace of the man.

Dak felt a sudden wave of concern wash over him. The feeling came from his gut, a sense of fear that kept him alive through the years when in dangerous situations. Back then, he had a team that watched his back. Now, he was on his own, and he suddenly felt very exposed on the edge of the cornfield.

He retreated, almost involuntarily, pushing with his toes to gain cover behind the browned stalks.

Nate wasn't just a ferocious killer with a machine gun. He was an expert marksman with a rifle. If he survived the blast, odds are he was regrouping. There was the outside chance Nate might consider the explosion an accident, but that was unlikely. Those kinds of things didn't happen often. And Nate wasn't stupid.

As Dak continued to withdraw from the burning yard, he noticed something lying on the ground about forty feet from the center of the explosion. He stopped and peered through the stands of corn at the anomaly and realized almost immediately what it was.

Nate's hunting rifle, the one he'd been holding prior to the blast, lay on the grass. The explosion must have knocked it out of his hands. But where was Nate? The concussion would have sent him flying, perhaps into the cornfield? No. That was too far. It might have knocked him fifteen or twenty feet if he was close, but that probably would have killed him, or at the very least, rendered him unconscious.

Dak's senses tingled. His heart tore at his ribcage as it pumped hot blood through his veins.

He retreated another ten feet, leaving only portions of the house visible through the smoke swirling around the yard. Then he turned and picked up his speed, circling around the farmhouse toward the driveway. Dak hedged his bets that if Nate wasn't in the yard and was somehow alert enough to move, he would try to escape or, more likely, regroup.

FIFTEEN

BROWN'S FERRY

For several minutes, Nate wasn't sure what had happened. He'd been standing on the lawn in front of his farmhouse, counting down the minutes and seconds until he could begin his hunt.

Then something happened.

The ringing in his ears, dreadful and high-pitched, wouldn't stop. He felt warm, but as his vision cleared, he could see his body wasn't on fire, despite feeling like his skin was burning.

He rolled over and saw the fire, the black and gray smoke churning toward the sky above his roof, carried high on a gentle Kentucky breeze.

When he pushed himself up, the world tilted in his vision and he felt himself being tugged back toward the ground as though gravity had doubled.

What happened?

Another look at the propane tank and he knew the answer. An explosion? How?

In his mind, he ran through the possibilities. There were only two plausible ones. The first was an accident, something that went wrong in the pipes or in the tank itself. That was extremely unlikely. He'd recently had maintenance done on the entire system due to the approaching winter. If there were issues with the tank or the lines, the expert would have addressed them.

That meant only one thing.

Sabotage.

Nate spun around in a drunken fog, scanning the cornfields that surrounded him. He remembered having a rifle, but he didn't see it. The pistol remained on his hip, though, and he could shoot the legs off a fly from a good distance with that.

Even in the haze clouding his memory, and even his judgment, Nate knew he was way too out in the open if it truly had been sabotage.

He stumbled away from where he'd been thrown by the blast, hurrying around the corner of the house even as the flames sparked on the grass behind him.

Nate leaned against the corner wall for a breath, then another. His head throbbed, and the ringing hadn't weakened.

Guns, he thought.

He knew he needed to get more of his weapons, but they were inside the house. If someone had sabotaged his propane tank, they may have done something to the house. But who would do this? Who would target him? And how would they?

His train of thought halted as the answer bubbled to the surface. It could be only one of two people: Bo or Dak.

Bo had no reason to come after Nate. He had several million reasons, actually, but Bo wasn't stupid. He couldn't take the risk of coming here and squaring off with Nate. Bo knew everyone on his team feared Nate Collier in some way.

No, Nate thought, it had to be Dak.

Dak Harper had every reason in the world to want Nate dead. He didn't have to replay the events that transpired in the Iraqi cave. Nate and the other members of their team had betrayed Dak, leaving him for dead.

That, it turned out, was a huge mistake.

Nate had always known that. Given the circumstances, there wasn't much else they could do. They'd been forced to seal the cave and hurry back to base, having completed the mission, but with a casualty.

Fortunately, Bo had the foresight to have a plan. Bo informed the colonel of Dak's betrayal, and how the team had barely managed to escape before being stabbed in the back. The colonel bought it, and Dak became the target of condemnation.

Nate shrugged off the unproductive thoughts. He had to get a rifle out of his house. He kept an AR-15 in the downstairs closet, just a few long strides from the door. The rifle was equipped with a red dot sight. It wasn't a scope, but it would do.

He waited for several seconds, even after deciding to make a run at the rifle. It was his best hope for survival.

Nate took a long breath, then darted around the front corner of the house, not stopping to look around as he ripped open the screen door and burst into the building. He rushed to the closet, anticipating an explosion or a gunshot—some harbinger of his demise.

Nothing happened.

He scanned the kitchen, his eyes jumping from point to point. He stood perfectly still for at least ten seconds, listening for the slightest sound: a breath, a creak, the crack of a joint.

Again, nothing.

Nate scurried to the closet and flung it open. The black rifle sat on the ground, propped against the wall. The muzzle leaned against the left interior corner. It wasn't the proper home for such a fine weapon, but he kept it there for a reason. If anyone ever had the idiotic idea to invade his home, he'd have more than just a pistol to handle the job.

A shotgun sat in the opposite corner. But he wasn't going to need that. His plan isn't for an up-close kill. If Dak were responsible for the explosion, Nate would have to take him out from a distance. The red dot sight on the rail of the AR-15 would be good enough. He could take out minuscule targets from a good distance with it, and he had every confidence that hitting a human would be even easier.

With the rifle in hand, Nate crept toward the door, making sure to stay low with every step.

He reached the exit and pressed his shoulder into the frame, then leaned around and peeked out through the glass partition in the lower part of the screen door. He peered into the cornstalks, searching for any sign of the trespasser, but all he could see were dried stands of old corn.

Satisfied there was no immediate threat, Nate burst through the door, flew down the flight of steps, and landed on the ground. He never missed a step, his feet pounding the grass as he sprinted to the safety of the cornfield.

Nate darted to the left and right, moving as erratically as possible to make for a more difficult target—in case someone had their sights on his back.

No shot ever thundered through the valley, and with every step, he gained confidence knowing that his long legs could cover a significant distance in a short amount of time.

He'd never let himself get out of shape—constantly maintaining a strict exercise regimen. He worked out six days of the week, lifting weights and doing cardio, just as he'd done in the military.

Nate was glad he'd kept up the rigorous program. He didn't feel winded at all as he steered his body slightly to the right, in the direction he knew the bridge would be. Whoever his attacker was had lost their chance at taking him out. The element of surprise was gone. Now, Nate could turn the tables and eliminate the one person he considered an equal. After that, he could finish the hunt—beginning with the McDowell boys.

SIXTEEN

BROWN'S FERRY

Dak knew he was taking a huge risk.

By circling around to the driveway, Nate could sneak up from behind and shoot him in the back. Every second, every hurried step he took, Dak wondered when the crack of the rifle would pierce the valley's silent embrace.

He'd picked up his pace to a near sprint through the cover of the cornfields. He stayed just far enough away from the edge that spotting him from the open would be difficult, but kept close enough that he could see the gravel driveway intermittently through the stalks as they blurred by.

Initially, he'd considered his maneuver as a counter to whatever Nate was doing. As he considered it further, though, Dak realized that the second part of his reasoning was more important.

The McDowell kids had come this way, rushing away from the farmhouse along the driveway—probably thinking that would be the simplest path to escape.

They might have been right, even with the long distance to the end of the gravel road.

When Dak emerged from the cornfield, the bridge came into

view and he instantly realized that the McDowell boys weren't going to be able to escape that way.

Nate had sabotaged his own bridge, removing wooden planks that typically covered the bridge.

Dak sighed, trotting to a stop at the creek. The water babbled under the bridge's frame. Under different circumstances, the setting might have seemed serene, peaceful, but not now.

The clear water spanned at least twenty-five feet across, and was easily two or three feet deep in the center. If the boys tried crossing in this chilly weather, they would risk getting sick and, at best, be slowed down significantly by their waterlogged clothes.

Dak twisted his head to the left, then right, looking for a flash of clothing or maybe a sound. The boys had a significant head start, and if they'd kept moving at a steady pace, it could take an hour for Dak to catch up. In that amount of time, the likelihood of Nate catching up also increased.

Standing out in the open, Dak felt the fear of exposure tingle across his body again, the same way it had when he was in the yard by the farmhouse. He snapped his head around, looking back down the driveway, knowing he couldn't stand out here for long.

Maybe Nate went in one of the other directions, after the other boys. Doubt snaked into Dak's brain. *He'd overplayed his hand, or thought the explosion would drive Nate this direction.*

"No," he barked, shaking the thoughts from his mind. "He'll come this way."

Dak shuffled toward the edge of the creek and then froze. Two distinct sets of footprints in the mud tracked from the bridge down to the water.

He imagined being in the boys' shoes, running as fast as they could to get away from the farmhouse. He envisioned them arriving at the bridge only to realize they couldn't cross it. They might have dipped a hand in the water to test the temperature, deciding it was too frigid to risk crossing.

The older McDowell boy probably suggested they keep going

upstream and try to find another place to cross. That's what Dak would have done if he were in their position.

He bent down and, squatting over the footprints, traced them to the right, heading toward the ridge. The indentations disappeared onto narrow strip of grass that separated the rows of corn from the stream. If the kids didn't find a place to cross, they would be forced to keep going until they reached the hillside. Dak knew from his recon the night before that the creek bent around the base of the small mountain and ran next to it for a few miles. He didn't stay long enough to find the source of the water.

A distant sound spurred Dak into action.

It came from the direction of the farmhouse and swelled with every second, growing louder and louder.

The groan of a truck's engine along with the crunching gravel under the tires, signaled that Nate was coming.

I guess the rules went out the window, Dak thought as he darted to the right and ran at full speed into the tall grass.

He didn't stop to look back as the truck rolled ever closer to the bridge. There was no time for looking back.

Dak realized he was leaving a wake in the long blades of grass, easily trackable by an expert such as Nate. In front of him, Dak also noticed similar, smaller indentations left by the two boys.

The path escalated slightly over a knoll and then sloped back down again. The undulating terrain made the run more challenging, but it was a challenge Dak met with the determined ease of a battle-hardened soldier.

He met another rise with the same grit, pumping his legs faster. He knew with every step he was gaining on the two boys. His legs were longer and the younger McDowell kid would have trouble keeping up the pace. Even if they spent hours running every week, Dak doubted they'd trained as hard as he did.

At the crest of the next hill, Dak felt the muscles in his legs warming, but he still had plenty of strength left. He slowed, however, as he saw something moving among the trees, just above where the creek steered to the left at the mountain's base.

The two boys' shirts made them easy to spot even from a thousand yards away. Dak's lungs filled and emptied in a steady, quick rhythm. He started to jog down the hill toward the mountain. When he reached the bottom, he opened the throttle to a full sprint.

His weapons and bag felt heavy, but he pressed on, forcing himself to run that much harder toward the two kids who were climbing toward the top of the ridge. A single concern raced through his mind as he cut the distance between himself and the boys.

Will I get to them before Nate's in range?

SEVENTEEN

BROWN'S FERRY

Nate slammed on the brakes and the truck's tires ground to a crunching halt a few yards short of the bridge.

He quickly opened the door and stepped out of the cab, clutching the rifle in his right hand. The overt smell of smoke filled his nostrils as thin, gray tendrils wafted by on the breeze.

A look back toward the farmhouse revealed the source. The single plume of black smoke had dissipated and been replaced by a wider column of smoke that grew with every passing second.

Nate clenched his jaw angrily—the explosion had caused a fire to break out. With the recent lack of rain and the dry rows of corn, it wouldn't take long for the inferno to reach the forest. The dry leaves that covered the forest floor would easily ignite. The entire area would be ablaze before anyone could stop it.

Fury raged inside him, burning hotter than the grass and cornstalks ever could. Dak had destroyed everything he'd worked for. His nostrils flared with every breath as all his plans, his detailed preparations, literally went up in smoke.

He reeled in his thoughts and returned to method; deliberate actions he could control when everything else around him spun wildly.

Nate trudged hurriedly down the bank where he found the soft dirt near the creek. Even with the dry conditions, the dirt left clear imprints, or should have. There weren't any on the left side of the bridge, so he quickly strode to the other side and investigated the soil there.

He noticed the footprints immediately and raised his eyes, following the three sets that trailed away into the strip of grass alongside the stream.

Two sets of prints were smaller; clearly belonging to the boys he'd planned on hunting. The third set, however, caused him concern. They belonged to a full-grown man, at least a size 10, perhaps a 10.5. The evidence couldn't have been clearer in Nate's mind. Dak wore that size. Nate would swear on his life to that. When they served together, he'd watched Dak put on his boots a hundred times.

Nate needed a new plan. Actually, he needed a new mindset. Instead of being concerned with Dak's surprising presence, Nate shifted his thinking. It was a bonus to have Dak here. Nate could take out the only threat to his way of life—assuming Bo was keeping as low a profile as possible.

Bo had tried, Nate thought.

Considered by everyone in the team to be the least clever, Nate let them all believe that. The truth was much different.

Nate had attended extremely good schools as a young man, and had often been at the top of his class in all his studies. He didn't let people see that side of him, though, choosing to allow them to think he was stupid. He put on the disguise of aloofness and naivety, sometimes to surprise people, but most of the time to keep expectations low. High expectations brought responsibility. Nate didn't want that. He held other desires close to the vest, along with his brilliant mind.

That resourcefulness and high level of intelligence served him well during his life, and especially during his search for Bo.

Nate knew that Bo was potentially as big a threat as Dak, even though Bo had openly advised none of them using their real names or contacting each other ever again.

So, Nate worked diligently to find where Bo Taylor had gone. It took months of searching, but he'd managed to initially locate the man in Southeast Asia. Bo wasn't stupid. He'd changed his name, forged papers, just like the rest of the team. But Bo took extra precautions, never staying in the same place for more than a month. He migrated like a nomad, sure to leave no trace he'd ever been in any of the locations.

Even with all his efforts, Nate was able to track him down.

Bo recently moved to one of the Cyclades Islands off the Greek mainland. Andros was one of the quieter, less populated islands in the Aegean Sea. It maintained a steady flow of tourists every year, but nothing compared to some of the more popular destinations, such as Naxos, Santorini, and Mykonos.

The move from Thailand to the rocky island of Andros was a drastic one, and one that few would have caught. Bo had taken every possible precaution, but he couldn't avoid Nate forever.

Nate had no plans to go after Bo, not yet. He believed that Bo would leave him alone, afraid of what might happen if he made a play for the tall, dark-minded member of their team.

Keeping tabs on Bo would be enough for the time being.

Nate twitched his head and focused on the present. Dak was here, and Nate knew why. He was going to exact revenge for how things went down in Iraq. It was fair. Nate knew as much. If their roles had been reversed, Nate would have scorched every inch of earth to burn out his enemies and repay them for what they'd done.

But roles weren't reversed. Nate was here, on the land he'd purchased, and Dak had intruded, both onto the property and into the hunt that was several months in the making.

Nate started to jog along the trail, following the prints until they disappeared in the tall grass. From there, he continued on, tracking the flattened grass the kids had trampled, and probably Dak as well.

It was then that Nate realized there was another possible piece to

Dak's intrusion. Was he going to try to save the boys? How could he have known they were here? Based on the footprints at the water's edge and the distinct pattern of the flattened grass, it was easy to know three people had gone through this area.

Nate pushed himself harder, his long legs chewing up yards at a time with every step.

He ran up a slight rise and down the other side, careful to observe the pattern in the tall grass. It remained unchanged as he reached the next valley and continued straight ahead toward the next hill.

Nate breathed steadily, but now at a faster rate. He knew he was catching up and refused to stop until he had the boys and Dak in his sights.

When he reached the top of the next knoll, he slowed down and then came to a halt. Peering up into the forest, he could see the McDowell boys' shirts against the backdrop of dying leaves and brown tree trunks.

The two kids moved slowly, the older one pausing to help the younger boy now and then. The boys were more than a thousand yards away, but at their speed and in their condition, Nate could be within shooting distance in mere minutes.

His heart pumped harder with the thrill of the chase as he ran down the next slope and charged ahead toward the forest. Halfway there, he skidded to a stop and immediately dropped to the ground amid the tall strands of grass.

The boys were alone. He cursed himself for getting caught up in the hunt. Where was Harper?

Ten feet away, the indentations in the grass narrowed, as if the boys and Harper had fallen into a single file line before reaching the forest two hundred yards away. Except Harper was nowhere to be seen.

Nate twisted his body around, leaning on his left shoulder to look into the rows of corn. He found it difficult to see anything through the grass, so he belly crawled over to the edge of the field and poked his rifle through, then his head. Free of the blinding grass, he surveyed left to right, but found no signs of Harper.

Dread nipped at him, but he didn't give in. Nate never let fear get the best of him. He was the predator in every scenario, and he reminded himself of that fact.

Slowly, he inched his way into the cornfield like a jaguar on the prowl. His first prey would be Dak. Then he would finish the boys.

EIGHTEEN

BROWN'S FERRY

Dak's legs felt like the smoldering fire in the valley below. With every step up the steep slope, the muscles grew heavier, more gelatinous.

He saw the boys up the hill and to his left. He purposely veered to the right once he reached the forest so he could catch the two kids from the side rather than from behind.

His reasoning for the approach was simple. Nate was chasing them and would come directly down the same path they'd forged through the grass. That meant Nate would focus on the mountain directly ahead instead of bothering to look to the right or left. The fact that the boys weren't doing a very good job of hiding reiterated that, but Dak knew Nate wouldn't be so foolish. He'd sense the danger and probably detour, perhaps into the corn rows—thinking that's where his ex-teammate had ventured.

Halfway up the ridge, Dak peered out over the valley. The fire had died down, which was fortunate. While it still burned, the sporadic and mild breeze aided its containment to no farther than fifty yards beyond the farmhouse yard. The smoke, however, hung in a haze that covered the property. While it hadn't thoroughly permeated the woods, the scent of burning grass and cornstalks still seeped into Dak's nostrils.

Dak slowed to a stop behind a thick oak tree to catch his breath, then turned to locate the boys gain. They were moving at a snail's pace up the ridge, halting frequently to allow the younger of the two to take a break.

Averting his gaze to the field below, Dak pressed his shoulder into the rough bark and peered through the misty smoke. He saw the truck down by the bridge, but there was no sign of Nate in the narrow strip of grass by the stream. He turned his attention to the cornfield, figuring his old teammate would have taken cover there to move faster. He could have stayed in the grass, but that would have left him far more exposed on his feet. And on his belly, it would have taken him too long to advance.

Then Dak spotted him.

The tall, lumbering figure of Nate Collier glided through the rows of dried corn like a snake, weaving back and forth. To his credit, Nate tried to keep a low profile, but from his vantage point, Dak had a clear advantage and his target was almost within range.

He raised his rifle and pushed the side of it against the tree to stabilize it. Looking through the sights, Dak lined up his target with the red dot in the center of the glass. His finger tensed on the trigger and he was about to fire when he heard a yelp from behind.

Dak twisted his head and saw the younger boy had fallen and was grabbing his ankle. The kid yelled in pain as his brother scurried around through the leaves and knelt down to check the injured appendage.

Dak clenched his jaw in frustration. The boy could wait another minute. One shot would drop Nate, then he could tend to the kid.

He turned and resumed his stance, peering down into the cornfield through the mini-scope. The target, however, was gone.

Nate had vanished.

Dak moved the rifle down toward the beginning of the tree line, then back again, but there was no sign of Nate anywhere.

Dak felt his pulse quicken. Panic wasn't in his vocabulary, but a sensation very close to it coursed through his veins.

He looked back to the boys. They were still on the ground, the older tending to the younger's wounded ankle.

Dak cursed their luck and took another glance down the slope to the edge of the forest. Still no sign of Nate.

He had two choices. The first was to traverse the ridge, reach the boys, and try to help them get to the top where Dak would regroup and defend their position. He didn't like that plan. It exposed him on his left flank. If he were lucky enough to make it to the boys, reaching the top of the hill would be slow and leave them vulnerable. They would be fortunate to get twenty yards before being shot in the back by Collier.

Dak decided to go with the second option.

It was a gamble, and his wager was the lives of the two boys on the hillside.

He would have to move fast, and while that could make him a more visible target, it was the play with the best chance for an optimal outcome.

He skidded down the slope, veering away from the line he'd taken before to circle around, creating a little more distance between himself and Nate—he hoped. He watched for roots and patches of dirt to land on, doing everything he could to remain silent as he skirted along the biggest of trees to keep out of sight.

Halfway down the slope, Dak caught something out of the corner of his eye. He stuck out his right hand and grabbed a tree trunk to halt his momentum.

Sixty yards away, he saw the hunter.

The forest camouflage jacket and matching pants made his body nearly impossible to spot, but the pale flesh of Nate's cheek stood out against the brown backdrop on the ground. The black rifle also gave away the enemy's position where he lay prostrate on the ground.

He was aiming at something up the hill.

Horror filled Dak's mind as he instantly realized Nate was about to shoot one of the boys.

He raised his rifle and shouted, fearful he might not get the shot off fast enough to keep Nate from firing.

"Looking for me, Nate?" The words blasted out of Dak's mouth loud enough to echo down into the valley.

Nate abruptly twisted with a full-body twitch, snapping his rifle away from one target to seek another.

Dak's weapon was already nestled in his shoulder, the sight climbing as he braced himself against the tree trunk. Through the sight, Nate looked almost panicked as he searched for the source of the voice.

Dak positioned the red dot on the mini-scope attached to Nate's rifle and squeezed the trigger just as Nate settled his weapon and prepared to shoot.

The rifle recoiled against the inside of Dak's shoulder. The loud boom thundered up over the ridge and throughout the valley, piercing the dying smoke around the farmhouse to reach all the way to the surrounding hillsides.

Nate's head slumped instantly to the ground, the rifle falling in limp hands.

Dak kept his sights on Nate for another second, his heart still pounding in his chest. He didn't breathe for ten seconds. Then he exhaled and sucked in a huge gulp of air.

He stepped out from behind the tree and moved toward the dead man, keeping the rifle aimed at Nate's head—or what was left of it. As he drew near, Dak saw that the bullet had gone through his eye and out the back of his skull.

Once he reached Nate's body, he kicked the rifle away out of habit. Not that there was any threat of the man suddenly rousing to life and using it.

Dak exhaled again as he looked down at his kill. He wondered what had driven Nate to such a place of evil, of absolute and total disaffectedness toward good or innocence.

Whatever the reason, whatever terrible things had happened to him in his early life to cause Nate to become this monster, at least now it was all over. And more importantly, the eight boys would be safe.

Dak turned away from the body and looked up the mountainside at the two brothers who stared with terror in their eyes at the new gunman who'd appeared—seemingly out of nowhere.

"It's okay," he said, raising a hand. "You the McDowell boys?"

Dak trudged the hill, careful to move slowly with each step so he didn't spook them.

The boys stared at the stranger with a mix of fear and confusion in their eyes. They stole a glance at each other, as if questioning the other as to whether or not they should trust the man. Even from up the slope, Jamie McDowell could see the green in the stranger's eyes. It was a disarming color that matched the grin on the man's face, an expression that told them everything was going to be okay.

The older brother nodded, still supporting his brother with one arm wrapped around him.

Dak stopped when he reached the two boys and exhaled with a nod of his own. "You're safe now," he said. "Let's get you two back to your parents."

NINETEEN

BROWN'S FERRY

Dak pulled up to the motel and stopped the SUV outside the last room on the end as the sun dipped toward the horizon in the west, surrendering its warmth to the cool evening air.

For a moment, Dak simply sat with his hands on the wheel, staring at the door to the McDowell's room. He imagined the gambit of emotions pummeling their souls with every waking second. This week had been their own personal hell. As a guy with no children, he couldn't truly reach the point of utter anguish they'd been living in for the last several days. He felt even worse for the other kids' parents, though he'd never met them.

After neutralizing Nate, Dak helped the McDowell boys back to his SUV. It took him nearly an hour to reach the vehicle due to the distance and the younger McDowell boy's sprained ankle. Dak had given Oliver a quick check and suggested that it wasn't broken, though the kid would need an X-ray to confirm it. He took it as a good sign that Oliver's ankle wasn't turning black and blue, though that wasn't always an indication of a fracture.

When they arrived back at the SUV, Dak was pleasantly surprised to see the other six boys waiting for him. The oldest one held up a stick when Dak and the McDowell brothers approached. The kid was brave. Dak had to give him that.

The second the boy saw it was Dak, he lowered his "weapon" and let out a sigh of relief.

Dak dropped the other kids off first, just outside the police department, with a request they not tell the cops who brought them there. At the moment, only two officers occupied the building, the rest of the department had been dispatched with a group of fire-fighters to investigate a potential wildfire at a farm near the Daniel Boone Forest.

The boys agreed, though Dak wondered how long they could keep his secret. He'd be leaving town that evening, after he dropped the McDowells with their parents and picked up his meager belongings.

He turned and looked over his shoulder into the back seat. The two kids wore sheepish looks of trepidation. Dak didn't know why. They should have been relieved, overjoyed, happy, any number of positive emotions. Instead, they appeared afraid.

"You boys okay?" Dak asked.

He'd never been the best at understanding emotions. That played no small part in the destruction of his relationship with Nicole. He knew that now. He wished he knew it back then.

"Yeah," Jamie said after a second of thought. "I just never realized how much I took our parents for granted. Our lives, too." He looked over at his brother then back to Dak. "We're definitely going to be better from now on."

Dak snorted and smiled at the boys, resting his elbow on the top of his seat so he could see them both better. "I have a feeling you two were already pretty good kids. Everyone makes mistakes. The great thing about moms and dads, as far as I understand them, is that they will always forgive you."

"They didn't want us to leave the campsite," Oliver muttered. "We told them we'd be okay."

"And you are," Dak said. "No one can hurt you now."

"We should have listened to them," Oliver whimpered. Tears formed in the corners of his eyes. "We shouldn't have wandered off."

"Hey, it's okay, kid." Dak tried to use a comforting tone, but that wasn't really his style. With every syllable, he felt like he was doing it wrong—another flaw that probably sabotaged his relationship. "Everyone makes mistakes. Your parents are going to be so happy to see you. That's all they are going to feel. Okay? No guilt. No punishment. Just love."

Oliver accepted his words with a nod.

"Go on," Dak encouraged. "Go give your parents the biggest hug you've ever given them."

Oliver opened the door first, then stopped when he realized his brother still hadn't moved.

"Thank you," Jamie said, looking at Dak's face as if studying it, searching for answers. "I don't know who you are and I know you said we can't know your real name. But you saved our lives. And those other kids, too. I will always appreciate that."

Jamie's comments overflowed with the purest sincerity. Dak felt something strange. The sensation accompanied a thought that was equally bizarre. Kids like these two still held onto something pure, a fragment of innocence the world had yet to rip from their soft hands. In the distant hopes of his mind, Dak wondered what it would be like to work for a kid, to be some kind of bodyguard or... he didn't know what.

He'd considered the private security industry a few times in the past. It was a pretty standard fallback for a guy with his kind of resume, but he'd let those thoughts go.

He didn't want to be a babysitter for some rich pop star whose one smash hit skyrocketed them to overnight stardom. Dak would be miserable working for someone like that. He didn't see himself serving any adults in that capacity, either.

A young person, though, he could see that. They needed protecting and guidance. It would have to be the right circumstances, though, and he had a feeling those stars would never align.

"Take care, kid," Dak said to Jamie. He turned to Oliver. "And keep watching out for your big brother. He needs all the help he can get." He winked at Oliver. The gesture produced a meek smile from the kids. Then Jamie rushed around to help his brother hobble to the motel room door.

Dak shifted the vehicle into reverse and slowly backed away. He turned the SUV around, pointing it toward the road to the left, and then watched as the door to the motel room opened.

The reaction on Mrs. McDowell's face was one Dak would never forget. Utter confusion, then pure ecstatic joy washed over the woman's face. Timothy McDowell joined her in the doorway mere seconds later, and the two scooped up their sons in their arms.

Dak didn't dare linger another breath. He stepped on the gas and eased the SUV out onto the road, disappearing around the corner where a thick outcropping of trees and bushes blocked his view to the reunion.

He was sure the McDowells would want to thank him, to shower him with praise or adoration or something that would make him feel beyond awkward. Dak couldn't risk that. The longer he stuck around, the better chance the cops had of catching up to him.

The fact was, he'd shot a man on the man's property. The kids would corroborate the story, make sure that everyone knew the truth, but there would be an investigation, questioning for days, maybe weeks.

That could not happen. The less time Dak spent in this town, the better.

He steered the SUV out of town and into the countryside, leaving the smoldering memories of Brown's Ferry in the rearview mirror.

Dak tried to shift his thoughts away from the families back in the little town, parents who were reuniting with their lost children, some getting phone calls from the local sheriff about the mysterious arrival of their kids. Letting his mind linger on those things wasn't helpful. He had one more person to find before he could clear his name.

Bo Taylor needed to be the center of Dak's focus. He could sit here in the eye of the storm and enjoy the temporary peace, but the storm was far from over.

An hour out from Brown's Ferry, his phone vibrated in his pocket. He looked down at the screen, but didn't recognize the number. With a confused scowl, he pressed the answer button.

"Who is this?"

Audible, steady breaths came through the speaker.

"I said, who is this," Dak stated authoritatively, ready to hang up. "No one has this number."

"I do now," the voice said, the serpentine sound slithering through Dak's ear.

He didn't have to ask. Dak would recognize that voice anywhere.

"Before you ask how I got this number, Dak," Bo said, elongating the name, "is it too much for you to say thank you?"

"Thank you?" Dak asked, deciding to play along.

"For killing Trask. You would have never gotten to him. You know that, right? He had that mountain rigged to blow sky high if any of us tried to get to him."

Dak didn't give him the satisfaction of asking how he did it. He'd heard enough about Trask's killing, along with the murder of the sheriff in Cuchara, to figure it was either Taylor or Collier pulling the trigger. In his head, the arrow always pointed toward Bo, even though showing up in the States could have been a huge mistake.

"Playing coy?" Bo asked. "Fine. Well, now that all the others are gone, I suppose it's just down to you and me, eh, Dak?"

"The others?"

"Coy again? You took out three elite soldiers, Dak. Guys you trained with, and in some cases, actually trained. You should be proud."

"What do you want, Bo? Calling to apologize? Because you're doing a poor job of that."

Bo laughed. "Me? Apologize? No. Deep down, though, I always knew I couldn't let the others live. I'd be on the run forever, never knowing when the target was on my back, always looking over my shoulder. That's no way to live, Dak. I'm sure you can relate."

"How did you get this number?" Dak growled the question through gritted teeth.

"Oh, that? Easy. You only have so many underground connections. I knew of two."

A sickening thought entered Dak's mind. "If you hurt Will—"

"Relax, brother. I didn't hurt Will. He's too well-connected with all the wrong people. But his apartment's security is lacking. I found what I needed and got out of there. Quite the view he has."

Dak could hear the familiar sounds of the Portuguese coast through the speaker. Bo was on the move, no way he'd be in that town or country longer than another hour.

"Before you think of trying to warn him, don't. I'll be long gone before you have a chance to put up any roadblocks."

Dak sighed through his nose. "Then what do you want, Bo?"

"I want this to end. Once and for all."

Dak inhaled slowly again. "It looks like we finally agree on something."

THANK YOU

Thank you for reading this story, along with the others. If you're trying to find Brown's Ferry, Kentucky on a map, you probably won't. As far as I know, the place doesn't exist, but I did base it on an area near the Daniel Boone National Forest. There are many gorgeous places to visit there, where the rolling hills seem to go on forever. I highly recommend it if you get the chance. Just be careful. You never know if there's another Nate out there....

OTHER BOOKS BY ERNEST DEMPSEY

Dak Harper Origin Stories:

Out of the Fire

You Only Die Once

Tequila Sunset

Purgatory

Scorched Earth

The Heart of Vengeance

Sean Wyatt Adventures:

The Secret of the Stones

The Cleric's Vault

The Last Chamber

The Grecian Manifesto

The Norse Directive

Game of Shadows

The Jerusalem Creed

The Samurai Cipher

The Cairo Vendetta

The Uluru Code

The Excalibur Key

The Denali Deception

The Sahara Legacy

The Fourth Prophecy

The Templar Curse

The Forbidden Temple

The Omega Project

The Napoleon Affair

The Second Sign

Adriana Villa Adventures:

War of Thieves Box Set

When Shadows Call

Shadows Rising

Shadow Hour

The Adventure Guild:

The Caesar Secret: Books 1-3

The Carolina Caper

Beta Force:

Operation Zulu

London Calling

Paranormal Archaeology Division:

Hell's Gate

ACKNOWLEDGMENTS

Big thanks to my editor Anne Storer and all the readers who helped out while the book was being written and posted each day on my website. I can't thank you enough. There were so many of you kind enough to send your comments. I appreciate you.

THE HEART OF VENGEANCE

A DAK HARPER THRILLER

ERNEST DEMPSEY

ONE

KENTUCKY

"How do you want to do this, Bo?" Dak asked as he pulled the SUV onto the side of the road.

He lowered the device and turned it on speaker, then found Will's number. He started to send a text message, but was cut off.

"I'll tell you how it's going to go down, Dak. And before you try sending your friend a text, don't."

Dak's fingers froze, hovering over the letters on the screen. He didn't say anything, unwilling to give away his intention. He hated that about Bo. The guy always thought he was a step ahead of everyone else. What really got under Dak's skin—he was usually right.

"You probably thought you could put me on speaker and send Will a quick message to let him know he'd been compromised or might be in trouble."

"That's actually a good idea, Bo. Can you give me a second while I set that up?"

"Funny. At any rate, it won't do you or Will any good."

Dak didn't like the sound of that. "I thought you said you didn't hurt him."

A short, forced laugh came through the speaker. "I didn't. Not yet, anyway. What happens to Will depends entirely on you, old buddy."

"What's that supposed to mean?" Dak didn't want to ask, and he was certain he didn't want the answer.

"Your friend is... tied up at the moment. With a timed explosive device attached to him. No tricks here, Dak. You'll find him in his apartment in Nazare. Just be sure you get there in the next twenty-four hours or its boom boom for our old friend."

Dak knew better than to question the sincerity of the threat. "That doesn't give me much time to find a plane ticket."

"You're a resourceful guy, Dak. I have faith you'll figure it out."

"Why are you doing this, Bo?" Dak probed. "Leave Will out of it. This is between you and me."

"Oh, no," Bo countered. "He has everything to do with this. You think I don't know what happened to the others? Luis? Carson? Now, Nate? Of course, I eliminated Billy. I didn't trust you'd be clever enough to get past that sniper. Especially on his mountain strong-hold. What was your plan with him? Scope out the property, figure out a way in? You know he had sensors and cameras all over that place. You wouldn't have made it fifty yards onto Purgatory before he spotted you and took you out."

"You looking for me to say thank you? Because that's not going to happen."

"I know it won't, Dak. You were always ungrateful. If you'd just played along and helped yourself to some of that gold—"

"You'd still be trying to kill me and take it all for yourself."

Bo snorted audibly through the speaker. "Is that what you think this is about? Me taking everyone else's share?"

"Sounds like you."

Another laugh echoed from the device. "I suppose you're right. Thanks to you, I wasn't able to recover much of it, except Billy's of course, and a little of what Luis had set aside. Thankfully, he wasn't terribly clever with how he hid his money."

"And Nate?"

"Oooo, well, there you go, Dak. Now you're starting to get it."

"Not even close."

"Eh, well. Some dogs can't learn new tricks. I'll get around to Nate's holdings, eventually. After you're dead, obviously. I do appreciate you taking those guys out for me, though. You certainly made things much easier."

Something about Bo's tone sent a shiver through Dak's spine. The back of his skull tingled and pebbled the skin on his arms. He exhaled, pondering the way Bo made the statement.

"What are you getting at, Bo?"

An old blue pickup truck growled by, the muffler sputtering smelly exhaust in its wake.

"Oh, come on, Dak. You don't see it? Seriously?"

Dak didn't answer. He wasn't going to give Bo the pleasure.

"Fine," Bo relented. "Do you think it was through sheer skill or even a little luck that Will was able to track down the others? They covered their tracks, man. You honestly think Will would have been able to find them if he didn't have a little help?"

What was he saying? Was Will helping Bo all along? Dak shoved the thought aside. He got his answer a second later.

"I fed him the information, Dak. I had to make it look legitimate, though. I couldn't just push everyone's locations and new names to him all at once. You would have figured it out. At least, I hope you would have."

"Why would you do that? So I could do your dirty work for you, take out the others?"

Distant mock clapping filled the SUV.

"Very good! Jane, show him what he's won!" Bo paused to snicker at his own humor. "Yes, Dak. You have been a marvelous puppet during all of this. Honestly, when I found out you managed to escape the cave, I was disappointed. Surprised? Moderately. But I'd taken precautions."

Dak knew exactly what he meant by that. Bo told the colonel it was Dak who'd betrayed the team, and the rest of the guys corrobo-rated that story. Bo had covered the bases extremely well, and Dak never realized who was pulling the strings, or that he and the others were all being played.

"So, now you're luring me into a trap. I go to save Will, if I can even get to Portugal in time, and then we both blow up when I get there."

"Now, Dak. You sound defeatist. That's not the plan. I hope you save Will. But I need you to jump through a few hoops for me before I let you have a shot at me."

"You don't have the guts to face me man-to-man."

"There he is! There's the Dak I know. So brazen. A touch misguided, but brave. If you manage to slip through my tests, of course I'll face you. I've always been the better of us, Dak. You know that. How many times did I beat you when we sparred?"

Dak knew the exact number. He knew that Bo did, too. The maniac held it over him like a bucket of hot oil, always ready to dump it all over Dak. In training, Bo had been the better of the two hand-to-hand combat fighters. The margin was thin, but it was certainly there. Dak had managed to best his ex-teammate occasion-ally, but the number of positive outcomes for Dak had been only one in three.

"I'm sorry I can't chat more with you, Dak. This has been a wonderful little reunion. I do hope that we can have the chance to square off in the near future. I'd love to finally be able to take you down without having to hold back like I did in the sparring ring."

"I look forward to it."

The call ended before Dak could say anything else. "Bo? Hello?" Dak slammed his fist down on the passenger seat. He felt his heated blood pumping through every vein in his body.

He forced himself to breathe, calming his fury. Those wasted emotions wouldn't save Will. And right now, that was all that mattered.

He merged back onto the road, heading toward Lexington. He'd need to get a flight to Portugal no matter the cost. Will's life hung in the balance.

Something else tugged at Dak's thoughts as he sped down the country road leading to the highway. Bo had said there were a few hoops to jump through before he would face him.

What else could there be?

TWO

NAZARÉ, PORTUGAL

Dak stepped out of the cab with his rucksack slung over one shoulder. He quickly paid the driver a fistful of euros and hurried toward the apartment building entrance.

The driver must have thought him a crazy person, hunched over and rushing forward with knees bent to stay low. If the cabbie thought anything of it, the man didn't stick around long enough to ask. He sped away, probably anxious to get to his next fare, though with the money Dak tipped him, the guy could take the rest of the day off and still end up way ahead.

Dak gave no thought to the exorbitant amount of money he'd spent just to get to Will's doorstep. The first class flight probably cost more than the cab driver would make in a month, but it was the only seat left on the only flight that could get Dak to Lisbon in time.

He stopped at the door and crouched low, digging his old key out from the front pouch of his bag. He hoped it would still work, but if it didn't, he'd still find a way in—whatever it took.

The building, with all its upgrades and amenities, still utilized an old-style key system instead of a digital keypad like most modern apartments and condominiums, though he'd seen the same in several places across Europe.

Dak inserted the key into the lock and then paused as he considered the possibility that Bo could have rigged the door to blow when someone opened it.

He grunted in frustration. Will probably had a device inside the apartment that could detect an electronically detonated booby trap. The irony twisted Dak's gut into knots.

It took a second for Dak to get a grip on the situation. He was being incredibly paranoid. Bo couldn't have rigged this door to blow. It was a central entrance. By the time he left the previous day, hundreds of people would have come and gone through this doorway. Dak shook his head for the idiotic oversight, though he wanted to give himself a break due to the exhaustion of travel and the lack of sleep.

He twisted the key in the lock and opened the door. A tendril of relief trickled over him, even though he'd already talked himself off the irrational ledge. He lowered his shoulder and barged through the door into the foyer. Forgoing the elevator, Dak charged up the stairs, giving no thought to the heavy sound of footfalls echoing throughout the stairwell.

He must have checked his watch a hundred times between the airport and the apartment, and a hundred more on the flight to Lisbon. Every glance renewed the tightness in his chest, throwing jet fuel on the anxiety that racked him with every passing second.

Luck, it seemed for now, was on Dak's side. He'd arrived at the apartment with more than an hour to spare, but he knew that would evaporate in a blink if he didn't move fast.

Dak rounded the first landing, taking the steps two at a time as he bounded upward. He ignored the warming in his leg muscles as he whipped around the second landing, then the third. His pace slowed slightly just before he reached the top and burst through the door into the corridor.

No need to check the clock now, he thought.

He sprinted to the end of the hall and scuffled to a stop at Will's door. If Bo had set a trap, it would be here. Bo didn't care about collateral damage. If he destroyed the whole top floor, it wouldn't bother him.

There'd been a couple of missions in Iraq when Bo called in airstrikes while civilians were still in the area. Fortunately, his orders were overridden and no one was hurt, but those occasions told Dak everything he needed to know about Bo and the way he viewed human life.

Dak needed to know if this door was rigged to blow or if Bo had given him half a chance to get in and save his friend.

Raising his hand, fearful that there could be an audio sensor attached to the door that would set off the explosives, Dak rapped on the door four times. He hit the surface hard enough that even if Will had been in the bathroom, he would have heard it.

Dak cupped his hands to his mouth and pressed them against the door as he yelled. "Will? You okay?"

"Dak?" Will's muted response was barely audible through the door.

"Yeah, it's me. Did he set any traps around the entrance?"

"Get out of here, Dak. No reason for you to die here."

"Answer my question or I'm coming in."

Silence answered. Then a reluctant "No, it's not booby trapped."

That was good enough for Dak. He inserted the key into the keyhole and twisted it. He winced as he turned the key, then again when he heard the click. No ball of fire consumed him. Not that he would have known if it did. But he still stood there in the hall, alive—for the moment.

"I'm coming in, Will." Dak made the announcement as he turned the knob and gently nudged the door inward. He immediately checked the doorframe for anything that could be used to trigger a detonation. Relieved that the trim was clean, Dak pushed the door open until he could slip through the gap, happy to swing it only as far as needed.

Dak flashed a look across the room and found his friend strapped to his desk chair with what looked like forty feet of duct tape.

Will stared back at his friend with eyes full of exhaustion and apathy. He bore the look of a man who'd given up all hope and resigned to the fact he was going to die in this room.

"You stubborn moron," Will spat. "I told you to leave me alone."

"Actually, you told me to get out of here."

Will shook his head and lowered it to his chest in disbelief. "Just go, Dak. There's nothing you can do. Call the manager of the complex and tell them to evacuate. Call the cops, too. They'll need to set up a safe perimeter around the building. There's still time to save people."

"Everyone except you," Dak countered. He closed the door silently and then padded across the room, setting his bag down next to the desk. "What are we working with here?" He knelt down and craned his neck to the side to investigate the explosive device.

Clusters of wires stuck out from underneath the seat, all attached to an aluminum box strapped to the support post. A red light next to a switch glowed dimly. Beside that, an LED screen displayed a count-down. Dak's estimate had been too generous. The screen displayed less than thirty minutes until detonation.

"It's no use, Dak. I'm telling you. He used a pressure sensitive detonator. If you get me out of the chair, boom. We're gone."

"Well," Dak said as he inspected the device's rigging. "There is some good news."

"What's that?" Will arched an eyebrow suspiciously.

"He also installed a failsafe so that if I try to bypass the system and replace the signal, that will also set off the bomb."

Will eyed him as if he was insane. "I thought you said there was good news."

"Yeah, but I didn't say for who." Dak stood up and shifted over to the desk where a collection of phones festooned the surface. "These burners?"

"Of course. You know better than to ask that."

"Had to be sure."

Dak picked up a flip phone and held it precariously in front of his friend, a judgmental look twisting his face. "A flip phone? I thought these were going out of style."

His statement only received a shake of the head from Will.

Dak dialed the number he recalled from his time living in the building. He set the phone on speaker just as the manager answered in Portuguese. Dak dropped the phone in Will's lap. Will spoke fluent Portuguese. While Dak had picked up a little while he lived here, it wasn't enough to tell the supervisor what was going on.

Then Dak rushed over to the kitchen and grabbed a knife from a bamboo holder. He returned as Will explained to the manager that there was a bomb in the building and everyone needed to be evacuated. He finished by telling the man to call the police.

"Oh, I'm sorry about that," a familiar voice said over the phone. "Calling the cops would be cheating, now wouldn't it?"

"Bo?" Dak asked, his face burning with red heat.

"You didn't think I'd let you just call the apartment manager and let him get you out of this mess with the local bomb squad, if they even have one."

"You're here?" Will asked.

Dak knew Bo wouldn't be so stupid.

"No, I'm nowhere near Nazare now, my friend. But I did take the liberty of rerouting calls to the manager to my phone. You're so predictable, Dak. You really are. Of course, now you'll call the cops. But is that really what you want? Are you going to risk getting caught? You call the police, they're going to want to know how you knew about this, why you were here. Seems awfully convenient, doesn't it? I mean, you'll have to be removed from the premises while their inept team works to disarm the device. They will fail and your friend will die. So, you really only have one play here, Dak. Disarm the bomb yourself or go up in flames with your pal."

"Why don't you just face me," Dak sneered. "Why go through all this? Huh? You like to play mind games?"

"With you, Dak? Absolutely."

The call ended and Dak found himself staring down at the bomb, his mind wandering in a thousand directions.

Will looked up at his friend. He peered into Dak's green eyes with sad sincerity. "It's okay, man. Just go."

Dak stood there in contemplative silence. A seagull squawked as it flew over the balcony. In the silence, the waves of the ocean crashed against the shore.

"No," Dak said, an idea sparking in his mind. He took the knife and sliced through the layers of duct tape.

Will let his hands fall and shook them to get the circulation back into his fingers. He shook his head. "It doesn't matter, Dak. You can't get me out of the chair. I already explained it."

"You're not dead yet," Dak cut him off and checked the timer on the bomb. "I do have a question, though."

Will looked at him curiously. "What's that?"

"Can you swim?"

THREE

NAZARÉ

"What is that supposed to mean?" Will asked. "Yes, I can swim. How is that relevant right now, Dak? I have a bomb under my butt and you're wanting to know if—"

"Good. Shut up." Dak looked over at the far wall where a paddle board hung over the sofa. "Aren't the waves here too big for that thing?"

"Dak? What are you doing?"

"Okay, this is going to sound crazy, but you and I are going to the beach."

Will searched his friend's eyes for any sign of the harebrained plan simmering in Dak's skull. "What?"

Dak didn't answer. He grabbed the back of the chair and rolled it toward the door.

"Dak, seriously. What is your plan?" Will gripped the edges of the chair so tightly that it could have left a permanent indentation of his fingers in the baseplate.

Dak maneuvered carefully to the door, aware that any bump could alter the pressure sensitive detonator and literally blow the roof off the building—and the two of them with it.

When they reached the door, he opened it and shoved Will into the hall. "One second."

Dak stepped back into the apartment and hurried over to the paddle board.

"Hey! Dak. What are you—" The door closed on his friend and muted the question.

Dak grabbed the paddle board off the wall and rushed back to the entryway and flung the door open again. He was greeted with a loathing, irritated glare from Will.

"What are you doing with my paddle board?" Will tried not to yell, but his impatience only swelled with every passing second.

"You're going to need to pull yourself along with your feet. Come on. We have to get to the elevator." Dak spun around and started toward the lift. Will followed more slowly, still confused as he rolled along—pulling his way forward with his heels.

Dak hit the down button and turned to his friend. "We need to get you in the water."

"What are you talking about? I have a bomb. Under. My butt!"

"Yes, I noticed. So, the chair is pneumatic. If we can get the pressure equalized, it should keep it from changing what the sensor on the detonator detects. So we fill it with water."

Will stared at him. "Seriously?"

"Maybe."

"Maybe? I need a little better than maybe, Dak."

"A minute ago you told me to leave. You'd resigned yourself to a fiery death. You don't sound so sure now."

"Yeah, okay. I don't want to die. But if you wanted to fill the pneumatic cylinder with water, why didn't you just use the hose in the sink?"

"Won't work that way," Dak said.

The elevator dinged, and the doors opened. A young couple in summer wear stepped off and looked at the two men with curious bewilderment, then meandered down the hall to their apartment, occasionally looking back at the odd sight of one man taped in an office chair and the other with a paddle board.

Dak pushed Will into the elevator, then tilted the paddle board at an angle to work it into the corner. "Could you hit the button?" Dak said. "My hands are full."

Will rolled his eyes and pressed the button for the ground floor. "You were saying?"

"Right. To make sure we keep the pressure distribution even, it's probably safest to submerge the entire chair."

"Okay... so why do you need the paddle board?"

"Sand. You won't be able to roll across the sand in that. So, I'm going to roll you onto the board and pull the board across the sand until we reach the water."

Will shook his head in disbelief. "I'm dead. Actually, we're both dead."

"It's going to work, Will. You just have to trust me."

"Why can't we just get in the pool. You know there's a pool here, right? Or did you forget?"

"It has to be gradual. If you rolled off into the pool, the chair would shift suddenly on impact, the pressure sensor would detonate, and, well, you know the rest."

The elevator dinged on the second floor and the doors opened. A middle-aged man with a thick graying beard and matching locks stepped in. He clutched a six-pack of Czech Pilsner in his right hand and a baguette with steak and cheese in the other.

He looked at the buttons, noted the one for the ground floor was illuminated, and turned around to face the doors.

"You boys goin' for a swim?" he asked in a sharp Irish accent.

"Something like that," Dak answered.

The Irishman nodded without turning around. Dak got the distinct impression this wasn't the strangest thing he'd seen, perhaps even that week.

When the lift dinged again, the doors opened into the lobby, and the Irishman strolled out. "Enjoy your swim, boys," he said with a nod of the head. Then he strolled toward the exit.

"Thanks. We will."

Will dragged himself off the elevator and into the lobby. Dak followed with the paddle board, banging it against the sides of the lift's doors on his way out. He rushed across to the main doorway leading out to the street and pulled open the glass doors. Will followed, albeit much slower, and carefully rolled over the threshold and out onto the sidewalk.

The two continued another twelve feet until they reached the main walkway. To the left, the sidewalk stretched toward town where restaurants, bars, and markets catered to tourists and locals. To the right, the path led down to the beach where a sparse collection of sunbathers warmed in the radiant sun and surfers waited for the waves to pick up.

Will stared down the hill in abject terror. The slope of the sidewalk was a five or six percent grade, and if they weren't careful, Will could easily roll out of control and crash.

"You better be sure about this," Will said, knowing his friend faced the same trepidation.

Dak nodded, ignoring the tidal wave of doubts to his plan. "Yep. It's going to be fine." He glanced down at Will. "Just, you know, go slow."

He didn't mention that a stolen glance at his watch told him they were down to less than fifteen minutes until the bomb detonated.

FOUR

NAZARÉ

Dak's guesstimate at the steepness of the sidewalk was a touch on the conservative side. He quickly realized that the gradient changed about eighty feet down the hill. The gentle slope turned into a precipitous nightmare.

Will found it increasingly difficult to keep a steady pace without losing control. He dug his heels, careful to keep the weight distribution even on the seat as he rolled forward.

Dak checked his watch more than once on the way down. Time was running out at a terrifying pace.

"Uh, Will?" Dak said, "not to make you panic or anything, but we only have about seven minutes left, so, if you could move a little faster...."

Will glowered at him. "I'm moving as fast as I can, man. You try rolling down a steep sidewalk with a bomb attached to your butt in an office chair and see how fast you go?"

"Yeah, I. I'm just... keep it up. You're doing great." Dak sounded like he was telling a 14-year-old he was proud that the kid learned to tie their shoelaces.

"Don't patronize me while I have a bomb attached to my butt!"

"My bad. Just... keep going. You're... we're almost to the beach."

Dak continued to backtrack down the slope, staying in front of his friend in case Will lost control and started to roll too fast. The paddle board hung under his right armpit while he kept his left hand extended to brace Will. The awkward maneuver made Dak's progress slow as well, but it was necessary to keep the delicate balance required to prevent an explosion.

The two men reached the bottom of the hill after what seemed like an hour of excruciatingly methodical progress. To the right, where the concrete met the sand, a cart with a yellow umbrella sat beside a palm tree. The vendor sold frozen treats to beachgoers, and a line of three children waited to get their desserts with a cluster of adults.

Dak briefly doubted his plan. The slightest mistake would now jeopardize more innocent lives. Thankfully, the beach wasn't crowded yet, but with every passing minute new visitors arrived.

Will rolled to a stop near to the sand and looked up at his friend. "Okay, we're here. Now what?"

Dak tilted to the side and glanced at the ticking clock under the chair. "Five minutes."

There was another problem, though, and he wasn't sure how to fix it. He cursed himself for not thinking of it before.

"What?" Will asked, sensing something amiss.

Dak ignored him, turning his head in every direction, scouring the area for a solution. He found it in one of the local power company's trucks sitting on the other side of the street.

Two workers were busily inspecting cables hanging from a telephone pole and had left a toolbox sitting on an open shelf on the driver's side.

"One second," Dak said.

He sprinted across the street and stopped next to the truck. The men were still busily talking on the passenger side, pointing up at the lines. They never saw the American reach into the toolbox and take out a roll of duct tape, then dart back across the street.

"More tape?" Will asked. "I hope you're not thinking about strapping me to this thing again."

"The thought crossed my mind," Dak said with a wink. "Hold on to the chair."

Will gripped the edges of the chair even tighter, fighting against the fatigue building in his tendons and ligaments from already holding on so firmly for the last several minutes.

Dak flipped over the paddle board and kicked off the fin attached to the bottom.

"Hey, man," Will whined. "I just bought that."

"You want me to save your board or you?"

Dak didn't wait for an answer, and none came. He flipped the board back over and shoved it onto the sand. Then he stepped behind the chair and eased Will forward, tilting the chair back slightly to ride the wheels up onto the paddle board's top surface. Once Will was in the center of the board, Dak set to work with the duct tape. He stripped off several pieces and wrapped them around the front wheels first, attaching them to the top of the board. Then he repeated the steps with the rear wheels.

"This should keep the chair from slipping off."

"Um, Dak? I'm not so—"

Dak didn't wait for him to finish. "Hold on," he cut in. He rushed back to the paddle board's nose, sand kicking up around him. He grabbed the cord attached to the board and started pulling.

"Try to keep your weight distribution even," Dak said. "And don't wiggle too much."

"Easy for you to say."

Dak pulled on the rope, his face flushing red almost instantly from the strain. He feared the cord would break under the burden, but as the paddle board began to inch forward, the taut line held true.

One step at a time, Dak burrowed his heels into the sand as he dragged his friend across the beach toward the sea. Waves rolled steadily into shore, churning white foam with every rhythmic crash.

On a good day, the waves at Nazare were some of the biggest in the world. It had become a surfer's paradise during peak times, but today, the cresting waters didn't rise more than ten feet off the surface.

The swells were still dangerously high for Dak's plan, but if he could get the chair deep enough between them, it could buy enough time to get Will clear.

Dak's forearms and thighs burned, and a quick over-the-shoulder glance told him he was only halfway to the water. He didn't need to look at his watch or check the display. That would waste precious seconds at this point, and every single tick of the clock counted.

He pulled harder, careful to keep his movements as smooth as possible. Jerk the rope too hard, and Will could tip backward. The duct tape keeping the wheels in place would only stabilize the chair. Too much force would rip the fragile bonds and send Will reeling.

A few of the beachgoers looked on at the bizarre sight. Will didn't pay attention to any of them. He kept his feet out to either side of the board and gripped the chair with every ounce of strength he could muster.

With every step, the sound of the waves hitting the shore grew louder in Dak's ears. He knew he was getting close. But would there be enough time?

The paddle board cut through the soft sand like a rusty blade, grinding against the gritty beach.

"Almost there, Dak," Will said in an attempt to encourage his fatigued sled dog.

Instead, the statement caused Dak to risk a glance back over his shoulder. When he did, his right heel slipped and skidded on the sand. He fell backward. With the sudden extra tug from his weight, the board would have lurched forward, but he had loosened his grip slightly and let the cord slide through as he hit the ground with a bump.

"Well, you were," Will offered.

Dak had at least five smart-aleck responses he wanted to use, but he kept them all to himself. The look back told him he was less than ten feet from the wet sand where the tide pushed against land.

With renewed energy, he started to pull again. This time faster. The clock in his head ticked down the seconds and he knew they didn't have long. After six steps, he felt the cool water of the ocean lap against his left heel, then his right. Within two heavy breaths, his ankles were covered in salt water and his toes dug into the submerged sand.

When the nose of the board touched the water, Dak dropped the cord and maneuvered to the back. Will kept his feet out wide for balance.

Dak reached the rear of the board and got down on his hands and knees. He ripped off the duct tape from the rear wheels, then the front. "Put your feet down and slowly inch your way into the water," he ordered. "I'll keep you steady from the rear."

"I don't like the way that sounds," Will quipped nervously.

"Glad you can keep your sense of humor at a time like this," Dak replied. "Okay, together. Here we go."

He carefully nudged the chair forward, rolling it on the surface of the board until it reached the tip. Will guided it with his feet under the shallow water.

Dak spun the chair around with the greatest of caution so that Will faced the shore.

"Going in backward, okay?" Dak asked.

"Do I have a choice?"

"Not really. These caster wheels won't roll very well in the sand. So, I'm going to have to drag you."

"Dak..." Will faltered.

"Don't even try to give me some sob speech about how I don't have to die and how I've done enough. Just save it."

Dak pulled before Will could counter. The water rose up to the back of Dak's knees, slapping against his jeans. He kept his muscles tight as he pulled the chair, plowing the wheels into the sandy beach beneath. Every step brought Will several inches deeper until half the cylinder holding the seat was submerged.

"Almost there," Dak said over the sound of a crashing wave. The surge of water hit him in the back. He could have been knocked forward by the powerful liquid wall, but he braced his right leg at the last second and steadied his arms to keep Will from moving too much. Dak's body broke a portion of the wave, but not all. Will was struck by some of the water and felt his torso lurch toward the shore. He squeezed the seat with every last ounce of strength. His forearms tightened, and he thought he might be dethroned a split second before he was consumed in fire.

Then the wave passed, dying out as it reached the shore.

Will slumped back in the seat, momentarily relieved.

Dak smashed that relief with a sledgehammer. "We're going to have to time this just right!" He yelled over the ocean. "We need to get between the waves to get this deep enough!" He pointed at the chair, noting the cylinder was almost there.

"Okay!" Will shouted back. "When are we going?"

"Now!"

"What?"

FIVE
NAZARÉ

Dak strained against the weight of the chair as it protested his efforts. The water and sand made moving the thing all but impossible. But as he plunged deeper into the sea, the task eased with every step.

"Hold on!" Dak shouted above the sound of the waves.

"Do you really think you need to tell me that?" Will yelled back.

He clung to the seat beneath him. The water was nearly up to his knees now, and both men knew that if this harebrained plan was going to work, it would have to be soon.

Dak looked back over his shoulder and saw the next wave building. The water beneath him sucked back out to sea, lowering enough that more than a third of the piston's cylinder remained exposed. The oncoming wave continued to rise, swelling higher and higher until it dwarfed him by three feet.

In less than ten seconds, the wave would be on them, and this time there was no way Dak could keep Will from being blown off the chair.

Knowing it was now or never, Dak pulled through the fire in his arms and legs. His fingers almost felt numb, like the first time he'd been put through a marathon round of pull-ups. They remained curled, almost gnarled, on their own, as if he'd lost all control. Now, though, Dak kept control through it all, dragging his friend deeper into the sea.

Will looked back and saw the incoming wave. To the man in the office chair, it may as well have been a tsunami.

"Dak," Will said, elongating the name.

"I know, Will. Just... another... few feet." Dak gave one last, hard pull.

The chair dragged through the water, its wheels plowing into the sand until suddenly, the weight lightened. The chair felt lighter, and Dak realized the seat was causing the chair to float.

Two seconds before the wave smashed into them, Dak shouted, "Now, Will! Jump!"

Will slid forward, planted his feet in the sand beneath the churning water, and leaped as far as he could.

The last thing Dak saw before the wave slammed into his back was the completely submerged cylinder as it drew back into the wave to join the liquid wall as it charged toward the shore.

Dak's limbs went limp. He exhaled and then sucked in one long breath before his world was swallowed by saltwater.

Everything around him swirled and twisted. He felt invisible forces tugging at him from multiple angles—the strongest of which pulled him away from the bending, shimmering light above. On a normal day, Dak could easily hold his breath for ninety seconds. After the exertion of dragging his friend across the sand and into the ocean, however, he'd be lucky if he could manage for half that.

A powerful current jerked him downward. His shoulder hit the sandy bottom with a thud. Then the tide ripped him forward, rolling him along the ocean floor like an underwater tumbleweed.

Dak's vision blurred. Everything spun around him. The flickering sunlight overhead twisted and curved under the rippling surface. The surface, Dak thought. I have to get to the surface.

He kicked his legs, but the fatigued muscles flopped impotently in the water. His arms felt like socks filled with pudding. Dak's lungs tightened with every passing second. He didn't have long before he'd need to inhale.

With the last gasp of strength he could summon, Dak shot his right hand toward the surface. Something slapped onto his wrist and pulled him up. When his head breached the waters, he spewed air out of his lungs and inhaled deeply several times. As the salt water cleared his face and eyes, he saw who held on to his arm.

Will squeezed Dak's forearm tight until Dak felt the sand dragging beneath him. He regained his orientation and stood up.

They were chest deep in the water, now deep enough to catch the next wave in. As the waters swelled again, the two men started swimming toward shore. They body surfed to shallow water and came to a stop.

Dak had never been so glad to see and feel wet sand, and for a moment, he was overwhelmed with gratitude for making it out of that scenario alive.

He glanced over at Will and nodded. His friend returned the gesture. Then after a few seconds of silence, Dak started to laugh. It began as a chuckle that crescendoed into a series of booms.

"What is so funny?" Will asked. His face twisted in confused disbelief.

Dak snorted. "Just the visual of you in that chair. We must have looked ridiculous with the paddle board, the chair, all of it."

He pressed the back of his hand to his lips to quiet the laughter.

Will merely nodded and bit his lower lip. "I still can't believe that worked."

"Me, either," Dak agreed.

Will's head froze and he lowered his eyebrows. "Wait. What?"

"Speaking of," Dak detoured. "Where is that chair?"

He looked past Will and got his answer. Two hundred feet down the shore, the chair tilted over at an angle, gradually burrowing into the sand with every wave that splashed by. A sparse collection of onlookers stood along the beach, away from the water, pointing at the oddity.

"Oh. There it is."

Dak pointed to the floating furniture. Will rolled his head the other direction and looked, just as the chair exploded in a fiery blast. Water and black smoke shot fifty feet into the air. The people on the beach screamed and retreated with reckless abandon, running toward the street.

Dak winced. Will snapped his head back around, glowering with accusation. "I thought you said the water would diffuse that thing!"

"Yeah. I mean. I did, it did," he corrected. "Honestly, I wasn't sure it would work at all. Or for how long."

He shrugged at his friend's silent fury.

"Anyway," Dak continued. "Glad you're okay. Now, we need to figure out where Bo Taylor went."

SIX

ISTANBUL

Bo sat at a street-side table under a red and white umbrella. He sipped a cup of Turkish coffee, never taking his eyes off the building across the street. A young man in a black apron appeared for the third time to ask him if he'd like anything else. Bo's head only twisted an inch to the side, still keeping his eyes on the apartment building on the other side of the street. He knew the waiter would keep coming back, probably hoping to free up the table for the next customer.

"I'm fine," Bo said. "But I'll tell you what..." He reached into his pocket and fished out a wad of cash, thumbed through and found a couple of hundred euros, then held them out for the server. "Take this and bring me another coffee every thirty minutes. Other than that, I'm not to be disturbed. Understood?"

The young man took the money from his hand with a grateful reluctance. "Yes, sir. Of course."

The waiter turned and hurried back inside the café with more money than he would have made in two or three shifts.

Bo sighed, exhaling through his nose at the irritation. He couldn't complain. Good service was hard to find these days. If he wasn't staking out the building opposite, he'd probably have been kinder to the young man. Circumstances as they were, however, he needed to focus. The stop-and-go traffic on the street in front of him was more distraction than he cared for. The only distraction he permitted was to check the news reports coming out of Portugal during the last hour.

The headlines were easy enough to discover with a quick search. "Bizarre Explosion Rocks Nazare," "Two Men Seen With Office Chair Prior To Blast" were a couple he'd noted.

The articles didn't provide any information, though, on whether there had been any casualties. The reports were still coming in. Bo assumed Dak and Will had somehow managed to escape unscathed. He wondered why the two decided to take the chair down to the beach. That particular curiosity itched at Bo's brain for minutes. Dak must have been trying to save anyone who might have been in the building, Bo reckoned.

He'd rigged the bomb to blow with a shift in pressure less or greater than five pounds, and most attempts to bypass the current in the wiring would have the same result.

There were, of course, ways around every explosive device, but Dak wouldn't have access to those means—not on such short notice.

The only explanation that made any sense was that he'd tried to get the bomb as far away from the building as possible, potentially saving a few dozen or more lives.

Still, with every subsequent search, the updated articles detailing the events on the beach in Nazare suggested there were no injuries, and more disturbingly, no deaths. Were the Portuguese media outlets covering up the real story? Would it hurt tourism too much to have two Americans die in an explosion? Is that why they're sweeping it under a rug?

Those thoughts rattled Bo's mind as he raised the coffee mug to his lips and took another long sip. The Turks liked their coffee strong, almost bitterly so, and they didn't typically use cream or milk in it—at least not the Turkish people he knew. And there were several. Some utilized sugar to smooth out the taste, and he'd done so liberally.

He peered over the mug's rim at the apartment building. Even if

Dak had managed to survive the ordeal in Portugal, as he suspected, that would make this chapter of their story all the sweeter.

Bo had never met Nicole, but he'd seen pictures. The woman mesmerized him, even just the images of her. Dak spoke of her sparingly, but when he did, Bo knew this woman still held his heart in a steel vault, unwilling to let it go.

She was beautiful, of that no doubt existed, but beyond her exterior beauty, Dak spoke of her spirit, her untamed passion to squeeze every drop of juice from the lemon of life.

That particular piece excited Bo the most. After all, the best hunt was always feral game.

He caught a glimpse of a familiar face gliding down the sidewalk. It blinked in and out between the pedestrians walking in the other direction. Bo perked up and leaned forward, peering at her through the aviator sunglasses perched on his nose. He let them slide down a little and gazed over the rims at the woman as she gobbled up the sidewalk with long strides.

She walked with the purpose of a businesswoman about to engineer a hostile takeover. Bo knew that wasn't her, though. Dak had been elusive about her career, but he knew enough. She could be dangerous if he wasn't careful. That cautionary thought only heightened his excitement. He was going to enjoy this.

He stood and slung his backpack over the right shoulder and walked to the sidewalk, where he turned and quickly scurried down to the crosswalk. The city street was too busy for him to cross here. Traffic started and stopped too frequently. He doubted he'd be hit by a car with the log jam going on, but the honk of an irritated diver's horn would startle his quarry. She would look to see the source of the trouble on the street and then spot him.

Not that she'd know who he was or why he was there, but the element of surprise was his primary advantage at this point. Getting her alone, in her building, was the goal.

The light changed and the walk signal illuminated on the street sign opposite where Bo stood. He hurried through the intersection and veered left as the woman slowed, nearing the entrance to her apartment building.

Bo cut left again onto the sidewalk, twisting and sliding past the oncoming pedestrian flood until he could see the woman just ahead. She'd already unlocked the front door, and while Bo certainly had his methods to break into people's homes, doing it the easy way would be preferable.

She stepped in through the apartment door as he cleared through the last of the people. The door inched its way toward closing. If he didn't move fast, he'd miss it.

Bo stumbled toward the steps and rounded them in a flash, his left leg whipping out behind him before planting it on the second step and vaulting his weight toward the closing door. At the last possible moment, Bo reached out and grabbed the edge of the door a split second before it closed. He felt the cool air of the entryway lobby against his knuckles, and with it, a tendril of relief.

He looked into the lobby, but the woman was gone. The stairs and the room beyond were vacant. And there was no sign that anyone was on the elevator.

"Where did you go?" he hissed.

SEVEN

ISTANBUL

Bo stared into the lobby, scanning it for any sign of the woman. If he lurked much longer, he'd arouse suspicion from passersby. Step inside, and he could be walking into a trap.

Trap? What was he thinking? The mark didn't know she was being followed. He was 99 percent certain she hadn't seen him approaching on the sidewalk. That wasn't a hundred, though, and there was always that one percent that gnawed through the best-laid plans.

He made his decision and stepped through the door, silent as a gentle breeze, and eased the door shut behind him.

Bo stood in the lobby, his hand shifting to the pistol concealed in his gray button down jacket. He drew the weapon and leveled it at his waist, then froze. He listened intensely and heard the sound of footfalls ascending the stairs. It was the repetitive click of shoes on steps, and he knew from the sound they were women's shoes—the kind he'd seen his target wearing the second before she disappeared into the building's entrance.

He snapped into action, padding quickly over to the stairwell. He wrapped his hand around a black metal knob on the railing and propelled himself upward, taking two steps with every stride. Bo carefully placed his feet on the edge of each step to keep his movement silent. His jeans rustled slightly, but by keeping his legs wide, that inhibited most of the sound to a nearly unnoticeable swish.

At the second floor landing, he paused and listened. The clicks echoed down from overhead. He pressed upward, continuing his ascent, his ghostlike movements drawing him nearer to his mark by the second.

Then, beyond the midway landing between the third and fourth floors, he caught sight of the target. Her red dress fluttered for a second, and he knew he had her. As he rounded the next corner, he skidded to a halt, freezing his place.

She'd stopped halfway up the next flight of stairs. Her laptop case hung from her left shoulder and her head drooped, as if she stared idle at the next step.

Was she taking a break? Had she heard him? Bo gripped the pistol in his hand and trained it on the target, aligning the barrel with the middle of her back. He narrowed his eyes, curious as to why the woman stopped. If she knew he was there, why wasn't she saying anything? As the seconds ticked by, her intentions blurred further.

A sniffle broke the silence, and she wiped her nose with the back of her free hand. Was she crying? The question hung in Bo's head. He didn't move, barely breathing through his mouth as he waited to see what she did next.

She whimpered. The pathetic sound bounced off the hard walls, reverberating through the stairwell in both directions.

What was she doing?

"What are you doing here?" she asked, choking on the sobs she couldn't hold back any longer. "Why do you keep doing this to me?"

Bo frowned at the question. He didn't understand. Had she seen him? And if so, how did she know who he was? And what did she mean, keep doing this? He hadn't done anything to her. Not yet.

"I told you to leave me alone, not to come back here. So why? Why do you do this? I was moving on with my life. I got a great gig here, started all over again. And you keep popping up, carving out fresh wounds. Do you have any idea what you've done to me, how this hurts all the way down to my core? I loved you. More than anything."

She paused, and the crying resumed for almost a minute.

Bo didn't know what to do. He always knew what to do. Her emotional breakdown, however, threw his plans into a tailspin. It didn't change his intentions. He was still going to do what he came here to do.

He inched one step closer to her, keeping the pistol aimed squarely at her spine.

"You told me you wouldn't come back, that you'd let me be. I can't go through this again. You know that. So why are you here? I thought you were supposed to be disappearing. You said that being here would put me, could put me in danger. If you truly cared about me, you wouldn't be here."

Bo realized who she thought he was. She hadn't seen him. She thought he was Dak. He hadn't realized the depth to how badly his ex-teammate had screwed things up with this woman. From the sound of it, she didn't realize how much ending the relationship had hurt him too.

This was too perfect.

"Well? Are you going to say anything or are you just going to stand there?" Her head drooped. "Answer me, Dak? Why did you come here?"

She whirled around and faced the man. Realization stretched across her face. She stared into the eyes of a killer. Her gaze fell to the weapon in his hand.

"You're not Dak," she said, her voice cracking at the epiphany.

"No, darlin'. I'm definitely not."

"Who are you? What do you want?"

A sickly grin creased his lips. "You'll find out soon enough."

EIGHT

NAZARÉ

Will and Dak stepped onto the elevator in the apartment building with their clothes still dripping wet. They'd managed to escape the beach without being noticed by witnesses, utilizing the explosion and the subsequent panic to sneak away.

First responders arrived on the scene within minutes, sirens blaring from every adjoining street.

Emergency crews didn't pay attention to the two sopping wet men as they climbed the hill back to Will's building.

Dak was grateful no one occupied the elevator on their return journey. He had no doubts that the people they'd seen before would recall the two men with the paddle board and the office chair. From there, it would only be a matter of time until those witnesses connected the dots and started feeding information to the authorities.

Will pressed the button for his apartment's floor. The doors closed two seconds later and the lift started to ascend. For a second, neither of the men spoke; both still breathing hard from the hike up the hill combined with the harrowing experience prior.

"Thank you," Will said, staring straight ahead at the doors per the social custom in elevators. No one ever seemed to make eye contact in the sacred space. Perhaps it was too intimate.

"You're welcome," Dak said.

"Although it's kind of your fault."

"Kind of?"

"Okay, it's entirely your fault."

The lift doors opened and Dak poked his head out through the opening, checking both directions before he stepped onto the floor. Will followed and then took the lead, heading toward his apartment.

Dak didn't say anything until they were safely back inside the flat.

The second the door closed behind him, Dak locked it and continued the conversation. "Yes, I know. And I'm sorry. You're right. It's all my fault. I should have never brought you into this."

"Relax, brother," Will said. He went to the refrigerator and opened it, pulled out two bottles of beer, and set them on the counter. "I'm just messing with you." He used a steel bottle opener next to the fridge to open both bottles, then handed one to his friend. "Although, it was your fault. For the record."

Dak grinned, shaking his head as he accepted the proffered pilsner. "Yeah, well, I know you would have done the same for me."

Will took a sip as if contemplating the insinuation. After he swallowed the cool liquid, he shrugged. "Maybe."

Dak pulled a swig from the bottle. "That was close, though. Too close."

"Yeah, next time you ask for help with hunting for a psychopath like Bo Taylor, remind me to tell you no thanks."

"Where's the fun in that?" Dak said and took another sip.

"Touché."

"Besides, it's not like your current line of work is some sort of cushy office gig. I'm sure you deal with plenty of crazies."

"Yeah, but none of them have strapped me to a bomb in my apartment."

"Yet."

Will rolled his eyes and took a big gulp from his bottle. He walked by Dak who stood next to the entryway with the bottle in his hand and a satisfied, smug look on his face.

When he reached the balcony door, he pulled it open and stepped out. Will peered down to the coastline where the chaotic scene still unfurled on the sand. Police had taped off the area to keep out curious gawkers. A bomb squad consisting of four specialists in protective gear inspected different spots along the beach where fragments of the chair and the explosive device sprayed out from the blast site.

A few hundred feet away, more than a dozen cops interviewed witnesses—some individually, some in groups. Will chuckled at the thought of people telling the police what they'd seen: one guy pulling another guy into the water atop an office chair riding a paddle board. Just before the chair blew up.

"What's so funny?" Dak asked. He sidled up next to his friend and drew in a deep inhale of the sea air. The events of the day notwithstanding, he could never get enough of that smell. It cleared his mind and his senses, like a soothing aromatherapy. He'd joked in the past about wishing he could bottle that, but it was more than merely a scent. It was a feeling that permeated the soul.

"Just thinking about those people down there telling their tall tale about two idiots with an office chair and a paddle board, then a huge explosion."

"It wasn't that huge," Dak countered. He took a long pull from the bottle. He normally wasn't a beer guy, but his frayed nerves needed calming and the inside of his mouth felt like the Mojave Desert.

"Big enough to kill both of us. Honestly, we're lucky no one else was hurt. If the beach was busier...." His voice trailed off.

"Yeah, we're fortunate there weren't more people around." Dak's voice took on a pensive tone.

Seagulls squawked nearby, cutting though the silent breeze with their annoying calls. Tree branches along the sidewalk and next to the building across the street danced in the wind. The moment gave the two men a respite, a much needed breather after such an emotionally, mentally, and physically draining encounter.

Neither of them said anything for two full minutes, both fully absorbed by their individual thoughts.

Will broke the silence after his nerves started to settle. It was one of his concerns swimming amid all the others, but now it bobbed to the surface.

"What's his play here, Dak?" he asked. "Is he testing you or something?"

"Testing me?" Dak considered it. That didn't make sense, though, and he shrugged it off. "I doubt it. That's not his style. He's not trying to make me jump through hoops to prove I'm a worthy adversary or anything like that. He's bitter." Dak's expression hardened. His jaw set firm and the next sip he took from the bottle was a shallow one. "Bo has an ego the size of Texas. He wants it all, including the loot the others took from that cave in Iraq. And he likes to manipulate people, make them jump through hoops for him. Gives him some kind of feeling of power or authority. He loved being a leader, played it up whenever he could."

"I know some guys like that, but they're criminals, dudes that run underworld organizations."

"Bo would be a perfect fit for that. He also has a sadistic side. It comes from a place of misplaced righteous indignation. If I had to guess, I'd say when he was younger he was largely ignored by his parents, disregarded by peers, perpetually overlooked."

Will cast a sidelong glance at his friend. "You almost sound sad for him, the guy that strapped a bomb to me yesterday and left me here to die—along with a bunch of other innocent people."

Dak's vacant gaze never wavered. His head only twitched slightly to the side. "No, he knew I could do it. And if I didn't get here in time and figure out a way to diffuse the bomb, all the better. He'd get rid of the lone threat to his safety and the guy who helped me—you were a loose end too."

"Thanks for reminding me. You're a dangerous guy to be friends with."

"I suppose so." He was about to add a smart-aleck comment to the back end of his admission when Will's statement blasted through the cloud of thoughts in his head.

"Nicole," Dak blurted.

"What?"

Dak spun on his heels and went for the phone on the computer desk. He dialed the number from memory. After the fourth ring, a voice answered on the other end. "Well, well, well," Bo said. "I see you managed to figure out a way to not die. Again. You're getting pretty good at this, Dak?"

Dak's jaw clenched to the point he nearly cracked his teeth. A vein pulsed in his neck, rising under the skin. His face flushed red with fury.

"If you touch her—"

"I'll do whatever I please, Dak. She's not your girl anymore. Remember? And besides, it's not like you can stop me. I'd love to see you try. I really would."

"You won't fight me straight up," Dak said.

"Quite the contrary," Bo argued. "I would love the chance to beat you to a pulp, but you're in Portugal and I'm... well, you know where I am."

"Stay there, Bo," Dak ordered. "I'm on my way."

Will stood nearby in the open balcony doorway on full alert, trying to take in as much of the conversation as possible. He listened with determined interest, eyes unwavering from his friend.

"Oh, Dak. I don't think so. I mean, I really would love the chance to fight you man-to-man, but I doubt you'll make it out of the country, or even out of Nazare for that matter."

A sickening feeling crept into Dak's chest and fell into his gut. "Oh, yeah? Why's that?"

"Because, unless I miss my guess, I'd say the colonel has a team en route to your location right now. They may already be there."

Dak's heart raced and his breath quickened. He shifted toward the balcony, sliding past Will who watched closely, mouthing "what" as Dak passed.

Dak stopped at the railing and looked down both ends of the street. "I'm not worried about the colonel or his men," Dak said, doing his best to sound convincing even as concern mounted.

To the right, toward the beach, the scene looked the same and the street running by it presented no threat. Then he turned to the left and saw the three black SUVs rolling down the hill toward the building.

"I wish I could believe you, Dak. I really do. But we both know that's not true. I wonder, are they already there? Are they on their way up the stairs or elevators right now? Dak? You there?"

Dak twirled his finger at Will, signaling that it was time to leave. Will immediately understood. He lived under the constant threat of having to bug out at a moment's notice.

He rushed into the bedroom and returned seconds later with a rucksack he kept next to his bed.

Dak shouldered his gear and made for the door. "Sorry, Bo, I lost you for a second there. Seems like the connection is—"

He ended the call then broke the phone in half. On his way to the door, he tossed it in the sink and ran water over it to make certain any data could never be recovered.

Will held the door open for him and the two men left the apartment, hurrying into the hallway.

NINE

ISTANBUL

Nicole's eyelids peeled open. She immediately regretted waking as her dry eyes felt like they'd been sandblasted. In her mind, she imagined a sound like rusty hinges creaking on a door. Blinking didn't make things any better, not at first. She closed her eyes again and kept them shut for several seconds, counting in her head until she reached ten. It didn't help that the lights in the room were bright.

Room? What room? She didn't know and had to open her eyes again. As before, opening her eyelids caused a scratching sensation, but this time it wasn't as bad. She blinked again, and it finally began to bring soothing relief.

Nicole looked like a caged bull as perspiration beaded on her nose. The gag tied around her mouth kept her quiet.

Then everything crashed into her memory like a tidal wave: the man, the stairwell, the conversation, the confusion.

She'd thought it was Dak. Did she even dare admit to herself that she initially hoped it was him? Even with all she'd said, the way she'd spoken to him, the angry tone she'd used, the truth was, Nicole wished she could do what Cher suggested in her hit song. If she could turn back time, she would, she would listen more and argue less, be less narcissistic, less bitter at Dak for wanting to serve his country more than her.

But she couldn't. It was too late to fix anything on her end, and yet she felt as if a good amount of her indignation was justified. He could have made more of an effort too, could have decided not to join the military. She had even offered to support him while he figured out his path.

She cursed the confusion racking her soul, twisting around her heart like boa constrictors suffocating their prey. One second she loved him, pined for him in ways she never had for anyone else. The next, she hated him, hated that he'd left her to fight a war she didn't understand.

Nicole felt something wrapped around her waist. Her wrists and ankles, too, felt tightly bound, causing the fingers and toes to tingle with numbness. The sense of smell returned, and she detected the scent of lilac. She recognized it immediately as one of the candles sitting atop the counter in her kitchen. After a few more seconds of blinking, the scratchy feeling on her eyeballs subsided. Her blurred vision made it difficult to see anything familiar, but she doubted the man had taken her anywhere. At least, not yet. And the candle was definitely a giveaway. She doubted he had something like that in his place, wherever that was.

She struggled to recall what happened after she'd turned around to find it wasn't Dak she'd been talking to in the stairwell, but a stranger with a gun and a menacing face to match. She didn't remember much about what happened next. He'd closed the gap fast. He was on her in seconds, pouncing like a cat that had been stalking her for the last hour, waiting for a slip-up before taking his prey. Her head ached. Deep, throbbing pain pounded the back of her skull and rolled up over the top of her head. Along with the blurry vision, that told Nicole everything she needed to know.

She'd been drugged.

Nicole recalled trying to take a step back, but he'd warned her to freeze. Then there was the pinch in her arm as his left hand whipped around and stuck her with the needle.

"Oh, good. You're awake." The voice shook her from the fog. She turned her head and found the man from the stairwell standing in the kitchen, her kitchen. The rest of the apartment appeared through the haze, her vision clearing by the second. The visual confirmed her initial suspicions.

Questions floated to the front of her mind, several of them. Nicole couldn't collect her thoughts enough to ask a single one. She wanted to know who he was, what he wanted, why he was here, but none of that came out of her mouth. Even if the gag wasn't choking back the words, her mind still couldn't decide on which question to ask first. Instead, she just sat there, sneering at him.

"You must be wondering who I am," he went on as he strolled around the kitchen counter and stopped in front of her. He'd placed one of her dining table chairs across from her. She also sat in one, though she was bound to it with extension cords wrapped around her waist and chest. She wasn't sure what the man had used to bind her hands and feet, but it felt like it was probably duct tape.

"Not much for talking?" the stranger asked. "Oh, right. The gag in your mouth. Well, it's probably for the best. We can't have you screaming for help or getting all hysterical, now can we?"

She stared into two round icebergs, eyes as crystal blue as she'd ever seen. They would have been beautiful had they not been so full of evil. His eyes were cold, calculating, emotionless—the opposite of Dak's, though he certainly had the calculating part as well.

"I am Bo Taylor," the stranger said with an odd sort of pride in his voice, as though he were giving himself some kind of grand introduction to speak at a TED talk. "I used to work with your ex-boyfriend, Dak. He and I had a little disagreement. Maybe you heard about that."

She didn't respond, merely glowered at him from her chair.

"At this very moment, Dak and his friend are being pursued by some men who very much want him dead. They will stop at nothing until he is. Or until he kills them. The beauty of all that is, either way, Dak loses. If he is killed, perfect. I let you go and I disappear with my new identity, never to worry about looking over my shoulder for the rest of my life. On the other hand, if he kills the men who are after him, he becomes the monster they already believe him to be. More will come for him until, inevitably, he dies."

Bo shrugged and tossed his head to the side. "You may be wondering why I'm here with you. Let's just call it a little insurance policy. Dak has the tendency to be lucky. If, by the remotest chance, he's able to slip through the fingers of those who are chasing him, I'd prefer to have a bargaining chip."

"You won't get away with it," she managed through the gag. Her voice was muted, choked, but her words were clear enough. "Dak will find you. And he will end you."

Nicole had no idea if she was right. She didn't have a clue what kind of people were trying to corral the man she loved. There it was. An admission. Even in her private thoughts, she knew it to be true. She still loved him with all of her being. Dare she hope he still felt the same, after all the things she'd said to him, all the reckless, bitter darts she'd flung from her mouth?

She wasn't sure, but at the moment, hope was all she could hold on to.

TEN
NAZARÉ

Dak heard the problem before the door to the stairwell was completely open. Footfalls, multiple pairs of them, echoed up from below. He stood in the doorway for a moment, listening. No one was barking orders. If the hit squad had radio communications—and he was sure they did—no words were said.

This team knew the plan and every person in the group operated as a single unit, an extension of command.

The group did their best to stay silent, but there was no mistaking the sound, not to Dak's well-trained ear. He and Will were out of time. The elevator would be covered. Maybe they could get off on the second floor and find a way out through a window. Dak doubted that notion's plausibility. It didn't matter. He knew the assault team would have the elevators covered, and probably shut down. If they hadn't done that yet, it would come.

Dak knew he had to make a decision. Will looked at him, silently begging for answers.

If they went down, they'd have to shoot their way out. Dak didn't like the idea of killing other American soldiers. Maybe they weren't

American. The colonel could have brought in bounty hunters from all over the globe to track down Dak and his friend. Even then, Dak loathed the idea of killing people who'd been hired for a job, a job they believed to be just. Some mercenaries didn't operate with a conscience. He'd seen those types before, but without a way to distinguish the bad apples from the good, he preferred to run rather than fight his way out.

His thoughts instantly flashed back to the current predicament. There was no way down to the main floor that didn't involve a bloody gunfight. That left one option: they'd have to go up and risk a daring escape across the rooftops.

"Come on," he whispered to Will. Without waiting for a reply or a breath of protest, Dak slipped into the stairwell and started to climb.

Will had no choice but to follow. He hurried after his friend, staying close behind him, using the edges of the steps to keep silent. The two kept their feet apart as they climbed to prevent their pants from swishing together as they moved. They rounded the top landing and slowed at the doorway to the rooftop. Dak pushed gently on the bar, then waited.

Will's eyebrows knit tightly together at Dak's hesitation. "What are you doing?" he mouthed.

"Wait," Dak ordered silently.

Will drew his weapon and aimed it down the flight of stairs, certain the assailants would appear around the corner of the next landing below. He didn't dare look over the railing in case one of the men below happened to look up.

Dak listened intently. The sound of a door being jerked open reverberated from below. The second it did, Dak pushed the rooftop door open and stepped out into the warm, bright sunlight. He winced and wished he had time to get his sunglasses from the bag on his back, but that was a luxury he couldn't afford.

He hurried out onto the roof and surveyed the immediate area.

The next building was fairly close, and one story below Will's, but after that, he recalled the gap between the second apartment complex and the third spanned at least sixty feet, separated by a small court-yard in the middle.

Dak pictured the attackers' approach to Will's apartment. He visualized them moving down the hall with every second he stood still on the roof. They would enter the apartment soon, breaching the door and sweeping every room until they realized their quarry was gone.

"Come on," Dak urged quietly. He held the door open and then eased it shut after Will passed.

"Where are we going?" Will demanded, indignant now that it appeared they had nowhere to run.

"Next building."

"What?"

Dak didn't answer. Instead, he sprinted across the rooftop and stopped abruptly at the edge. The lip of the building was shin high. He looked down at the deadly drop, knowing that a mistake here would be the end. He'd been in worse spots before.

He knew the death squad downstairs were entering the apart-ment. Every second counted.

Will skidded to a stop next to Dak and looked down, then over at the next building. "You're gonna jump?"

"No choice," Dak said. He had no time to argue. Instead, he took a few steps back, trotted to the edge, and planted his left foot on the flat top. He launched himself through the air, easily clearing the distance.

Will watched as Dak landed on the rooftop below, hitting the surface with a thud. The second his boots struck the roof, Dak's legs crumpled, and he rolled to his feet.

Dak turned and looked back up at Will, motioning his friend to hurry.

Will stepped back and copied Dak's move, leaping over the gap like an Olympic long-jumper to the next rooftop. Midway through the air, Dak heard a noise just over his right shoulder and instinctively dove to his side.

The access door to the rooftop burst open and a man in a black mask and tactical gear stepped out, military-grade rifle in hand. He raised the weapon, aiming it at Will as he struck the ground and rolled forward.

The gunman's finger tensed, ready to fire.

Dak sprung from behind him and kicked the hand guard an inch in front of the man's left hand. The muted pop escaped the suppressor on the end of the barrel and fired the bullet harmlessly into the sky.

The guard reacted, but slowly, both out of confusion and fear. He started to turn, but it was too late. Dak grabbed the weapon, ejected the magazine from the rifle, and head-butted the gunman in the nose. The man staggered back for a second, loosening his grip on the weapon. It dangled from the strap over his shoulder, and Dak used the moment to pull the charging handle. The last of the live rounds ejected onto the ground.

Dak tilted his body at the hip, and kicked the man in the chest, driving him back through the open door and into the stairwell.

Will had recovered from his landing and aimed his pistol at the gunman, but Dak stepped in the way and held up a hand.

"Don't shoot him," Dak said.

"What?" Will's bewilderment boiled over and seeped out of his eyes. "Why not?"

Dak slammed the door shut and motioned to a metal-handled broom leaning against the access portal's exterior wall.

"Give me that, quick," Dak barked, keeping his right foot wedged against the closed access door.

Will grabbed the broom and passed it to his friend.

He didn't have time to ask another question. Dak took the handle and threaded it through the latch and a lamp post hanging to the side of the door. When the gunman recovered and tried to get through, the door would be barred shut.

"Come on," Dak said.

He started toward the far wall. Will followed, but called after him. "Dude, you realize there's no way we can jump to that next building."

Dak knew he was right, and the realization was only confirmed when he reached the edge. A courtyard below separated the two buildings. After that, there were no other structures for a full block. A park sprawled beyond the next apartment complex.

"The hit squad," Dak said, "are they on the roof yet?"

Will glanced back at his building. "No, not yet."

"Good. Come on."

Dak ran to the back corner of the rooftop where a set of cables ran down over the edge.

"What are you doing?" Will pleaded.

"How many times are you going to ask me that?"

"As many as it takes for you to tell me exactly how you're planning to get us out of this mess."

"Fine," Dak said. "Watch." He grabbed the cluster of cables and flung his legs over the ledge. "We're rappelling down."

"What?"

"Stop saying that and grab the cables." Dak's eyes flashed to a row of rooftop water heaters. "They won't see us if we hurry."

A second later, he was gone.

Will leaned over the edge and saw his friend rapidly walking his way down the exterior wall. The building was shorter than his, but only by one story, and the fall from here would still be deadly.

He looked back over his shoulder and saw the access door shuddering at a steady cadence as the man inside tried to break through. Then Will saw the door to his apartment building burst open. He ducked down and grabbed the cables, then crawled over to the edge.

Will eased himself over the side of the building as he whispered a quiet prayer that the wires would hold. He doubted they were intended to carry the weight of two grown men, but he had no choice.

Will lowered his feet until he felt the hard wall, and then, hand-over-hand, began walking his way down the building.

He'd been rappelling before, but with a harness, handbrake, and other safety gear. Here, if he slipped or lost his grip, he'd fall.

Down below, Dak neared the bottom. Their combined weight and uncoordinated movements caused the cords to vibrate and shake in his hands. He didn't know how long the wires would hold.

When he reached the second floor, he quickened his pace, almost to a backward, straight down jog. A few feet below the top of the first floor, he took one more big step and then let go.

Dak hit the ground with a thud. He'd underestimated the drop, and the jarred landing sent a dull pain through his knees and hips. He'd be fine. He knew that. His eyes lifted to Will who had just passed the top of the second floor.

Dak felt a pounding sense of urgency. He looked around the empty courtyard and out onto the street. So far, no one seemed to notice the two men climbing down the side of the apartment build-ing. Thankfully, most of the town's attention was focused on the beach where the explosion had occurred.

Still, Dak knew the team hunting him would figure out where they'd gone and make their way down to the street. If they were smart, and he had to assume they were, the killers would cordon off the area, probably claiming they were with local authorities searching for another explosive device.

It's what he would do.

Will made it to the top of the first floor.

"One more step and you can jump," Dak urged.

"One step? You serious?"

"Fine, two steps. Come on, man. We gotta go."

Will kept moving, albeit much more deliberately than Dak would have liked.

After four steps, he reluctantly released the cables and dropped to the ground. The wires slapped against the side of the wall as Will's feet struck earth with a thump. The landing didn't hurt him as much as it had Dak, at least from what Dak could tell.

"You good?" Dak asked.

Will nodded. "Yeah, I'm good. I can't believe—"

"I know. Rappelling down an apartment building. Crazy. But we're not out of this yet. Let's get out of here and we'll reminisce later."

ELEVEN

NAZARÉ

Colonel Cameron Tucker watched everything on the eight monitors in front of him in a remote location just outside of Lisbon.

Two months after the debacle with Dak Harper in Iraq, the colonel was reassigned. While his superiors told him, it could have happened to anyone, and that the new job had nothing to do with his failure to bring in the rogue Harper, it was just lip service.

He'd been placed in charge of a head-hunting unit with the specific purpose of tracking down AWOL soldiers like Harper, and Tucker would be lying if he said he didn't spend most of his time and resources trying to locate the man who'd betrayed his team in Iraq. More than a year had passed since then, and with every passing day his impatience pooled near the brim of his cup of iniquity. He'd become grumpy, easily agitated, going from a man most of his soldiers looked up to and admired, to a figure who barked orders like some kind of authoritarian dictator.

Tucker was self aware enough to realize the changes he'd experienced, and he didn't care. The longer this manhunt dragged on, the more pressure mounted on him. The higher-ups demanded results, and after so many months of coming up empty, he felt more and more like he was on borrowed time.

He kept his eyes glued to the team leader's body cam, watching as the man maneuvered through the apartment building's lobby and up into the stairwell. As ordered, two men were stationed near the elevators with one more at each of the two main exits. Based on multiple layouts of the building, Tucker was confident they'd secured every possible way out.

Every way except one.

Tucker's team entered the floor where Harper's friend, Will Collins, had an apartment. Tucker knew of Collins, but only by reputation. He couldn't find much on him now, which in Tucker's mind meant the guy was up to something illegal. If he had to guess, he'd say running guns to militants, rebels, or even ambitious drug lords. Nazare was a strange location for something like that, though, and he wondered what the logistics nightmare must look like from the small fishing village.

Those distracting thoughts had taken very little of Tucker's focus during the recon effort. One of his former operators, Bo Taylor, had given Tucker everything he needed to put his team in place. Dak Harper would fall right into their net, and the colonel envisioned accolades from his peers. They would honor his perseverance and innovation in getting the job done.

But he hadn't gotten the job done.

Colonel Tucker watched with dismay as his team entered the corridor, then breached the door into Will Collins' apartment. Tucker's men swept the entire place, searched every room. They ripped blankets off beds, cushions from the sofa and chairs, scoured the kitchen, and even checked the cabinets despite the fact that neither Harper nor Collins were small enough to fit inside.

The apartment was empty, and Tucker felt a sudden wave of anxiety flood his body. His chest tightened and his breath shortened. He shifted his view to the other screens, monitoring the exits where his men stood guard. They hadn't moved, hadn't even twitched since taking up their stations.

Where was Dak Harper?

The answer to his unspoken question came to him within seconds. "Check the roof," Tucker ordered into the comms link. "Swanson, get to the roof. If you get eyes on the target, take him down."

A sharp "Yes, sir" barked through the earpiece.

Tucker's placement of Swanson in a vacant, top level apartment in the building next door provided the team with a sniper in case Harper managed to escape to the street. While Swanson was equipped with a military-grade rifle, it wasn't the usual sniper version he preferred. Still, it would be more than enough to take down the rogue operator and his friend.

While Swanson hurried up the stairs to the roof, the team left the apartment and rushed back to the stairwell, leaving one man standing guard in case Harper and his accomplice thought they could hide out in one of the other apartments until it was safe to leave.

As the men ascended the stairs, Tucker's eyes remained fixed on Swanson's screen. His body cam bounced and shook as he ascended the stairs. The screen brightened momentarily when Swanson opened the door. When the lens adjusted, a foot shot out of nowhere just as the gunman was lining up the shot to take out Collins, who'd landed on the rooftop and rolled to a stop about twenty feet away.

The blow from the boot knocked the rifle loose in Swanson's hand. Then a familiar face appeared on the screen.

Tucker watched in rapt horror as Dak Harper disarmed the soldier, disposed of the weapon's ammunition, and knocked Swanson back into the stairwell. When Swanson recovered, he couldn't open the door again, no matter how many times Tucker urged him to get back out there and stop them.

Try as he might, Swanson couldn't get the door to open. He pushed and barged against it with his shoulder, but it didn't budge.

Tucker slammed his fist against a nearby counter, causing the rest of the operators in the room to jump with a start. He let loose a sting of obscenities born of monumental frustration.

"Someone stop Dak Harper!" he shouted.

The team in Collins' building emerged into the daylight and fanned out to cover the entire rooftop. There was, of course, no sign of Harper or his friend.

"Cooper? MacFarland? Tell me you have eyes on the target," Tucker sneered, forcing himself to keep at least a sliver of calm.

"Negative," the two men echoed. "No sign of either target."

"They're on the roof next door. Get someone over there and let Swanson out of the access stairwell."

"Sir?"

"What, Cooper? What's the problem?"

"That's a dangerous jump, sir. And there's no sign of either target on the other roof."

Tucker's mind raced. Where could they be? Had they jumped? No, Harper wouldn't do that.

He spoke to a man in an SUV. "Mills, do you have any visual of the targets?"

"No, sir. They didn't come out this way, and I have eyes on the next building. They didn't come out of there, either."

Of course they didn't. They vanished into thin air like ghosts in a breeze. "Circle around the block and make sure they didn't get out another way. I know we had all exits covered. Do it anyway."

"Yes, sir."

Tucker watched the feed from the camera in the SUV as the driver sped around the block. He already knew what was coming. There would be no sign of Harper. He'd managed to slip through their fingers.

Another thought needled at his brain, though, and he couldn't shake it. Why, if Harper was the man Bo Taylor claimed him to be—a reckless, self-serving killer who was happy to betray his own men—didn't he kill Swanson on the rooftop? Harper was armed, and he'd disarmed the sniper easily. He could have shot Swanson in the face, used the man's own weapons against him, but the techniques Harper used were all non lethal.

Perhaps Tucker was looking into it too much, overthinking things.

One fact remained, he needed to catch Dak Harper, and somehow, the man had wriggled out of his net.

TWELVE
LEIRIA, PORTUGAL

Dak and Will climbed out of the gray sedan and onto the street in front of a row of steps leading up to a church. The paint on the white, stone building had faded in places, and displayed dark, mottled spots in others where the weather had tarnished the walls, both those wrapping around the church property, as well as the building itself. Some sections of the cracked retaining walls looked as if they might crumble away. The steps climbed ten feet, then made a sharp left, leading to the entrance of the old building perched atop a slight rise.

Will tipped the driver through the window and thanked him in perfect Portuguese before the man drove away, speeding down the antiquated street in search of his next fare.

It was the second such ride Dak and Will had taken. The first landed them in Marinha Grande, just to the north of Nazare.

After running from the apartment building, the two men considered disappearing in the park, or perhaps blending in with the locals. Dak struck down the plan the second it passed through his own lips. The colonel's men would be thorough. They would scout the town until they found what they were looking for.

Instead, Dak and Will took a cab north, figuring Colonel Tucker would be watching the way to Lisbon—the largest city, and the one with the most travel options. Lisbon would make sense as a getaway route.

Dak doubted the man would look to the north, toward the smaller towns and villages.

Once they reached Marinha Grande, they had paid the driver and immediately secured another ride, this one taking them to the town of Leiria, a short ride east.

The Castelo de Leiria stood high on a hill overlooking the town of winding streets and pedestrian walkways. Its terracotta-tiled roof contrasted with the gray stone walls. Square-shaped parapets towered over the main portions of the fortress. The nearly 900-year-old building had been renovated and restored multiple times during the centuries, most recently after the 1969 earthquake.

Dak admired the view as the afternoon sun shone brightly on the gray walls. He longed to visit it. A lover of history, both obscure and mainstream, Dak had always wanted to travel the world, visit historical locations such as this one and thousands of others. That dream was another rift between him and Nicole. She always looked to the future, to technology, innovation, the next generation of everything. Dak gazed into the past, studying and learning all he could. Whether it was to admire millennia-old architecture, the history of war, or the evolution of art throughout humanity, he indulged in all of it. Their worlds were too different.

That microcosm of their relationship only flashed for a second in his memory, and then it was gone.

"Where are we going?" Dak asked, jerking his eyes away from the castle.

"You said we need to get to Istanbul."

"I said I need to get to Istanbul. You need to get somewhere safe and lie low."

Will peered at him with derision. "Seriously? You think I'm just going to put you on a train or a plane or whatever to Istanbul and hide out here while you go get yourself killed?"

"I haven't died yet." Dak's matter-of-fact tone was cool, even, and hinted at no fear of death.

"Fine. You haven't died. Yet. But in case you haven't notice, you brought this little war of yours to my doorstep, too. I'm in, whether you like it or not. And whether I like it or not."

A white compact car drove by that looked like something Dak had seen at the circus when he was a kid. He couldn't believe two adults could even fit in the thing, though he'd seen at least eight clowns get out of the one at the circus.

Church bells rang from a bell tower in the distance, signaling the change of the hour. He felt his stomach grumble, and the beer he'd consumed at the apartment had done little for his parched throat.

Dak sighed. "Fine. What's the plan? The colonel will have people stationed at the airport in Lisbon. If I had to guess, he'll have security cameras tapped at the smaller ones, too."

"I have a friend in Madrid," Will said. "Well, technically, he's been in Ecuador for a while, but recently he returned to his family estate."

"Estate?" Dak's response was only half-cynical. "I didn't know you kept such lofty company."

"Believe it or not, I don't just hang out with the dregs like you."

Dak snorted. "I don't hang out with dregs."

"I meant you... you know what? Never mind."

"I see what you did. You meant I'm one of the dregs. It came out wrong, though."

Will shook his head and laughed. "You're an idiot." He started walking down the sidewalk toward a restaurant with wooden chairs and tables beneath blue and white umbrellas, all clustered next to the street like so many other places they'd seen throughout Europe.

"Where are we going?" Dak asked hungrily.

"I don't know about you, but I'm starving. And I need another drink. Probably some water, too."

Dak laughed at the joke. "Yeah, same here." He caught up and walked alongside his friend, perhaps one of the few people he trusted in the world at that moment.

"Your connection in Spain," he said, "what's his deal?"

A red five-door hatchback sped by, the tailpipe grumbling loudly. When the noisy car had disappeared around the bend in the street, Will answered. "His name is Diego Villa. He was hiding out in Ecuador for a few years. Still has a place there, I think. Real low key. I guess you could say he's a private intel guy. Sells information to the United States and its allies. Heck, you probably ran at least one mission based on—in part—something he discovered."

"A guy who does that kind of stuff has an estate? And how have I never heard of him?"

Will stopped at the host stand and greeted a young woman with dark brown hair and a bright smile with a pleasant Portuguese hello, then requested a table for two in the back corner of the patio.

She scooped up a couple of menus from the sleeve attached to her podium and led the two to a secluded table in the back, far from the street. She set down the menus and informed them the server would be there shortly.

"You never heard of him," Will finally answered, "because like I said, he keeps a low profile. Lots of people want him dead. Wouldn't be smart to pop up from his hole too often. Lately, though, I hear he's been at the old homestead more frequently. China and Russia have their own issues to deal with right now. Same with some of the other less stable nations in Europe and Asia. As to his estate, it's a family-owned operation. Been there for generations. They have vineyards for wine, and I heard they've dabbled in growing coffee, though I'm not sure if that region is suited for it."

"Doesn't sound like an intel guy."

"He's eccentric."

"Indeed."

"Not as eccentric as his daughter, though. I hear she was trained by some ultra-elite fighter or martial arts expert or something, and that she hunts art stolen by the Nazis in World War Two for a hobby."

Dak's right eyebrow climbed up his forehead. "Sounds like a strange hobby. Or a tall tale."

"I know, right? I've never met her. And I've only met Diego once, several years ago when I was just getting started... you know, after I left the service. Good guy. He'll help us. We just have to get to Madrid. Once we're there, he can get us a flight to Istanbul. Guaranteed."

Dak considered the information. It all sounded fantastical and outlandish, but if Will thought it was the safest play and the one with the best chance of working, he'd go with it. There was no chance they could risk going into Lisbon. Maybe if they went farther north, they could outrun the colonel's reach. Then what?

"We get a bite to eat and then we head to the train station here in Leiria. We'll have to dump our weapons, but Diego can get us more."

"If he's in Madrid, like you say."

"True. I guess you're just going to have to have a little faith."

Dak sighed. He'd been putting faith into a lot of endeavors lately. He picked up the menu and scanned the offerings of food and drink. As he pored over the list, he thought; Might as well put my faith in one more.

THIRTEEN

"Wake up," Bo snapped.

Nicole slowly rolled over until she felt something cold jerk on her wrist. For a minute, she didn't understand what was going on or why she couldn't move her arm. As she blinked away the remains of slumber, her bedroom came into view, as did the handcuff on her wrist.

The abduction. The hostage situation. Whatever it's called. The thought could have caused panic in most people, especially a woman in this situation. The blond man standing over her had not been abusive, other than to drug her at least once, then cuff her to the bed. She still wore the same clothes as the day before, but there were no signs of the aftereffects of being drugged the previous night.

She remembered him making threats, a conversation with someone, then the name he'd said with disdain—Dak.

He'd mentioned a colonel and some men or a team or something along those lines. They were going after Dak and his friend, the man she'd helped him find in Portugal more than a year ago.

She knew struggling against her bonds would produce nothing but pain in her forearm, so she sat up as gracefully as possible, glancing over at the shackles attached to the wooden bedpost. For a second, she wished she'd gone with a modern headboard from IKEA, one with a flat surface and no posts for binding.

A smell filled her nostrils and soaked her brain with the need for caffeine. Bo stood over the bed holding two steaming cups of coffee.

"I hope you don't mind," he said. "I took the liberty of making coffee."

She inched backward, despite having nowhere to go, retreating like a frightened animal.

"It's not poisoned," he said, extending the cup toward her. "You want me to take a sip?"

Nicole hesitated for a moment, then shook her head. She was thirsty and hungry. Her stomach grumbled, as if hearing the thought.

Her captor put on a warm face. At least that's how she interpreted it. The expression looked uncomfortable on him, like a hungry tiger attempting to be sympathetic to its prey.

"You're not the one I'm after," he said. "I am going to kill Dak, but I'll let you live. Probably."

She didn't like the way he added that last part at the end. She didn't believe him, not entirely. Nicole wasn't stupid. Her career in the tech industry lent no knowledge of hostage situations, but she'd seen enough on television, in books, and in the news on occasion to understand that he would keep her alive as long as she was useful. Once that usefulness was gone, she was expendable.

"You want the coffee or not?" Bo pressed, interrupting her thoughts. "I'd hate for you to get a caffeine headache."

"Why do you care?" she hissed, still staring suspiciously at the proffered mug.

"I don't. But if you start getting cranky with me because you're head's pounding, then I'll have to take more drastic measures. And I don't want to do that."

She considered it for another twenty seconds, then reluctantly took the cup.

"There you go," he said cheerfully, then helped himself to a seat in a light blue chair next to a black dresser.

Nicole looked down at the dark brown liquid. She let the aroma fill her senses.

"It's okay," Bo said. "It's not poisoned, though if I was in your position I would wonder the same thing."

What's the difference, she thought. I'll end up dead one way or the other. Poisoning would be bad for a minute or two, then it would be over.

Resigned to her fate, Nicole took a sip from the mug. It tasted just like she usually made it, maybe even a touch better. She swallowed, then greedily took another sip, and a third, slurping the hot liquid through her lips.

"See? Not bad, huh?"

She didn't respond. She was too angry. And her right hand was still cuffed to the bed.

"What's your plan?" she asked between sips. "Obviously, you're going to use me to lure Dak here."

"Obviously." He took a sip of his coffee and grinned devilishly.

"My apartment isn't a big place. No room to maneuver in a fight, unless you're planning to shoot him when he gets here. And if you did that, someone would hear the gunshots." She held back mentioning that Dak's friend Will might come with him for backup. There was no way to know that for sure, but if Dak was smart, that's what would happen.

"You're correct, for certain. Though the suppressor on my pistol would make certain no one on the street heard anything."

She'd forgotten the silencer. "Still a lot of people down there who could give a positive ID on you. You'd have to disappear pretty fast."

"That's also true, which I have covered, but I see where you're going with all of this. I'm not luring Dak here. Right now, if he's still alive and managed to slip through the colonel's ambush, he will probably be on his way out of Portugal, heading here. When he arrives, we will be gone."

Nicole didn't like the sound of that.

"Gone? Where are we going?"

"There's a small town east of here. It's in the mountains. Honestly, it's little more than a sparse village. Out there, no one will be around to interrupt our confrontation."

"So, a showdown at high noon, then?"

"Something like that. I will have the advantage, of course. He will ride in like the knight in shining armor to save his lost love. And he will die."

Several unpleasant thoughts pierced her mind. She wondered how he would do it. Sniper rifle? Explosives?

"You'll shoot him like a coward? Pick him off when he arrives?"

Bo shook his head. "No, nothing like that. I don't need to kill him that way. And honestly, Dak deserves better. He deserves a fighting chance."

"You would fight him straight up?" She sounded dubious.

"Of course. Dak only bested me on rare occasions when we trained together. On his best day, I would give him a thirty percent chance. But he hasn't been training lately. He's probably rusty. I'd say his odds of beating me now are more like one in twenty. If that."

Her eyes flamed and nostrils flared. She'd finished half the cup of coffee, but suddenly didn't feel much like the rest. The smell of something cooking in the kitchen—toast, from what she could tell—didn't appeal to her growling stomach.

"So, when you're done eating and drinking your coffee, we'll head out to the mountains. On the street, if you make a scene or try to get help, I will shoot you. No one will know what happened. With all the noise down there, not a soul will hear the muted sound of my pistol. You will collapse in my arms and I will yell for help, insisting someone has a gun. Chaos will ensue. People will run in a panic. And I will melt into the crowds and make my way to the rendezvous point without you."

He leveled his gaze at her, piercing her armor with his icy blue eyes. She couldn't find a bluff, try as she might.

"I would prefer it not go down that way. That's up to you. Live and watch Dak die at my hands, or die on the sidewalk like a street urchin."

She inhaled sharply through her nose and forced another sip of coffee down her throat. "He won't lose."

FOURTEEN
MADRID

Dak sat uneasily at the bistro table within the confines of the court-yard. Surrounded on three sides by dark sandstone walls, he felt like a trapped feral animal. He did his best to remain calm, but it was a vain effort.

Meanwhile, Will sat a few feet away in another chair, sipping on a red wine provided by their host. The vintage apparently came from the estate's vineyard. The bottle lacked a label, further signaling the homemade nature of the drink.

He appeared to be enjoying himself, leg crossed over one knee, looking around and admiring the scenery.

It was beautiful here. Dak had been struck by the same thought. The rolling hills of forests stretched out away from the vineyards surrounding the Villa estate. By all counts, Dak should have felt a moment of relief sitting there in the shade, inhaling the dry, warm air.

But he couldn't relax, not when he knew Nicole was being held captive by his nemesis. He shuddered to think about her condition, how she was being treated. He hoped his read was correct on Bo, that the man wouldn't stoop to other lows. The possibility was always there, though, and it was that sliver of potential that caused Dak's anxiety to run wild.

He also felt a touch uncomfortable in the confines of the mansion, even though they were seated outside.

Dak had never been around much money. He'd saved up what he could and stashed it away to keep safe in case of... emergencies. He'd used some of that during his mission of vengeance, but there was still plenty left if needed, and now that he knew where he was going— where the final act would play out—money was the last of his concerns.

The biggest was how to take down Bo and save Nicole, especially in the confines of her apartment. It wouldn't be that simple. Dak knew as much, but he didn't know Bo's angle, and that needled at him.

"Hello, gentlemen," a new voice said from behind.

Dak and Will started, the latter nearly spilling wine on his lap.

They turned and stood slowly as an older man approached. Dak sized him up within two seconds. The man's thick, black mane looked as if it had been painted with thin strokes of gray. The same was true of the dense mustache over his mouth. The dark eyes witnessed to a life well-lived, full of wisdom, love, joy, but laced with concern. He wasn't short nor tall, but somewhere in-between that gave him a level of comfort as he walked, knowing that he had to look up or down to few.

"Señor Villa," Will said. "Thank you for meeting us on such short notice."

"Of course," the old man replied with a genuine smile. He embraced Will and slapped him on the back. "It's been a long time since we've spoken."

"Yes, sir. It's been a minute."

"Is that what the kids are saying these days? A minute? I recall it's been more like two or three years since you tried to convince my daughter you were worthy of her attention."

Will bit his lower lip, bracing for the onslaught he knew was coming.

"You tried to date his daughter?" Dak asked, temporarily loosed of the bonds that wrapped him in anxiety.

"It wasn't like that," Will tried.

"Oh, so my daughter isn't good enough?" Diego Villa cocked his head an inch to the left and winked at Dak, who was enjoying watching his friend dig himself into a hole.

"He said she was kind of weird," Dak prodded, essentially dousing the fire with jet fuel.

"What?" Will's eyes widened. "I did not say she was weird. And besides, she's with someone else now. Right?"

Diego's face turned to stone as he stared at Will, holding his guest's gaze with an icy grip. "You know what? Come to think of it, she is."

Will sighed. "That's what I thought. And it wasn't a couple of years ago, Señor. It was like seven years ago."

For a second, Diego had let down his guard. Then he feigned offense. "You think to correct me in my own home? The place where I gave you sanctuary?"

Will looked off into the distance at nothing specific, then nodded and dropped his head. "You do this every time. You know that, right? Make me feel guilty?"

Diego's tight scowl flipped back to the friendly grin again. "Sí. I know. And it makes me laugh every time."

Will held back for a breath, then started laughing with the older man.

"Please, my friend. Sit down. Sit down," he repeated, motioning to the chair.

There were no bodyguards, no security detail scoring Diego around his home. Dak knew there were some in hidden places, but the two he'd seen weren't watching the interior of the property. Their eyes were focused outward, scouring the landscape beyond for a potential threat.

"You must be Dak Harper," Diego said, extending a hand.

"Yes, sir." Dak gripped the proffered hand for three seconds, then let go. "Thank you for meeting us. Will says you can help us. I hate to be a bother."

Diego shook his head vigorously. "No bother at all," he said and put up his hands. He sat down next to Will while Dak took his seat. The morning sun climbed into the clear sky to the east, peeking up over the wall.

The Villa family mansion was a formidable home, built like a small castle, its U-shaped design only left the western end open to sprawl out into the vineyards. Still, the way Diego dressed in a pair of linen slacks and a light blue linen shirt, he gave the impression that he preferred to live life simply.

Other than his dangerous lifestyle working intel, Dak thought.

"You're lucky you caught me here when you did. I have some pressing matters and I fear I'll have to return to Ecuador soon."

"This must be a difficult place to leave so often," Dak sympathized.

Diego's eyes wandered across the walls, then drifted out onto the rolling vineyards. "Sí," he admitted. "It is. But not because it's lavish. It's a part of me, my family. Villas have lived here for centuries on this very land. The place in Ecuador is fine for me. It has a roof, good food, warmth. And it allows me to work without drawing too much attention to the rest of my large family."

Dak nodded, understanding. He didn't need to ask why the man continued to work. Diego clearly didn't need the money. The family business appeared to be doing just fine, and any additional money he brought in from doing private intel work would merely add to the pile. It was clear to Dak that Diego did what he did because he believed in it. He believed in freedom and fighting against those who would oppress it.

"So," Diego said, interrupting Dak's thoughts. "You two are looking to get into Istanbul, huh?"

"And fast, sir," Dak said.

"Pressing appointment?"

"You could say that." Dak hoped he didn't have to say more.

"I see." Diego's face turned grave. "I assume you had to leave your weapons in Portugal before you took the train to Madrid?"

"Yes, sir," Will and Dak answered together.

"Will you be needing more when you get to Istanbul or is it a peaceful appointment?"

The two guests looked at each other and then back to their host.

"That looks like a yes," Diego surmised. "I'll have them waiting for you when you land. It's pretty last minute, so I don't know what kind of stock my man in Istanbul has, but it's better than nothing."

Dak felt a twinge of hope flutter in his chest. "Thank you so much, sir. I truly appreciate it."

Diego waved off the praise. "It's nothing. I'm happy to help a couple of good soldiers like you two."

Dak's face must have looked surprised, because Diego noticed.

"What, you didn't think I did a little research on you before you came to visit my abode? I have enemies, you know."

"Hey!" Will said, perhaps feeling a touch hurt at the comment. "You think I would bring someone into your home who intends to do you harm?"

Diego shrugged. "You do have some shady dealings, Will."

Dak laughed. "He's got you there, pal."

Will sighed. "Fine. When do we leave?"

Diego leaned forward and lifted the bottle, tipped it toward an empty glass, and poured until the glass was half-full. He set the bottle back down and raised the drink in a toast. "As soon as you leave here."

FIFTEEN

ISTANBUL

Dak peered out at the busy city street from behind the steering wheel, his eyes searching for signs of trouble.

Istanbul was one of his favorite cities to visit. It had been the crossroads of every major civilization and culture throughout human history, and there was much to appreciate from food, to drinks, to ancient ruins and monuments throughout the city.

He and Will weren't here for sightseeing, though Dak allowed his imagination to wander through his brain, casting visions of dinners and enchanting conversations with Nicole.

There was no sign of the colonel's men. They were probably still scouring the Portuguese countryside or perhaps infiltrating the towns near Nazare. Those endeavors would have proven fruitless, even if the two marks were still in that country. There were a million places to hide in the little villages, hills, and cities. While the two men might stick out compared to the locals, Dak and Will could have stayed on the move indefinitely. With open borders throughout most of Europe, and the knowledge of how to exploit them, they could have driven the colonel around in circles until he lost his mind.

Time, however, wasn't on Dak's side. Bo had Nicole, and he

needed to get to her. He prayed it wasn't too late, but a nagging, painful feeling continued to throb in his gut. He picked up the white and red cup of coffee from the cup holder and sipped it conservatively as he stared through the windshield. He hoped the coffee would shock his senses back to his old battle-hardened self. It did little.

"You see anything?" Will asked in a hushed tone, as if he spoke too loud Bo would hear him.

"No," Dak said. "I don't expect to. Not until we get into the apartment."

"How you want to do it?"

Dak had been considering that since they boarded the plane out of Madrid. Diego's contact picked them up at the airport and provided them with a pair of pistols and a car, along with instructions of what to do with the vehicle when they were done with their visit.

The guns, the man had said, they could keep. There was, of course, a slim chance that would happen. Once Bo was dead, Dak planned on heading back to the United States, and taking a sketchy firearm with him wasn't an option. He detested ditching good weapons, and the Glocks that Diego's man provided were quality guns.

Dak longed to be back in his cabin on Monteagle Mountain, far away from this mess. One more, he thought.

If he could save Nicole, he wondered if the same salvation was possible for their relationship. Oddly, he doubted that more than his ability to take down Bo, despite the advantage the enemy held.

He was thinking too much. It was time to act.

"I'll go in through the stairwell," Dak said finally. "You take the elevator."

"Split up then?"

"He could be watching the building. I know I would be. He'll know when we get there. If he tries to take me out in the stairs, you can get the drop on him from behind, via the elevator."

Will eyed his friend with concern. "But then you'd be dead."

"That doesn't matter," Dak said. "All that matters is Nicole is safe."

"Look, man. I appreciate the sacrifice and selflessness and all that, but you know I'm your friend too. I realize we haven't known each other that long. Still, I can't let you just run into an ambush on some suicidal down-in-a-blaze-of-glory charge."

"I don't want to die," Dak laughed. "But you know how it is. When you sign up, you're taking on that risk. When we joined the military, we assumed that death was part of the deal. We didn't want it to be part of the deal, but if we save someone else, someone who can't defend themselves, then it's our burden to bear."

Will knew Dak was right. They'd both taken the same risk when they signed up. But they weren't in the service anymore, and things were much different out here in the real world. None of that mattered. But Will knew his friend's mind was set.

Perhaps he'd overestimated the value of their friendship. In truth, the two rarely spoke, except when Dak needed Will to find the next target for him. Still, he'd grown to like Dak. Trust him, even. And trust, in Will's world, was a difficult thing to come by.

He shook off the sentiment and inclined his head. "Okay, I'll take the elevator. Just watch your six. Okay?"

"I always do."

The two men exited the vehicle and made their way up the sidewalk, keeping their weapons out of sight—tucked into their pants and covered by lightweight, long-sleeved button-up shirts, Dak's black and Will's white.

The city's nightlife was in full throat. Motorcycles growled by, car horns honked, and people reveled in the sights and smells of drinks, street food, and the promise of more around every corner.

No one seemed to notice the two men as they approached the building. Will and Dak, however, noticed everything. They caught each and every irregular movement and sound, though they never overreacted.

When the two reached the steps leading into Nicole's apartment, a slew of emotions smacked Dak in the chest. He paused for a second, staring at the door. Will waited patiently, his head on a swivel as he checked the street for trouble in both directions.

Dak sighed and raised a finger, then pressed on the number of Nicole's apartment on the call box.

Immediately, the door buzzed, and the lock clicked. A deep frown tightened on his face.

He couldn't recall that happening before.

Will pulled on the door's handle and held it open. He slipped in ahead of Dak and subtly drew his weapon, keeping it low and out of sight of pedestrians on the sidewalk. The empty lobby's silence grew as Dak stepped in and let the door close behind him.

"Okay," Will said. "I'll see you upstairs."

"You remember which apartment number, yeah?"

"Yes, I got it. Thank you for the reminder." Will made no effort to hide his sarcasm.

"Good. I'll see you up there."

SIXTEEN

ISTANBUL

Dak peered through the narrow window of the stairwell door and waited. He kept the pistol in his hand low and by his hip in case someone else came into the building. The last thing he needed was to send a child into hysterics at the sight of a gun in the apartment complex.

The elevator doors closed, and the lift began its ascent, carrying Will to Nicole's floor.

Dak saw nothing through the window except the steps ascending to the left and an empty corner to the right. He turned the latch and jerked the door open, hoping that the sudden, jarring movement would lure out any danger lurking in the shadows.

The only sound that escaped the stairwell was the sound of the door opening as it echoed up through the shaft. Dak entered the room, leading with his pistol. He swept to the right first, checking the minuscule blindspot in the near corner, then shifting to the left and up, making certain the next landing and stairs were clear. The back corner of the ground floor was last.

With no sign of trouble, he cautiously made his way to the steps and began to climb. He moved deliberately, but quickly. He made no sound as he scaled the stairs. When he reached the first landing, he rounded and swept the next section; still no sign of Bo or any mercenaries he might have employed.

Dak felt overcome by the silence and the lack of a threat. He didn't stop, though, despite his concerns. Pressing forward, he continued up the stairs, repeating the process each time he reached another landing. When he finally arrived at the door leading into Nicole's floor, he paused and waited.

Will would already be there.

Diego's man had given them a pair of radios to use for situations just like this, but Dak insisted on staying silent during their invasion of the apartment.

Dak wrapped his fingers around the door latch and waited. Seconds ticked by so dramatically he could almost feel them. He inspected the bolt and receiver, the edge where the door met the frame. There was no sign of an explosive device. He'd considered Bo might booby trap one of the entry points, but that would be foolish—a random stranger living in the building could have been blown to bits. There was no way to control who came and went, and in which direction they chose to go.

He shook off the consideration, realizing he'd already been over that before.

Dak pulled the latch down and pulled the door back. He checked left first, using the door as a shield against any threat that might be to the right.

Will stood in an alcove next to the elevator, weapon in hand and held high near his face. Will gave a nod, indicating the corridor was clear.

On the signal, Dak rushed out of the stairwell and down the hall, stopping in the opposite corner of the alcove where Will was concealed. He only waited a moment before advancing again, this time creeping hurriedly toward Nicole's door.

At the entrance, he stopped. He'd planned everything up to this point, but wasn't sure now what he should do. Should he knock?

Then Bo would know he was there. He already knows, Dak thought. You rang the buzzer downstairs, idiot.

He decided to be more direct. Reaching down, Dak grasped the doorknob and twisted.

The knob turned without resistance. Unlocked.

Dak glanced back at Will and motioned for him to make his move. Will did as instructed and hurried over to the apartment doorway. He waited there, lowering his weapon in case another tenant appeared unexpectedly. Will's job was to cover the exit. If something bad happened, he was the backup.

Dak eased the door open, praying silently the hinges were well-oiled. For some reason, that mattered. He didn't know why. Again, he reminded himself that Bo knew he was there, knew he was coming in.

Upon entering the little foyer, Dak's eyes shot toward the far end of the room where a door led onto the balcony. It was closed, but he could see through the open curtains that no one was out there. He expected to see Nicole in the living room, tied to a chair or something with a gag in her mouth and Bo standing behind her, holding a gun to her head. As he moved into the space where the kitchen and dining area merged, he searched the apartment, but found no sign of either his enemy or Nicole.

"You okay?" Will whispered into the radio. Dak didn't respond.

Something was off.

He continued deeper into the apartment, checking the office, bedroom, and bathroom, before returning to the living room. It was empty.

"No one's here," Dak said into the radio. He kept his weapon ready, but relaxed slightly.

"What do you mean, no one's here?"

"Get in here and see for yourself."

Dak noticed something on the coffee table. A piece of paper sat in the center with a hand-written message splayed across it.

He moved closer and picked up the note as Will burst into the room, his weapon drawn and sweeping the apartment.

Upon realizing Dak was right, he lowered his pistol and eased the door shut. "Where are they? I thought they said to come here."

"They did," Dak answered. Then he held up the note.

"Looks like Bo wants to do this the old-fashioned way."

SEVENTEEN

ULUPELIT, TURKEY

"Are you sure about this?" Will asked.

Dak shook his head. "No, but what choice do I have? He said come alone. He'll know if I don't."

Will looked out across the rolling hills of Ulupelit, pondering what he should do.

Dak also stared at the landscape. It reminded him of the foothills back home in Tennessee, where his cabin awaited him. He wished more than anything he could take Nicole back there with him, but he'd resigned himself to that being nothing but fantasy. Even if he were able to rescue her, she would never return to Tennessee with him. Her life was here, in Turkey, in the sprawling city of Istanbul.

He didn't blame her. The appeal was undeniable with so much to do, so many cultures mingling in one place. He wondered if he could stay there with her, but that would be denying who he really was. None of that mattered at the moment. He still had the issue of taking out Bo to worry about. "Don't put the cart before the horse," his grandpa always said, using the same cliché the old man must have used a hundred times in his life, and that he likely heard twice as often.

Dak still had the note in his back pocket. It had instructed them to come to this obscure, tiny village, to an old farmhouse at what seemed like a random address. According to the GPS, the address was just up the road—the next driveway on the right.

Will had done as much recon work as he could before they arrived. He looked up satellite images of the farmhouse and barn on his phone to get an idea of what they were heading into.

The house looked abandoned, and the barn actually appeared to be in better condition. Will wondered why, out loud, why Dak's ex-teammate wanted to rendezvous there, when there were plenty of other locations in this part of the country.

The village spread out through the hills. Red terracotta roofs interrupted the forests, along with a few church steeples poking up above the canopy.

It wasn't just the location that concerned Will, nor the fact that Dak had been instructed to come alone. The other part worried him more than anything.

"I don't like the idea of you going in unarmed," Will growled. "You're going to walk in and he will shoot you. Game over, man. You can't trust him."

"I know that," Dak said. "I also know that I don't have a choice. The note was clear. If I show up with someone else or with a weapon, Nicky dies."

"You think playing by his rules is going to change that?" Will considered adding "if she's still alive," but that wouldn't help and it would only anger Dak. For the time being, all he had to go on was hope, and Will knew he couldn't strip that from his friend, even if it meant Dak was walking head first into a firing squad.

"The note said he wants to face me," Dak explained. "Bo may be a lot of things, but he's a warrior. I think he wants to settle this like men."

Will shook his head. "So, what? You're going to duke it out, beat the crap out of each other until one is dead?"

"I don't know what his plan is," Dak admitted. "But I know he has one."

He looked off to the right at a clear, still lake. The water snaked its way through the densely forested hills until it disappeared around a mountain in the distance.

"My parents think I'm a traitor. They think I betrayed my brothers in Iraq. I never got the chance to tell them the truth." He left the words hanging.

"I'll find them and tell them. I mean, if you don't make it out of this alive." Will tried to sound optimistic, but his tone betrayed what he really felt.

"It's okay," Dak said. "Even if Bo is telling the truth, and wants to face me man-to-man, I still only have like a one in three chance of beating him."

"You trying to make me feel better?"

Dak shrugged. "You got to go sometime, right? Everyone dies sooner or later. Better to go down swinging."

Will nodded and sighed. "Yeah. That's what we tell ourselves."

"Come on," Dak said. "Drive another five hundred feet and I'll get out. Remember, don't interfere. I can't risk anything happening to Nicole."

"I know. I know."

Will wanted to tell him that she was probably already dead, and if she wasn't, she would be after Bo executed him. He didn't for a second believe that the villain would keep his word, that he would face Dak like he said in the note.

He did as Dak requested and drove a little farther down the road before stopping when more of the farmhouse driveway came into view.

"Good luck," Will said, unwilling to meet his friend's gaze.

"Hey, it's going to be okay." Dak slapped him on the shoulder and stepped out of the car. His boots crunched the dry dirt and gravel underfoot.

"Hey, Dak," Will said.

Dak was about to close the door. He held the top edge and waited. "Yeah?"

"Kick his butt."

EIGHTEEN

ULUPELIT

Dak walked on the gravel verge next to the ancient asphalt road. He kept his eyes forward as he lumbered toward the driveway. The farmhouse came into view on the right, forty feet away, tucked back into the corner of the property. The dark brown barn on the left stood next to a rolling field. Tall grass wavered in the breeze in the unkept pasture. It looked like it hadn't been maintained in years. A weathered wooden fence wrapped around it with rotted wooden pieces dangling precipitously from posts in multiple places.

Birds squawked and chirped in the trees, but he couldn't see the animals. Their songs mingled with the wisp of a warm breeze that brushed against his hair and ears, tickling the back of his neck.

Dak kept his breathing at a steady cadence as he ambled up the driveway and toward the farmhouse. The gentle slope leveled off and Dak noticed a sedan parked behind the farmhouse.

He kept walking toward the derelict home. Some of the windows were cracked, or shattered entirely. Several shutters hung crookedly. The faded paint peeled and cracked like a dried skin around the building. It was evident no one had lived there for some time, or if they did, the tenants didn't care much for its upkeep.

"That's far enough," a sickeningly familiar voice shouted across the gravel parking area.

At least he didn't shoot me without saying a word, Dak thought. Part of him wished Bo had just shot him. No bull. No banter. Now, Dak had to listen to his monologue.

He turned his head toward the barn, where the sound of Bo's voice had come from, to see a second-floor window-door swing open with a loud creak. Bo stood just inside the opening. Another figure sat close by in an old wooden chair. There was no mistaking who struggled against the bonds wrapped around her arms and torso.

Nicole stared back at Dak with pleading, apologetic eyes.

He felt a familiar, sickening feel drop into his gut like a bomb. His heart pounded, as if attempting to leap out of his chest with every heartbeat.

Dak sighed, averting his gaze to the pistol in Bo's right hand, hanging next to his hip.

"So, you get to have a gun but I don't?"

Bo looked down at the weapon, raising it above his waist. His eyes roamed over it momentarily, as if he hadn't seen the pistol before. "Oh, you're right. I'm sorry, Dak. I forgot I had this. Silly me."

Dak glowered at the man, but said nothing. In his flashing moments of fantasy, he envisioned leaping up to the second story and snapping Bo's neck.

"Down on your knees, Dak," Bo commanded. Even at this range, Dak knew his ex-teammate would be lethal with the pistol.

"That's it?" Dak protested. "I thought you were going to face me in a fair fight."

"Oh, yes. I am. Terribly sorry," Bo hissed. "But before we do that, I have to come down this ladder back here." He motioned to a rickety wooden ladder that led down to the barn's main floor. "See?"

Dak rolled his eyes. "I don't like the idea of getting on my knees for anyone, Bo."

"Fine. Turn around."

Dak huffed at the continuing awkward moment. "So you can shoot me in the back? What's the difference?"

"I've already told you," Bo exclaimed. "If I were going to lure you here to shoot you, I'd have already done it. I want to kill you with my own hands, Dak. The old-fashioned way, hand-to-hand combat. Sure, you could get lucky and beat me. But there's something pure, and at the same time barbaric, about two men fighting to the death. I haven't had the pleasure in so long."

The words sickened Dak. Perhaps he'd underestimated the level of evil that possessed Bo. Maybe he was just trying to be intimidating. That came next.

Bo turned the pistol to Nicole and pushed the muzzle into the side of her skull. "Look, Dak. You're going to die one way or the other. She doesn't have to. So, please, pretty please, turn around and stop being an idiot."

Dak stared into her frightened eyes. No tears formed, but she looked tired, more than he'd ever seen before. And he'd worn her out emotionally on several occasions—usually when being stubborn.

"Fine," Dak surrendered. He turned around slowly with his hands in the air. Three thumps of boots on wood, followed by a slightly different thud, reached Dak's ears. He looked over his shoulder to see Bo was already on the ground and walking toward him, pistol leveled.

"You can turn around now, Dak."

Dak pivoted around until he faced his old teammate. He lowered his hands to his sides, knowing Bo had already checked for firearms, simply by analyzing Dak's form. Had he been concealing a weapon, Bo would know it, and Dak would probably already be dead.

"I don't blame you," Bo said as he slowed to a halt a mere ten feet away from Dak.

"For what?" Dak sneered.

"Wanting revenge. I mean, if I were standing there in your shoes, I'd want the same thing. Me and the guys, we probably deserve the vengeance you're looking to mete out."

"You killed Billy."

Bo nodded. "Yeah, that's true. But don't get sentimental on me." He extended the pistol in a feigned threat. "I didn't do that one for you. I did it for me."

"You didn't think I could take him out."

"Affirmative. As I said before, Billy's fortifications were considerable. He had a tight net around that entire property. The only way in was a Trojan horse—one who's son had just been murdered."

"I suppose I should thank you," Dak quipped.

"Not necessary. All a means to an end. You're the last loose string, Dak. The last piece I need to tie off so I can rest easy, stop looking over my shoulder."

Dak smiled, an odd gesture at that moment.

"What's so funny?" Bo demanded, curiously.

"Just the thought of you unable to sleep each night. Waking up with every bump in the night. Walking down the street, glancing behind you every time you think someone is on your tail. Those are the thoughts that make it all worthwhile, Bo."

Bo let out a humph. "Yes, well. When this is over, I won't have to worry about that."

He pulled the release button on the side of the pistol, and the magazine slid out of the grip. Bo meticulously ejected each round out of the mag until it was empty, then pulled the slide on the weapon which sent the last live round tumbling onto the ground.

Dak never liked seeing people do that. It made him nervous that a round would go off. Even though he knew it was unlikely, stranger things had happened. Relief took over as the last shell came to a rest amid the gravel.

Bo tossed the pistol aside and reached to his hips. Dak had already noticed the pair of hunting knives, each black handle concealed in gray sheaths. Bo's fingers unclipped the blades from the hand guards, flipping them open with ease. He unsheathed the weapons from their slumber and flipped them over in his hands. He caught one in his right hand by the grip and the other by the tip. It was a careless, showy move that could have cut his fingers open. Unfortunately, Bo caught it with graceful ease. He laid the knife down on the ground and took a step away from Dak.

"Shall we?" Bo asked.

Dak spied the knife with caution, wondering if the second he made for the blade, Bo might cut him down. He leaned over at the hips and reached for the weapon, keeping a watchful eye on Bo.

His enemy never flinched, never made so much as a twitch in the wrong direction. He stood like a possessed statue, his gaze locked on Dak like a hungry lion.

Dak's fingers brushed against the handle, then quickly snatched up the blade. He held the curved weapon with a comfortable ease. The hunting knife was much like his favorite one back in Tennessee, one he'd practiced with often.

"I didn't want things to go down the way they did in Iraq, for what it's worth." Bo's confession did nothing to ease Dak's mind. "But you left me no choice. You should have taken your share of the treasure with us."

"Then who would've done your dirty work, taking out the others while you sat back and played?"

Bo chuckled and wagged his knife. "You make a good point. Eh, maybe you're right. This probably worked out perfectly for me."

Dak was done talking. The time had come to end this.

Last one, Dak thought. Then he twisted his body into a fighting position and surged forward.

NINETEEN
ULUPELIT

Dak fought two enemies. The first he had to overcome was the rage burning inside him. Not only had Bo left him for dead and kidnapped the woman he loved, he had used Dak to do his dirty work.

He lashed out before he got control of his emotions. The blade swiped recklessly through the air in front of Bo as he easily stepped back to avoid the strike. He countered with a slash of his own, drawing first blood with his initial attack. The blade slipped across Dak's forearm, opening a four-inch slit just above the wrist.

Dak snapped back, retreating at the sudden sting that screamed from the wound.

"That was stupid," Bo snarled. "Have you really gotten that rusty?"

Dak grimaced. When the pain numbed a little, he stepped to the left. Bo mirrored his movement, and the two circled as if in a deadly dance, each studying their opponent for a weakness.

"Maybe I have gotten rusty," Dak said. "But the rest of your crew might beg to differ if they were still alive."

Bo huffed. "None of them were ever as good as me, not at this.

They all had their strong points, but you and I were the most well-rounded. Fitting, I think, that the two of us are the last ones standing."

Bo took a quick step toward Dak, feigning a stab to the gut. Dak recognized the fake. Instead of buckling backward, as instinct would dictate, he spun away from the strike before Bo could offer a secondary punch to the face with his free hand. As he twisted, Dak used his backhand to rip the tip of his blade over Bo's shoulder and down his tricep.

He could have gone for the killing blow a second later had Bo not reeled away at the last possible moment.

Bo growled like an angry dog. He grasped at the wound that oozed blood through his Rush T-shirt.

"This was my favorite shirt," he grumbled, glowering incredulously at Dak.

"Appropriate since you wore it to your funeral."

Bo's expression tightened into a smug grin. "Don't get cocky, now, Dak. We both know this is a fight you can't win."

"Your torn shirt and cut arm beg to differ."

Bo clenched his jaw and lunged again. He swiped and slashed in a flurry of movement. Dak jumped back from the first attack, then dipped away from the second to avoid getting a gash across the neck.

As Bo's fury wore on, the attacks grew less vigorous. Dak ducked away from another stab, but this time Bo anticipated the move and kicked Dak in the gut.

The blow knocked the wind out of Dak, and he cursed himself for not seeing it coming. His plan had been to let Bo wear himself down, then counter with a quick attack of his own and finish the fight.

Instead, it appeared Bo had been ready for that plan, and now he didn't seem fatigued at all, aside from the shallow panting for air.

Dak wished he could get even a minuscule amount of air in his lungs, but his chest remained locked as his enemy stalked toward him.

"You get too caught up in what's right in front of you, Dak," Bo preached.

Dak scooted backward along the gravel, still clutching the knife as he retreated.

"When you narrow your focus, you forget the big picture, the grand scheme of things." Bo extended his hands out above his shoulders. "Just like with how you found yourself in this predicament." He pointed the knife at Dak, letting it bob as if chastising a child with a ruler.

The air abruptly returned to Dak's lungs and he sucked it in with huge gasps. Relief flooded him and he glared at Bo again while clawing himself back to his feet.

"I don't think you should be telling anyone how to live their lives, Bo. You're a murderer and a liar. I'm not sure which is worse."

Bo pouted his lips as if he didn't care that his opponent was correct. "Yes, well, that may be true, Dak. But don't act like your hands are so squeaky clean. You've killed. I'm not just talking about Iraq either. You killed men you served with, men you knew. You're no better than me."

"I didn't say I was better," Dak responded. "I know I have sins on my ledger, ones that I'll live with for the rest of my life. But your boys got what they deserved. Just like you will."

Bo snorted a derisive laugh. "Perhaps, but not today. And not from you."

He launched an unexpected strike, stepping quickly toward Dak and then leaping. Dak didn't anticipate the attack, but he reacted in time to dive onto the gravel again. Instead of trying to get away, he rolled directly at his enemy, who flew by before he knew what had happened.

Dak and Bo stopped suddenly, but Dak recovered faster and from a crouching position drew the blade's sharp edge across the achilles tendon of Bo's right leg. The knife sunk deep as it carved through skin and tissue, easily slicing the tendon in two.

Dak heard an audible pop followed by a scream of pain.

Bo fell onto his side, grasping at the wounded heel. A look of anguish stretched his face, replacing all of the bravado he'd worn just seconds before. Amid a flood of profanities, mostly directed at Dak, the air around the two men grew heavy, as if the reaper himself had descended into the hills to collect another soul.

Upon sensing the change in the air, Dak glanced around and realized it was just a cloud overhead, giving them shade, though he could have sworn something else loomed in the ether around him.

It didn't matter.

He would finish this fight.

Dak trudged toward Bo, who kicked his good leg out to push himself away. He repeated the process, looking like a wounded animal.

"What were you saying about not getting cocky?" Dak asked.

"You got lucky," Bo said. "But it's not over yet."

He scrambled to his feet... or foot, and leaned on it with all his weight. Bo grimaced in agony, but he would not surrender, not even when he had to fight on one leg.

"Maybe I got lucky," Dak admitted. "Or maybe you never had control of your emotions. You let them get in your way and make rash decisions, just like in Iraq."

Bo's eyes gleamed hungrily. He still believed he would win, that he would kill Dak. He couldn't believe he'd been so foolish, so careless.

Dak stopped five feet from his ex-teammate. Bo flashed his teeth. Ever the predator, he had no intention of going down easily.

"Come get it, Dak."

He flicked his fingers, beckoning Dak forward.

Dak knew better. He'd already calculated the five potential moves Bo had in his now limited arsenal.

Seconds ticked by as Dak decided what to do. Leaves fluttered through the air around them as a breeze swelled to a gust. Dak knew Nicole was watching from the barn's second floor, but he didn't dare look at her. He focused only on Bo and the attack.

Bo licked his top lip to relieve it from the dry air, but Dak only took it as a disgusting gesture from a back-stabber.

Dak lunged abruptly, the knife in his right hand diving toward Bo's upper chest. Bo reacted, but a fraction too soon. He overcommitted, turning his body to avoid the strike and counter with his own backhanded stab. Dak's motion changed in an instant. As his body twisted, he tossed the blade from his right hand to his left. When his fingers and palm made contact, he squeezed and jerked the knife toward himself.

Bo's exposed neck stood in the way, and the man only realized what was about to happen a fraction of a second before the tip pierced his skin.

Dak felt the blade resist for a second as it plunged into his enemy's throat. He pulled through that resistance effortlessly, driving the long hunting knife into Bo's neck and up into the bottom of his skull.

Bo's eyes blinked once and then remained open, staring lifelessly into the sky over the farmhouse. His body went limp and fell to the ground. Dak let go of the knife handle and let it drop to the ground with his victim. Bo's body lay on the ground, his head on a gravel pillow.

Dak's breathing slowed again. The scene around him returned to the peaceful tranquility from before. The birds' songs resumed, and it was only then Dak realized that nature itself seemed to have watched the duel between the two men.

He tore his gaze away from the dead man at his feet and looked up to the second story barn window. His eyes met Nicole's. An ocean of emotions rushed over as he hurried over to the ladder. He climbed it in seconds, then untied the old rope binding her to the chair.

When he removed the gag from her mouth, she stood and immediately wrapped her arms around him. He hugged her back, squeezing her tighter than he ever had before.

"I'm so sorry," he said. Tears streamed down his cheeks and soaked into the back of her shirt.

"I know," Nicole replied. "I am too."

He pulled away and locked eyes with her again. "You don't have anything to be sorry about."

"I could have done better. You know, with us."

Dak shook his head. "Maybe we both could have."

Then he sighed, as if bearing a two-ton weight on his thoughts. Gripping her shoulders, he never took his eyes from hers. "I have to go. We'll get you back to Istanbul. You should be safe now. But this isn't over for me."

She puzzled at the statement. "But you just—" she faltered at the thought of what happened, how she'd seen the man she loved brutally kill another.

Dak's head shook again. "I know he's the last one of my team, but there's another threat."

He held up his phone and pressed a finger to the screen to stop the audio recording. "This will clear my name with the military. But when this goes to the higher-ups, there will be questions. Colonel Tucker will not take it well. My guess is, they'll give him some kind of an honorable discharge, but if I know Tucker, that won't stop him."

"What are you saying, Dak?" She searched his eyes for a truth that would somehow put them together again, a new life where they could live happily ever after. That fairytale ending was nowhere to be found in his jade gaze.

"It's not safe to be with me, Nicky. It never will be. Maybe I'm wrong, but the colonel doesn't strike me as the kind of guy to take losing gracefully."

"But you said you have the recording of Bo's confession. Whoever this Colonel Tucker guy is, surely he'll take that as proof you were innocent. He'll be glad. Won't he?"

"That's not how it will go down, Nicky. I've seen it before. The military is all Tucker has. Once that's gone, he will either end up at the bottom of a bottle, or he'll try to figure out a way to make me pay for the destruction of his career."

"So," she choked back a sob, "you're going to leave me again?"

He nodded. The gesture was subtle, almost unnoticeable. He didn't want to. He wanted to return to Istanbul with her and start a new life, but that couldn't happen. Not yet. Maybe Tucker would bow out and disappear. Dak doubted it. He'd already seen the lengths the colonel would go to on a few occasions.

Now, he wouldn't be shackled by the rules of the United States military, not that he was playing by those rules anyway.

"Where will you go?" Nicole asked, realizing there was no changing the course of their tattered relationship.

"I honestly don't know," he said. "I'll hop around some. I've always wanted to see the world, study some history in the places where it actually happened. Who knows?"

He could see she had a question still waiting in reserve, and he wondered why she held back.

Finally, she set it free. "Will you... kill the colonel?"

Her eyes wandered to the body on the ground below and Dak followed her gaze. "If I have to," he said. "I don't want to, though. I hope I'm wrong about Tucker, that he'll take his retirement to his grave and be happy with the life he's lived. I can't plan on that, though."

"When, then? When will you know if it's safe? I want to be with you, Dak. When can that happen?"

The pleading in her eyes as they met his again nearly broke him.

"Someday," he said. "I promise."

TWENTY

SEQUATCHIE COUNTY, TENNESSEE

Dak sat perfectly still. Warm breath escaped his nostrils, billowing into the cool, late fall air. He watched the forest below—unmoving, ever-patient, like a statue.

From his tree stand, he had a clear 180-degree view of the woods without having to turn his head.

While he focused on detecting even the slightest movement, his mind wandered to a city far from Tennessee. On the other side of the world, Nicole would be having a late lunch, or perhaps she'd already returned to her job. He wondered what she ate during her break. He smiled, knowing there was probably some baklava to finish off the lunch menu. She loved that stuff, especially with a little afternoon espresso or just black coffee.

He enjoyed it too, but it always tasted better when he ate it with her. It was as if her intoxicating smile sweetened everything.

Not everything, his brain reminded.

That was true. Dak and Nicole had gone through their rough spots, but they'd always worked it out, until they didn't.

His heart ached at the thought. After years apart, they'd finally reconciled, and she'd even told him she wanted to be with him.

Dak believed, or thought he believed, that Nicole didn't want to have anything to do with him. She'd put on a good show to that effect, but it turned out she loved him after all.

He couldn't risk being with her, and he knew it. He'd meant what he said when he surmised the colonel would never stop hunting him, even after his career tanked. And it did.

Dak sent the recorded message to an officer he trusted, one that wasn't under the command of Colonel Tucker. His friend delivered the audio higher up the food chain. When it was verified, the cover up began immediately.

Dak found out that Tucker had received—as predicted—an honorable exit from the military. He was even given accolades for his service, all to cover up the man's ineptitude in bringing in a rogue soldier who ended up being an innocent victim.

Tucker was, no doubt, furious. Innocent or not, Dak was the reason his career came to a grinding crash. Tucker enjoyed the control, the perception of power that accompanied his position. It was no secret the man had eyes on becoming a general someday, and likely was on track for the promotion.

Now, he was finished.

In his quest for revenge, Dak had opened another can. He pondered a quote from the Bible his mother read to him when he was a child. "Vengeance is mine, says the Lord," she'd say. When he asked about it, his mother explained that when humans seek revenge, it engulfs them. It takes away everything else from life and replaces it with an unquenchable thirst for revenge. Such negative energy, she said, could eventually drive a person crazy. Not only that, when revenge was taken, it opened an unending chain.

Dak realized that had come true. By eliminating Bo and clearing his own name, he'd brought about a new danger from someone who perceived their own injustice. Tucker would stop at nothing to find Dak.

He noticed a subtle movement about fifty yards away. The rustle of leaves confirmed something or someone had ventured into Dak's forest.

"You hear that?" Will hissed. "I think I see it."

Dak rolled his eyes and twisted his head to the right. "Can you shut up? You're going to scare the deer away."

He looked through the scope on his rifle, raising it gradually until he locked on to the animal. The buck's antlers had grown since he'd last seen the creature. Dak smiled, admiring the animal's beauty. It's dark, black eyes stared blankly into the woods to Dak's left. Its light brown and white underside looked perfectly groomed, as if the deer had been brushed down earlier that morning. The buck twitched its fluffy tail, and then went back to nosing around the ground, searching for a snack.

"You gonna take the shot or what?" Will asked.

Again, Dak suppressed the irritation swelling inside him.

With his Nazaré apartment compromised, there was no way Will could return there. He and Dak both knew that Tucker would have gone through everything, ransacking the place for information. Even after Tucker lost his role with the military, Will assumed that the man would have someone permanently stationed there just in case he slipped up and decided to swing by the old residence.

Will wasn't stupid.

While he did have some valuables in the apartment, mostly computers and gadgets, those could be replaced. His fake passports and the bulk of his underground operations took place in another location; in an old knitting mill on the outskirts of town. There was nothing in the apartment to link the two places, so Tucker and whatever mercenary thugs he sent in there would find nothing useful.

Will also performed a remote scrub, erasing anything on his computers' hard drives that Tucker might find useful.

"I don't kill for sport," Dak said. "Only when I need to."

Will twisted his head to the left and eyed Dak with surprise.

Dak lowered the rifle and turned to face his friend.

Will shivered in the early morning chill. "Why do you have the gun, then?"

"Practice," Dak shrugged. "Always pays to stay sharp."

A snort escaped Will's nose and he shook his head. "Yeah, I guess so." He remained silent for a minute as the two men watched the buck meander closer to the tree stand. "They really are beautiful animals."

"That they are. Innocent. Pure. Unlike us."

"We do what we have to do to survive."

"True. Speaking of, what do you think you're going to do? I know you have a scheme somewhere in the back of your head."

Will pretended to be insulted. "Scheme? You make it sound like I break laws or something."

Dak narrowed his eyes and bobbed his head from side to side. "Eh, maybe you operate in more of a gray area."

"Thank you," Will said, and went back to watching the deer. "I have a few things cooking."

"You're not going to stay here in the States, are you?"

"Nah. I found a nice place in Serbia. Beach town, too. Not many tourists come through there. I'll be able to set up shop there within a few weeks."

"Serbia, huh? I hear the beaches are nice. When I get a chance, I'll come visit."

"Please don't." Will looked at him with serious eyes. "At least give me a couple of months to get settled in."

"You act like I'll ruin everything. I'm hurt, Will."

Will chuckled and the deer's head perked up. The black eyes stared at the two men for a few seconds, then the creature darted off into the forest, disappearing in three bounds.

"Let's just say, you have a tendency to draw attention."

"That's fair," Dak surrendered.

"What about you?" Will asked. "Gonna stay here?"

"As long as I can. This place is owned by a shell, so Tucker likely won't find it, but I don't want to hole up forever. That's no way to live."

"So, what then?"

Dak lost himself in the forest again. He loved this place. Tennessee was his home, but something called to him. It was a distance voice, echoing in the canyons of both his memories and his potential.

"I've always wanted to travel," he confessed.

"Didn't get enough of that in the army?"

Dak huffed. "Not the same thing. They mostly just took me to deserts. And I didn't get a chance to investigate the local history."

"Sounds like you want to be an archaeologist," Will offered.

"Maybe. I don't know. That sounds kind of boring to me. Have you ever been to a dig site?" Will shook his head. "Lots of scraping and brushing and digging with small tools. I need a little more adventure, more mystery than that. I like a good mystery."

"So, what then?"

"I don't know," Dak said, still staring into the distance after the buck. "But I'll figure it out.

TWENTY-ONE

TWENTY-TWO

TWENTY-THREE

THANK YOU

Thank you for taking the time to read this story. We can always make more money, but time is a finite resource for all of us, so the fact you took the time to read my work means the world to me and I truly appreciate it. I hope you enjoyed it as much as I enjoyed sharing it, and I look forward to bringing you more fun adventures in the future. If you this story kept you up late, on the edge of your seat, or burning your fingers as you swiped or turned the pages, swing by Amazon and leave a review. I'd appreciate it and so would other readers.

See you in the next one,

Ernest

OTHER BOOKS BY ERNEST DEMPSEY

Dak Harper Origin Stories:

Out of the Fire

You Only Die Once

Tequila Sunset

Purgatory

Scorched Earth

The Heart of Vengeance

Sean Wyatt Adventures:

The Secret of the Stones

The Cleric's Vault

The Last Chamber

The Grecian Manifesto

The Norse Directive

Game of Shadows

The Jerusalem Creed

The Samurai Cipher

The Cairo Vendetta

The Uluru Code

The Excalibur Key

The Denali Deception

The Sahara Legacy

The Fourth Prophecy

The Templar Curse

The Forbidden Temple

ACKNOWLEDGMENTS

Big thanks to my editor Anne Storer and all the readers who helped out while the book was being written and posted each day on my website. I can't thank you enough. There were so many of you kind enough to send your comments. I appreciate you.

For Edward

SECRET CHAPTER

TWO YEARS LATER | COLIMA, MEXICO

Dak sat back in his desk chair and flipped open the gray laptop.

Through the huge window pane beyond the desk, the titanic volcano Volcán de Colima spewed a steady stream of ash and smoke into the crystal blue sky.

He'd been here for the last year, finally settling down for more than a few months in one place. Prior to arriving in Colima, Dak had bounced around from place to place. He spent three months in Ecuador, just outside of Quenca. Then there were stints in Split, Croatia, the New Zealand countryside, the Greek Island of Andros, back to South America and Chile, Panama, and finally Mexico.

His movements were random and sporadic enough that it would make tracking him nearly impossible. After two years of running, he was ready to plant his feet somewhere. Unfortunately, with the former colonel still out there and desperate for revenge, settling down wouldn't be the smart play. Then again, staying on the run all the time was hardly living. It was surviving, sure, but it was no way to live.

He'd been getting by, mostly on the money his ex-teammates had

left behind. With the exception of Carson, whose money went to the bookkeepers in Miami, Will had managed to track down most of the funds the guys from the team had squirreled away. Bo had been a little more creative with where he stashed his money, but the others had gone to the usual places where that people tried attempted to hide their dirty money. Their lack of creativity had made it fairly easy for Will to get all the proper authorizations to make huge withdrawals.

Dak had told Will he could keep everything he found, but Will wouldn't hear of it, and he split the money with Dak.

With all of his basic needs taken care of for the rest of his life, Dak could have rested a little easier at night, but he knew that would be folly. Colonel Tucker would never give up, chasing Dak relentlessly until judgment day arrived.

Something else crept up on Dak through the days, weeks, and months. It was a sinister enemy, one that had appeared innocently enough initially, but had grown into a troublesome adversary. He was bored.

Coming from a life where he was almost always on high-alert, perpetually ready for action, his new life—he discovered—had become overrun with boredom. He felt the itch to do something. He played the guitar a little, but not enough to be professional. A few other hobbies occupied some of his time, but for the most part, Dak felt incomplete. He'd been channeling most of his mental energy to surviving, watching his back, making sure he was careful. Come to think of it, Dak couldn't recall doing something just for the fun of it in in—forever.

He sighed and turned on his VPN, then opened the browser and logged into his email account.

There wasn't much to see.

Dak had started a private security firm, more to occupy the his time than anything else. That kind of work paid well for ex-military guys like him, but it was difficult to get clients without popping his head up above water where Colonel Tucker could might see it. He'd worked a few jobs for Carina Perez, the scourge of Mexican cartels. She paid well, but the jobs she had to offer were few and far between, which put Dak on his rear for long stretches.

He scrolled through the usual minutia: bills, spammy offers that should have gone to junk mail, discounts on various products he used, and then, he stopped midway down the first page page,when an email subject line caught his eye.

It said, "Adventurer wanted."

Dak's eyelids narrowed and his forehead tightened at the strange subject line. He didn't recognize the sender, but from the looks of his email server's analysis, there was nothing threatening about the message.

He clicked it and waited, half-expecting a warning to pop up alerting to alert him to of a virus being downloaded to his laptop.

Instead, a normal text email appeared.

"Dear DH Security Services." Dak read the first line aloud, and his puzzlement deepened. "I am looking for someone, someone with the ability to recover ancient artifacts from bad people. These artifacts have been stolen or bought in black markets around the world, and I want them for my personal collection."

Dak shifted in his seat. The email read like a child had written it. Not a young child. Perhaps an eight eight- or nine-year-old. He kept reading. "I have more than enough money to pay you for your services and would like to discuss a job, one where you get to travel the world, find adventure, and bring ancient relics and artifacts to someone who will appreciate them. And, if we can find the people they belong to, even better."

He paused and looked around, as if he might find the person responsible for the strange message. His little apartment was vacant and gave no answer to the conundrum.

"If this sounds interesting to you, and you're up for it, reply to this email and we can make arrangements to meet and discuss terms. I know that you're trying to lie low. And I know why. Don't worry.

I'm not a creeper or stalker. You come highly recommended by your friend, Will Collins. He thought you might need a little work to keep you from being bored."

Dak chortled at the line. *So this mysterious person knew Will. That explained a lot.*

"If you're not interested, no big deal. I do hope you are interested, though. Would be cool to meet you and Will couldn't say enough good things about you, and it would be cool to meet you. I'll leave you alone. Have a good day, and I hope to hear from you soon."

Just below the last line, Dak read the name Boston McClaren.

He held his frown, facial muscles locked in a tightly sculpted scowl as he stared at the message, reading it two more times.

"Boston McClaren," Dak wondered. "Who in the world is that?"

He opened a new tab and entered the name into the search bar. The page filled immediately with articles and pictures featuring a young boy with shaggy, blond hair and black-rimmed glasses. The kid was some kind of video game legend in the gamer community, being the youngest ever to make seven figures playing video games. Boston McClaren, it appeared, was some kind of savant.

As Dak read through the various articles, he learned that the boy had a keen interest in history, particularly ancient history.

Dak leaned back in his chair as he finished reading the last of the articles nearly an hour later., and he leaned back in his chair. He laced his fingers behind his thick, dark hair,hair and looked up at the ceiling. He blew air out of his mouth, flapping his lips in the process.

He thought about the last several months, the loneliness he'd endured for longer, and the sense that his life didn't really have much purpose—at least not at the moment.

His mind wandered to Nicole, far away in the city of Istanbul. He wondered what she was doing at that moment. *Was she eating? Chatting with a coworker? Looking at silly videos on the internet?*

Dak didn't know if he would ever be able to see her again. If he did, would she be waiting for him?

He sighed and sat up straight in his chair, positioning his fingers over the keyboard.

He paused, considering how he should reply, then simply typed, *So, you need a relic runner? I'm interested. Let's talk.*

DAK HARPER WILL RETURN **as *The Relic Runner*.**

.

Made in the USA
Monee, IL
08 September 2020